Good Friends
are everything

love now & alway

Patty b

SWEET AGE BEFORE REASON

Reminisces of an Anglo-Indian Childhood

PATRICIA BROWN

iUniverse, Inc.
Bloomington

Sweet Age Before Reason
Reminisces of an Anglo-Indian Childhood

iUniverse books may be ordered through booksellers or by contacting:

iUniverse
1663 Liberty Drive
Bloomington, IN 47403
www.iuniverse.com
1-800-Authors (1-800-288-4677)

ISBN: 978-1-4502-5545-5 (pbk)
ISBN: 978-1-4502-5547-9 (cloth)
ISBN: 978-1-4502-5546-2 (ebk)

Printed in the United States of America

iUniverse rev. date: 11/11/2010

For my grandchildren, Maya, Sara, Isabella and Andrew,
to explore and discover their past.
And for Winnie, who loved a good read.

The acrid scent of dust and dung,
Evening mist in winter's chill.
Burning leaves, jasmine trees,
Saris flapping in the breeze.
Sola topees, parasols,
Army rum and tea.
Faded silk, bright parrot wings,
Langurs bounding through the trees.
Cloying scents, excrement—
Bodies floating out to sea.
Marble Rocks, Western Ghats,
Sun-baked plains, and the Nilgiris.
Echoes from a distant place in time,
Carried on the wind by temple chimes,
Reach icy halls in northern climes ...

Patricia Brown
March 2007

Contents

PROLOGUE
High Tea Looking Glass

Sunday. High tea. Andrea continues the tradition in much the same way as her family did in England. I always thought it a charming ritual that lent an air of festivity to the day. Fussing in the kitchen, basting a roast, baking sausage rolls, pouring cake batter into parchment-lined pans. Always rewarding. But that time has long since passed—for me. Now, more often than not, I have to be led to the table.

"Here's a slice of pie, Mum."

My rheumy eyes, dimmed with seventy-six years of age and diabetes, can barely make out Howard's proffered hand.

"Thank you, son."

The plate trembles in my hand as I take it from him. I salivate, contemplating the sweet, melting portion of pie—vanilla custard, brimful with ground almonds, raisins, and desiccated coconut, baked in a rich, buttery pastry. Gingerly spooning a morsel into my mouth, I vainly attempt to keep the crumbs from falling, but they do however, clinging to my chin and settling on my frock. Hastily I dust them off. Brandy, the dachshund, is busy in a feeding frenzy at my feet.

"Was that good, Mum?" Leaning towards me, Howard inquires solicitously.

"Very good, son. Coconut-custard pie always does turn out well. That was delicious, Andrea."

She ignores me.

"Is the old lady making a mess with crumbs all over the place?" She frowns across the table at Howard.

There's a hard edge to that daughter-in-law of mine, which she tries to compensate for with periodic acts of kindness.

"Brandy's doing a fine job of cleaning up."

"I wonder, should we be giving her so much sweet? I'm pretty sure it's not good for her."

"What difference does it make at her time of life? Let her enjoy the few pleasures left. God knows she can't read any more, and she hardly ever gets out with her legs being so bad. Ah! Let her have her sweet. I don't think it's going to do any great harm."

"I guess not."

They are discussing me as if I am an inanimate object or some moron with no powers of comprehension whatever. I belch loudly, without excusing myself. The grandchildren giggle, then lower their heads, intent upon the food on their plates. Andrea rolls her eyes, and Howie doesn't hear me. Or does he?

Sarah, my granddaughter, passes me a sausage roll, which I refuse.

"Look at that, she's being tiresome again!" Andrea exclaims, exasperated. "Have a roll, Mother. You can't go to bed on just a piece of pie. I'll make you a bowl of soup later, but for now, come on, have a sausage roll," she coaxes. Turning to Howie: "Try and get her to eat something, will you? All she's had since breakfast is a cup of tea and two digestive biscuits."

"She'll eat when she's hungry."

What's her problem? I wonder. Most days I exist only on tea and biscuits with a bowl of soup and crackers for lunch. During the endless afternoon hours, when hunger pangs gnaw at my belly, I quell them by dreaming of meals long-since digested—splendid repasts I cooked to perfection, and served up to family and friends.

Each evening, as lengthening shadows slant across the windowsill, I listen for the sound of their footsteps in the hall. The dining room clock chimes the half-hour, keys rattle, and the front doorknob turns. Andrea arrives home with the children and Brandy greets them boisterously. Sarah and her brother dash up the stairs to wash and change; their mother hastily discards her coat and scarf, shucks her shoes, and pads into the kitchen to fill the kettle for tea. Bringing a cup into the library on a tray.

"Hullo, Mother. Here's your tea."

Her greeting never varies; she never tells me about her day, she does not stop to inquire about mine. Setting a cup down on the coffee table, she hastily piles my collection of dirty dishes onto the tray and carries them out into the kitchen briskly, efficiently. I hear her set them down on the counter with a clatter. The kitchen is out of bounds for me now and has been for a long time, ever since I left the stove on.

It happened last summer. I awoke one morning with a hankering for a breakfast of bacon and eggs. Oatmeal wouldn't do, nor any one of those low-calorie cereals that Andrea stocks her kitchen shelves with. I fancied eggs fried over easy, with rashers of crispy bacon and, to top it all off, a couple of slices of bread, fried golden brown in sizzling bacon fat. The family was all out, and I had the house to myself. Shuffling into the kitchen, I set about to satisfy my craving, and then eagerly sat down to enjoy the meal, forgetting to turn off the stove. I can't imagine how I was so careless, but careless I was and there was hell to pay. I have also become clumsy with age—dropping a package of biscuits the other day, I created a mess with crumbs all over the floor. Fortunately, Brandy cleaned that one up nicely and so my little accident went undetected.

Searching the faces around the table, I realize they are family and yet I feel like a stranger seated in their midst. All except for Howie, that is; I am close to him. Watching my grandchildren munching on sausage rolls, gulping down their tea, I feel no sense of kinship, no thoughts of love surface and beg to find expression. Why is that? I wonder, recalling the tender smile that creased Granny Connie's face as she smoothed my sister Moira's hair in passing. "Petty Boo," she'd croon. Moira, squirming in her chair, would smile shyly. Special feelings have a way of showing themselves. People can't hide them. Granny Connie, God bless her, is up there with the angels, no doubt, gazing down at me with a look of disapproval on her face.

But there is no such connection here. These children mean nothing to me. And their mother even less. Our relationship was tainted from the start. I never liked Andrea and found her to be a cold, calculating woman, who married my son because she was afraid of being left on the shelf at the age of thirty-two. And Howie, himself no spring chicken, must have seen something he was searching for in her. Or was he desperate as well? Their children are well-behaved and obedient, but bear not the slightest resemblance to any member of my family. Nothing betrays their ancestry or even remotely suggests who they are or where they came from. They are homogenous—your very ordinary garden-variety type of child. Nothing sets them apart from any other kid on the block. In speech and mannerisms they are typically North American. I stop myself—where am I going with this crazy train of thought? It's leading me nowhere.

Tiredness seeps through my bones, saps my strength, and I slump further into the dining-room chair. *This is hard* ... old age; it's crippling and, worse still, one can't do a damn thing about it. However, one has to be grateful for small mercies, and I have it good here—comparatively. Howard loves me, this I know, and Andrea, well, she cares in her way, I suppose. Besides, I know I'm not the easiest person in the world to get along with—petulant and demanding on occasion, that's me.

"Come along, Mum." Howie's chair scrapes back from the table as he rises. "Would you like to sit in the library?"

Nodding, I struggle out of the chair and follow him.

A faded, velvet-covered rocker, pillows, a blanket, books and other paraphernalia litter the room. This is my universe. A pale afternoon sun filters through the blinds. Warmed by its streaming rays, I close my eyes, adjusting to the light. Howie tosses another log on the grate and asks if I would like some more tea.

"If it's not too much trouble."

He goes to get it and I gaze after him with a soft look. How good and patient he is. He would like nothing better than to have this little arrangement work, run smoothly. But, of course, it cannot with two temperamental creatures like Andrea and me in the mix.

Picking up a leather-bound copy of Zola's *L'Assoimmoir*, I trace the gilt, raised lettering of the title. Nowadays I don't see well enough to read, but no matter, for I've digested the entire volume several times. As I lovingly smooth the edges, it rests like a weight of solid comfort on my lap.

The teacup rattles as Howie sets it down. I reach out and caress the aging contours of his face.

"You're a difficult woman, Ma, you know that?"

"I'm sorry, Howard."

"Have you finished with that book?" He takes it from my lap. "Would you like another?"

"Pass me *The Cloister and the Hearth*, I like the heft of it."

My mind's eye follows his finger as it travels up and down the bookshelf, searching for the title. I am intimate with all of them and grateful for their company—precious friends, they help ease the long lonely hours. A cavalcade of characters slide off the pages and crowd the room: rogues, buccaneers, knights and ladies of high quality. Some arrive bedecked in finery, having spent long hours in the corridors of power. Courtesans come warm from a bishop's bed, bringing with them the odour of sanctity. Strumpets, rumpled doxies, reeking of filth and stale vomit, straggle in from the stews of Southwark, to amuse and delight with their droll stories, dirty deeds, gossip and intrigue. John Taylor's poem comes to mind and I titter, reciting it.

The stews in England bore a beastly sway
Till eight Henry banished them away.
And since these common whores were quite put down,
A damned crew of private whores are grown.
So that the devil will be doing still
Either with public or with private ill.

"What's that?" he asks absently. "You said—"

"Nothing at all."

Finding the title, he hands it to me.

"I bought this for you at the Antiquarian Book Fair, remember? It was your birthday present."

"Of course, I do. We traveled there by streetcar with your brother Randy."

I wipe away a tear.

"Are you all right, Mum?"

"Right as rain, my son. It's my eyes, you know they tear all the time. Such a nuisance! How is Randy, by the way? He and Jane haven't come around for a visit in ages. I really wish he'd marry that girl. Ah! But he was always the stubborn one, had to have everything his own way, could never make up his mind about anything. Too many choices I expect ... Give him a call, Howie dear, I'd like to know how they're doing."

"We lost Randy five years ago, Mum."

"Ah, yes."

My voice breaks. A silly old woman filled with emotion. I always thought I'd be the first to go and here I am bringing up the rear, sipping tea, and eating pie, if you please—enjoying every bit of it.

"I miss your brother."

"We all do."

Outside it has started snowing. Falling in thick, heavy flakes, it blankets trees and hedges and muffles the sound of cars plowing past.

"Howard, how is Aunty Moira? Have you heard from her, my son? Please give her a call to see if everything is okay. And your cousin Stella, where is she? Such a rolling stone."

"Don't fret, Mum." He takes my hand between both of his and rubs it gently. "Stella's fine. She may pay us a visit next summer."

"And Aunty Moira?"

"For that you'll have to wait."

I nod in understanding.

"Comfy?" He tucks the old blanket in around my legs.

I nod again.

"Well then, I'll leave you and go give Andrea a hand in the kitchen with doing the dishes."

"You go along. Don't mind me."

I close my eyes for a brief moment.

The ghost of Teresa flounces in and sets herself down in the winged-back chair, occupying a brooding corner of the room, beside the mantel. She looks serious; I just know she's here to lecture me.

"Try and maintain an attitude of gratitude, my dear," she intones gravely. "Think of how much better off you are than the poor souls down at Happy Acres—just like you, they're all waiting to die, but in different circumstances. You wouldn't want to be confined in one of those institutions now, would you?"

"No, I would not. But you seem to forget that I've heard all this before, on innumerable occasions. Whenever we met, you never tired of recounting your sordid little experiences at that old-age home. Is that the reason for your visit?"

"Why, Sarah, old thing, I just dropped in to cheer you up."

"Could have fooled me."

A broad grin spreads across her face, illuminating her saucer eyes.
We understand each other perfectly, Teresa and I. Countless years
of friendship, morning chats, gossip, laughter, and the exchange of
clever repartee vanished—pfft!, like a puff of smoke. Dear Teresa.
With us at Christmas and taken by Easter—carried off by the dreaded
cancer. I mourned her passing for several months. Long after the pain
left me, the emptiness remained. I never did make another friend like
her, didn't care to. Friendships take too much effort.

Fluttering her lashes, she gives me a knowing grin before evaporating
into thin air.

Logs crackle, spit and flare within the grate. The fire's warmth
seeps in through my heavy woollen socks. It's cold most all the time
these days and it never used to be that way. How many years has it
been since we came over? I can't remember exactly—forty, maybe fifty
years since we came to Toronto. Time has very little meaning anymore,
it just drags on.

Ancient history, that's me—existing in the present and all the while
living in the past. Primary memory rules, nourishes, and sustains—
enables me to cross the bridge of time that leads from one day to the
next. Silence can be deafening as the world goes about its business,
leaving the old and infirm to age like furniture—except furniture
appreciates. There you go again, feeling sorry for yourself. Steer away
from self-pity. Be content.

"Umm ..."

"Is something the matter, Granny?"

Round-eyed, little Sarah, my namesake, is standing before me.

"Do you want a sausage roll?"

I shake my head.

Andrea enters the room and Sarah runs to the safety of her mother's
skirt.

"Granny's talking to herself again," she informs her in a hushed
voice.

I chuckle, past caring.

What I had for breakfast this morning escapes me, yet I can vividly
recall a breakfast shared decades earlier with Mummy, Daddy and
Moira in the restaurant car of the Frontier Mail as it traveled from

Bombay, racing across the plains, towards Amritsar. Moira and I were busy prattling away to one another, while Mummy was looking around in awe, admiring the white damask tablecloths and napkins, the silver cutlery, exquisite crockery and crystal fruit platters on the tables. She was terribly excited to be traveling on "the elite train," as she called it, "the pride and joy of the BB&CI."[1] Smartly uniformed waiters served us tea and coffee, followed by kidneys on toast, fried eggs, bacon and tomato wedges. When we were done, they cleared away our plates, served more coffee, more toast and three kinds of jam.

Settling into the soft pillows of the rocker in this darkened room with a winter storm raging outside, I give myself up to reminiscing, smiling softly as I recall an anecdote Daddy recounted that morning. There was a story doing the rounds in railway circles, he said, that gentleman keen on making a conquest often lured their lady loves into taking a journey with them on the Frontier Mail. The crowded, dusty environment of most Indian cities often lacked that special atmosphere so necessary to entice a lady into their arms, whereas the elegant surroundings and sheer adventure of traveling by train at great speeds was guaranteed to arouse feelings of passion. After that, it was but a short distance to the cozy coupes that offered so much privacy and just a matter of time before love was declared and sometimes consummated before journey's end. This is why so many couples, upon arriving at their destination, hurriedly made straight for the preacher.

"Reg, the children!" Mummy declared, rolling her eyes. But we knew she was not serious, for she giggled girlishly as Daddy leaned forward and brushed her cheek with his lips. Moira and I stared out the window intently, watching smoke from the engine drift upwards and disappear like ghosts into the sky.

Haunted by the phantoms of my youth. Childish voices, echoing through the years, find me in this present time.

We play hide-and-go-seek, Moira and I, with a servant child—racing through the vacant rooms of a rambling army-issue bungalow. Dodging bedding rolls and tin trunks piled high in the front veranda, we are unmindful of Mummy's harried cries to settle down or go play outside.

"We are gypsies!" I cry out, draping a discarded scarf over my head. "Gypsies never sit still. They're rolling stones."

---

1   BB&CI Bombay Baroda & Central India

"You look like an old witch," Moira taunts.

Daddy's been posted and we are on the move again, seated on the platform at Jhansi Station amidst the clutter of bedding rolls and boxes. The clickety-clack rhythm of the rails rings in my ears. Mummy hates postings and I see it in her weary smile and by the way she runs her fingers tiredly through her hair. I hate them too; although sometimes I find the prospect of new places, fresh faces, fascinating. Moira doesn't mind either way; so long as we all stay together, its okay with her. I chase after her, up and down the platform, dodging the many stalls, jumping on and off the huge platform scales.

That is our life. Army brats, governed by the whims of HQ, our schooling constantly disrupted by postings. Stops and starts across the length and breadth of the great subcontinent. Nights spent in musty army mess accommodation—sleepy-eyed, gazing through mosquito netting at noisy geckos on the ceiling, busy with their mating rituals. Splat! One falls to the stone floor, wriggles, loses a tail and scurries into a corner. Days spent journeying to another cantonment—to the outer reaches of the Empire. I watch the landscape slide by: swollen rivers after monsoon rain, bullocks at the yoke, the villages and farms of agrarian India. Night falls and we stop at a dimly-lit railway station. Fruit and cigarette vendors stir from their lethargy to race up and down the platform, hawking their wares with hoarse cries. Mummy instructs Radha, our ayah, to help us wash up. Moira and I look like a pair of pickaninnies, our faces blackened with grit and coal. Dinner is carried into our compartment by a couple of waiters from the dining car.

What spurred me to leave India? I struggle to recollect. Somewhere in the passage of time, between adolescence and womanhood, I was swept up by the tide of change and set down in a new arena—but keeping the door leading to the past always slightly ajar, I could at will don those magic robes sewn into the fabric of my being and, like a modern-day Alice, disappear through the looking glass, to revisit dear familiar haunts. Elements of my past, entwined with the present, I see whirling in the winter storm that rages outside—strange, inviting, and fanciful!

Stuart, my grandson, informs his mother in a loud whisper, "Granny's dozed off."

"Take the book from her lap and put it on the table beside her so she can pick it up again when she wakes up," the soft side of Andrea instructs him.

He does her bidding.

"Hello, Moira, you silly, where have you been? I've been searching for you all over the place."

She giggles and we slip easily into that time before time, into that sweet age before reason, when I was eleven and she was eight years old.

PART ONE
Saltair-By-The-Sea

Ranga twisted the lid off the large glass jar and lifted the scorpions out of it by the strings he had attached to their tails. Moira shrieked with fright and raced around the garden in a panic.

"*Bitchoo* dance, *baba*,[2] see bitchoo dance. *Juldee khana khao*,[3] then bitchoo no bite baba," he yelled, chasing after her with a spoonful of food, scorpions trailing in the dust behind him.

I stood rooted to the ground as he dropped them onto the soft white sand, string ends twisted around his bony fingers. Moonlight streamed down and illuminated their hairy, dark-shelled backs, which glowed like burnished mahogany. Tails curled upward, poised to inflict deadly venom, they scurried around, seeking refuge under flower pots and large stones. Howling with demented laughter, Ranga danced a circle around them, his skinny legs flying in every direction. Hungrily spooning the remains of Moira's dinner into his mouth he exclaimed: "All gone!"

I imagined the crunching sound of scorpion backs being crushed by a Tommy's heavy boot, scorpion ooze all over the sand, thick and white like toothpaste. Ranga would be the next to go—splat! We would then be rid of both him and his hateful pets. Skilfully, he lifted each one and dropped it back into the jar. I gasped with relief.

"Radha!" I cried out.

"What, darling?"

She waddled into view from out of a patch of darkness. Our beloved ayah, who watched over us, protected us when danger threatened and comforted us after the painful experience of parental discipline. Radha was a force to be reckoned with. The other servants were afraid of her, but disguised their feelings in the belief that she had Mummy's ear and could have them dismissed at a moment's notice. A notion she did nothing to discourage.

Moira sat whimpering on the top step of the front porch, her knees held tightly together. I knew she had wet her knickers, since she was always afraid to go to the bathroom after dark. Running to the safety of Radha's arms, she left a dark, wet patch on the smooth, stone surface.

"I'm going to tell!" I cried out vehemently, hating Ranga and determined to break the conspiracy of silence surrounding this frightful ritual with the scorpions. All the servants were terrified of him; I

---

2   *bitchoo* scorpion *baba* child
3   *juldee khana khao* hurry up and eat

couldn't understand why. He was, after all, only "the boy," engaged by Mummy to placate Hamid the cook, who kept whining about how difficult it was to maintain the kitchen without the assistance of a *chokra*.[4] Skinny and malnourished, with dark, saucer eyes that blazed out of an oversized skull, Ranga had a maniacal laugh and the ability to cast spells which (according to Radha) kept the servants in a state of constant fear. Drawing us into the ample folds of her sari like an old mother hen, she glared at him.

"Why don't you say something?" I asked, puzzled. "Tell him to stop frightening us with those horrible scorpions. Say you are going to tell Mummy, and have him sacked."

"Shush!" She placed a hand over my mouth. "Shush, now!" Herding us to the safety of a corner in the garden, she sat us down on a couple of *morras*[5] and explained: "Ranga, he is child of devil, making big, bad magic. Be quiet, my sweet, no tell Mummy." Holding her forefinger to her lips, she looked around fearfully. Then, in hoarse whispers: "Radha take care of Ranga, okay?"

"Then do so," I declared vigorously.

Moira snuggled in her lap, cradling her head against an ample bosom.

"Sarah, you be *chup chaap*,[6] listen to me."

"Yes, Sarah, otherwise he'll let those scorpions loose into our beds," Moira whimpered, her eyes filled with fright.

Helplessly I nodded, hating Ranga all the more.

Sirens wailed in the distance. Air raid!

"Japanee coming!" Radha hurried us into the house, which was pitch dark, since all the windowpanes were plastered with tarpaper, and we were not allowed to switch on the lights. A lantern flickered on the dining-room table; picking it up, she carried it before us into the bedroom. We undressed in silence and she tucked us in, moving between the beds in that funny waddling way of hers. Jamming a wad of tobacco into her mouth, she sighed, rolled out her bedding on the floor between our beds and lay down. There she remained, the faithful ayah, until our parents returned from the club.

The night was fraught with fear. Outside, the sky was filled with

---

4   *chokra* boy, servant
5   *morras* round bamboo footstool, with a woven jute top
6   *chup chapp* quiet

enemy planes. Huddled beneath the covers, I tried to shut them out, but could still hear them droning overhead. Trembling, I lay awake with the memory of those dreadful scorpions still fresh in my mind. A gust of wind rushed in through the open window, sending the lantern flame on a wild dance. Mosquito netting billowed all around and bedroom furniture transformed, assumed bizarre proportions. Ghoulish figures draped in trailing gossamer raiment traipsed across the ceiling.

Ek kauwa pyaasa tha
Jug me paani thoda tha
Kauwe ne daala kankar
Paani aaya upar
Kauwe ne piya paani
Khatam hui kahaani

I sang softly in Hindi. Moira giggled in the bed beside me.
"Go sleep now or I call Ranga," Radha threatened.
We were silent.
Although this was wrong, each night I prayed that something awful would happen to Ranga. Admitting my wickedness to Father Humphrey one Saturday—in the hope of adding weight to my confession, which always suffered from a dearth of transgressions—I nervously awaited my penance within the darkened confessional that smelled of stale sweat and tobacco. After an awful silence, Father peered at me from behind the grill and shaking his finger, scolded me severely for having broken one of God's commandments. I lowered my head, pretending contrition, and he fell silent for what seemed like an interminable time. Watching his fleshy face lying crumpled on a shaggy beard, I wondered whether he had fallen asleep and was startled when he looked up and delivered a hefty penance of one complete rosary. Back in my pew, I was kept on my knees for half an hour by the penance, under the dreadful scrutiny of the holy family and a pantheon of saints.

The war was on and Daddy was in it too, since he was an officer in the army. We had been recently posted to Saltair-By-The-Sea, a tiny coastal town on the Bay of Bengal, which owed its importance to its strategic location. Ocean-going vessels, carrying provisions for Allied troops, anchored in the harbour for refuelling. It was a military port, all swagger sticks, spit and polish. Canteen stores, barracks, officers' quarters, parade grounds and sentries on duty. Massive shade-giving trees lined the avenues of the cantonment, their trunks neatly circled with rings of white paint. My parents fitted in perfectly. Even though Mummy moaned about our many postings, she enjoyed the social whirl of army life and joined the bridge club and sewing circle within a week of arrival. Daddy was in Movement Control; this kept him pretty busy all day and sometimes late into the night. He was not a tall man, my father, and rather stout, but he projected a quiet dignity that was easily recognizable. Reticent, he could look quite glum when something displeased him. When he smiled, he positively beamed and you could see the wide gap between his two front teeth. Mummy, on the other hand, was slim, rather tall and fair complexioned with silky brown hair that she held in place with bobby pins. Mummy had lovely chiselled features and high cheekbones. She was outspoken and at times impatient and uncharitable where other people's foibles were concerned. Loyal and true, she was an avid correspondent and claimed a wide circle of friends. A gracious hostess, she was always trying to further Daddy's career by entertaining his fellow officers and their wives. At parties her laughter could always be heard ringing out, loud and clear, for she enjoyed a good joke and a few drinks—nothing, though, that would prompt her to indulge in "crude and salacious behaviour" as she put it. Unlike some of the other ladies in the club.

The bungalow we lived in was built of stone, surrounded by high walls draped with bougainvilleas in vibrant colours. Iron gates at the front were bolted shut at night to keep out intruders. The garden was plagued by blood-suckers (lizards), lying torpid, sunning themselves in the white heat, when not hunting for prey amidst the tropical blooms and palm trees. I watched in awe as the chameleons changed colour as they scurried amidst the foliage and clambered up the trellis. Inside the bungalow were numerous rooms filled with heavy, army-issue furniture—a drab universe of olive-green, khaki and grey. Around the clock, continuous columns of military vehicles, fifteen hundred weights, three tonners, jeeps and motorcycles moved in convoys down the dusty road outside. They bumped and rattled forward, churning the sandy soil, sending myriad little dust devils spiralling upwards into the brilliant sunshine. Fine white sand settled everywhere—on the flowers and creepers, on freshly washed clothes hanging from the line. It powdered our hair and invaded our mouths and nostrils.

Throughout the day we heard the intermittent wail of sirens, followed by the all clear, mostly in practice. But, when the droning Japanese planes flew low overhead, one could detect a subtle change of pitch in their long persistent cries and then everyone scrambled for the trenches, except for Grandpa and Granny. Grandpa would simply look up from his paper and refuse to budge.

"I'll die when my time comes and not a moment before," he proclaimed philosophically. Granny nodded in agreement and continued with her knitting.

Grandpa and Granny Watkinson were Daddy's parents. They spent long holidays with us each year. I heard Mummy remark fondly to Daddy that the old people were becoming a permanent fixture, but that she didn't mind at all. Daddy smiled thoughtfully and informed her that their presence gave her plenty of free time to gallivant with her friends and indulge her passion for bridge. Moira and I, of course, just loved having them there. Grandpa and Granny owned a farm on the outskirts of Stanton Station, in the Central Provinces, but since Grandpa was a hopeless farmer, it was constantly plagued with crop failure. As he explained it, this was mainly due to the fact that the Deccan was a dustbowl. Granny disagreed, however, saying most of the fault lay with Grandpa, who was a city boy and clueless on how to work the land.

"I am a country girl," she'd say, "and my ancestors who settled there understood farming. But not him." She dismissed Grandpa with a wave of her hand.

"I took up farming as a hobby," he defended himself, ignoring Granny's disparaging remarks. "Actually, I'm a man of letters, a deep thinker, and was known as something of a dandy in my day." Drawing himself up to his full height, he'd swagger up and down the room. Slim and tall, with iron-grey hair held in place with Brilliantine, Grandpa cut a dashing figure, even at the ripe old age of seventy. Moira and I giggled, whilst Granny shook her head and scowled over her glasses.

Grandpa was very proud of Daddy's commission and would boast about it at the drop of a hat. "My boy has a King's Commission," he'd declare pompously to anyone who would listen.

Granny Connie was petite with tiny hands and feet. She had long silver curls that escaped from her bun by the end of the day. Granny was a woman of few words, who could look severe when she was cross. Whenever Mummy was at one of her bridge club sessions, Granny was placed in charge of us, to ensure we ate our meals on time.

"I haven't got patience for any dawdling, step to it now!" she'd order us brusquely. We ate in silence, finishing every scrap on the plate; only then were we allowed to engage in "table conversation." Strict as she was, we were not afraid of her, for she loved us both dearly. Moira, however, was clearly her favourite. She doted on her, a fact that was plain to see.

"Petty Boo, sit by me," she'd call out and Moira would come and squeeze in beside her, spending hours in that position, sucking her thumb.

Knitting and crocheting kept Granny busy all day. Moira and I received cardigans and sweaters galore for birthdays and at Christmas. She also loved to crochet socks, which we detested, because they itched. Mummy insisted we wear them though, out of respect for Granny's effort.

Moira and I wished our grandparents would never leave because we loved having them around. Grandpa read the newspaper and enjoyed listening to BBC Radio. When the news came crackling over the airwaves, we children had to be very quiet, so he could pay full attention to "the latest developments on the war front." At times I completely forgot they had another home and took it for granted they would always be with us.

The bus arrived each morning at 7:00 o'clock to take me to the Convent of the Holy Name, a Catholic school for girls. The bus was painted all over with splashes of olive-green and khaki with a strip of glass left clear on each window to look out of. The drive to and from school took an hour each way, but I didn't mind. We followed the coastal road and I enjoyed passing through the tiny fishing villages along the way, watching the children at play while their elders mended fishing nets strung out between the palm trees. I gazed at the tide as it rolled onto the shore from the Bay of Bengal, sunlight dancing on its back. During the monsoons the sea turned dark and angry and monstrous waves came crashing in to dash themselves furiously against the rocks. Fishing boats bobbed in the water like crazy corks.

Even though we had never experienced an air raid on the way to school, we were prepared for the eventuality. Ignatius, the driver, had orders to park the bus in a palm grove and wait for the "all clear."

Just before the road reached the rocky cliffs that plunged into the sea, our bus turned into an avenue fringed with casuarinas, which led up to the gates of the school. Once inside, we rolled down the gravelled path and came to an abrupt halt before the great stone building. Weathered and streaked by the elements, it stood against a backdrop of coconut palms and bright blue sky. Tumbling out, we ran towards the assembly hall at the rear for morning prayers. Only parents and visitors were admitted through the large wooden doors at the front entrance, which led into the parlour. The parlour was out of bounds for students. I remember being ushered in on my first day at school. Fearfully clutching Mummy's hand, I gaped in awe at the splendid surroundings, never having seen anything quite so grand in all my born days. Many years later, however, when my voracious appetite for the written word led me down strange and different paths, I happened to read about a brothel in France, the description of which brought this very parlour to mind, with Mother Superior a dead ringer for the Madam.

Inside was dark and cool, cluttered with heavy, brocaded furniture, potted palms in elaborate brass jardinières and an ornately framed picture of the Sacred Heart on the far wall. Below it, on a gilded shelf, votive candles flickered in crimson glass holders, casting a rosy glow. Here, Sister Pauline, the secretary-nun with her whispering, white habit, greeted visitors who wished to meet with Mother, who sat in the hushed silence of her office, behind plush bordello-red drapes. Only the rustling of rosary beads spoke of her presence.

Outside, a garden filled with neat beds of cannas, crotons, marigolds and bright orange nasturtiums that tumbled over red brick borders, formed a walkway from the parlour to the classrooms at the back. Identical in shape and size, they were large and airy with desks arranged in rows and open windows facing the sea, inviting it in. We girls formed a line in the hallway connecting the classrooms and were shepherded in by a nun with a ruler in her hand. I was assigned a seat beside a window and delighted in the damp, salty breezes that blew in. Suspended over the blackboard at the head of each classroom was a crucifix.

"Jesus is watching you," the nuns constantly reminded us and we shivered at the thought.

The school compound dropped away to a stretch of beach, at the very edge of which stood an abandoned lighthouse surrounded by a patch of smooth, grey rocks. Edged by frothy white ripples, the gentle lapping waters suggested calm and serenity. Mummy and I walked over to the beach on that first day of school and she was charmed. "Land's end!" she exclaimed. I rather liked that phrase. The words rolled off my tongue in much the same way as did "falling into an abyss"—another lovely expression. I desperately wanted to explore the inside of the lighthouse, but a heavy padlock and a sign that read *Do Not Enter* prevented me. I decided to make this little area around the lighthouse my sanctuary and, whenever I could, I would slip away after lunch to enjoy the solitude it offered—to read, to dream or just to catch a glimpse of the white, lateen sails of the fishing boats gliding over the deep, blue waters of the Bay of Bengal. Fortunately, I was never discovered and my daydreams went undisturbed, since the nuns took attendance just once a day and forgot all about you afterwards. Besides, Evelyn Dunstan, who became my best friend, always allowed me to copy her homework at the end of the day. I was a hopeless student.

Our school day started with catechism, Sister Rita presiding. She would limp into the classroom and we snickered. I named her "Dot and Carry One." The name stuck.

"In the name of the Father and of the Son and of the Holy Ghost, Amen.

"Who made you?" she then asked in a high, tremulous voice.

"God made me," we replied in unison.

"Why did God make you?"

"To know Him, to love Him and to serve Him in this world. And to be happy with Him in the next."

Christine Turner often fell asleep at the back of the classroom; with her head cradled in her arms, she was dead to the world. On one occasion, Sister Rita spotted her and limped over. Thwack! Down came the ruler on Christine's back, and she woke with a start, gasping, "Sorry, Sister!" But it was too late.

"Wretched little misfit. Did you come here to sleep? Or to learn the word of God?" Sister Rita sprayed her words when she was in a fury.

"Say it, don't spray it," I muttered from my seat near the window. My desk mate, who heard me, giggled.

"Devil's spawn!" Sister Rita's voice cracked with rage. "Probably up to no good all night." Grabbing Christine by the collar, she pushed her forward between the rows of desks, depositing her in a corner like a heap of dirty clothes. The wretched girl's glasses slipped down her nose, exposing pale, grey, red-rimmed eyes brimming with tears. Bullies tittered, but others looked away. I for one never understood why Sister Rita picked on Christine, an orphan who lived with her Aunty Jean, whose husband had gone off to the war. Christine wore a perpetual woebegone expression on her face, and was the butt of many a practical joke. It was awful. I promised myself from that day forth to share my sweets with her every time I had any.

"You'll come to a bad end, my girl, no doubt about that!" Sister Rita snapped at Christine. "What's bred in the bone comes out in the blood."

Looking up at us she barked, "Back to your books, the rest of you!"

One day I told Mummy about the promise I had made, to share my sweets with Christine.

"And have you?" she asked.

"Have I what?"

"Why, shared your sweets, of course."

"I haven't got around to it yet," I replied lamely, immediately regretting the confidence. Mummy could take you to task about such things. She had the memory of an elephant and would continue reminding you long after you'd forgotten the whole thing. "When I'm at school it always seems like such a long way to tea," I explained, "and so I hang on to my sweets, just in case I get hungry on the way home."

"H'm ..." She was not convinced. "Remember, Sarah, the road to hell is paved with good intentions."

I didn't quite get that, so I ran outside to play.

Every afternoon Evelyn and I ate lunch together in the boarders' refectory. Mummy said it was too far to send daily tiffin. I wouldn't have minded bringing sandwiches, but she insisted I needed a hot meal. I was served a different lunch from Evelyn with extra fruit, either a banana or an orange.

Peering into my tray, Evelyn would remark "You get the nuns' lunch tray, Sarah; my parents can't afford it." She shrugged matter of fact. "Your daddy's in the army, so you must be well off."

"What's that got to do with it, silly?"

Evelyn had a squint and I was never very sure whether she was looking at me or at someone else. Refectory Sister Marcella was often mean to her. Tugging at her hair, she would complain to the other nuns that Evelyn was cheeky and stubborn. But I thought her very brave, especially since she never cried out when her hair was pulled or when Sister smacked her for having her elbows on the table, for not sitting up straight, for pushing the bowl of watery dal soup aside. I remember an occasion when I felt particularly sorry for her. The school bus had arrived early at our house that morning and, since I didn't get to finish breakfast, Granny hurriedly packed two omelette sandwiches and placed them in my satchel. I shared one with Evelyn at the break, which must have satisfied her. At lunch that afternoon, I watched her flinch and turn away from the watery gruel she was served. We looked around for Sister Marcella, since I felt bold enough to toss it out the refectory window, but she had noticed Evelyn's grimace and was watching us. Coming right over, she stood poised with a foot rule in her hand.

"You'll finish that, young lady," Sister yelled at her, pointing to the bowl.

Evelyn stared up at Sister, her crossed eyes brimming with tears. "I can't, Sister."

"You can and you will." The ruler came down on Evelyn's back.

Stoically, she bore the punishment. I knew it hurt, for she bit down on her lower lip until it bled. Deliberately, she began spooning down the gruel, taking sips of water between each spoonful. When the bowl was empty, I passed her a toffee to remove the putrid taste, but the effort had proved too much—her chest heaved and she vomited violently, spewing out the messy gruel, spattering it all over our uniforms. Sister Marcella was in a fury. Lifting us out of our chairs, she marched us over to the boarders' dormitory, where we were told to undress, and our uniforms were given for cleaning to the convent *dhobi*.[7] We sat in our petticoats all afternoon, lolling around on the neatly turned down beds.

Evelyn had beautiful hair, bright red ringlets that tumbled down her back in a cascade of curls. I always felt Sister Marcella was jealous

---

7   *dhobi* washerman

of her, especially since her own hair had all been chopped off and under her wimple she was as "bald as an egg," according to Grandpa.

"Why do they have to shave off all their hair?" I asked him once.

"So they won't perspire, I suppose. I'll bet it gets hot under there."

"Oh, but they do!" I exclaimed. "All of them. They smell of sweat and could do with a dab of eau de cologne."

"Don't be sacrilegious, child," he chuckled.

I told Grandpa everything—well, nearly. I confided in him that I wouldn't mind having Evelyn's hair. "Red ringlets would be nice," I said. "I'd toss them all the time."

"And what would you do about the squint?" he inquired. "You can't have the one without the other, you know. You've got to take the whole package."

I decided against the package. I couldn't go through life with a squint, other people wouldn't be sure of whether I was looking at them or not, which in time could lead to all sorts of confusion. I wasn't prepared for that.

"Exactly," said Grandpa, when I informed him of my decision.

My report cards were a disgrace. I did well in history, spelling and composition, but failed miserably in maths, geography and botany. Being an ace in English didn't seem important to my parents; maths was all that mattered to them. Reading was my passion. With my nose buried in a book, reliving daring exploits in far-off lands, I often found it difficult to return to the present, especially if it was to complete a boring arithmetic assignment. I kept putting it off endlessly and sometimes homework never got done.

"Sarah, get down to your maths!" Mummy would scold, snatching my storybook away from me. But it was useless. After that I found it even harder to concentrate on times tables and boring sums. Of course I received a big fat duck's egg the next day in class and would sometimes have to spend the entire lunch hour working on corrections.

Grandpa said, "One good book is as good as two good teachers." I was in complete agreement.

"Stop filling the child's head with rubbish, Cliffy," Granny yelled at him. "But will he listen?" she then asked herself. "Not him." Granny often asked a question and answered it herself all in one breath. It was her way.

Grandpa peppered his conversation with sayings all the time. I loved them and tried to memorize as many as I could. Mummy called them "hackneyed phrases," and warned me not to use them, but I couldn't resist trying a few out on Moira. They failed miserably because she didn't understand what I was getting at, so I dared throw one in Mummy's direction, which annoyed her immensely.

"If you're going to persist in using those terrible clichés, Sarah, at least learn to apply them in the proper context."

I darted out of the room to look up "context" in the *Oxford Dictionary.*

I could recite Keats and Shelley at the drop of a hat, but this failed to impress Mummy, who said that if I was as smart in arithmetic there'd be no telling what dizzying heights I might reach.

Always keen to perform on stage for the school concert, I raised my hand when a teacher requested contributions for the tryouts, but since there was a lot of favouritism in school, I was never asked. It was no different here at the Convent of the Holy Name. After being overlooked for the hundredth time, I mentioned this fact to Mummy, but she brushed me aside with: "Try not to be a show off, Sarah, your turn will come."

When?

My dream was to get all dressed up and recite the poem "Miniver Cheevy" or "Meg Merrilies" for the concert.

"Old Meg, she was a gypsy—"

"Sit down, Sarah Watkinson. It's not your turn," barked Miss Staples, her lips compressed in a thin line. "Let's hear what Jane Allan has chosen for the tryouts. Read from the book, Jane, my dear, you can always polish it up later."

Opening her book, Jane read, "The Pobble who has no toes had once as many as we—"

"Ha!" I laughed out loud. "Imagine that."

Miss Staples glowered at me.

Jane Allan, with dark curls and pink cheeks like Rose Red, was her favourite.

Each afternoon, when I returned from school, we all sat down to tea. Moira who was younger by three years, attended a junior school nearby and was always home early. Hopping off the bus, I'd see her seated on the top step of the front porch waiting for me. She'd never own up to that, though. After tea we washed up and went with Radha to a garden that stood at the very edge of the cantonment grounds. The area was all spruced up and enclosed by a chain-link fence with an iron gate, painted olive green. It wasn't much of a garden really, just a patch of lawn surrounded by neat beds of flowers in regimental colours standing to attention. A tidy clump of trees shaded one corner and in the middle of the lawn stood a large iron cannon, painted black, with cannon balls arranged around. We would scramble all over it, engaged in childish games. Darting in between the trees, we played hide-and-go-seek. Other children, accompanied by their ayahs, frequented the place as well, and with the passing of time we became close friends. There were four of us altogether: Rosie Findlay, Adrienne Pemberton, Moira and me. Donny Hill was the only boy and he was a pest, continually chasing us around the cannon, screeching "lipstick ladies" at the top of his voice. He told me he was different down there and I wanted to know how.

"First you show me," he whispered in my ear, "then I'll show you."

"Don't!" yelled Rosie when I told her what he'd asked. "You'll have a baby just from that."

Rosie knew about such things, so I listened, but was curious.

Moira and I were forbidden to set foot outside the garden. Radha had filled our heads with terrible tales of wild dogs, who, she said, roamed the harsh, dry landscape covered with thorn scrub and stunted trees, which stretched out from the garden boundary all the way to the low hills in the distance. We were told to beware of the wild man who lived among the animals. I caught sight of him once at the close of evening, as I sat apart from the others, dreaming, watching a crimson sunset. A rustling sound disturbed my reverie and looking up I saw a dark, hairy creature peering out at me from behind a craggy rock. Our eyes met for a brief second, before he turned and ran into the bush. A few evenings later, as Radha sat chatting with the other ayahs, I ventured out, filled with curiosity, to see if I could get a closer look at the man and I did. We startled one another, actually, for I came upon him unawares. He took a step back in surprise and, as for me, I turned and raced headlong to the safety of Radha's lap. He looked quite fierce, hairy and naked, reminding me of a Bushman from the Kalahari Desert, which I once saw in Daddy's geographical magazine. Radha had a fit on observing my trembling body and flushed face.

"Where you been? ... Ha!" She pinched me cruelly.

"Ouch! I'm telling Mummy you hurt me!" I cried out, rubbing my bruised arm.

"Go tell! *Badmash*[8] girl! Sit quietly now!" She flung me away from her and, shaking her head, she rejoined her gossiping ayah friends.

Sullenly, I listened as she recounted for their benefit a litany of my misdemeanours. Gazing over in my direction from time to time, they shook their heads and clucked in sympathy with Radha for having such a troublesome child in her charge.

"Winston Churchill is the most important man in the world," declared Rosie one evening, as we sat around in the garden playing five stones.

I asked Mummy if this was true.

"Very nearly," she replied.

"Where does he live?"

"London, England."

"With Dick Whittington and his cat?"

"Don't be cheeky, Sarah!"

Rosie and I chattered endlessly on a variety of subjects, but the one that stirred our curiosity the most was where babies came from. She had her theories and I had mine and we could never agree on any one of them. Adrienne and Moira were excluded from these conversations, since we felt they were too childish to take part.

One evening, tired out after a game of kick the can, Rosie, Adrienne and I collapsed in a heap beside the clump of trees. Giggling, we watched as Moira circled timidly, trying in vain to find a space between us to wedge herself in. Closing in, knee to knee, we kept her out.

"Can I join you?" she whined. "Please, pretty please."

We ignored her.

"Where do you think babies come from?" Adrienne inquired out of the blue, startling both Rosie and I.

"They come from the belly button," I informed her importantly.

---

8   *Badmash* naughty, rascal

"Everybody knows that a long string attaches the baby from its belly button to the mother's belly button. In this way it gets to share the mother's food. After nine months, the mother gets an awful tummy ache, after which her belly button pops out and she has a perfectly lovely newborn child." They looked at me aghast.

Moira pouted and gave me one of her hangdog looks. Feeling sorry, I made a little space for her. "Sit down and be quiet," I ordered. She smirked.

"Where did you hear that story, Sarah Watkinson?" Rosie challenged.

"I read it in a book," I replied defiantly. It was, of course, a lie, since, try as I might, I had not been able to lay my hands on any book dealing with the subject. But I was determined to brave it out and get the better of Rosie, who always thought she knew everything.

"And I just know that isn't true. It comes from another part," she proclaimed. Rosie resented being upstaged.

"Another part?" Moira looked shocked. "Is there another part? Which part?"

"I'm not telling."

"That's because you don't know," I scoffed. "Because if you did, you'd tell, Miss know-it-all Rosie Findlay."

"It's a secret and I just won't tell you."

"Why?" wailed Adrienne. "You know I can keep a secret. Here, tell me in my ear." She edged closer to Rosie.

"No!"

Ayahs called out, and we made haste to join them as the sun dipped in the western sky, bringing an abrupt end to the day.

The next afternoon Moira asked Grandpa if he knew where babies came from.

"Sarah says it's the belly button. Is that true?"

"Oh! The belly button theory; I've heard that one before." He nodded wisely.

I looked up at him, shifting uncomfortably.

"There's lemon pound cake for tea, let's all have a slice." Grandpa shuffled towards the dining room and we followed.

"Rosie Findlay says she's English, Mummy. Are we English too?"

I asked one afternoon. She looked up from her sewing, an impatient frown creasing her forehead.

"No, we're not."

"Then what are we?"

"We're Anglo-Indian."

"Does that mean we're Indian?"

"Not quite. Now, how shall I put it? We're a blend, Sarah; the best of both races actually and that's all you need to know for now. Run along and play and don't bother your head with things that don't concern you."

"But they do. I have a right to know who I am," I declared vigorously.

"Suffice it to say, you're a fortunate little girl who needs for nothing, who should be more than happy with her lot in life, considering there are so many poor people in this world."

I let the matter pass for the moment. Mummy could get really cross if one persisted. Besides, Anglo-Indian sounded interesting. I gathered we had a little bit of both, British and Indian blood; in short, we were not a hundred percent pukka.

A large mango tree stood behind the house, its branches sprawling over the back garden wall. It was out of bounds to Moira and me. Radha told us that a huge, lazy python had decided to call it home. Draping himself across the branches, after polishing off a goat or two, he liked a dessert of sweet mangoes. On full moon nights, *cherails*[9] danced around the tree and cast all kinds of wicked spells on behalf of their "familiars", a word I'd just learned. Ranga was one, I was sure. I knew he broke fresh coconuts and scattered jasmine around as offerings to the devils. In exchange they granted him all sorts of favours, giving him power over snakes, scorpions and centipedes.

Govind, the goatherd, was in total agreement with me on the subject of Ranga. I came upon him one afternoon as I slipped out of the compound to do a bit of exploring. He was sitting under the guava tree, playing cowrie shells. I asked him about the fresh coconut.

"Devil food!" he warned. "Leave it alone."

He offered me half a raw mango rubbed with chili powder and

---

9   *cherails* she devils with feet that turned backwards

salt, which I accepted gingerly. It tasted hot, sour and salty—quite good, really.

"You are stealing the python's mangoes," I warned him. "He will eat you and your goats."

"Never!" Govind shook his head. "I have just eaten the antidote and now the snake will not harm me."

"What's the antidote?" I asked.

"You are eating it," he chuckled. "Chili powder and salt." I didn't believe him, but promised myself to test the truth of his words when the mangoes were ripe.

The mangoes finally ripened into the sweetest, roundest, most luscious ones I had ever eaten. Grandpa called them *"Banganapalli."* [10] Hamid, the cook, brought a small galvanized tub out of the godown and placed it under the dining table. Every morning after breakfast, he filled it with fresh, cold water, then, after wiping the mangoes carefully to remove all the turpentine, he dropped them into the tub. During the season we were allowed a mango for dessert every day, after lunch and dinner.

Creeping out of the house one afternoon, when I was sure Moira was asleep, I gorged myself. The tree was groaning with fruit, its branches low to the ground. Taking care to stay away from Ranga's devil offerings, of course, and since the python was nowhere around, I seized the opportunity. I would really have liked to bring a few back for Moira, but was afraid she'd tell.

The next day I suffered for my greed, waking to find my chin and cheeks covered with mango blisters.

"Turpentine sores," Granny called them. "The girl needs some ointment, Emma," she yelled out to Mummy.

"You greedy child!" Mummy scolded and slapped me very hard. "Didn't you hear me when I said you were not allowed to go near that tree?" She slapped me again. After applying ointment all over my face, she sent me off to school. It was horrible. The blisters were yellow and full of pus. I looked like a leper and felt like one. Everyone avoided me like the plague, even Evelyn kept her distance. I was devastated.

"How did you get those boils?" Veronica Fleming asked.

"They are turpentine blisters," I moaned, "from eating too many mangoes."

---

10 *Banganapalli* a mango variety

"Greedy gut, your belly go phut, with twenty maggots in your gut," she chanted and the bullies joined in. Girls can be very cruel. Someone aimed a paper aeroplane at my head.

That day, after lunch, I headed for the solitude of the lighthouse and spent the entire afternoon looking out to sea, feeling very sorry for myself.

The next day Mummy kept me home from school because I had diarrhea. Grandpa put a cake of jasmine soap in the bathroom.

"For every time you need to wash your bottom," he said. He knew I liked the perfume.

"Sarah. Go to your Room. You're punished," Daddy ordered sternly. "There'll be no dinner for you tonight. The next time you'll learn to listen when your mother gives an order."

Crawling into bed, I spent a pleasant evening reading *The Curly Wee Annual* and *Anderson's Fairy Tales*. After dinner Mummy and Daddy left for the club and Radha crept into the bedroom with a chapati wrapped around some of her hot mutton curry. It was splendid. Moira was asleep.

The rains came in June and so did the holidays, but they sped rapidly by and we were back in school for the second term. The hot, dry winds of August breathed fire and white afternoon glare hurt the eyes. At times the wind drifted in from the Bay of Bengal, heavy and damp. Languorous, we wanted to lie down and sleep. Movement was an effort. This natural lethargy often heralded a severe rain storm, a deluge, when Moira and I were allowed by an indulgent Mummy to prance around like mad caps in the garden, our rain-soaked frocks clinging to burning bodies.

One Saturday morning as we sat around the breakfast table, Mummy entered clutching a telegram. She said it was from Grandpa Reagan, her father, and he had written to inform us of Aunty Maggie's arrival. She was Mummy's youngest sister, the "daring one," they called her. Moira and I liked her immensely and looked forward to her visits. She always arrived loaded down with gifts for us. She had presented me with my very first bottle of perfume. Working as a secretary in Bombay, she was up on the very latest of fashions, which she modelled for us on every visit. Aunty Maggie was very generous and shared her makeup with us. We borrowed her scarves, glare glasses and hats. Tottering all over the house in Mummy's high heels, trailing wisps of organza, Moira and I tripped over ourselves and fell to the floor time and again, shrieking with laughter. She had even allowed me to sneak a puff of her cigarette when no one was watching.

"Does she still work in Bombay?" I asked.

"No," Mummy replied, preoccupied, "she's been staying with your grandfather at the Serendipity Lodge on Bell Island. I guess, she's coming here for a change of scene."

"When is she coming?" inquired Moira, excitedly.

"Well, it seems this afternoon. Your father and I will go and pick her up at the train station at around 4:00 o'clock.

"Today?"

"Yes, Sarah, today."

"Who lit a cracker under Maggie?" asked Grandpa, looking up from his newspaper. "What's her all-fired hurry?"

Mummy rolled her eyes, picked up the telegram and stalked out of the room.

I didn't understand why Mummy was so flustered at the prospect of Aunty Maggie's visit; they always got along so well. In fact, Mummy never tired of reminding us of how sisters should behave towards each other, holding up her relationship with Aunty Maggie as an example to Moira and me. We were fed up of hearing how they never went to bed cross with each other. I was sure it was Aunty Maggie who made the first effort because Mummy, I knew from experience, could hold a grudge. But that didn't matter right at the moment. What worried me was Mummy's apparent discomfort at the thought of her sister's imminent arrival. Uh-oh, I thought, it smells like trouble brewing. I had a good nose when it came to such things and something was definitely fishy here. Nevertheless, Moira and I were thrilled and hurried with our baths that evening so we could sit on the front verandah and wait for Daddy's jeep to turn into the compound.

They arrived in a cloud of dust. Mummy was the first to step out and then she carefully helped Aunty Maggie down. I was surprised to see how stout she had become. Her flushed face broke into a happy smile as she caught sight of us and, after innumerable hugs and kisses, she turned and greeted Grandpa and Granny rather primly, before disappearing with Mummy into the bedroom.

"She's knocked up for sure," I heard Grandpa confide to Granny, who nodded, knowingly.

I didn't quite get that, but I was afraid to pry. Granny looked disapproving and kept shaking her head.

Aunty Maggie was definitely changed, as both Moira and I discovered in the days that followed. Normally vivacious, she now appeared pale and dull. Her silky brown hair, that she styled in a fashionable bob, now hung down her back, stringy and unwashed. She dressed in large shapeless frocks and her body looked swollen.

"You look a mess, Margaret Mary Reagan," Mummy took her to task in the bedroom one morning, addressing Aunty Maggie by her full name. "I suggest you start taking better care of yourself. If it's a tonic you need, we'll get that and some vitamins as well. No use wallowing in self-pity. What's done is done. Now let's get on with it and make the best of a bad situation, shall we?"

Aunty Maggie nodded helplessly, hung her head and wept silent tears that streaked her cheeks. She sniffled audibly and I ran to fetch a handkerchief. I wondered what could possibly have gone wrong. How had she changed so much? Both Moira and I were disappointed to find her continually depressed and not her usual giggly self. She cried a lot and showed no interest at all in exciting things like actresses, clothes and lipstick. Her new love was food and she certainly packed it away. Where previously she had just picked at her food, now at both lunch and dinner she polished off great quantities of curry, rice, and side dishes, returning to the sideboard for seconds at every meal. She also did quite well with afters—blancmange with jam sauce was her particular favourite.

"Eating for two?" Granny inquired, eyeing her up and down.

Aunty Maggie burst into tears.

"What's the matter with Aunty Maggie?" I asked Mummy. "She's very weepy."

"None of your business, Sarah. Go out and play," Mummy ordered. So, of course, I didn't find out right away why she was so broody, but I was confident that it would all come out sooner or later. In our family, it generally did.

Afternoon lie-downs on weekends and holidays bored me to tears.

After a heavy lunch of curry and rice, we girls were required to have a *charpoy bash*,[11] until it was time for tea. Moira had no trouble with this arrangement and was generally asleep within a few minutes. I, on the other hand, would lie in bed wide awake, watching the fan as it sluggishly redistributed hot air. Tossing and turning in the unbearable heat with all kinds of improbable ideas passing through my head, I could stand it no longer. I would rise and creep out of the room to do a little exploring. This habit persisted right through my teenage years and I must confess that I made my most remarkable discoveries during those afternoon forays.

On one occasion, it was a blazing October afternoon when I crept out of the house through the back gate and went for a walk through the coconut groves. I came upon a maidan with olive-green tents pitched all over and a Tommy seated on a stool before a barbed-wire fence. I knew he was the sentry because army officers' daughters know about such things. There were always a lot of sentries around when we visited the mess and they saluted Daddy. Although I was not supposed to talk to strangers, I did to this one, who appeared quite friendly. He had smiling eyes.

"Hello, little girl," he greeted me.

"Hello," I replied nervously.

"Out for an afternoon stroll, are you? Like some sweeties?" He offered me a packet of sugar cubes and a couple of bull's eyes. They were hard to resist, since I was hungry from all that walking.

"What are you all doing here? Hiding from the Japs?" I inquired inquisitively.

"You might say that," he grinned. "We're waiting to be shipped out."

"Where are you off to?"

"Africa."

"My Daddy's an army wallah," I informed him importantly. "We live in the big house with the mango tree in the back."

"Uh-huh," he nodded, dragging on a cigarette. "So, what are you doing out here at this time of the afternoon? Shouldn't you be resting?"

"I'm exploring," I answered boldly.

---

11   *charpoy* string cot   *charpoy bash* sleep on a charpoy

"I think you're out of bounds, so you'd better run along home. Little girls are not allowed in army camps."

Clutching my treats in sweaty palms, I thanked him and turned tail for home, afraid of being late for tea. Besides, Radha said snakes, she-devils and God knows what else prowled around the coconut groves at dusk. Munching along the way, I was left with just two sugar cubes when I arrived home, so I shared them with Moira, hoping she wouldn't ask me where I'd got them from. She didn't.

Aunty Maggie adored sentimental love songs. She'd place a record on the turntable, wind up the gramophone, hop into bed and start bawling. "Good Night, Sweetheart" and "Now is the Hour" particularly depressed her. Her pillow was always drenched with tears. She also had a disgusting habit of leaving snotty hankies all over the place and this bothered Granny to no end, for she felt it was "most unhygienic."

Lonely and lost, she wandered about the house aimlessly, flopping down in an armchair whenever she got tired. Mummy tried her best, but did not succeed in cheering her up. Grandpa and Granny made friendly overtures, but Aunty Maggie kept her distance, because, I felt, she was filled with shame about the way she looked. All in all it was a miserable state of affairs, which Daddy stayed away from, altogether. Setting out for work early each morning, he returned home just in time for dinner. Moira, as quiet as a mouse, said very little, while I on the other hand tried endlessly to cheer her up. I tried to understand how she must feel without a friend in the world and kept questioning her about her life in Bombay, her friends and did they go dancing every day or only on weekends?

"Clear off, Sarah, and leave me alone!" she'd snap at me.

I forgave her, every time.

One afternoon, however, she could hold it in no longer and spilled the beans. Between blowing her nose and drying her eyes, Aunty Maggie tearfully informed me she was desperately in love with a soldier named Danny Groat. They were having a romantic affair in Bombay, when suddenly, out of the blue, he received orders and was shipped out to the front, leaving her behind. Of course, she was devastated and, what was worse, she had heard nothing from him since the day he sailed away.

"If only he would write," she moaned.

I gazed at her, feeling sad and helpless. All I knew of love was found in fairy tales and they always ended with marriage, and living happily ever after. This was somehow different. I turned away from her misery, not knowing what to say.

"He'll return from the front, Aunty Maggie, don't you worry," I consoled. "The war can't go on forever." I hugged her.

Moira, who was lying on the bed beside us, eavesdropping as usual, suddenly chirped up: "Which front? Back to front?"

Aunty Maggie glared at her and, with quivering lips, clung to her pillow and sobbed wretchedly.

"Now see what you've done, Moira Watkinson," I scolded. "Run along and play." But she refused to obey. Moira could be quite stubborn. I changed the record and played one of my favourites, "You Are My Sunshine", in an attempt to cheer things up, but it had the opposite effect.

"Sarah, how can you be so insensitive?" Aunty Maggie wailed.

Moira and I loved the gramophone and played all of Mummy's records—waltzes and jazz tunes. Granny said, "Jazz corrupts," whatever that meant. We didn't care, we loved it anyhow. One evening Moira and I got all dressed up in Mummy's old gowns with high-heeled shoes. We dusted our faces with powder, rouged our cheeks and lined our eyes with pencil. We had arranged a concert and it was going to be held in the sitting room. The entire household was invited, even the servants. Chairs were placed in a row and a *dhurrie*[12] spread over the floor for the servants to sit on. Both Moira and I were terribly excited. Lights were dimmed and I entered, parting the bedroom curtains. Dressed as a show girl, draped in a silken stole, with rouged cheeks and carmine lips I came slinking into the room and did my best imitation, singing in a high childish voice:

Oh, I wish that I could shimmy like my sister Kate;
She shimmies like a jelly on a plate.
My mama wanted to know last night,
What makes the boys think Kate's so nice.
Now all the boys in the neighbourhood,
They know that she can shimmy and it's understood;

---

12   *dhurrie* cotton mat

I know that I'm late, but I'll be up-to-date
When I shimmy like my sister Kate.
I mean, when I shimmy like my sister Kate.

Grandpa clapped and laughed uproariously. Mummy leaned over and tapped him on the back.

"Who taught her the words?" she inquired, looking annoyed.

"Haven't a clue," he replied, wiping away tears of laughter.

Moira came on next. She was Shirley Temple with ringlets. Bowing, she sang:

On the good ship, Lollipop
It's a sweet trip to a candy shop
Where bon-bons play
On the sunny beach of Peppermint Bay.

We were called back on stage to take a bow, but were laughing so hard we collapsed in a heap onto the floor. Everyone was in high spirits and even Aunty Maggie seemed to be having a good time. Hamid served refreshments, cheese sandwiches, and lemonade for us, something stronger for the grown-ups. Then Mummy played Granny's favourite record, the one that always brought a dreamy look into her eyes.

"When I was a girl," said Granny, reminiscing, "we used to dance to this tune with the young chaps down at the *gymkhana*.[13] They had a lively band there, well up in every kind of music, quicksteps, sambas, and waltzes. There was nothing they couldn't play. In between dances we sat around and sipped lemonade, just like you girls are doing now, and when it was all over, our blokes took us home in a *gharry*.[14] I shall never forget those carefree days in Bombay," she sighed.

I imagined Granny looking beautiful in her dance dress, with high-heeled shoes and a lacy shawl draped around her shoulders. Her dark, curly hair swept back, and held in place with a tortoise-shell comb.

"Did you have a fan, Granny?" Moira asked.

"No, child," she replied softly, but Grandpa contradicted her.

---

13   *gymkhana* club
14   *gharry* carriage with two horses

"You did so," he covered her hand with his. "It was the fan that did it."

"Come now, Cliffy, did what?"

"Bewitched me, woman. Batting your eyes at me from behind that fan—I was captivated."

Granny laughed. Moving her hand gently out from under his, she picked up her knitting needles once more and began to unravel the silken yarn from the small tightly wound ball lying on her lap.

If there was one place I loved above all others, it was the kitchen. Mummy said, "Proper young ladies do not linger too long at the back of the house, in kitchens and around the servant quarters."

I paid her no heed. I was headstrong and found it impossible to resist the dark, smoky interior. The wood fire crackling in the old cast-iron stove mesmerised me. As Hamid stood fanning the flames, they spread out, licking the base of every pot simmering over the fire holes. Curry, dal and vegetable *foogath*,[15] released their delicious smells into the air, mingling with the pungent aroma of spices being ground on the masala stone. Plopping down into Radha's lap, as she sat leaning against a pillar of the back veranda, I was soon lost in the separate world that existed behind the bungalow. Outside, servant children played hopscotch in the dust and called out to me: "Baba, *aow khelo*,"[16] and sometimes I would join them. Watching Hamid, as he carefully poured out cooking oil from a large can, I giggled, as Dilip, the sweeper boy, shoved a thick little bottle, topped with a funnel, under the scoop. "Humph," Hamid grunted, pushing it away when it was half full. Carefully wiping the mouth of the bottle with the end of his shirt, Dilip corked it before scooting out of the kitchen. Granny poked her head in from time to time, checking on the meal, but she never seemed to notice me. When Grandpa passed by, he'd eye the mound of garlic I was often busy peeling and exclaim, "You have enough there, girlie, to choke a family of vampires!"

Hamid was the son of one of Grandpa Watkinson's old retainers. He was born on the farm at Stanton Station and had grown up there. In his youth he had been my father's gun bearer, following him into the jungles when he went out to hunt for deer or wild boar. Skinny

---

15   *foogath* stir-fried vegetable
16   *aow khelo* come & play

and not very tall, Hamid had iron-grey hair, a solemn face and smoked countless *bidis*[17] throughout the day. He had a wracking cough and would run out of the kitchen every so often to clear his throat and spit violently into the dust. This worried Mummy, who tackled Daddy on the subject on innumerable occasions.

"He cooks all our food, Reg. Please arrange for him to have a few X-rays taken at the hospital. I'm always afraid of TB and would feel so much better knowing there was nothing wrong with him."

"I'll see to it," was Daddy's standard response, but I don't recall him ever doing anything about it. They shared a silent bond, Hamid and my father, forged at an early age when they had been playmates. Since Daddy was an only child, I guessed, he had looked on Hamid as a brother. When he joined the army, Hamid went along with him and proved to be an indispensable and versatile retainer, capable of producing an omelette and a cup of tea at a moment's notice. After my parents married, he was immediately elevated to the position of cook, since Mummy didn't know her way around the kitchen. There he remained, following them all over India, from posting to posting. Taking up residence in the kitchen, he slept on a mat kept rolled up in one corner. Each day the household was awakened by loud splashing, gargling and spitting, as Hamid performed his morning ablutions under the back garden tap. The rest of the time he went about his culinary chores in silence.

Mummy was determined to turn him from a very ordinary cook into a master chef. Set on impressing the commandant and his wife with Hamid's culinary skills, she began subscribing to an array of ladies' home magazines. Before one of her dinner parties, they could be found scattered all over the house, pages opened to lavishly illustrated recipes of mouth-watering entrées and desserts. Since her own talents in the area of haute cuisine were very limited—she could barely manage buttered eggs on toast, according to Daddy—the rest of the family found her efforts laughable. Over dinner one evening, Grandpa joked that Mummy in her eagerness was bent on achieving an overnight promotion for Daddy. "From captain to colonel, bypassing major!" She was, of course, not amused and gave him the cold shoulder for several days afterwards.

Hamid became quite distraught when he got wind of an upcoming

---

17   *bidis* raw tobacco leaf

burra khanna[18] and everyday "plain fare" suffered as a result, which put Daddy in very bad humour. Mummy, however, continued undeterred, ordering choice cuts of meat and other delicacies scarce in rationed times, but freely available at exorbitant prices in the black market.

"It's worth the extra expense and effort, Reg, believe me," she confided to Daddy. "It'll pay off in the end. Besides, having a prized chef on the payroll is nothing to sneeze at."

"I gather you're referring to Hamid?"

She nodded.

He smiled indulgently at her and left the room.

One particular burra khanna comes to mind. It was Daddy's birthday and invitations were sent out to the commandant, a few fellow officers and their wives. A couple of days before the event Hamid was called into the dining room and listened intently as Mummy gave him precise instructions about the preparation and presentation of the main dish.

"Ha, memsahib." Naturally shy, Hamid wobbled his head from side to side. He then retreated with the magazine tucked under his arm. Since he could neither read nor write, his inspiration would have to come from the profusely illustrated pictures.

On the morning of the dinner, Mummy followed him into the kitchen and I watched as she proceeded to make puff pastry on the large marble slab that Hamid used to crumb cutlets and tenderize tough cuts of meat. Referring to the recipe repeatedly, she rolled out the pastry and folded it into a neat square. Wrapping it in waxed paper, she set it in the icebox. A perspiring Hamid hovered anxiously. After giving him some last minute instructions, she departed the kitchen and he, looking in my direction, heaved an audible sigh of relief.

That evening at dinner—to begin with—all went well and according to plan. The guests were seated round the table, making polite conversation. Moira and I were seated at a "kiddies' table" set up in a corner of the dining room. The tinkling of glasses and a toast was raised; they all wished Daddy a happy birthday and he beamed, raising his glass to his lips several times, acknowledging their good wishes. Soup was served and it was excellent. Ranga cleared away the plates, as Hamid mutely carried the pièce de résistance in to the expectant guests. An awkward silence followed. A fuming Mummy toyed with

---

18   *burra khanna* big feast

her portion while the company made polite conversation. It was only after they had all departed that the proverbial custard hit the fan.

Somewhere between the time he had received his instructions—amply illustrated—and dinner, the *ghabraud*[19] Hamid, having failed to grasp the intricacies of the dish he was required to prepare, had created his own interpretation of it. A tough cut of beef swathed in greasy puff pastry was served up as beef Wellington, alongside a cheese soufflé, which had sunk to new lows.

"He'll never amount to anything!" Mummy fumed afterwards. "It's no use trying to make a silk purse out of a sow's ear!"

"Why do you persist then, when you know his limitations? After all, he was only a gun bearer and field hand," Daddy said sensibly.

"I don't understand it, Reg. Here I am trying so hard to turn him into a decent cook, but he shows no interest. Do you think he does it deliberately?"

"Don't be ridiculous, Emma, of course not. You can barely manage that fancy stuff yourself. As for Hamid, it's all over his head. For God's sake, the man can't even read and write. All he has ever been capable of producing is a fair chicken curry and a passable brown stew—both of which he learned from my mother, by the way. Country Captain, cutlets, et cetera, he has picked up along the way. And, besides, did you think to go into the kitchen before dinner and check on the meal yourself?"

She shook her head, "I was busy and there were other things to attend to."

"I guessed not. Anyway, it's all water under the bridge now and the next time you'll know better than to give Hamid instructions that you yourself find difficult to follow." Daddy stomped out of the room, refusing to be drawn into any further argument pertaining to Hamid's cooking skills.

I was the firstborn child and Hamid loved me unconditionally. In his eyes I could do no wrong. I often caught him scowling at Radha when she scolded me for being insolent or for bullying the servant children. Whenever I got the opportunity, I'd creep into the kitchen and he'd allow me to remove the lids from the cooking pots to inhale the delicious aromas. Deftly trimming the crust of a sandwich, he'd

---

19   *ghabraud* confused, excited

hand it to me and point to the milking stool in the corner, where I was allowed to sit. Before a burra khanna, there was always a lot of masala to be ground. On those occasions, when I got the chance, I would slip into the kitchen. Hamid would solemnly hand me a tin plate filled with garlic pods and knobs of fresh ginger. Labouring at the task of peeling, scraping and cleaning, I chattered endlessly to him. Never looking up from his chores, he'd nod from time to time, acknowledging my running commentary. Only Mummy's footfall sent me scurrying out of the kitchen, smelling divinely of wood-smoke and spices.

An open passageway, overhung with corrugated sheeting, connected the kitchen to the main house. It was a dangerous crossing for someone armed with a cutlet or a roast beef sandwich. Kites and king crows circled overhead and perched upon the roof, watching hawkishly. If one was not careful, they swooped down and snatched the food right out of your hands. It happened to Moira once and she ran bawling into the house, crying for Daddy to get his gun and finish off the thieving bird who had swiped her sandwich. Of course, he did nothing of the sort, which upset her even further.

Grandpa said: "Moira must learn to hang onto her grub."

Harry De Boer drove his father's Hudson over to our place every Saturday morning; "a very dangerous practice," according to Aunty Maggie. Mummy agreed with her. You see, Harry was just thirteen years old and could barely see over the bonnet. When we spotted a large dark car barrelling down the road towards our house with no driver in sight, we knew it was Harry. Moira and I would run out to meet him. Coming to a full stop before the gate, Harry would emerge from a cloud of dust.

"Hello, Sarah-Moira. Wanna come for a ride?"

Mummy said it was shameless the way he was allowed to drive around in that car at his age with no supervision at all. But I thought it pretty wonderful. Actually, I didn't like the way Mummy and Aunty Maggie gossiped about Harry's family. After all, he couldn't help it if his mother was a "shameless hussy, who had a different pair of shoes under her bed each night." Or if his "father was an old toper." Harry promised to take me exploring anytime I could slip away, but I knew this was impossible, since Moira was a spy watching my every move. I did try and give her the slip on several occasions, but it was impossible.

Running to Mummy, she would whine, "Have you seen Sarah? I have no one to play with."

Radha would then be dispatched to discover my whereabouts.

"Tale, tale tit, your tongue will be slit and all the little doggies will have a little bit," I teased Moira unmercifully. "Little Miss Goody Two-shoes." I stuck my tongue out at her, but it was useless: she was thick-skinned.

Harry's parents lived in the railway colony, not too far from the church. Mummy once said that Harry came from the wrong side of the tracks and I took it to mean that he lived on the other side of the railway tracks, which he did. He was an altar boy and Father Humphrey sometimes sent him over to our house with a message for Mummy. He also brought over messages from the "Ladies' Circle." On weekdays he'd come on a bicycle, pedalling down the road at a furious pace. It was only on Saturdays that he had the use of his father's car. In the hot weather Mummy would have Radha squeeze him a glass of fresh lime juice and he would be allowed to stay and play with us. No doubt his drooping grey eyes and waiflike appearance won her over. "Just look at him," she would sigh, gazing fondly at Harry as he sat at the dining table munching on a raisin bun, gulping down a glass of milk, "the poor child looks woefully neglected." After a time Harry became a fixture in our house and we soon got used to seeing him sit down for Saturday lunch with us. Daddy too felt sorry for Harry and would smile indulgently at him.

Granny, however, was not convinced. "He's a clever little monkey." She scowled at him. "And up to all sorts of tricks. I'd watch him around the girls, if I were you."

"How can you think that?" Mummy glared at her. "He's just a poor, lost boy and for the moment a guest at our table." Harry gave her a soulful look, as he slid deeper into the chair.

Later, however, I heard Mummy, in an attempt to mollify Granny, inform her that she had already instructed Radha to ensure that neither of us girls set foot in Harry's car.

Harry knew that Mummy had a soft spot for him, so he wheedled extra change out of her. Each time he came over with a message, I'd watch her disappear into the bedroom and return with a few annas, which she would drop into his hands, whilst ruffling his straw-coloured hair. He'd beam up at her and dash out of the house.

I liked Harry immensely and over time came to know him quite well. He was not the angel Mummy thought he was, neither was he a devil. He was lonely, having no brothers or sisters to play with, and his parents really didn't care much about him, allowing him to wander all over town and in the bazaar on his own. Sitting beside me under the custard apple tree, he would pass me a few communion wafers, which he had filched from the church.

"I'd bring you some of the wine, Sarah, but I haven't got a bottle."

"What does mass wine taste like?" I asked. "Does it taste like blood?"

"Not at all. It's sour and a bit sweet. Not bad really."

I couldn't spend much time alone with him though, because Radha was always on the prowl and, like Granny, she was suspicious. Appearing out of nowhere, she'd grab me by the arm, saying: "Sarah, come quick." Then rudely, turning to Harry: "You go home. Sarah busy now."

"Those darn sirens again!" Aunty Maggie moved heavily down the back stairs towards the trenches. There were two of them at the rear of the house, one for us and the other for the servants. Moira and I didn't like climbing into them because we were afraid there might be scorpions lurking inside. Grandpa said the place was crawling with them. He and Granny decided to wait it out on the front veranda and Mummy said this was okay because their minds were made up. I guess, it didn't matter very much what happened when you were old. I resolved to stay away from trenches when I grew old.

Japanese planes roared overhead. We heard an incredible boom, followed by a flash of light that brightened up the sky. A thick plume of black smoke curled upwards in the distance.

"I think they've bombed the harbour!" exclaimed Mummy.

She pulled Moira and me closer to her. I liked it when she did that, it made me feel so much safer. This was all very exciting! Another boom and then another—more flashes of light! A surge of dense cloud hung over the horizon, blocking the sun. Aunty Maggie whimpered, she was shaking and inched closer to Mummy, who put a protective arm around her shoulder. I tried to put my arm around her waist, but it didn't get very far because she had become so large. She was crying very hard.

"You poor thing," consoled Mummy, "in your condition—"

"What condition?" I blurted out. Mummy looked down at me severely.

"Do you think Winston Churchill will hear about this?"

"Sarah, don't start—"

We heard a motorcycle approaching; it was Daddy. He drove around to the back of the house and I was surprised to see him, since he seldom came home at lunchtime. Moira was feeling itchy because she had been bitten all over by red ants. She began wailing at the top of her voice and jumping up and down.

"Stop fidgeting!" Mummy scolded, but Moira paid no attention and continued scratching her arms and legs.

We heard fire engines in the distance.

"Just came home to make sure everything was okay." Daddy leaned down and kissed Mummy's cheek. "Keep the girls in. They've bombed a cargo ship anchored out in the harbour and there's lamb, bully beef and hunks of cheese all over the place. I believe those rations were meant for our chaps in Africa."

"Africa!" I exclaimed. "Gosh! What will those poor soldiers eat now?"

"There are a couple of fires burning out of hand, but we'll eventually get them under control." Daddy sounded tired, but excited. "Don't wait up for me; it's going to be a long night." He turned and was gone again in a billow of dust.

I regretted taking those sugar cubes from the Tommy in the maidan and kept wondering if he was already in Africa. With no cargo ships in sight, what would he do if he needed to sweeten a cup of tea, or a sweetie just to suck on? I detested my greediness.

News of the yearly poetry competition was posted on the bulletin board at school. It was open to all students and divided into three categories: Junior, Intermediate and Senior with a prize for the best poem in each category. I had quite a collection, since I scribbled all the time. However, I noticed that Miss Staples was one of the judges and this was a bit worrying, since she told Mummy I was an "unsettling influence" in her class. Now, every time she entered the room, she glared at me fiercely and I was forced to be quiet. Deciding to give it a go anyway, I resolved to show my effort to absolutely no one, not even

Grandpa. After a week, I handed in my poem and tried to forget the whole thing.

"Sarah Watkinson!" The booming voice of Mother Superior echoed through the Assembly Hall.

"Yes, yes, Mother—" I stammered.

"Will you come up on to the stage, please?" I hurried, scurrying between the ranks of girls. Climbing the three high steps, I stumbled onto the stage in full view of the entire assembly.

"Sarah, did you write this?" Mother shoved the poem under my nose.

I nodded.

"Your poem has been judged the best in the intermediate division. Please read it aloud for everyone to hear."

I cleared my throat and nervously began:

> Where's Madge?
> Heaven knows, she's out somewhere among the orange groves.
> Busy with chores most of the time, Madge is a difficult girl to
> find.
> From early morn 'til setting sun, she feeds the chickens and
> rakes the hay,
> She leads the cattle to the pasture. Attending to her tasks all
> day,
> I can sometimes hear her shrill clear voice and the tinkle of her
> happy laughter.
> But if you asked me, I couldn't say, where Madge might be at
> any given time.
> She might be here, she might be there, Madge is a difficult girl
> to find.

My fellow students clapped and, becoming very shy, I started to chew my lower lip. Mother Superior handed me a gift-wrapped package and I murmured my thanks. Then, racing off the stage, I made my way to the back of the hall, flushed and shivering with happiness. Skipping afternoon classes, I spent the entire time sitting on the smooth rocks beside the lighthouse examining my gift, a copy of *Heidi* by Johanna Spyri. Opening the book, I read the first page over and over, savouring every word.

"Where were you all afternoon?" Evelyn pinched me.

"Ouch!" I cried. "Why?"

"Mother was looking for you—Mother Superior!"

My eyes went wide with fear. "What did you say? Did she ask you where I was?"

"I'm glad she didn't; I would have told."

"Where did she go?"

"I don't know, she just swept out of the class and disappeared down the corridor. I'm really getting tired of covering for you, Sarah Watkinson. One of these days I'll tell."

"I hope she thought I was in the infirmary," I stammered.

On the way home, I was filled with mixed emotions, joy and fear for the different things that had happened to me during that day. Leaping out of the bus, my satchel flying behind, I rushed up the stairs, ignoring Moira who was waiting patiently on the top step. I wanted to show my prize to everyone. Mummy hugged me, her eyes shining with pride.

"O Lordy!" I exclaimed, looking heavenward, "please don't let her find out I wasn't in class this afternoon."

"Humph," said Grandpa. "Little vixen. Kept this one under your hat, eh! No matter; it's a wonderful effort. I'll have to get you to read the poem for the entire family after dinner."

Suddenly, remembering Moira, I ran to find her.

The next day at school, before the English literature period began, Miss Staples called out: "Sarah."

"Yes, Miss Staples," I answered gravely, standing up at my desk.

"Come to the front of the class please, will you?"

At that precise moment, Sister Bernard walked in carrying a large tea cozy.

"Sarah, since you've always wanted to perform, I have a spot for you in the concert. I would like you to recite a poem."

I eyed the tea cozy nervously and took a step back. Sister Bernard moved towards me and slipped it over my head, pulling my arms through the openings on either side.

"Yes, Sister." Miss Staples nodded approvingly, circling me. "A perfect fit."

My classmates snickered behind their hands, but I pretended not to notice.

"Now," said Miss Staples, "repeat after me":

I'm a little teapot, short and stout
Here is my handle, here is my spout
When I get all steamed up, hear me shout
Just tip me over and pour me out

I mumbled the words after her. Removing the cozy, she handed it back to Sister Bernard. Passing me the sheet of paper with the poem written in pencil, she instructed me to take it home and memorize it.

"Say it with feeling, Sarah," she continued. "Believe you are a teapot. There's a smart girl!" She patted me and I was humiliated beyond belief.

Miserable, I cried all the way home in the bus, my head stuck out of the window, since I didn't want anyone else to see me bawling. Darting out at my stop, I flew up the steps to the bedroom and collapsed on the bed. Pulling the covers over, I sobbed uncontrollably.

"What's the matter child?" asked Granny, agitated. "Come on, have your tea."

"That's the matter!" I cried, flinging the poem across the bed in her direction.

"Looks easy enough to me," she remarked, examining the soggy piece of paper. "You should be able to learn it in no time at all. After all, you are the house poet. Come on, stop fussing and settle down to tea." Granny tugged at my arm. "We have some nice raisin buns; let me butter one for you."

Moira came in and sat at the edge of the bed, sucking her thumb, a thing she was absolutely forbidden to do. If Mummy had caught her, she would have received a wallop for sure.

"Here's my dolly," she offered, shoving Ronny the rag doll over, but I was miserable and turned away.

Granny led me to the table.

Grandpa looked up from his newspaper. "What's all the fuss about?" he asked.

"Something about a poem," Granny muttered, as she shuffled over to the *doolie*[20] for the golden syrup.

"The biscuit man came by this afternoon and we have raisin buns

---

20   *doolie* meatsafe

for tea," Grandpa declared cheerfully. "Butter two for Sarah, Connie, and warm up that tea."

I stared at the tea cozy with a look of hatred on my face.

"Sarah, what's the matter?" asked Grandpa.

"It's this poem," I sobbed, handing over the sheet of paper.

"It's a perfectly simple poem, child, and you should know it by heart in a matter of minutes."

"No, you don't understand, Grandpa," I wailed.

"What don't I understand?"

"I am the teapot. They've chosen me to be the teapot for the concert. I have a tea cozy for a costume."

Moira burst into gales of laughter. I gave her a withering look.

"Oh! Oh!" said Grandpa, suddenly grasping the complexity of the situation. "Well." He cleared his throat. "There is no reason for you to get upset. After all, you did want to be in the concert, didn't you?"

"Yes, I did, but not as a teapot."

"Well, Sarah, it's a start, isn't it? You go up on that stage and imagine yourself to be the most magnificent teapot they've ever seen. Queen Victoria's teapot, in fact, made of pure silver. She would pour Earl Grey tea from it every afternoon, when entertaining dignitaries, and foreign ambassadors. On days when she had a particularly boring audience and felt a headache coming on, she'd pass her cup to her faithful retainer, John Brown, and he'd add a splash of brandy to the tea. I think you will be most impressive, Sarah, and next year they'll remember your excellent performance and who knows what part you may be offered. This is your chance, child. Seize the opportunity!"

But I was crushed and tears of self-pity continued to stream down. My nose was running and the raisin buns got soggy.

"Go wash up," Grandpa urged. "Radha is waiting to take you to the garden. Hold on! On second thoughts, maybe you should skip the garden for today."

Radha quietly took Moira by the hand and I watched them disappear down the road.

When Mummy returned, she wanted to know why I was at home. Grandpa took her aside and explained.

Mummy, however, was most unsympathetic and refused to understand. She was impatient with him. "Pay no attention to her tantrums; Sarah can get quite dramatic at times."

Mummy could be quite heartless.

"First things first, Sarah," said Grandpa. "You must learn this poem so that you know it forwards, backwards and sideways."

I giggled. Grandpa was funny.

"Then, we'll work on the expression and acting. You'll be the star performer, I just know it."

I was cheered up already.

The next day at school was hellish. Climbing down from the bus, I was quickly surrounded by the bullies, who chanted:

> Fat little Sarah Teapot,
> Has a nose that's full of snot.

And:

> Bessie Bunter the fat boy's sister,
> Was so large they couldn't lift her.
> So she sat on the floor and ate some more,
> Got as big as a house—
> Couldn't fit through the door—

They yanked at my pigtails and pinched me black and blue. I darted away and sought sanctuary in the chapel. There, in the quiet gloom, under the protection of the Sacred Heart and the Virgin Mary, I opened a library book and read until the bell rang for classes.

After lunch I retreated to the lighthouse and spent the entire afternoon imploring Mother Mary to grant my wish and give me flowing red hair and sultry good looks like Rita Hayworth, but all in vain. Gazing into the mirror that evening, I saw fat little Sarah with poker-straight hair staring back at me.

"Moira has a kink in her hair," Granny said pointedly, "but you don't." Did she hold that against me? I wondered. I knew Moira was her favourite, for she called her "Petty Boo", even though it was a name that Moira absolutely detested. I called her "Hollywood Coconut Scrapers" because she wanted to become an actress and Mummy said that if she continued sucking her thumb she would have bucked teeth. Moira called me "Billy Bunter's Sister" in retaliation and I tried not to mind.

Concert day rolled around and by that time I was feeling much better about things. Mummy, Daddy and Moira were going to be attending at the school auditorium that evening, but Grandpa and

Granny stayed at home because Aunty Maggie was feeling unwell. Besides, Grandpa said he had already seen the star performer and was not interested in anyone else. I loved him for that. Hugging him, I ran to catch the bus.

After school, we performers were taken backstage and Sister Bernard painted our faces. She slipped the tea cozy over my head and steered me in the right direction.

"Seize the moment, Sarah," I heard Grandpa's voice. It was my turn. I tottered onto the stage, and the recitation went smoothly. Mummy and Daddy clapped very hard and grinned at me from across the footlights. Curtsying, I nearly toppled over, but managed a successful exit.

"Wonderfully executed!" Sister Bernard exclaimed, rushing to help me out of the cumbersome cozy. I was perspiring profusely and my face burned as I flushed with joy.

Every Saturday we had to go to confession, so we would be pure to receive communion at mass the next morning.

"It's expected of all good Catholics," said Mummy. "Especially convent girls."

"But I haven't any sins," I whined.

"Stop complaining, Sarah. Kneel down and make a good examination of your conscience; I am sure you'll find a few."

But try as I might I couldn't think of any. I promised myself to make a special effort the following week and collect a few. After all, Mummy did have a point—and it would be dreadfully boring for Father Humphrey, sitting in the confessional for all that time, if everyone was like me and had no sins to confess. The poor man could go clear out of his mind and start talking to himself.

Moira didn't like going to confession either. "Examine your conscience," I teased.

"Shut up, Sarah, or I'll tell on you."

This was no idle threat, I knew, so I buttoned my lip. Moira had a habit of stowing away every little infraction of mine in that head of hers and she had no qualms about passing this information on to Mummy, when the need arose.

Before the end of the school term we had a raffle and the prize was a porcelain shut-eyed doll, wearing a burgundy velvet dress, with a bonnet to match. I didn't care for dolls, but this one was a real beauty; so I spent half my pocket money and bought two tickets, which I gave to Granny for safekeeping. The draw was to be held on the day before school closed for the Christmas holidays.

At assembly, Mother Superior put her hand into the drum and pulled out a ticket stub. "Two hundred and fifty-three," her voice boomed out across the hall. There was a rustling throughout the assembly room, as each student examined her ticket. Suddenly, I remembered I had forgotten to bring my tickets to school that morning. "Two hundred and fifty-three," she called out again. A hushed silence followed.

Evelyn frantically tugged at my sleeve. "Look, Sarah, look!" she exclaimed excitedly, shoving her ticket in front of my face. "I have two hundred and fifty-two, and you bought your tickets directly after me. You must have two hundred and fifty-three. Put your hand up quick, before Mother draws another number."

"I've left my tickets at home," I wailed. "It's too late."

But Evelyn, undeterred, jumped up and down waving her hand in the air, until Mother finally took notice.

"Evelyn, do you have two hundred and fifty-three?" Mother inquired.

"No, no, Mother," stammered Evelyn, "but Sarah Watkinson does."

"Can't Sarah Watkinson speak for herself?" Mother looked sternly down at Evelyn. She hated for us girls to get out of hand.

"Come here, Sarah." I walked up to the front of the hall. "Can I see your ticket, please?"

Mother leaned forward.

"I've left them at home, Mother; my tickets are in Granny's pocket for safekeeping."

"Well, they're not much good there today, are they? What makes Evelyn think you have the lucky ticket, anyway?"

"She bought ticket number two hundred and fifty-two and I bought the next two tickets," I explained.

"Well then, that's settled," said Mother. "I shall hold this doll for a day and tomorrow when you fetch me your tickets, if you have two hundred and fifty-three, the doll is yours."

"Thank you, Mother," I beamed.

The doll was mine and I named her Elizabeth, after you-know-who. Mother carried her into the classroom and presented her to me. The girls crowded round and Veronica Fleming wanted to undress her immediately to examine her underthings, but I wouldn't allow it. I brought her home in a large box which Ignatius, the driver, stored under his seat and handed to me as I stepped down from the bus. Trembling with excitement, I rushed passed Moira to show Mummy the doll first.

"She's lovely!" exclaimed Daddy. "You lucky girl!"

Mummy offered to sew a new dress and Granny, no doubt, would knit her some socks and a cardigan. Moira wheeled her pram into the room. Unceremoniously, she dumped Ronny, the rag doll, onto the floor, dusted off the seat, and offered it to Elizabeth. Granny suggested we call her "Lilibet," for short. I thought that was a good idea.

I could never abide a teddy bear or doll in bed with me, but Moira, who loved to cuddle up, kept pestering me to allow Lilibet to sleep in her bed each night and I finally relented. I would have given her the doll, but held back because that would mean the end of all my privileges. Moira had started fagging for me and, lately, had become quite good at it.

Besides, Lilibet and I were constantly being invited to lunch. Hamid provided the meal, rice, dal, *papads*[21] and a peeled banana sliced up for dessert. She would set the table on the back veranda with her toy dinner set, and Radha lowered the *chicks*[22] to keep the crows out. "There's plenty for everyone," Moira assured us, agreeably, as we sat down to lunch.

I remember getting into an argument with her one afternoon as she entertained Lilibet and me. It was over something trivial, but I shouted at her, calling her a brazen hussy, a name Aunty Maggie used when referring to Rita Haslem. With tears streaming down her face, Moira ran in search of Mummy to find out what a "brazen hussy" was.

"I'll wash your mouth out with soap and water, young lady, if I ever hear you talking like that," Mummy scolded sharply.

Moira returned, snivelling.

"Maggie, you'd better watch what you say in front of the girls," Mummy yelled. Then she took me to task for being unkind to my sister. Moira was becoming a pest and so I grabbed Lilibet away from

21   *papads* short for pappadums
22   *chicks* bamboo curtains

her and got quite strict about where she slept. Moira soon wised up and promised she would never tell on me again. Nevertheless, I decided to hold off giving her the doll for a bit longer and thought maybe I would present her with it on her birthday.

We awoke one morning to a sad, unsettling day. Lying in bed, I could hear the grown-ups speaking in hushed voices and a loud sob came from the dining room. Coffee cups rattled as Ranga washed up in the back veranda. Why was everyone awake so early? I wondered. Creeping into the room, I noticed glum faces all around. Somebody had died for sure. My heart sank. I tiptoed past them and peered through the curtains into Granny and Grandpa's bedroom. I was afraid Granny may have expired during the night. After all, she was very old and never stopped repeating: "My end is near." Her favourite expression was: "Eat while my eyes are open," and this she always said while passing someone a paratha, or serving us with a dollop of guava jelly. When she asked you to fetch something, she always followed her request with: "Hurry, child, my days are numbered."

I was relieved to see her sticking hairpins into her bun before the dressing-table mirror.

Back in the dining room, I heard Mummy sigh: "How dreadful! It's that wretched woman's fault; she never did take proper care of the poor lad." Blowing her nose, she dabbed her eyes with a handkerchief.

"Which lad?" I inquired.

With a surprised look on her face, she strained to give me a cheery, "Good morning, Sarah." She then looked over at Grandpa.

"Come here, Sarah." He made room for me beside him on the easy chair. "This is about Harry De Boer, your little friend." I glanced at Grandpa nervously. Moira climbed up on the arm of his chair.

"You know how Harry liked to drive that bucket of bolts belonging to his father, even though he could barely see over the bonnet?" I nodded. "Well, we won't be seeing Harry around here any longer. Yesterday evening he drove his father's car right off the cliff. They found it at the bottom, smashed against the rocks."

"And Harry?" I asked, my heart sinking.

"He's with Jesus," Mummy replied, sobbing. "I wish I had done more for the boy." She sniffed, dabbing at the tears streaming down her

face. "But it's too late now; he's with the angels. It may be all
best; he had no future with parents like that."

Suddenly wanting to be alone, I slid off the chair and ran outside.
Sitting in a quiet spot under the custard apple tree beside the pond, I
felt like crying, but somehow the tears would not spill down. Instead,
a tight, squeezing sensation gripped my chest. It suddenly dawned on
me that I had never before known a person who had died. Harry was
the first and he was just two years older than I. The realization left me
feeling helpless, since there was nothing I could do to bring him back.
He was gone and I would never see him again—this was frightening. I
wondered what being dead felt like. I thought only old people died and
that was perfectly okay, according to Grandpa. They were tired after
spending all that time on earth and so God called them back to their
reward, sending them to heaven or to hell, depending on how they had
behaved themselves on earth.

"When one gets old and crotchety, it's time to move on," he had
explained.

"Where's hell?" I wanted to know.

"Live long enough, sweet Sarah, and you'll discover hell right here
on earth. Everyone experiences hell at some time or the other, I'm pretty
sure of that." He nodded wisely.

I thought one had to die to go to hell, but hell on earth? It was all
very confusing. In that case, I didn't want Harry back; I wanted him
safe in heaven with the angels. We were chums and he would have taken
me for a ride anytime.

"I can take you as far as the market, Sarah," he had offered, wanting
me to come along.

"Won't your mummy mind?" I asked.

"She doesn't care."

"What about your daddy?"

"He's very busy. You see, he's a mail train driver."

"She's a bad lot." I could hear Mummy and Aunty Maggie
discussing Harry's mother.

A slight breeze brushed across my face and a dragonfly settled on
my arm. I knew it was Harry, telling me he could fly and didn't need
a car to get around. "I'll miss you," I whispered, as it flew away and
settled on a rose bush. Overcome with a strong urge to explore the cliffs,
I wanted desperately to see for myself the place where Harry's car had

leaped over the precipice. I wondered if it would still be there lying at the bottom, all smashed up on the rocks with the waves rolling over the broken bits. I knew the cliffs to be not more than half a mile down the road, since I passed them every day on my way to school. An easy walk, I could be there and back in plenty of time for tea. My mind made up, I rejoined the others sitting out on the front veranda.

"Feeling better, child?" Grandpa asked, his eyes shining.

Climbing onto the chair beside him, I requested a story.

"Yes, tell," said Moira squeezing in.

"Can't think of a thing," he replied gruffly. Setting down his newspaper, he rose from the chair. "I think I'll have a lie-down now; maybe later, girls." He limped slowly over to his bedroom.

It was a searing hot afternoon, but I sneaked out of the compound without a hat. Grandpa often said: "Mad dogs and Englishman go out in the midday sun," but I didn't care. The sky was a pale, washed-out blue, with a few clouds scudding about. Harry was sitting on one of them, I was sure. Granny had called him "a little angel" at breakfast. That's a switch, I thought; when he was alive, she had always referred to him as "the devil's spawn." I remembered the time she had caught him stealing mangoes from the tree behind the house. On that occasion, showing him her fist, she had yelled, "Dirty little thief!" after him. Of course, now the tables were turned and Harry could put in a good word for her in heaven. I chuckled to myself as I tripped along, kicking up the pebbles that crossed my path.

A rubble-strewn patch of bleached grass marked the end of the earth, which dropped sharply down to dark, jagged rocks. The sea below was rough and churned up into great frothy pools. Peering over the cliffs, I tasted salt spray on my lips. There was no sign of the De Boer's "bucket o' bolts," just three men in gumboots and raincoats, busy with a measuring tape. They shouted to one another while darting between the slippery rocks.

Gazing out across at the immense expanse of water that met the clear blue sky on the horizon, I felt myself a mere dot upon the barren landscape. Sweat poured down and a queasy feeling rose up inside my tummy; I began to feel sick. Poor Harry, I thought, he had literally fallen off the face of the earth, without knowing it. Feeling light-headed and delirious, I stared up at the sun as it went into a crazy spin, whirling in the sky, creating a giant funnel that slurped up the sea and carried it rushing towards me. Seized with a sense of panic, I turned and bolted out of there, running as fast as my feet would carry me, along the path leading back to the house, shrieking like a *puglee Mary*[23]: "Mummy! Daddy! Moira!"

With pounding heart, I slowed down, approaching the lane leading up to the house and stopped before the front gate to catch my breath. Hearing a terrible commotion in the compound, I peered in and saw Mummy on the front steps. She was calling my name. Suddenly, Aunty Maggie came hurtling out of nowhere and grabbed me by the arm, twisting it cruelly. I screamed in pain. Radha appeared on the scene. She was beside herself.

"What's the matter?" I asked. "Surely, it's not time for tea."

"Where have you been, Sarah?" Aunty Maggie panted, out of breath and quivering all over like a jelly. Without waiting for my reply, she dragged me through the garden and up the front steps, muttering, "A licking for sure." Sick with fear, I found myself suddenly looking up into Daddy's stern face.

"Where have you been, Sarah?" he asked between clenched teeth.

I looked up at him, mutely.

"Answer me, girl!"

I was dumbstruck; my heart filled with fear. I could say nothing and looked away. It was then that I felt the belt come down on my legs and buttocks repeatedly with thick, solid sounds.

"Stop it, Reg!" Mummy's voice was harsh. I fell limply to the floor as Daddy let go. Mummy half lifted, half dragged me into the bedroom. Closing the door, she asked severely, "Where were you this afternoon, Sarah? I want the truth." It was impossible to reply since I was crying so hard. "You must tell me," she insisted, "or I shall have to punish you further."

"I went to the cliffs," I blubbered, "to say goodbye to Harry." Crouched on the bed, I rubbed the welts on my bruised legs.

"Well I never!" she exclaimed, incredulous. "What possessed you to go there? ... Never mind. You are to stay in bed until I return." Pulling the covers right up to my chin, she drew the curtains and swept out of the room. After a while, Moira slowly pushed open the door and came in. Her lips were quivering, but she did not cry. Depositing Ronny, the rag doll, on the bed beside me, she curled up on the rocking chair,

---

23   *puglee Mary* crazy woman

cradling Lilibet in her arms. The room was heavy and grey in the filtered light of evening, but it soon grew dark and as silent as a tomb when night descended. Moira dozed off, but I remained wide awake. Radha entered and switched on a light.

"Where's everyone?" I asked.

"Gone for Harry baba's funeral," she replied morosely. "*Baba log*,[24] please to undress and make ready for bed, I going to bring dinner here. When Mummy, Daddy coming home, I tell baba log gone asleep."

"Can I eat here as well?" asked Moira.

"Why not." She turned and left the room.

The next day it was difficult getting out of bed. I was sore all over. A great cloud hung over me and I hated Daddy for what I felt was an unjust beating. Lingering in bed long after Moira had left for school, I turned my face to the wall when Mummy tried to rouse me.

Her voice was kindly, cajoling. "Come along, Sarah, it's time to shake a leg. Hamid has prepared a lovely omelette for you and there's plenty of toast. You wouldn't want all that to go to waste now, would you?"

"My tummy aches," I complained.

"A wandering fart," Grandpa teased playfully, entering the room. "Give the girl an opening dose and allow her to stay home. She has to be confined to the bathroom, of course."

I giggled. Mummy looked at Grandpa severely. She disapproved of "vulgar talk." I had once overheard her complaining to Daddy about Grandpa being crude.

Daddy shrugged, replying, "He tells it like it is."

Rising heavily, I took a bath, but did not change into my school uniform. Arriving at the breakfast table in my nightdress, I enjoyed Hamid's delicious omelette, which I washed down with sweet, milky tea.

The newspapers and radio broadcasts had proclaimed the war was over in Europe, but Japanese planes continued to shriek overhead. Mummy ignored the wailing sirens and made no move towards the trenches at the back of the house. She didn't seem to care and neither did I. Absorbed in her music, she reclined on the sofa with eyes closed, as symphonic strains from the old gramophone rose up and filled the

---

24   *Baba log* children

room. Classical music was her enduring passion and she particularly enjoyed the works of Mozart and Chopin. Curling up beside her, I too allowed the music to wash over me and drown out the warring world.

"Are you enjoying this piece, Sarah?" she asked softly.

I nodded.

"Who is it?" I asked hesitantly.

"Why, it's Mozart, of course, one of his great piano concertos. Do you know that Wolfgang Amadeus Mozart began composing at the age of five? And during his lifetime gave the world some of the most beautiful music?"

"How did he remember all those notes?"

"As I see it, Sarah, Mozart was an old soul who was first born at the dawn of musical expression, but died before completing his life's work. He was reincarnated and as a child he began furiously composing, completing a large body of work by the time he was a young man. The spirit within him may have known that this also was to be but a short journey. Mozart never lived to see old age."

"Do you think he will come back again?"

"Who knows? Musical genius is a gift from God that He bestows on men like Mozart, so that they may share it with the world, touching our hearts and making us aware of Him. Wordsworth once wrote: 'trailing clouds of glory, do we come, from God, who is our home.'"

I shivered, hearing those lines and promised myself to read more of Wordsworth's poetry.

"Be still, Sarah, and enjoy it." She touched me with a gentle fluttering motion.

There were hundreds of questions swimming around in my head, but I didn't dare disturb her. When the record ended with the scratching sound of the needle against the groove, I slipped off the sofa and turned it over. Winding up the gramophone again, I placed the needle on the reverse side. Once more the glorious strains soared heavenwards, filling the entire room with magical sound.

"*The Marriage of Figaro!*" Mummy exclaimed, before lapsing into silence.

That night, I hopped onto Grandpa's lap and asked, "Did you know what you were in your previous life?"

"H'm, let me think." He scratched his head. "Ah yes, now I remember. I was a majestic tiger, lord of the jungle."

"Did you know me then?"

"Of course, you were a comely village maiden named Tara, which by the way means shining star. I watched over you constantly—that is, until you were carried away by the Raja of Sonapur."[25]

"Why did he carry me away?"

"Well, you see it was like this—" Grandpa settled back into his chair and Moira scrambled up on the arm, anxious to hear the tale. "There was this comely maiden named Tara, who came down to the village well every day to draw water for her sick mother. Once, while the Raja was out hunting, he became very thirsty and passing the well he noticed the young girl with a bucket of water. 'Can I have a tumbler?' he asked and, as she handed it to him, he gazed into her sparkling eyes and was promptly smitten."

"What did she look like?" I asked breathlessly.

"Why, like you, silly. She had long, black braids, bright eyes and a lovely smile. The Raja accompanied Tara home and asked for her hand in marriage. Her mother readily agreed and a magnificent celebration followed. Soon after, he carried her away on his horse to live in his castle. They had many handsome sons and beautiful daughters."

"Who was I?" asked Moira.

"A dainty fawn of the forest that grew into a beautiful doe. No hunter was ever able to aim his arrow at you because you were under the protection of the gods of the jungle. One day the majestic stag, Bara Singha,[26] spotted you grazing on the Adol Maidan in the heart of the Satpura Hills.[27] It was love at first sight and, after a brief courtship, marriage followed. After that both of you spent many long years together, wandering the grassy slopes, nibbling on tender shoots and drinking from the crystal streams. And now, since you know all about your previous lives, old Sher Khan is toddling off to bed."

The war was really over, and the allies were victorious. Everywhere there were signs of jubilation. On the radio, in the newspapers and on the streets, people were babbling about it to one another.

"We whipped the living tar out of the Germans and the Japs!" Grandpa exulted, rubbing his hands together in satisfaction. He had the radio tuned to the BBC all the time.

---

25 *Sonapur* land of gold
26 *Bara Singha* a deer with 12-point horns
27 *Satpura Hills* in Central India

"Are we friends now?" I asked Aunty Maggie.

"With whom?"

"With the Germans and the Japs, of course."

"Not on your life. What a nerve, Sarah!" Aunty Maggie was indignant. She waddled off in the direction of the kitchen.

Of course, what she said made sense. After all, what was the point of all that bombing and fighting if they were just going to turn around and be the best of friends?

"What was all the fuss about, anyhow?" I asked Grandpa.

"The Japs and the Germans had to be taught a lesson," he replied seriously.

"Why?" I asked. "What did they do?"

"It's that madman Hitler's fault. And that crackpot Japanese emperor had no small hand in it as well. If they had won, can you imagine the world kowtowing to a bunch of gooks? No, siree. I'm glad we settled that, once and for all! Put them in their place, we did." He strode up and down the dining room, looking self-righteous and important. Moira and I gaped at him.

"Do we know any Japs or Germans?" I asked.

"No, Sarah, I don't think so and I don't imagine we are likely to know any in the future, either. Anyway, don't worry your pretty head about it now; plenty of time to read up on the war when you're grown up."

"I shan't be reading up on any war when I grow up; I'll be much too busy with other things. And as for trenches," I declared importantly, "why, I'll avoid them like the plague."

"Me too," echoed Moira.

Grandpa laughed out loud.

"Well then, that's settled. Now get on with your breakfast." Granny was supervising and she didn't approve of too much chatter.

I loved sitting in Granny's old rocker, which stood beside an open window in the sitting room. From there I could look out at the bushes in the garden and watch the birds as they soared in the sky or came to rest upon the highest branches of the trees. I would nestle close to her cushion that smelled of Pears soap, just like her, and begin to rock. Lulled by the motion, I'd fall asleep and dream the most wonderful dreams, from which I was always sorry to wake. In them, Grandpa stood tall and imposing and Granny wore a delicate lace dress with a shawl draped around her shoulders. Together they waltzed around the great gymkhana hall in Bombay. Occasionally, I paid a visit to their ground floor flat, where they had lived when they were first married, and it was just as they had described it. A light breeze made the chintz curtains billow and the flat smelled of salt sea air. Delicious odours streamed out from the kitchen, of crumb chops, chicken curry and a Dundee cake that Granny had baked for tea.

"Wake up, sleepy head, enough of catnapping in my chair."

It was Granny, reclaiming her seat.

"I had a lovely dream."

She smiled knowingly, sat down and continued with her knitting or crocheting. I had recently got into another argument with Mummy because I absolutely refused to wear the socks Granny made, since they had a habit of rolling down my ankles and by the end of the day were eaten by my shoes. I took to holding them up with rubber bands, but Mummy disapproved of them as well, saying, "Rubber bands cut off the circulation." After school, both Moira and I ran all over the house with lacy patterns etched into our bare feet. I felt they looked disgraceful, but there was nothing I could do. Besides, deep down I knew Mummy was right: Granny's knitted socks were a special gift from her to us, her granddaughters. When she handed us a pair, we had to put them on and stand before her shoeless. She would beam, exclaiming, "Don't they look pretty! Now, put your shoes on and let me see what you look like all dressed up." It was the same with the cardigans she knitted; we modelled every one of them for her, which gave her no end of enjoyment. The downside of all this, of course, was that we received countless more pairs of socks. I prayed the shop would run out of yarn.

Every time the postman swerved into the compound on his bicycle, Aunty Maggie rushed out to meet him, but she always returned empty-handed, looking sad and disappointed. She confided in me again one night, while Moira was snoring. Mummy and Daddy had gone off to the mess and we could not get to sleep.

"I'm going to have a baby, Sarah," she whispered.

I looked at her belly, then at her face, round-eyed with disbelief.

"Is that why you're so fat? Is there a baby in there?"

She nodded her head miserably.

"When is it due?"

"In a few months," she sobbed and I tried to put my arm around her, but it was useless, she was huge.

"Please don't cry, Aunty Maggie," I begged. "I'm sure it's not good for the baby."

"Oh, I wish Danny were here," she blubbered. "I miss him so."

"So that's why Granny keeps saying you're eating for two. Do they all know?"

"Yes."

"You mean to say that we are going to have a little boy or girl cousin and no one even bothered to inform Moira and me about it?" I hated everyone for keeping us in the dark. Despite that, I tried to cheer her up with words of encouragement: "I'm sure Danny will be here very soon. A letter is going to arrive any day now and it will be the happiest day of your life. Just you wait and see."

A few weeks later a letter did arrive, but it was not from Danny Groat. It was from Grandpa Reagan, who wrote to inform us of his impending visit. I was surprised. We hardly ever saw him these days, since running the Serendipity Lodge for retired British pensioners kept him busy all year round. This suited me perfectly, since he was not a particular favourite of mine or of anyone else in the family, for that matter. Grandpa Reagan was a short little man with a pale humourless face, a pointed chin and thin wet lips that hardly ever cracked a smile. He had a large drooping moustache and bright blue, darting eyes. His days were spent going to church, giving orders and disapproving of the way things were done. "A thoroughly disruptive influence," according to Daddy. That evening, after reading Grandpa's letter, Daddy flung it on the teapoy and stormed out of the room in a huff.

Returning a while later, he asked Mummy: "And why, pray, is he honouring us with his presence? What does he want this time? … Emma, your father is welcome to visit, but I really don't relish the idea of him coming around here and giving orders like a *burra sahib*."[28]

"He's coming to take our Maggie back to the lodge."

"Ha! And that's another kettle of fish. She should've known better than to get herself knocked up by a BOR[29]. I wouldn't be holding my

---

28   *burra sahib* big sir
29   *BOR* British Other Rank

breath if I were her, waiting for that bounder to return. It's a sorry state of affairs and a bad example for the girls. However, since she's your sister—"

That was quite a mouthful coming from Daddy, who generally never had a lot to say about Mummy's side of the family.

Mummy was silent.

The servants had a difficult time of it as well, when Grandpa was around. He was never happy with the way Radha made up the beds and continually gave Hamid orders to prepare special dinners for him. During his last visit he pushed Daddy's patience to the limit when he took a whip to Ranga and gave him a sound thrashing.

Livid, Daddy fumed, "Who does he think he is?"

I timidly ventured to ask Grandpa why he had beaten Ranga. "The boy has the devil in him," he replied severely.

I couldn't argue with that.

Grandpa Reagan had a daily ritual that began with mass in the morning and ended with church service at night. He would have liked to have dragged Moira and me along as well, but Mummy put her foot down and insisted, "Once a week on Sundays is quite enough."

A fortnight before Grandpa Reagan was due to turn up, Grandpa Watkinson informed us that he and Granny Connie would soon be returning home to Stanton Station. The news upset both Moira and me and we spent the entire day moping around the house.

"Why can't you stay on?" I asked that evening.

"I've got to get back and tend my failing crops," Grandpa sighed.

"Why are they failing?" inquired Moira.

"Because I don't tend them, silly, and the field hands do pretty much as they please when I am away."

"I have an idea," I chirped up. "Why don't you write and ask Uncle Cyril Fenwick to look after things for you. I heard you reading Aunty Hilda's letter out to Daddy the other day, in which she complained that Uncle Cyril was being his usual lazy self. Looking after the place until you get back would give him something to do."

"It wouldn't work." Grandpa shook his head. "If your uncle even bothered to reply, he'd most probably say I should return and attend to my own land. He's a lazy fellow, that's a fact, and will never change."

"And neither will you; you're both tarred with the same brush,"

Granny butted in, reminding him sharply. "I don't know how we three sisters made such bad choices with our husbands."

"Oh, come now, girlie, don't take on so. We've had a pretty good run of things, haven't we? Everything considered," he cajoled.

"Humph! That's what you think."

"Another thing, we must hire a new supervisor for next year," Grandpa said, "Bill Pigott hasn't panned out at all. I had a letter from Dr Sohrab Pudumjee, informing me of the fact that this loafer does nothing all day but sit around and play *theen patta*[30] with his cronies, who by the way are swarming all over the place."

"And that again is your fault, Cliffy," said Granny accusingly. "You fell for his sob stories. Alison Munroe warned us he was a good-for-nothing bounder, but you wanted to give him a chance. I, for one, was against hiring him from the start. Saw right through him, I did. Scruffily dressed and liquored up, to boot! What is worse, you gave him a free hand and the run of the place. If you would but attend to matters on the farm yourself we wouldn't need the likes of Bill Pigott to swindle us out of the little we have. I am sure if he is allowed to remain for another season he will land us in the poorhouse or into the hands of moneylenders."

Grandpa listened silently to Granny's tirade.

"We are already in their hands," he laughed shortly. "Where did you think we got the money from to buy seed and another pair of bulls?"

Granny continued with her knitting.

They departed as planned, leaving empty spaces everywhere. Moira and I were very glum.

Grandpa Reagan arrived seated in a tonga with his tin trunk and a bedding roll beside him.

"Hope he's not moving in for a long stay," observed Daddy, as he watched the servants help the tonga wallah unload Grandpa's luggage and bring it up the front steps into the house.

"I hardly think so." Mummy sounded stiff and angry.

Grandpa wore his *sola topee*,[31] puttees, and shorts. He carried a walking stick. We greeted him on the front steps, but Aunty Maggie

---

30   *theen patta* a three-card game
31   *sola topee* sun pith hat

was nowhere in sight. Mummy showed him to his room, which a short while ago had belonged to Grandpa and Granny Watkinson. I felt a twinge of sadness, but cheered up pretty fast because something was brewing and it promised to be exciting. Grandpa Reagan, sooner or later, managed to cause a stir. I hated kissing him good morning and good night though, and shuddered at the prospect of the new routine that would now commence.

It wasn't long before Mummy wouldn't allow Aunty Maggie to leave the house, not even to attend mass on Sunday. She could only stroll around the compound and sit outside in the garden after sundown. Mummy said it wasn't wise for her to gad about in her condition. Grandpa disagreed. He accused Mummy of being embarrassed to be seen out with her pregnant sister in front of all her la-di-da friends, especially since there was no husband in sight.

"They have nothing to be snooty about," he snorted. "Our Maggie's better than the best of them. Trash, for the most part. Know they can't make it in old Blighty, so they continue to stay here and lord it over the natives. I'm very well acquainted with that type. Met them at the club in Bombay every day."

"Speak for yourself, Pa." Mummy was livid.

Daddy too was beside himself and they didn't join us for tea. Aunty Maggie sobbed all the time. The letter from Danny Groat never arrived. Grandpa Reagan didn't care a fig, of course; he had his tea, buttered toast and jam, took a bath and walked over to the church for evening services.

The brief cold weather had fled. By late February the dry, blustery winds of impending summer swept down the coast. Sea breezes only served to make conditions muggy and oppressive. I suffered in the cruel heat, but not so Moira. Jugs of lemon and barley were placed on the dining table at every meal and Mummy informed Aunty Maggie that she was to consume five glasses, at the very least, per day.

"And you too, Sarah," she said. "Moira seems able to better withstand the heat. In any case, I don't want to see either of you roaming around outside without your hats in this blasted weather."

Moira and I were covered in prickly heat and we squirmed when our starched frocks rubbed against the rash. Radha dragged us off to the garden each evening, looking like a pair of clowns with liberal dustings of baby powder over our entire bodies. The grown-ups, from what I observed, seemed to be even more than ever at odds with each other. Daddy was irritable and impatient with everyone and kept repeatedly referring to Grandpa Reagan as "General Smuts."

"He's become even more pompous since acquiring the Serendipity Lodge," he remarked to Mummy. "I pity his poor guests and can't imagine how they put up with him. The man gets on my nerves. When does he plan to leave, Emma?"

"I put up with your parents for months on end, Reg, now it's your turn to put up with the old man," she replied. "I know he can be annoying at times, but it won't be for long."

"Annoying at times, did you say? That's putting it mildly. There's not a moment of the day when he isn't annoying, strutting around as if he owns the place, giving orders, left, right and centre."

"Well then, see what you can do. As soon as you can book a coupe to Bombay, he'll leave with Maggie and that'll be the end of that."

"I'll see to it right away!" Daddy replied, striding out of the house. Hopping into a waiting jeep, he was gone down the road in a cloud of dust. Mummy shook her head, picked up her magazine and continued reading.

"Who's General Smuts?" I asked.

"Who wants to know?" she looked up, a smirk on her face.

"I do. I hear Daddy calling Grandpa Reagan by that name all the time."

Mummy snickered. "You don't miss a trick, my pet, do you? General Smuts was a leader of South Africa—a very opinionated sort of chap. Mahatma Gandhi—one of our great leaders—when he was campaigning against white prejudice in South Africa, had a run-in with Smuts. A man of peace, Gandhiji,[32] is a lover of truth and non-violence. Unfortunately, the same can't be said of General Smuts."

I examined her face closely and was surprised to see how soft it had become. "You really do like this Mahatma, Mummy, don't you?"

"Yes, Sarah, he is making great changes here in India. And sometimes, I think, his is the only sane voice in the clamour around us."

Heat poured down and the situation continued to deteriorate.

---

32   *Gandhiji* the added *ji* is a term of respect

Mummy and Daddy seemed frequently to be at loggerheads with one another. Daddy had difficulty booking a compartment on a train to Bombay and so Grandpa Reagan's stay dragged on endlessly. He, of course, didn't seem at all worried, but went about his business as always, looking cross and silent most of the time. Aunty Maggie kept to her bedroom and so we didn't see much of her either. One evening, upon returning home from the garden, Moira and I noticed that the stifling heat had driven them all out of doors. The entire family, including Grandpa Reagan, were seated out in the front compound, looking sullen and depressed. We were allowed to join them. Mummy had two morras brought outside to extend the circle, and Moira climbed onto one.

Moonface sailed over the rooftop and the cloying fragrance of *rath ki rani*[33] scented the evening air. The shadow of the rain tree threw a lacy pattern across the garden. I circled its giant trunk and tripped a fairy path between the bushes, surrendering to the magic of the night.

> Moon of the summer night!
> Far down yon western steeps,
> Sink, sink in silver light!
> She sleeps!
> Sleeps!
> Wind of the summer night!
> Where yonder woodbine creeps,
> Fold, fold thy pinions light!
> She sleeps!
> My lady sleeps!
> Sleeps!
> (Henry Wadsworth Longfellow, "Serenade")

The following day, after Daddy had left for work, Mummy and Grandpa got into an argument. Since it was a special saint's day and a holiday for me, I grabbed my stool after breakfast and set it down quietly beside Mummy's bed. I knew that if I sat very still with my nose in a book the grown-ups wouldn't notice me and would freely speak their minds.

---

33   *rath ki rani* queen of the night

"It's one thing not allowing Maggie to gallivant all over the place in her state and quite another objecting to her attending mass," complained Grandpa loudly. "After all, Emma, a child conceived on a dirty weekend is hardly in a state of grace, even in its mother's womb. They both need all the help they can get."

Mummy, busy with tidying her dressing table drawers, turned and casually replied, "I have asked Father Humphrey over for dinner this evening and he will bring the host with him for Maggie."

"Not good enough, my girl! The Eucharist alone will not suffice. She must go to mass. This is a sorry business, indeed, from start to finish. Anyhow, I want Maggie to return with me and have her baby at the lodge. It will be baptised a Reagan. I have already spoken to Doc Stewart and filled him in with all the sordid details. He has agreed to come up from Bombay at the end of her term and stay with us until the confinement. Barring any complications, the delivery should go smoothly. Also, if it can be arranged, I would like for us to leave here as soon as possible. I've left the running of the lodge in the hands of that fellow Turcotte, one of my guests, but I'm getting anxious now and would like to leave. I only came to see Maggie safely home. By the way, has she heard anything from that good-for-nothing scoundrel, Danny Groat?"

"Not a thing," replied Mummy. "I'm beginning to think he might be a casualty."

"It's her who is the casualty," sputtered Grandpa in a rage. "He's landed her in quite a pickle, he has. Left her holding the baby, literally! I would like to pack her off to your sister Lillian in Kent after the delivery. Things are more liberal in England and she may just be able to make a fresh start there. No one will marry her here, once this gets out. Humph! What do you think?"

"It's for Maggie to decide, Pa. We can only tell her what her options are, but I wouldn't force her into anything. As you know, she has always had a mind of her own. The final decision has to be hers, after the baby arrives."

"Options, poptions!" Grandpa sputtered. "She had options before and we are now seeing the bloomin' results. I wanted her to attend Teachers' College in Poona; heaven knows, she had the brains for it. But no, she wouldn't listen—went waltzing off to Bombay to become a stenographer, if you please. Found a flat, joined up with those WAC friends of hers and this is the outcome! Sashaying about until all hours of the night with unsavoury types, no doubt, and that's how she got knocked up. Then she comes home and tries to lay some cock-and-bull story on me, but I'm no fool. I wasn't born yesterday, you know. 'Take yourself down to your sister,' I said, 'and stay there 'til I come and fetch you. I need time to work things out in my mind and make the necessary arrangements.'" He marched up and down the room irritably, chewing on his pipe.

"It's all water under the bridge now," said Mummy tiredly. "Let's attend to the matter at hand, instead of dragging up the past."

"Do the old couple know about this?" he asked.

"Who? You mean Ma and Pa Watkinson?"

"Who else?"

"Of course they know about it," replied Mummy, "they've been with us all this time and it's difficult to hide a thing like a pregnancy."

"Jesus, Mary and Joseph!" Grandpa Reagan exclaimed, collapsing into an easy chair, holding his head. "She's gone and made a laughing stock of us. That toddy tapper's[34] son and his country wife, what must they think?"

"I've heard enough!" Mummy snapped. "I won't have you bad-mouthing those sweet old things. What have they ever done to you?" Her face was flushed and two dangerous red spots appeared on her cheeks. "I'll agree, the old man is a bit rough around the edges, but that is no reason to be unkind. Besides, you're hardly in a position to talk."

"Right, I'm sorry," said Grandpa wearily. "It's just that so much has happened in the last little while, I feel like I'm falling apart at the seams. In truth, things haven't been the same since we lost your sainted mother. And now, God knows what's going to happen in this country with those Congress wallahs marching about, shouting *Jai Hind!*[35] all over the place. It doesn't sit well on an old-timer like me and I don't mind saying so. Quite frankly, I'm afraid of this new India."

"There's nothing to keep you here if you don't want to stay." Mummy was angry. "You can always pack up and go back to England.

---

34   *toddy tapper* person who tapped palm trees for toddy, which was distilled into liquor
35   *Jai Hind!* Hail India!

You did it once before, so who is stopping you now? Reg and I will remain here with the girls. He has a commission and a job to do."

"Yes, there's England." A far away look crept into Grandpa's eyes. "Ah! but that wouldn't work," he muttered. "I'm very involved with the lodge now and that keeps me going. I can't envision a life in England at this stage of the game."

He looked tired and depressed. The room fell silent, as Mummy dragged a chair up beside him and began leafing through a magazine.

Turning to Mummy again, he continued: "I hope and pray, for your sakes, that things don't go wrong. One can never be certain in these troubled times. Gandhiji, poor devil, I am sure must be having one helluva time trying to keep it all together. What with this Jinnah bloke giving himself airs on one side—him and his Muslim League clamouring for a separate country. And Nehru on the other, with something up his sleeve, toadying up to the Mountbattens at every turn. I have an idea it's got to do with Kashmir. Jinnah wants it too, you know, and that's the root of the problem. A real pity all this, for the vale of beauty may very well end up being a vale of tears." Grandpa let out a great sigh. "It seems like every man for himself, but whom for India, eh? I keep wondering about that. I'm afraid it's all going to end in a great big bloodbath with tragic consequences for those who fall between the cracks."

"Nonsense, Pa!" Mummy said impatiently. "Who is going to fall between the cracks?"

"The Anglo-Indians, my dear, that's who. While the Hindus and Muslims are at each others throats and busy carving up the subcontinent, do you think they're going to spare a thought for the A.I's? Not a bit of it. And why should they, I ask you? After all, Anglo-Indian sympathies have always been with the British. In their enthusiasm to eradicate all vestiges of British colonialism, you all may end up being murdered in your beds. I hear there is already a great clamour for passages to Blighty and that they are selling like hotcakes."

"It's talk like that which causes the most confusion." Mummy snapped at him. "What would you have us do? Pack our bags and run away to England? I don't think so. Besides, if there is a general clamour for passages to England, its England's turn now, isn't it? Ha! Even when they are packed in like sardines and people start falling off the bloody island, she won't be able to turn them back and do you know why? They'll all be carrying British passports."

"Dear God!" exclaimed Grandpa, "I think I need a stiff drink and could go for a gin and tonic."

"So could I, at this point," agreed Mummy. "I'll join you."

A new girl joined our class and she was assigned the desk beside me. Uma was a princess, a real one, and the nuns were falling all over her, especially Sister Rita. This was okay by me because it left her with no time to pick on Christine Turner. Uma had a small, pointed face, large coal-black eyes and long plaited hair. Every morning a huge car rolled into the school compound and stopped before Mother Superior's office. The driver hopped out and opened the rear door, allowing Uma and a servant carrying her school satchel and tiffin carrier to step out. Arriving late, she never attended catechism class because she was a Hindu and had her own gods, according to Mother. Of course, it didn't matter to the rest of us, since we were used to seeing the Hindu and Muslim girls go for music lessons during our catechism period. Uma didn't take music lessons.

"She is here simply to study," said Mother, but she did very little of that and hardly ever completed a homework assignment. Sister Rita forgave her every time. Miss Staples, on the other hand, would have none of it. When it was Uma's turn to recite, she became very shy and refused to stand up. We could feel Miss Staples' blood boiling just before she exploded.

"Please understand, I will not be trifled with," she said, her lips forming the famous thin line. "Uma, you are here to learn and learn you shall!" she snapped. "There will be no recess for you today and you will have to remain in class during the lunch hour to master this poem. Sarah, will you help her?"

I was startled. "Very well, Miss Staples," I replied importantly.

Uma was a dunderhead and it was an exercise in futility. "It's easy," I explained, trying to sound like Mummy. "Just apply yourself and recite after me: 'I remember, I remember, the house where I was born—'" I led her through the opening lines of Thomas Hood's poem, but it was useless; she mumbled some of the words and swallowed the rest. I resolved to take her seriously in hand.

Writing to Grandpa about Uma, I mentioned the fact that she was a princess. Grandpa's reply made me laugh. "Is she the daughter of the *Rani of Kooch Parva Nai?*"[36] he inquired. I showed the letter to Evelyn who also thought it very funny.

"I would love to have a family like yours, Sarah Watkinson," she said, looking at me longingly with crossed eyes. "You live such an interesting life."

I whispered Aunty Maggie's secret in her ear. That really bowled her over.

Change was in the air.

Daddy came home with the news that he was being transferred.

Aunty Maggie was busy getting ready to leave with Grandpa Reagan at the end of the week, since Daddy had managed to find a berth on the Bombay Mail. She was going to have her baby at the Serendipity Lodge on Bell Island, which was off the coast of Bombay. She wasn't thrilled about the fact, but Mummy reminded her that beggars can't be choosers.

"You've got yourself into a sticky situation here, Maggie, and this seems to be the only way out. After you have the baby, we can discuss where to go from there. But for the time being, for God's sake, co-operate. Don't make things even more difficult than they already are."

However, Aunty Maggie was positively not going to England. "I will not be railroaded into that," she said determinedly, blowing smoke rings into the air. This was supposed to be her last cigarette before she stopped smoking altogether. I greedily inhaled her smoke and savoured the few puffs she allowed me when no one was looking. I would miss them. Aunty Maggie seemed her old self that evening and confided that if the baby was a boy she planned to name him Trevor and Amber, if it was a girl.

"Ooh—Amber!" I wrinkled my nose. "Where did you get that name from?"

"From a novel, silly, that you wouldn't be allowed to read anyway, since you're not grown up enough."

I was silent.

By nightfall, however, Aunty Maggie was a wreck. She burst into Mummy's bedroom sobbing as if her heart would break. Moira and

36 *Rani of Kooch Parva Nai* queen with no worries

I peered in from behind the curtains to see what the hullabaloo was about. Mummy held her close.

"There, there, now, everything is going to be all right, I assure you."

"I can't go through with this alone," she blubbered.

"You won't have to," Mummy consoled. "Old Doc Stewart will be there with you and Pa—"

"That's what I mean," she wailed. "It's just too much. I think I shall die. Please, please come back with us, Emma. School will be out and the girls can spend their holidays at the lodge. You know how Pa loves having them around."

"H'm," Mummy was not convinced. "I certainly can't travel with you next week, if that's what you're getting at, but there is a possibility we could follow later. You know how Reg feels about Bell Island; I'd have to convince him. With the war over, who knows, he may allow us to spend the summer there. At any rate, I'll have a talk with him. It will mean he'll have to go down to Delhi alone and live in the mess for a while. It's very unlikely we'll get accommodation right away, with things the way they are. Of course, he'll have Hamid along to do for him and Radha can travel with us." Even as she spoke, Mummy solved the problem in that efficient way she had.

"Leave it with me for the present, will you? We'll work something out, I promise. In the meantime, dry your eyes and try not to worry. It's not good for you to get all weepy so close to your confinement. This sorry state will sort itself out, one way or another. I know what you mean; I can understand how all those old-timers at the lodge can be intimidating. Cheer up, old thing!"

Aunty Maggie mopped her eyes with one of her snotty handkerchiefs.

"I thought we were going to the farm for the holidays, to be with Grandpa Cliffy," I whined a few evenings later, as we sat outside in the cool evening air.

"And who said otherwise?"

"You did. I heard you promise Aunty Maggie."

"You heard right, little miss inquisitive bob. Plans change. Aunty Maggie needs me. Besides, you both may enjoy the seaside for a change and there'll be plenty to keep you both occupied at the lodge. All in all, it promises to be a very exciting time for you girls."

"Will Aunty Maggie be having her baby while we are there?"

"Why, Sarah, what a question?"

"Well, will she?"

"Yes, my dear, you are about to have a new little cousin. Does Moira know about this?"

"I don't know." I shrugged.

"My, what a precocious little creature you are growing up to be. I shall have to watch you more closely from now on." Mummy stroked my hair.

Daddy glared at her.

Worse news was on its way. After the holidays, both Moira and I were going to be packed off to a boarding school, "to a proper convent," according to Mummy.

"And where are you all going to be?" I wailed when she informed us.

"Your father has been posted to Delhi, but he doesn't know as yet how long he will be there. We shall most probably be living out of boxes for ages, since I hear there is a shortage of accommodation in the capital. And if Daddy should be posted out again soon after—to God knows where—I don't want all this moving about from pillar to post to disrupt your education. So we have decided to put you both into a good boarding school, for the time being at any rate.

"No-o-o—" I wailed. "I shan't go. You can't make me. Why can't we go and live with Grandpa Cliffy on the farm until the army makes up its mind where it wants to post Daddy?"

"Don't be absurd, Sarah. Be sensible, child. You and your sister must have a proper education."

"Can I come with you?" asked Moira, looking up at me.

I put my arm protectively around her. "Of course you can and I shall take good care of you." I glared accusingly at Mummy.

"Now, let's have no more of these tantrums," she said tiredly, "I have an awful lot of planning ahead of me. There is packing for the move, your school kits and tuck box, not to mention the summer holidays. O Lordy, this means countless sets of clothing! "

"A tuck box each!" I exclaimed excited.

"No, Sarah, a kit box each, and one tuck box for the both of you," she corrected.

I felt suddenly excited, but sad as well to be leaving Saltair-By-The-Sea, school and all my friends. "What about the servants?" I asked nervously.

"Radha will be accompanying us to the lodge, of course, and Hamid will be with Daddy. As for the others, they are all expendable and will stay behind, with proper recommendations, naturally."

I hugged Radha; it would be impossible to leave her behind.

The end of term rolled around and with it my last day at the Convent of the Holy Name. After lunch I walked over and said goodbye to the lighthouse, the Bay of Bengal and the fishing vessels bobbing in the sea. We had shared so much.

I sat sadly beside Evelyn, waiting for the bus. Uma joined us. Over the past few months the little princess and I had become good friends. I introduced her to the lighthouse and she had slipped away on a couple of occasions to spend the afternoon with me. Of course, the nuns were not aware that we had skipped afternoon classes, but Uma's trusted guardian, Munshi, had to be told. He nodded and looked in my direction suspiciously, as Uma whispered in his ear. During one of our chats, I learned that Uma, prior to attending the Convent of the Holy Name, had been tutored by an English schoolmistress, a Miss Drummond, whose job it was to teach her English, music and deportment, but she had picked up nothing in two years of instruction. The teacher was horrid, she said, and treated her cruelly when her parents were away, which was almost all the time. "The Ogre," as I christened her, was eventually dismissed after a maidservant discovered her slapping Uma. One day, during the lunch hour, Uma shared a secret with me: her parents, it seemed, were searching for a husband for her.

"How do you know?" I inquired, bowled over by this piece of news. "Golly, aren't you a bit young for marriage?"

"I'm twelve," she replied simply, "old enough for the search to begin. It's very important they find the proper groom."

"Who told you this?" I asked.

"My ayah, of course; she knows everything that goes on. Besides, she wants to come along with me when I go to my husband's house.

And since I love her, I will ask for her to be my maid. In this way, I will always have with me someone that truly loves me from my home."

She sounded wiser than her years and very grown up.

"I think you're rather young to be having such thoughts, Uma. Maybe you should talk to your mummy about it and not listen to ayah stories. I for one can't imagine getting married and leaving home right now, although I know grown-ups do it all the time. Will you see your mummy and daddy after marriage?"

"I hardly see Papa at all, even now," she replied. "Mummy, of course, will come to visit and I will come home to have my babies."

"Babies!" I exclaimed, aghast, "you'll be having babies."

"Why not? My older sister has two and I am already an aunty."

"Uma, you're a wonder," I cried, "and very brave." She looked at me with shining eyes.

Now, seated between the two of them, I gazed at Uma's small, pinched face, and slipping my hand in hers squeezed it tight. I was going to miss her terribly and Evelyn as well. I bent over with a cramp in my stomach. "We'll always be friends," I whispered hoarsely, tears sliding down my face. "And I'll write; I promise you." Evelyn turned away and I knew she was crying. Thoroughly depressed, I could think of nothing to say and this in itself was strange, since I was known as "Sarah Jabberwocky."

"Moira and I will be going to boarding school after the holidays," I informed them mournfully.

"What's it like?" asked Evelyn.

"Dunno, but I'll let you know."

"Where has your father been posted, Sarah?" asked Veronica Fleming, on her way to a waiting car. Her father was an army officer as well and so she knew all about postings.

"To the capital, Delhi," I replied importantly.

Clambering into the old camouflaged bus for the last time, I felt someone tugging at my uniform. It was Christine Turner, looking up at me with red-rimmed eyes.

"Goodbye, Sarah Watkinson," she said seriously. "Here is my pencil with a rubber at the end, to remember me by."

Dumfounded, I muttered, "Thank you."

The bus turned out of the compound and gathered speed along the dust-filled road. I waved and waved until my friends were mere specks on the horizon. When Ignatius reached my stop, I quickly jumped out without wishing him well. Racing across the compound, bounding up the stairs, I fled to the safety of my bedroom.

Saying goodbye proved to be a horrible, stomach-churning experience. "When I grow up, I shall never, never move," I vowed to Mummy. "I'll stay in the same place until I am very old and then I'll just disappear, or something." We were seated amidst the confusion of tin trunks and bedding rolls. She put an arm round me and her eyes were moist. "I was settling in so nicely at school, even Miss Staples was starting to like me," I confided. "Why do we always have to move? Couldn't we stay here a while longer or at least until I grow up and get married?"

"Yes, that would be ideal, Sarah," she looked at me kindly, "but, unfortunately, your father has a career in the army that requires him to be posted at least once every two years. But you are right, leave-taking is never easy. Just getting your kit ready for boarding school has been very hard on me. Your father and I will miss this place as well; we have made so many good friends here. Unfortunately, leave taking is a fact of life and so we had better get on with it."

Ever practical, ever Mummy!

I sobbed into my pillow every night. Would I ever see my friends again? What about Grandpa and Granny Watkinson? Delhi seemed a million miles away. Would they ever visit? Besides, I would have to take care of Moira, a huge responsibility. She could be a crybaby sometimes, most times. I wept for days and days, but no one seemed to care. The custard apple tree beside the pond became my refuge. Mummy looked preoccupied and harassed and Daddy kept out of sight. I think he was avoiding Grandpa Reagan, who was himself getting ready to leave with Aunty Maggie. Radha must have noticed how broody I had become and informed Mummy, for she came into our bedroom late one night.

"Life is full of change, Sarah," she said softly, stroking my face. "You've had a lot of growing up to do in the last little while, but there's nothing wrong with that." She looked quite wan herself. "Saying goodbye is beastly business, I know, but there will be new friends and a whole new world is waiting out there for both of you. But first, of course, we have the summer holidays to look forward to. I think it's going to be quite wonderful by the sea. So, for the time being, I want no more sulking and talk about boarding school, you hear?" Mummy rose and moved towards Moira's bed, leaving her scent of sandalwood behind.

Moira started to wail. "I don't want to go to boarding school with Sarah. I want to stay with you."

"There's nothing to be afraid of. It's an excellent convent; it will help both of you to grow into accomplished young ladies." Kissing Moira good night, she slipped out of the room.

I tried to imagine what boarding school would be like, but couldn't picture it. My fears and uncertainty produced confusing dreams.

PART TWO

Serendipity Lodge

Upon arriving in Bombay, Mummy made arrangements for our journey to Bell Island to the Serendipity Lodge where we were going to spend our summer holidays with Grandpa Reagan and Aunty Maggie, who was going to have a baby. We set out late one evening as the sun went down in a blaze behind the Gateway of India. Boarding a launch at Ballard Pier, Moira and I slid about on the seats that were wet with sea spray and smelled of fish. As the city of Bombay receded in the distance, Radha opened the picnic basket and we helped ourselves to hard-boiled egg sandwiches. Eating with gusto, we washed them down with mugs of sweet, milky tea. Mummy had purchased a dozen large, loose-jacketed Nagpur oranges, which she shared with us. We sucked on the juicy segments and spat the seeds into the churning waters, while searching for jellyfish. There were none to be seen, of course, just sunset streaks of orange and gold, piercing the inky sea.

Night fell suddenly and it was pitch dark with the only light being the flickering flame of a kerosene lantern at the bow of the boat. In the distance I could see the twinkling lights of ocean-going vessels anchored out of Bombay harbour. Gazing at them, my mind drifted back to what I knew of Grandpa Reagan and to that weekend of confusion when he had first purchased the lodge.

A coffee planter for most of his life, Grandpa sold his plantation after the death of the "sainted" Sheila, his wife and our grandmother. She passed away when I was two years old and so I never did get to know her. Disgusted with the political unrest in India, he returned to England, but after a few years became disillusioned with conditions there as well. With the threat of war looming on the horizon, he sailed back to Bombay, rented a house and settled into a routine. After mass each morning, he would take a long walk to the club, where he had his breakfast and read the daily newspapers and other periodicals. Mummy said Grandpa was unsettled and grieving for her mother. She wished he would find something to occupy his mind and raise his spirits. Daddy very seldom offered his opinion but, when he did, it was only to say that Grandpa was a crusty old fellow and, at the best of times, very difficult to deal with. This was the main reason he had no friends because few people were willing to put up with his cockeyed opinions and high-handed behaviour. There always seemed to be tension between the two of them.

One morning, prior to Daddy's transfer to Saltair-By-The Sea,

Mummy had received a letter from Grandpa in which he asked my parents if they could come down to Bombay for a few days.

"I have made a sizeable real estate purchase," he wrote, "and would like your opinion."

Mummy and Daddy decided to make the journey and took us along as well. It would be a short holiday, Daddy said; we could spend a few days shopping and taking in the sights. Moira and I were excited. However, what was supposed to be a happy interlude turned into a series of heated arguments between the three of them.

We stayed at Grandpa's rented bungalow. The next morning the three of them started out early to look over the property Grandpa had purchased. It had once been an elite sailing club, but its owners had grown nervous with the sounding bells of approaching Indian Independence and had hurriedly placed it on the market. They wanted to sell, take their money and clear out of the country. The club was located on Bell Island, one of many dotting the coast, attached to mainland Bombay by a causeway. Grandpa Reagan intended to turn it into a home for retired British colonials who wished to remain in India.

That afternoon, as Moira and I sat lounging on the cane furniture set out on the front porch, we could hear Grandpa's raised voice as they approached the house. He was congratulating himself on his good fortune at being able to snap up such a splendid piece of land for "a mere pittance." Mummy said she was delighted for him and, as they drew nearer, I watched as she patiently listened to his eloquent recounting of the many desirable features and panoramic view from the garden.

"Most impressive, don't you think? Perched high on that rocky headland, overlooking the sea—at night, one can see the lights from ocean-going vessels anchored out in Bombay harbour. And the sunsets! Why, they're spectacular!" Chuckling, rubbing his palms together, Grandpa flopped down on the settee beside me and called for a beer to celebrate his good fortune.

Daddy was silent the entire time. When Rahim Khan, Grandpa's old bearer arrived with the drinks, he took a sip from his glass and seriously declared, "It's a scenic spot all right, but hardly a deal given its location. With the war on, no one in his right mind would have touched that property with a barge pole."

"Why?" asked Grandpa. "Not of any strategic importance is it? I just see it as a beautiful piece of land with an unspoiled beach. Besides, it has a lot to recommend it. There are countless little atolls fringed with palm trees just a boat ride away, excellent spots for picnics, I'd say. I've made inquiries, and the local fishermen are not averse to rowing a party out for a couple of chips. Oh! I've been busy. Scouting around, getting to know the lay of the land, buttering up the natives. It doesn't hurt, you know. Of course, the lodge needs a little work, but nothing a coat of paint and a few nails can't fix. The wood has rotted away in parts, but I've hired a carpenter for the job."

"It's not safe," said Daddy, adamantly. "Too many bays and inlets. Jap submarines can slip in with ease and lie undetected for weeks, even months. And if their planes decided to bomb Bombay harbour, guess who'd catch it as well? I'll never agree to Emma and the girls visiting, as long as the war is on. You can forget it!"

Moira and I were hurriedly packed off to bed, but even though I drew the covers over my head to shut out the sound of their raised voices, I could still hear Grandpa blustering away and Daddy making his point. Later that evening, I heard Mummy taking him to task, for being "harsh with the old man."

"The lodge is a good idea, Reg. If this independence thing ever materializes, I am sure there will be a lot of British retirees with no intentions of pushing off to Blighty. The truth is, many of them are ready for the glue factory and have nothing to go back too. India is all they know—*ma/bap*,[37] so to speak. The lodge will fill a need. Renting out rooms to a few 'guests,' as he likes to call them, will give the old man a purpose and something to do. He has been so lost since Ma passed away."

"Layabouts," Daddy snorted, "looking for the easy life. They've had it good here for far too long and now, of course, they're afraid to face reality and go back where they came from and that's the truth."

"I disagree," stated Mummy emphatically. "Many of them were born here and have given their all to India." She had the last word.

So, here we were, Mummy, Radha, Moira, and I being tossed about in a fishy smelling launch on the Arabian Sea. I had heard Mummy confiding to one of her friends from the bridge club that Daddy had

---

37   *ma/bap* mother and father

relented since the war was over and on "compassionate grounds." I guessed the last part had something to do with Aunty Maggie.

Arriving alongside the jetty, we discovered Grandpa had sent a porter to meet us and he helped with the luggage.

There were a great many steps with an iron handrail winding up to the gates of the lodge, which opened to reveal a garden and a cobbled path leading to a trellised front porch. Grandpa Reagan was there on the top step to greet us. He planted a moist kiss on our cheeks and ushered us into his stuffy sitting room, filled with heavy furniture.

"This is where my guests enjoy their R and R," he declared expansively. "I know you must be tired, but let me give you a quick tour so you'll know where everything is." He took the lead and we dragged wearily behind. Across from the sitting room was the dining room, where twelve straight-backed chairs stood arranged around a large polished dining table. A heavy sideboard cluttered with photographs and crystal stood against one wall and a tea trolley against another. In the passageway we passed a curtained door that Grandpa called his "private sanctum."

"Close enough so I can keep an eye on things," he remarked, winking. Further down the corridor was a library. "It's imperative to check out any book you wish to read," he said, looking directly at me. "In this way I have a record of who has what." A staircase led to further bedrooms upstairs and it creaked as we stumbled up after him.

"Now girls," he admonished, "on no account must you race up and down these stairs. As you know my guests are on in years and like their peace and quiet."

We halted on the landing as Grandpa rambled on, explaining how everything ran like clockwork at the lodge.

"It's shipshape and Bristol fashion around here! I insist on set meals at set times. For instance, *chota hazri*[38] is at seven in the morning. Not necessary for you two girls, but, Emma, would you like to have tea sent up? Breakfast is at eight-thirty sharp, lunch at noon and tea at four o'clock. Dinner is no later than nine. The servants have to get their rest, you know."

Mummy paid scant attention and asked, "Where's Maggie? I want to go to her."

"She must be in her bedroom, my dear." Turning to us, he

---

38   *chota hazri* little breakfast, served in bed

continued: "You both look ready for bed, so let me show you to your room. You'll be sharing the bathroom with your aunt; of course, the rest of the rooms are used by my guests. There are two more bedrooms downstairs, off the veranda, and they are occupied by the Dowling sisters and their brother Stanley."

Mummy made a beeline for Aunty Maggie's room, while Radha entered our room and opened the windows to let the fresh air in. We had a sea view and the limp cotton curtains stirred lazily, catching the cool night breeze. Moira declared the mattresses lumpy, as she busily tucked Lilibet in for the night. Ronny, the rag doll had been packed away and would travel to the next posting with the rest of the luggage. When the time had come to say goodbye to Lilibet though, Moira had created quite a scene and Mummy softened. I shuddered at the idea of carting her along with us to boarding school. It would be most embarrassing.

Radha dropped her bedding roll on the floor. "I sleeping here," she declared firmly.

Grandpa, standing at the door, informed her that there was a servant quarter at the rear of the house, which she could use.

"We want her with us," whined Moira.

"As you wish," he replied, stomping out of the room.

After a while, Mummy returned with Aunty Maggie, who looked bigger than ever. Her soft, round face seemed strained and she smiled wearily. We clamoured over her and she seemed happy to see us.

"Will you come catch crabs with me tomorrow?" Moira asked. Aunty Maggie looked pointedly at her stomach.

"Is there a baby in there?"

"Moira!" gasped Mummy. Glaring at me accusingly: "Sarah, you didn't?"

I shook my head.

"Is there?" Moira persisted.

"Yes," replied Aunty Maggie, simply.

Moira laughed, triumphant.

"Where's everyone?" I inquired, changing the subject. "The place looks dead."

"Very nearly is," Aunty Maggie laughed. "Just watch, they'll all come creeping out of their coffins for breakfast tomorrow morning," she giggled.

We hugged her.

"I'm hungry," I complained, rubbing my belly. "Can't we get something to eat?"

"The servants have all left for the day," Aunty Maggie mimicked Grandpa, "but let's see what's in the meatsafe."

While Mummy and her sister crept downstairs to rustle up some food, Radha laid out our nightclothes and we washed up.

Sitting up in bed, polishing off a potato cutlet sandwiched between doorsteps of buttered bread, I drained a glass of warm milk and burped with satisfaction. Looking around the room, I was content to see all my favourite people present.

Mummy and Aunty Maggie stayed up talking until all hours. Trying to stay awake with them proved impossible, as my eyes grew heavy and I drifted off.

The next morning Grandpa's guests were all assembled around the breakfast table: the two Miss Dowlings and their brother Stanley; Miss Skinner, a retired school teacher; and Major Edmund Turcotte. Moira and I joined them, decked out in brand new sundresses, with sandals on our feet. Miss Skinner looked us up and down, her lips compressed into a thin red line.

"Miss Staples!" I gasped, shocked at the uncanny resemblance.

Mummy frowned at me, as I slid into the chair beside her.

Quarter-boiled eggs, buttered toast and marmalade—tea, coffee, and milk, with fruit after. Rahim Khan, Grandpa's old bearer, shuffled in and out, setting down and removing plates. The two Miss Dowlings dabbed the corners of their mouths with napkins. Mr Stanley Dowling had large, bulbous fish eyes and an Adam's apple which bobbed up and down each time he swallowed a piece of toast. He watched us intently, a weak smile hovering about his pouting, wet lips. Miss Skinner simpered and batted her lashes at the Major while passing him the jam, but he didn't seem to notice her at all, since he was preoccupied with the newspaper and the "conditions in England after the war." I gawked at her, unable to turn my eyes away. She returned my gaze with a cold, hard stare.

Moira and I had porridge in which a banana had been sliced—we detested it. The toast was soggy and Moira slipped hers to Toby, the lodge dog, who sat under the table to receive all the scraps.

There was very little conversation at breakfast.

One of Grandpa Reagan's rules was that you had to close the front gate behind you to prevent stray dogs from venturing onto the property.

"They may have rabies," he declared, "in which case, if you're bitten, you'll get hydrophobia and die frothing at the mouth."

"Not if you reached the doctor first," I corrected him, "and he gave you several injections in the stomach. I learnt that at school."

"That's enough out of you, you cheeky girl," he snapped at me. "There is a standing rule around here: the gate must remain closed at all times. And I expect everybody to obey." He marched back into the house.

Of course, we forgot the rule. The rusty, old gate squeaked, swinging on its hinges as we darted in and out on our way down to the beach and back up again. Radha had a hard time controlling us and when Grandpa discovered the gate open she got bawled out for it. I thought it was most unfair, especially since the back of the lodge was not fenced in and, throughout the afternoon, umpteen ring-tailed pye-dogs sauntered into the compound to loll beneath the peepul tree. They were all friends of Toby's, who whined and wagged his tail in greeting as each one appeared.

I knew Grandpa had it in for Radha because she had refused to sleep in the servants' quarters. Having had enough of his *kitkit*,[39] she took herself off in a huff and found a quiet spot on the back veranda.

Muttering under her breath, she opened her little betel nut box and began the ritual of making paan. Smearing the leaf with lime, cracking an areca nut into tiny pieces, adding a hint of tobacco and secret spices to the leaf, she tenderly folded it and placed it in her mouth. Moira and I watched intently, salivating, as she went through the ritual of chewing and spitting. The intoxicants finally took hold and her mood improved. We persuaded her to make up two little sweet packets for us and shoved them to the back of our mouths, just as we had seen her do hundreds of times. I concentrated on the serious business of masticating—the juices flowed, flooding my mouth and dribbling down the sides. I spat

---

39   *kitkit* constant interfering

a furious torrent of red onto the bleached sand and Moira followed suit. We gazed intently as it ran away from us like a stream of blood. Consuming the "cud," I ran into the bathroom to examine my mouth and lips in the mirror, pleased to see them stained red all over. Moira drank a glass of water to try and get rid of her colour, since she was afraid of being found out.

The sea washed up debris all along the beach: dented cans, bottles, old leather chappals, coconut shells and large brown logs covered with moss. Monstrous rocks stood guard along the shore, like sentinels heaved up from the ocean floor, their surfaces dark and slippery. Some were jagged with deep fissures, almost cleft in two. Some were smooth with basins hollowed out in them. The tide rushed in, bringing with it huge waves that washed over the rocks. Retreating, it left behind crystal clear pools of sea water with soft-shelled crabs and tiny darting fish trapped in the basins. Moira and I filled our buckets, then racing to the deep wells we had dug along the shore, hurriedly emptied them, watching in fascination as the water vanished, leaving the poor little fish to wriggle about and eventually expire on the sun-baked surface. The crabs, however, disappeared, sucked up by the porous sand.

A particularly picturesque spot, where a palm tree curved over a large flat rock, was the favourite backdrop for photographic sessions. The ladies of the lodge, dressed in soft muslin, with white buckled shoes and parasols, posed alone or in groups, and were photographed by Mr Stanley Dowling with his box camera.

"What will they do with the pictures?" I asked Mummy.

"I imagine they send them to friends and relatives in England."

"To show what a good time they're having?"

"I suppose so."

"Oh! But that's not true," I disagreed. "They're always grumpy around the lodge, like they're having a bad day."

"Enough said, Sarah!" Mummy snapped at me. "Let's go in. These flies are driving me crazy."

Aunty Maggie kept to her room a lot, but sometimes I would find her brooding down by the shore. Leaning against a palm tree with a far away look in her eyes, she whiled away the hours, drawing patterns in the sand with a piece of driftwood. My heart ached for her. If only I could do something—send a message to Danny Groat, for instance.

I suddenly recalled Mummy's words: "He might be a casualty." In that case, he would never return, never know that Aunty Maggie had had a baby and that he was the father of a little boy or girl. I moved closer to her on the warm sand and placed my hand upon her arm. From time to time she heaved a great sigh, which brought tears to my eyes. It all seemed quite hopeless.

A few nights later, I overheard Mummy telling Grandpa that he had better send for Doc Stewart.

"Her belly has dropped, so the head must be in place. She could deliver at any time now," her concerned voice continued. "At any rate, it's a good idea for him to come and examine her."

Grandpa dispatched Rahim Khan with a letter.

Miss Esther Dowling liked to sit on a rocking chair near the low veranda wall and crochet all day. She made countless little squares that she shoved into a large bag, which in turn was made from countless little squares. Each time she completed six squares, she joined them together to form a row.

"What are you making?" Moira, asked.

"Wouldn't you like to know?" Miss Esther fixed her beady eyes on Moira.

"Yes, I would."

"Well, my dear, I have an order from the bogey-man to make a large bag."

"What will he do with it?"

"He will use it to carry away naughty, inquisitive little girls like you to a special horrible place where they never get to see their parents again. Now, if the both of you don't run along and play this minute, I might just give him your names." She glared at us malevolently. Moira ran to the safety of Radha's lap. I disappeared over the low wall.

A few days later, as I sat crouched against this selfsame wall, enjoying a handful of jambuls, whose dark, purple flesh stained my mouth and hands, peering over, I spotted Miss Esther busy with her squares. An opportunity for retribution presented itself and I was quick to seize it. Flicking the ickiest seed in her direction, I ducked as it caught her smack in the middle of her forehead. Startled, she lurched forward and let out a banshee scream. Her shrieking set Polly off in her cage.

"Bitch!" Polly screeched. "Bloody old bitch!"

Grandpa came rushing out onto the veranda, exclaiming, "What's the hullabaloo about? What happened here?"

Miss Nellie Dowling appeared upon the scene and led a flustered Miss Esther away.

Turning to Grandpa, she asked, severely, "Who gave you that bird, a drunken sailor?"

Retreating in a huff, he never bothered to reply.

Undetected, I slipped into the back garden, feeling as pleased as punch. Wanting to share my prank with someone, I went in search of Moira, but then thought better of it—she was known for carrying tales and could go to Mummy with it. A while later, I came upon Aunty Maggie, sprawled out on a deck chair in the garden, and she asked what all the fuss was about. I recounted the incident, with some embellishment.

"Serves her bloody well right, they're a pair of frustrated old biddies that don't approve of me, you know."

"Why?" I asked.

"Oh! Because of this," she poked her stomach. "Them and their stuffy old Victorian values. They can go to hell for all I care!"

Aunty Maggie was on a rampage and I was disappointed. She had failed to see the clever way I had wreaked revenge. Guessing that something more than just the two Miss Dowlings was bothering her, I kept very quiet. In a huff, she eased herself out of the chair and waddled down to the beach with me trying to keep pace as she strode along the shore like a sergeant major.

"What's the matter?" I finally asked. "Aren't you feeling well?"

"Buzz off, Sarah, will you? I want to be alone."

I was hurt beyond belief and fell back, watching as she continued walking along the shore, her heavy, swollen feet, sinking into the warm, wet sand as the tide rolled in.

I hated sleeping in the afternoon and crept out of the house every chance I got to play hopscotch in the back compound with the servants' children. One sultry Sunday, Gita, the dhobi's daughter and I were busy with our game, when Mr Stanley Dowling and Jamal, the kitchen helper, appeared upon the scene. Mr Dowling had an olive-green haversack slung across his shoulder, while Jamal trailed behind with a butterfly net.

Reaching into his haversack, he produced a handful of *curoundas*[40] and offered them to me.

"Where did you pick them?" I asked.

"That's my secret. Here's some for you."

I sat down and he dropped them into my lap. Biting into the tiny, tart, plum-like berries, I looked up and inquisitively inquired, "Have you been catching butterflies?"

"As a matter fact, I have. Would you like to see my collection?"

I nodded.

"Well, some afternoon when everyone's asleep, you can slip out of your room, like I've seen you do on countless occasions, knock on my door and I shall be more than happy to show them to you. I have an entire room of butterflies, fragile, delicate little creatures, impaled upon my walls." He had a peculiar look in his eyes. "Will you come?" he asked again.

"I'll think about it."

He squatted down beside me on the step and I tensed, feeling his hot breath on my neck. Beads of perspiration trickled down from under his sola topee and ran streaming into the furrows of his fat, flushed face. Mopping it with a large white handkerchief, he glanced around furtively and edged closer. "I keep sweeties, biscuits and chocolates hidden away in my room to share with my very special friends. What about it, Sarah? This can be our little secret." I concentrated on the curoundas, not bothering to reply. He stood up, dusted off his pants and walked away with Jamal following behind.

I knew Mummy would never approve of my visiting him in his room nor did I want to. However, I resolved to follow his trail the next time I spotted him leaving the lodge on a "butterfly expedition." It would be excellent to discover the whereabouts of the curounda bushes.

I didn't have long to wait. A few days later I spied him from my bedroom window, ambling out of the compound with Jamal in tow. Hurriedly, slipping out of the room, I raced down the stairs and followed discreetly. It was a wretchedly hot afternoon and the flimsy sundress clung to my body in awkward places, but, caught up in the adventure, I didn't care.

The way was scarred with deeply rutted cart tracks, on either side of

---

40   *curoundas* little sour plums

which lay parched fields baking in the noonday sun. A herd of scrawny goats nibbled on meagre tufts of grass and kites swirled overhead in the shimmering glare. Passing beneath a giant banyan tree, I noticed a family of monkeys busy at their toilette. I would have liked to have stopped and watched their antics for a while, but couldn't afford to lose sight of the pair ahead of me. Trudging forward, stumbling, as the trail dipped sharply into an area of scrubby undergrowth, I skipped over stones and avoided steamy dung pats before coming to an inlet of brackish water that reeked of rotting fish. A herd of buffalo, wallowing in a pool, seemed anxious not to be disturbed, so I steered clear of them, following a path that led to an open field. And there they were: bushes galore, packed with thousands of berries. Mr Dowling and Jamal were nowhere in sight; they seemed to have fallen off the face of the earth. Moving quickly among the shrubs, I plucked the sweet, tart curoundas, stuffing them by the handful into my mouth. Munching away and filling my pockets at the same time, I tramped along, blissfully unaware of sticky fingers and a fruit-stained dress.

Quite forgetting the butterfly gatherers, I was totally absorbed with berry picking, wandering across the field as it sloped upwards in a gentle rise. Stopping for an instant, I looked up and caught my breath, aghast! For there, in the distance, rising up before me like the summer moon, was the great white bottom of Mr Stanley Dowling. It sank down again behind some bushes and was lost from view. I could scarce believe my eyes. Edging closer, I noticed Jamal, face down, impaled beneath him, upon a large slab of rock. He cried out as Mr Dowling groaned. Turning, I lost my footing and slipped, landing in some brush, disturbing a family of grouse who took flight in a fluster. A *babul*[41] thorn pierced my palm and I hastily yanked it out, sucking on the sore spot. Mr Dowling looked up and our eyes met for a brief moment before I scampered away, breathlessly. Running as if the devil himself was after me, I quickly scanned the horizon once more and was relieved to find no one in pursuit.

Arriving at the lodge with full pockets and a heart pounding with fear, I leaned against the outer bathroom wall in an effort to catch my breath. Struggling with mixed feelings of confusion and turmoil, I realized that what I had just witnessed out there on the curounda fields was something I was not supposed to see or even to comprehend.

---

41 *babul* acacia

Dashing up the stairs, I tumbled into bed and lay frozen with fear with the covers pulled over my face, until it was time for tea.

Thank heavens, Mr Dowling was not at tea; it would have been unbearable.

Miss Skinner had agreed to give us music lessons and Mummy said we should try and be in by sundown, to get some practice in before dinner.

"Thank Miss Skinner, girls, she is giving up her evening for you." We did with the sweetest of smiles. She smiled back. Perhaps she was approachable.

That evening, as we played upon the beach, I was particularly careful to stay within sight of Radha. The incident with Mr Dowling had totally unnerved me. Flushed and feverish, I tried unsuccessfully to banish the awful sight that remained fixed in my mind. Finding it impossible to join with Moira in her childish games, I wandered away by myself and sat upon the flat-faced rock. As the sun dipped into the Arabian Sea and the quarrelsome crows cawed endlessly, seeking perches for the night, Radha steered us towards the garden tap to wash our feet before going in for dinner. Moira went on ahead, but I lagged behind, delighting in the warm water as it spilled over my toes. Rubbing them together in an effort to remove all the sand, I gasped as a pair of strong hands grasped my shoulders and pinned them to the wall.

"Well, well, well. Who do we have here?" It was Mr Dowling with a wicked gleam in his eyes. "I noticed you followed us this afternoon, you little hussy."

"I wanted to find the curounda bushes," I replied boldly.

"And you did, did you not?"

"Why was Jamal screaming?"

"Oh, that. I had to punish him for being disobedient, you see, so I goosed him rather severely. And the same thing can happen to you, you saucy brat, if I hear you haven't kept our little secret."

Wrenching free, I darted out from under him and into the house, my face flushed all over.

Mummy exclaimed, "Sarah, what's the matter? Don't you feel well?" Rising, she marched me upstairs and, after I undressed, she tucked me into bed. Radha brought up a tray and insisted I polish off my portion. Seated on her mat beside my bed, she crooned softly to herself until she thought I was asleep, but I fooled her. Outside, a *koel*[42] filled the night with its cry and even though the soft lapping of the waves encouraged slumber, for me it was out of the question. Feeling jittery and restless, consumed by a fire I did not understand, I arose from bed and sat on the window ledge. As still as a post, searching the shadows, I watched a waxing Moonface glide over the rooftop and come to rest upon the shining sea. There was something repugnant about Mr Stanley Dowling that thoroughly disturbed me and I resolved to stay away from him in the future.

The next day Miss Skinner smiled at me from across the breakfast table when I wished her good morning. "How are you feeling today, Sarah?" she asked kindly.

"Much better, thank you," I murmured, staring into my porridge.

"Not feeling up to the mark, are we?" Mr Stanley Dowling chortled. "Perhaps you have a touch of the sun. I've seen you wandering about all over the place without a hat."

The kitchen at the Serendipity Lodge stood beside a giant jackfruit tree that was home to a family of monkeys. The young ones flew through the air between the branches, while the old grandfather with grey whiskers sat humped upon a sturdy limb, nibbling on tender young shoots. Females busily groomed each other, chattered and suckled their babies, as long as the male was nowhere in sight. He was a solitary fellow, who kept to himself most of the time. Occasionally, he would swing down through the branches and then the entire family braced itself. A fierce disciplinarian, he snapped at the rambunctious young ones when they misbehaved. Every now and then he would go over to a female and "goose" her from behind. Sitting on the kitchen steps, I observed him.

"Sarah, what are you doing here?" Mummy's voice startled me.

"I'm watching Mr Monkey goose his wives," I replied matter of factly.

"Where in heavens did you learn such a word?" she asked, incredulous.

"From Mr Stanley Dowling. I saw him goose Jamal, out in the fields, among the curounda bushes."

42   *koel* a nightingale

There, it was out. I heaved a sigh of relief.

"When? Where?" Dangerous red spots appeared on Mummy's cheeks.

"Come here, child, I think it's time we had a talk." She led me by the arm into the house and sat me down in one of the library chairs. "Now, tell me exactly what happened. What did you see?"

"We-l-l," I mumbled hesitantly. Half afraid and yet glad to get it all out in the open, I spilled the beans and a sorry tale it was. I explained to Mummy that this was how Mr Dowling disciplined Jamal for being a bad boy.

"Did he tell you that?" she asked, her voice rising in anger.

I nodded, but neglected to mention that he had threatened to inflict the same punishment on me if I breathed a word about the incident. That part refused to come out.

Mummy's face was a mask of horror as she pulled me to her and held me close. I started to cry with relief and she wiped away my tears with a scented hankie. Sitting on her lap in the cool, dark library that smelled of leather and old books, I felt safe. Directing me to sit back in the chair once more, Mummy explained: "The large male monkey was having sex with the female monkey, Sarah. That is how little monkeys are made. His actions were not wrong. It is the same way with human beings. But what you saw the other afternoon was a very different thing. It was a wicked act performed on Jamal by Mr Dowling. He was not being punished for being a bad boy; nothing can be further from the truth. He was being used by Mr Dowling in a vile, unnatural way. I never want you to allow anyone to approach you or use you in such a manner. There is a time and place for everything, Sarah, and you will learn about sexual love as you grow older. For now, as long as we are here, I want you to stay away from Mr Dowling. Keep an eye on your sister as well, will you? I shall have a talk with Radha. That is all I can say to you right now, my darling." She smoothed the hair away from my face and looked at me with shining eyes. "Do you want to go upstairs and have a lie-down?"

I nodded and we climbed the stairs to the bedroom. I lay down and she pulled the covers over. Watching Mummy as she sat in the rocking chair beside the window, moodily staring out at the silver sea—at that moment I felt a great rush of tenderness towards her. Moira entered and lay down in the bed next to mine. Chintz curtains fluttered in the afternoon breeze and I grew drowsy, falling asleep to the rushing sound of the tide rolling in.

I awoke the next morning with a fever and spots all over my face and arms.

Mummy peered down at me. "Good morning, Sarah," she smiled cheerily. "How did you sleep?"

Moira shoved the looking glass in front of me. "See yourself, Sarah," she giggled; "you're spotty."

"And so will you be in a little while," said Mummy. "Put that mirror back on the dressing table at once, Moira, for if you break it we're in for seven years of bad luck, something we really can't afford at the moment."

"I have a headache," I complained.

"You have a fever and the measles, young lady. Doc Stewart will be in to see you later and, unless I am wrong, you'll soon have your sister for company. Radha has been instructed to serve you your meals up here. Both of you must stay away from Aunty Maggie because she can't afford to get the measles in her condition; it could be very dangerous. So try and keep to the room, will you?"

We nodded in unison.

"I'll send for some colouring books and paper dolls that you can dress up. Maybe we'll have a fancy dress parade when you're feeling better."

I smiled weakly.

My fever soared and I must have jabbered away deliriously all afternoon. I felt the sting of a needle in my arm, a cologne-scented towel upon my brow and Radha's anxious face beside the bed. Falling into a deep sleep, I awoke to raised voices in the room. Mummy was seated beside me, while Grandpa paced up and down the room in an agitated state.

"I don't see what all the fuss is about, Emma. The child is delirious and has been running a high temperature all day. At the best of times she is a precocious girl with an over-active imagination. If you paid greater attention to the children, instead of leaving them in the care of that halfwit Radha you would know by now that Sarah is often *away with the fairies*. How can you believe all that nonsense she's been babbling?"

What nonsense? I wondered.

"I refuse to accept it as nonsense," Mummy replied angrily. "You don't know the half of it."

"I can very well imagine! However, I cannot ask the Dowlings to leave. You know that. There are three of them and that's a lot of revenue every month," fumed Grandpa.

"I don't care how you settle it, Pa; I just don't want that man around the girls. And there's Jamal, too; how do you propose to handle the affair with him?"

"I'll send him packing back to his village and instruct Rahim to find a replacement. You don't have to worry about the boy, he's dispensable."

"I am sure he is," she replied tartly, "and his replacement will no doubt be a new toy for Stanley Dowling."

"Humph!" said Grandpa and stormed out of the room.

Moira got the measles after me, but her attack was not as severe. At any rate, we were confined to the bedroom for what seemed like ages. Then one day Doc Stewart visited and said it was okay for us to come downstairs again.

Miss Skinner bought each one of us a little gift and Mummy promised a picnic when we were feeling stronger.

Mr Dowling did not look up from his eggs and toast.

Moira had a passion for empty matchboxes. She liked stuffing them with cigarette and bidi butts that she found lying around the compound. I heard Radha lamenting that Moira's dresses smelled funny, even after the dhobi had washed them. Mummy didn't seem overly concerned and, shrugging her shoulders, dismissed the complaint.

One morning Moira and I came across Arun, the sweeper boy, sitting in a corner of the compound, smoking. Importantly, she reached into her pocket and pulled out her matchbox overflowing with butts, which she offered to him. He slapped his bony thighs and shrieked with laughter. Lighting three butts, he gave one to each of us and kept the third for himself. After a few puffs, Moira ground hers into the dust the way she had seen grown-ups do. Closing the matchbox, she replaced it in her pocket once more. Arun informed us that the best butts were to be found in the library, since sahibs and memsahibs who went in there to read and have a smoke were often distracted and hardly ever finished their cigarettes. Moira promised to check it out.

"Be careful," I warned, but she stuck her tongue out at me and ran away.

The collection grew and, since it was impossible to smoke all the butts accumulated in a day, Moira took to storing her matchboxes in an empty drawer of the dressing table. Putting away the dhobi clothes, Radha discovered them one day. She was led to the stash by the reek of stale tobacco. The jig was up and Mummy was furious. Washing Moira's mouth out with soap and water, she smacked her. Grandpa, hearing the commotion, was on the scene in a trice. Ranting and raving, he said Moira would break out with terrible sores if she persisted with her filthy habit. Grandpa blamed everything on Radha's slack supervision.

"Most of her time is spent seated on the back veranda, gossiping with the servants and ogling the *mali*.[43] She allows the girls to wander all over the place unsupervised. Why, I've seen them myself, up to all kinds of mischief. I turn a blind eye because I know they are on holiday. It's beyond me why you keep that slovenly creature in your employ. I'll never understand it at all, at all!"

Mummy turned on him and soon they were embroiled in a shouting match. Radha pulled Moira out from between them and carried her into Aunty Maggie's bedroom. I followed. There we sat shivering upon the bed until the confusion died down. The incident terrified Moira and she stopped smoking altogether. I did not. Besides, try as she might, Aunty Maggie could not give up the "filthy weed," and, from time to time, I was able to sneak a puff or two from her.

The summer days swept by in quick succession and boarding school loomed large on the horizon. Feeling wretched at the prospect of going off alone to God knows where with Moira, I tried to think of other things, but it was useless. I was incurably depressed. Besides, I missed Grandpa Watkinson and wondered how he was doing. We had written him two letters, but had received no reply. Thinking about friends left behind in Saltair-By-The-Sea—Evelyn, in particular—I despaired of ever seeing them again. They too had not replied to my letters.

Leaning against a pillar on the back veranda, I allowed the tears to slide down my face unchecked. Sparrows took a mud bath in the

---

43   *mali* gardener

compound. Miserably, I observed as Kusum, the *matherani*,[44] sauntered out of the bathroom carrying two aluminum chamber pots. She disappeared to the rear of the lodge and, after dumping the night soil in a pit dug for that purpose, she returned. I watched as she vigorously scoured the pots out under the garden tap. After rinsing them in a phenyl solution, she carried them inside. I wondered why commodes were called thunder boxes. Could it be that internal combustion caused our bottoms to explode while seated on them? The very idea made me laugh out loud. Perhaps I could ask Mummy, but then again, better not, for she invariably got annoyed and dismissed me with: "Sarah, it's not ladylike to be vulgar!"

Emerging from the bathroom once more, Kusum picked up her broom and proceeded to sweep the compound. Clouds of dust swirled about as she piled dried leaves into a heap against the compound wall and set them alight. Squatting a short distance away with her broom resting between her legs, she lit a bidi, inhaled deeply and, leaning back, relaxed. A cricket in the bushes started up a musical rhythm and I heard the incessant cry of the brain-fever bird as it flitted restlessly between the branches of the trees. I wondered how it came to be called thus—named by an Englishman driven mad by the heat, no doubt. If he had had some knowledge of Marathi, he would have understood its cry, '*paus ala*', to mean 'the rains are coming'. At any rate, I had come to the conclusion that they were all slightly daft, like Grandpa Reagan and his guests at the lodge. Another irreverent thought! I giggled. The odour of smouldering leaves, dust, coupled with intense bidi fumes caused me to swoon and I felt myself dissolve into the sum and substance of my surroundings. Soaring high above the earth like a bird with spirits uplifted, I floated free among the clouds. Circling the shining sea, I came to rest upon the tallest coconut palm. Awakening with a start from this strange, mystical experience, I felt as light as a feather and totally detached and walked around for the rest of the day with a silly smile plastered all over my face.

Monsoon clouds were nowhere in sight. The earth's surface cracked and split apart as harsh, glaring heat shimmered down day after scorching day to dance upon its crumbling crust. Cuscus tats were lowered along the length of the front and rear verandas and buckets of

---

44   *matherani* sweeper

well water were tossed over them—they helped keep the lodge cool and dark. We were not allowed out after breakfast.

"Get inside! You'll burn as black as coals," Grandpa yelled whenever he caught us stealing out through the back door. "Like golliwogs, they'll think you fell off the marmalade jar!"

At dusk, when the blood-red sun dipped into the sea, Moira and I strolled along the shore on either side of Mummy, holding her hands, as the lapping waves gently tickled our toes. But the nights were oppressive and sleep often eluded me. Creeping out of bed, I sat perched upon the windowsill, gazing out at the great, grey waves rolling in. The flutter of bat wings, the hoot of an owl and the listless swish of the palm trees were all I had for company.

"By Jove, it's another scorcher! We're in for a torrential downpour," warned Doc Stewart, taking his place at the breakfast table one morning. He was a large man and plates clattered as he pulled his chair in. "Yes, there's a helluva storm brewing out there, and when this one hits—boy, everybody lookout!"

"Some kind of an authority, are you?" Major Turcotte inquired, looking up from his morning paper.

Doc Stewart chuckled, "I'll say. I've spent too many years in the *mofussil*[45] not to know the signs. Besides, I begin to feel a bit under the weather myself. It's the old rheumatism you see begins to act up. I feel it in me bones, way before it arrives. Ha! What's for breakfast?" Rubbing his palms together, he eyed Miss Skinner's plate. "Ham and eggs, eh, great stuff!"

"How's the roof?" inquired Mr Dowling, delicately picking his nose. He looked across the table at Grandpa. "D'you think it'll hold up if we run into really foul weather?"

"And why should it not? It's just been fixed," Grandpa replied shortly, stabbing his streaming eggs.

Doc Stewart had arrived to stay at the lodge until after Aunty Maggie's confinement, and Grandpa hoped that wasn't too far off.

"The fellow rattles the guests with his loud laughter and bawdy jokes," he complained to Mummy. "Not to mention his hearty appetite. And, after all that, he sticks you with a bill. But what can one expect; he's an army wallah after all!"

---

45   *mofussil* the country

The barb was not lost on her and she smiled wryly. "He's not a horse doctor I hope, many army wallahs are, you know," she teased.

"Who? Old Sawbones? I don't think so."

I was bored. Moira had spent all day embroidering a doily she planned to give Mummy for her birthday. She had asked Miss Skinner's help with designing a card. They had grown quite close in the last little while. My head, filled with heavy, unhappy thoughts, found it impossible to concentrate on anything. Besides, I had nothing to read. The library was practically out of bounds, since every book I brought down from the shelves contained "adult material," according to Grandpa. Actually, I felt he didn't trust me to take care of the books I borrowed and this hurt because, if there was anything I loved, it was books. Respect for the written word was ingrained in us, as both Moira and I had been taught at an early age not to dog-ear a page or leave a book face down, since that would weaken the spine.

Radha, her face gleaming with Afghan Snow cream, a marigold set in her hair at a jaunty angle, sat on the steps of the back veranda, reeking of *Kanta*.[46] I caught a whiff of it as I passed by. She had set her sights on the mali and was leaving nothing to chance. Slipping past her in the early evening with a couple of hours to spare before dinner, I decided to skip out of the back compound and do a bit of exploring on my own.

Crossing an open field behind the lodge, I followed a deeply rutted path lined with babul trees, cluttered with bottle birds' nests. Gusts of hot air created tiny dust whorls and sent them pirouetting over the arid landscape. A string of village girls carrying large bundles of kindling on their heads passed by, giggling self-consciously. Ignoring them, I strolled on as though I knew where I was going. The trail snaked through a cotton field and ended up alongside a majestic grouping of trees, cloaked in green—a mango tope. Peering in, I caught sight of a tiny well within its cool, shady interior. The topes of the plains had for generations served as a refuge for weary travellers seeking shelter. Tranquil and filled with birdsong by day, they could, however, be dangerous places by night. Recalling Grandpa's yarns of thugs, devotees of the goddess Kali, who frequented such places, I hesitated for a moment before entering.

---

46   *Kanta* perfume *bottle birds* weaver birds

Belonging to the order of the *rumal*,[47] these vile bandits used the protective canopy of the tope to carry out their murderous deeds. Employing every type of disguise, they joined up with unsuspecting wayfarers on their journeys and, at dead of night, while their weary companions slept exhausted from a hard day's trekking, the thugs ruthlessly murdered them in their sleep. After plundering their baggage and stealing their horses, they rode off to join other groups and repeat their heinous offenses.

Shivering with excitement, I tiptoed in with some trepidation, only to find beneath an umbrella of green, lit by the filtered rays of evening sun, a cool, dark oasis—a shelter from the burning plains. The earth was covered with a blanket of dried leaves, which rustled underfoot. Whilst in the branches above doves cooed within the foliage. I looked around in awe at the heart of the mango tope, imagining weary travellers bedding down for the night—a *chaddar*,[48] some food and water. I offered up a prayer for those unknown wayfarers to the guardian of the tope and, even as I appealed to the deities, became aware of the murmuring spirits around me. It was as if my prayers had magically released them from their troubled slumber: men and women who had died brutally, butchered in their beds, their blood oozing into the soil beneath the blanket of leaves. Surrounding me, they filled the air with whispers, making their presence known. I stood transfixed, not knowing what to do, and bore their suffocating company. After all, I had released them. Leaning against the immense girth of an ancient tree, I gazed into its branches that reached up and spread wide like an umbrella overhead. Shadows lengthened and the sun dropped low in the western sky. The sound of weeping, stemming from the depths of an abandoned well, disturbed my reverie. What was that? I wondered, walking over and peering into its murky interior. Picking up a pebble, I tossed it in and it was a long way down before the stone landed with a plop. Jackals howled in the distance and the hair on the nape of my neck stood on end. Frantically, I began searching for a way out, as the wailing continued, wave upon wave. Finally, finding an opening, I hurriedly made my escape through the dense brush into a field of meadow grass. Looking around in dismay, I realized I had lost all sense

---

47   *rumal* handkerchief
48   *chaddar* sheet

of direction. Spotting what looked like a farmhouse in the distance, I ran towards it.

As I drew nearer, I noticed its exterior was overgrown with vines and wild lantana bushes. A large banyan tree with limbs like the tentacles of a giant octopus had spread out and encircled the place. Gingerly, I negotiated the undergrowth and stepped onto the front veranda. A single window gaped into its shadowy interior and I peered in, quickly crossing myself as a shiver ran through me. Something sinister surely lurked within. A battered front door, torn away from its hinges, lay upon the earthen floor. "Fools rush in—" Mummy often cautioned, but unmindful of her warning, I willfully crossed the threshold.

The roof had blown away in several parts, leaving the house exposed to the elements, and the ever-encroaching extremities of the banyan tree. The place was bare, except for an earthen, dung-washed *choolah*[49] in one corner of the room, with a few blackened cooking pots beside it. A niche held a discarded *charak*,[50] and an unstrung charpoy leaned against the wall. Stepping cautiously through the rubble, I trembled, as soughing from the canopy above gave way to soft moaning sounds that faintly called my name. The sharp scent of bat droppings stung my nostrils and even the rosy glow of evening could not dispel the sense of menace. I was sure that within these crumbling walls, at some point in time, an incident of unspeakable horror had occurred. My skin crawled at the proximity of such tangible evil. A rush of air swept dried leaves into a corner and I heard the patter of tiny feet, followed by a sharp intake of breath. Was it my own?

An unseen presence hostile to intruders insidiously filled the room with its scent of terror. Strange odours, sickly sweet and repellent, wafted in and settled like a filthy fog. Rigid with fear, I stood rooted to the earthen floor as the spirits of the house clamoured around me in one voice, with one intention. Cowering, I knew they meant to overpower and possess me, hold me there forever. "Mary, Mother of God!" I gasped, as a vision of a grotto yet undiscovered passed before my eyes. Then, turning, I fled, stumbling over the rotting timbers at the front door, in a mad rush to escape. Racing through the open fields, skirting the mango tope that loomed ahead, brooding and sinister in late evening shadow, I rushed headlong for the safety of the lodge.

---

49 *choolah* earthen stove with a half-moon pattern
50 *charak* earthenware vessel with a wick to the gods

Once inside the compound, I stopped, trembling beneath the sprawling jackfruit tree, to catch my breath and was discovered by Radha. She grabbed my arm and pinched it cruelly.

"Ouch!"

"Where you loafing, *hanh?*" she asked between clenched teeth. Her large, dark eyes were angry and full of fear. "Mummy calling!"

Wrenching free, I raced past her into the bathroom to wash up for dinner.

The next evening, as old Rahim Khan took his ease on the back porch, I crept up beside him and sat cross-legged on the floor. He drew heavily upon his bidi, ignoring me altogether. This was his private time, the lull between duties, with no meals to serve, shoes to polish, or errands to run.

"Who lived in the broken farmhouse beside the mango tope?" I inquired.

"Ha! Missy baba no going there. *Shaitan*[51] place! Nighttime *booth* coming. You going next time, Rahim telling Mummy," he warned, wagging his finger at me.

"Why?" I asked. "Why booth coming? Tell me." I tugged at his arm.

Moira joined us, clutching the grubby looking doily that she had been working on all day.

"Is he going to tell a story?" she asked.

"Maybe. Sit still if you want to hear."

Wiping his rheumy old eyes with a dishcloth, which he always carried slung over his shoulder (for polishing cutlery and drying plates), he stared morosely into the distance. It was a long silence and I was sure he resented our intrusion. The evening air was oppressive and I noticed banks of heavy clouds hanging low on the horizon, as the last shades of twilight quickly disappeared. Not a leaf stirred in the trees shrouded in darkness. I inched closer to Moira. Toby, lying sprawled out on the cool stone floor beside us, gave me a start. He had suddenly decided to disturb his tick population and began vigorously scratching himself all over. Rahim Khan cleared his throat and spat roughly into the mud, as we gazed at him expectantly. An evil grin lit up his weather-beaten old face and he chuckled to himself. Moira and I moved closer together.

---

51   *Shaitan* wicked, devil *booth* devil

"That house belonged to Shinde, a farmer. He lived there with his two wives—first one and then another. Shinde's first wife was very beautiful, everybody said so. They were happily married for a few years."

"Three years?" asked Moira.

"Hanh." His head wobbled from side to side. "But Lalita—that was her name—could not bear him any children. She was barren, you see, and this was a matter of great concern to Shinde's parents, since he was their only child. Who would inherit, they worried, if their son produced no male heir? His family owned a great deal of land, from here to Bombay." He gestured expansively. "'Will I never hold my grandchild in my arms?' his mother wept. His father urged him to consult with a doctor. 'We have tried everything,' Shinde replied, despondently. 'We do not know where to turn next.'

"As the weeks stretched into months and the months became years, the pressure mounted and Shinde was fast becoming desperate. Every time he returned home from a visit with his parents, he was rude and impatient with Lalita. One evening he went so far as to strike her. 'What have I done that displeases you?' she asked, hurt at his boorish behaviour.

"'My parents say that you are barren.'

"'That is not my fault. I pray everyday and make countless sacrifices to the gods, imploring them to bless me with a child. Sometimes, I even feel a quickening in my womb and I am happy, thinking they have heard me. But then my time of the month arrives and I am filled with despair again. *Hai Ram!*'[52]

"After eating his meal, Shinde rose silently and taking his mattress laid it down in another room.

"Sleeping away from Lalita, he had a curious dream. The Mother Goddess, to whom he prayed above all others, appeared to him in a seductive guise and urged him to take another wife—a younger woman named Asha, whom he had known since childhood, for she was the daughter of his neighbour, Marauti. Awakening with a start, Shinde mulled over her instructions, but dismissed them. I am overwrought, he reasoned, besides, I cannot afford two wives. Nevertheless, the dream persisted and would not leave him alone. Every night for a whole week the Mother Goddess continued to offer him the comely Asha, in

---

52   *Hai Ram!* O God!

many enticing ways. Seriously, in his waking hours, the girl began to occupy his mind, until he was obsessed, remembering her as a child during festivals, how she would dart between the guests—a skinny, frail-looking girl who did not fill her *choli*.[53] And then, a few years later, she blossomed into a fetching maiden. The last time he had visited her father—as she flitted in and out of the room with refreshments—he had noted her coy looks cast in his direction. When an opportunity presented itself, he gazed into her dark, glowing eyes. Smouldering coals, he thought, waiting to be ignited. Asha would do very well indeed, Shinde decided—she had nice, flared hips that could bear him many sons. After all, hadn't he suffered embarrassment enough on account of the barren Lalita? He had become the laughingstock of the entire community. It was now time for a change. Lalita, of course, would always be his first wife, the elder, and as such she could demand proper respect from the younger one. They would work together: Lalita running the home and Asha providing him with many sons. He was sure the idea would please his mother and, with her support, he would be able to convince the old man, his father, to loosen his hold on the purse strings, to give something extra every month; this would help ease the burden of running an extended household. There was also the matter of a dowry to be considered. Shinde felt he might be able to persuade the skinflint Marauti to part with a parcel of land. In particular, the plot adjoining his own, that would increase his acreage considerably. Pleased with himself, he made a special offering to the statue of the Mother Goddess, placing a garland of jasmine and marigolds around her neck.

"Resolving to make his proposal, Shinde paid a visit to his neighbour. Marauti was glad to see him and doubly glad to give his daughter, Asha, in marriage to such an affluent farmer. He hummed and hawed at first about the land Shinde requested as a dowry, but finally agreed. Avarice shone in his beady little eyes, as he cried '*Vah!*'[54] and concluded the deal. 'It is good; after all, our properties are adjoining.'

"Marauti secretly hoped Lalita would die of a snakebite or some other affliction, then nothing would stand in the way. 'Especially if Asha bears this fellow many sons,' he reasoned. Insisting Shinde stay and share the evening meal with the family, he discussed wedding plans

---

53   *choli* blouse
54   *Vah!* expression of happiness, great

with him and the date was set. It was not long after that the ceremony took place and was celebrated with much fanfare.

"Lalita watched from her bedroom window as Shinde arrived at the front steps of the farmhouse seated on a horse with his new wife following behind. They were escorted in by her relatives and a band making much loud music. Alone in her room that night, she shed many hot and bitter tears.

"The girl, Asha, proved to be a meek and lovely creature, who deferred to her senior in everything. Looking up to Lalita as the first wife, she was quick to do her bidding. However, pain and anger against Shinde festered in Lalita's heart and she grew hard and silent. At night she would leave her bed to sit upon the front stoop and would often fall asleep leaning against a pillar. Shinde was oblivious, wholly occupied now with making his beautiful new wife pregnant.

"A few years passed and Asha, too, remained childless. Shinde was beside himself and became a sour, mean man who ranted at both his wives. Nothing they did seemed to please him. Neighbours passing his house would snicker: 'Here lives a man with two wives, but not one single child!'

"He was desperate. It was then that he had his second dream.

"The Mother Goddess appeared to him again, but this time in a different guise. Her long wavy hair flew wildly about in a state of disarray. Her lips were stained blood-red and her eyes were dark hollows set in her sallow face. She appeared to have walked out of a storm into his dream. Her angry words were clear: 'Fool!' she cried out, 'why do you come pleading to me every day with your whining voice? Your wife Asha is still not with child and what should you do? Be a man, I say, and understand the forces that work within your household. Asha is not pregnant because the vixen Lalita has cast a spell over all. She spits venom in your food and must be killed if you are to succeed. Her death will be a suitable sacrifice to me. Then and only then, will I show you how to successfully exorcise the evil she has spread around your home.'

"'Ma!' screamed Shinde, in despair, 'how can I achieve this?'

"'Listen closely, and I will tell you how. Take Asha to her parents' home. Return from there and kill Lalita. Sever the head and throw her body into the poisoned well that lies within the mango tope. Take her streaming head and sprinkle the blood over your room and upon your marriage bed. This will remove the evil she has wrought. After some time go back and fetch your wife. She will bear you a son.'"

Moira shivered beside me and I swallowed hard, moving closer to her. Should we be listening to this gory tale? I wondered. I knew not, neither did I care. Rahim Khan rolled his red-rimmed eyes and continued.

"'What should I do with the head after I am finished with it?' inquired Shinde.

"'Burn it!' ordered the Mother Goddess, with a fierce grin. Then she disappeared.

"Shinde mulled over these instructions with fear and trembling for a full fortnight and his desperation grew into frenzy as his neighbours' mocking voices continued to echo in his ears. He decided the deed must be done and soon. It was the only way he would be vindicated.

"'I am a man,' he muttered to himself, 'and this thing that I do will prove it. I will satisfy the Mother Goddess.'

"A week later he bought some bhang from the liquor merchant. Then, taking Asha for a visit with her parents, he persuaded her to remain with them for a few days. As he walked home on the winding path through his fields, flooded with moonlight, he felt a great surge of courage. 'This night I will carry out the murder,' he resolved, loudly. 'This night I will appease the Mother Goddess.'

"Lalita watched, as he entered the house alone. 'Where is Asha?' she inquired.

"'I have left her for a few days with her parents,' he replied in surly tones. 'She was missing them.'

"'I miss my parents too.'

"'You can go and see them when she returns. Now, serve me food, for I am hungry.'

"While she rattled the pots by the fire, filling his plate with vegetables, dal and puris, Shinde poured out two tumblers of rose *sharbat*,[55] placing the bhang in one of them. Lalita entered, carrying the food and a *lota*[56] of water, which she set down before him. A smiling Shinde offered her the drink and she accepted. The sweet, scented sharbat slid easily down her throat like velvet and within minutes she fell swooning to the earthen floor. Amazed at his own callousness, he

55   *sharbat* rose scented drink
56   *lota* stainless steel drinking cup

continued to eat, without as much as a glance at his wife lying on the floor beside him. It is the power of the Mother Goddess come over me, he thought, casually taking sips of sharbat from the tumbler. When he was done and had rinsed his fingers, he sat down to enjoy a smoke. Then, lifting the woman, he carried her out to the mango tope, where he brutally murdered her. Hacking her head off with a single blow, he tossed the body into the poisoned well. Carrying the streaming head into the house, he anointed the room as the Mother Goddess had instructed. Moonlight streaming through the tope was the only light he knew, as he poured kerosene over Lalita's head, and set it on fire. The deed was done.

"Asha, returning from her visit, inquired after the first wife.

"'She has gone to see her parents and will be away for sometime,' Shinde gruffly informed her.

"Time passed and Lalita, of course, never returned. Once again, Asha anxiously asked after her.

"'She must have decided to stay on for a while,' Shinde replied nonchalantly. 'Good riddance! With her gone, we have one less mouth to feed. She was barren, anyway.'

"The Mother Goddess kept her promise and, in time, Asha became pregnant. Soon she was big with child and the proud father could be seen strutting all over the district, his chest puffed out like a pouter pigeon.

"'Where is your first wife?' inquisitive neighbours inquired.

"'She has gone for an extended visit with her parents,' he replied cheerfully.

"The year passed and Shinde was now the proud father of a healthy son.

"In Bombay, Lalita's parents were worried. They had not received any news of her for a long time. Letters had gone unanswered. One sweltering day, a few years later, a wandering, mendicant fakir entered the mango tope, seeking refuge from the sweltering midday sun. His rest, however, was disturbed by strange cries coming from the well. Rising, he searched the depths and was shocked to discover a headless body floating upon the murky water. He ran to inform the local police. But even before they could start their investigation, Lalita's father got wind of it. The news confirmed his worst fears. Taking matters into his hands, he hired some *goondas*[57]and dispatched them to Shinde's house.

"On a dark, moonless night, as Shinde, his wife and baby son slept soundly on their charpoys, the murderers crept in and butchered the entire family. It is said, if one looks very closely, one can still see blood stains spattered on the inside walls of the farmhouse."

I cringed in terror.

"The farmhands all ran away and the place was abandoned." Rahim Khan continued, pulling on his bidi. "Today, it is as you saw—wrecked and ruined. The single occupant, they say, is the body of a woman, who roams through the house and grounds, searching for her head."

Moira and I shook like leaves in a windstorm. She had twisted the doily into a wretched little rag. Rahim Khan gazed at us, an evil glint in his watery eyes. He had, after all, succeeded in scaring us half to death.

A strong breeze had started up, causing the coconut palms in the compound to sway crazily. Thunder rumbled and exploded, as streaks of lightning lit up the night sky. The unmistakable scent of monsoon rain touching down, filled the air and the parched earth, gasping with relief, rose up to receive it.

"*Barsath. Barsath agia,*"[58] Rahim Khan muttered.

Grasping Moira's hand, I hurried her into the house. Once inside, we scooted up the stairs like a pair of frightened rabbits being chased by a hunter with a blunderbuss!

It continued to storm through the night. The wind shrieked through wildly thrashing trees and the rain came pelting down in sheets, battering the old lodge that creaked and shuddered as the furies played around it. The sea was a roiling mass of water, angrily hurling itself against the rocks. Creeping out of bed, I pressed my nose against the windowpane and watched thin rivulets of rainwater as they streamed down to join the swollen torrent pouring out of the drainpipe. I thought I heard jackals howl in the distance and pictured a headless Lalita, drenched to the skin, sitting forlornly on the front stoop of the farmhouse—keeping a deadly vigil!

The bathroom door creaked open, as someone paid a visit. Low

---

57   *goondas* local thugs
58   *barsath* rain *barsath agia* rain has come

moaning sounds came from the hallway and I dismissed them as my imagination. Getting into bed and pulling the covers over didn't help; the moaning continued. Looking over at Mummy, I saw she was fast asleep. Radha was snoring on the floor beside me and Moira, who had kicked off her covering, lay sprawled across the bed with her nightgown around her waist. Someone tapped at the bedroom door.

"Mummy!" I cried out fearfully.

"Sarah!" The light was switched on. "Are you awake?"

It was Aunty Maggie, as white as a sheet and shaking all over.

Mummy leapt up. "What's happening?"

"It's time," said Aunty Maggie. Sagging against the wall, she clutched her belly.

"What are you doing up? Get back to sleep," Mummy ordered me. "Radha!"

Shaking off her sleep, she rose and followed Mummy, switching off the light behind her.

It was dark once more and I was left alone with only the howling wind and the spirits of the night for company.

Moira didn't count; she was dead to the world.

We awoke to sunlight streaming through the open windows. Gentle gusts of monsoon wind ruffled the curtains, bringing with them the damp, sweet smell of earth. Radha, with a wide grin, urged us to hurry up, bathe, dress and get downstairs for breakfast. "It is a good day," she exulted and I knew the reason why. Aunty Maggie had had her baby.

All the demons of the night were banished.

The house was a hive of activity. I heard the heavy footfall of Doc Stewart going down the stairs and Mummy's merry laughter in the dining room. Hurriedly, we bathed. No sundresses today! Radha had laid out our best voile frocks with the heavy satin sashes that tied in a large bow at the back. We had to wear shoes and socks.

"Is it a boy?" I asked in undertones.

"Hanh," she smiled, her head wobbling from side to side. "Trevor baba."

Bursting with joy, giggling uncontrollably, we danced around the bedroom in our petticoats. Radha smiled from luck to luck.

"Can I hold him?" Moira wanted to know, as we tumbled down the stairs for breakfast.

"Hush!" I said in my best grown-up voice.

Mummy was seated at the table, sipping a cup of coffee.

"Girls!" she beamed at us. "Aunty Maggie has had a lovely baby boy she's named Trevor. Mother and son are resting at the moment, but after breakfast you can both go up and meet your little cousin."

As the guests filed into the dining room for breakfast, Grandpa greeted them with the good news, proudly handing out cigars to Major Turcotte and Doc Stewart. Miss Skinner received a rose, likewise the Dowling sisters. He was glowing with pride; all the shame and humiliation of the past months forgotten. Everyone liked the name Trevor.

"Excellent choice." Major Turcotte nodded approvingly. "Couldn't have picked a better name myself. Trevor, eh!"

Doc Stewart, rubbing his palms together, inquired, "What's for breakfast? I could eat a horse."

Very nearly does, every morning. I knew what Grandpa was thinking.

Mr Stanley Dowling was conspicuously absent. He had asked for a tray to be sent to his room.

"Damned, peculiar chap," remarked Grandpa.

"Only just finding out?" Mummy raised her eyebrows.

Rushing through the meal, we raced up the stairs to Aunty Maggie's room and found Radha guarding the door.

Baby Trevor lay in his crib—creased, red and as bald as an egg. Not a very attractive package, I thought, but I was sure he would improve with time. Aunty Maggie, looking pale and tired, smiled softly as we kissed her.

"How d'you like Trevor?" she asked weakly.

"Can I carry him and keep him in my bed?" inquired Moira.

I knew she was ready to discard Lilibet the moment she set eyes on Trevor.

"We'll see. Maybe later," Aunty Maggie whispered.

Radha fussed over the baby. She kept pulling us away from the crib.

The two Miss Dowlings shyly knocked on the door before entering the room. One of them held a velvet box tied with a bow and the other carried a large satin bag. Tittering, they admired the baby and cooed a little in his direction. Depositing their gifts on the bedside table, they shuffled out again.

"Poor old ducks," sighed Aunty Maggie, "they don't know what to make of all this, I suppose."

"What's in the box?" inquired Moira.

"Let's see."

It was a beautiful silver mug, alongside of which stood a push fork and spoon, also made of silver. The large satin bag held an exquisite baby quilt, made from hundreds of colourful silk squares, all neatly sewn together. The card read simply: "For Trevor, from The Dowlings."

I looked up at Aunty Maggie and her face shone with tears. Drying her eyes, she whispered, "I don't know why I feel so weepy."

"You're happy Trevor's arrived."

She nodded.

Miss Skinner came in, followed by Major Turcotte.

"By Jove!" he exclaimed in a hearty voice, "What do we have here?"

They leaned over and watched baby Trevor as he slept in his crib.

Golden slumbers kiss your eyes,
Smiles awake you when you rise.
Sleep, pretty wantons; do not cry,
And I will sing you a lullaby:
Rock them, rock them, lullaby.

"Why, Sarah, that was beautiful!" exclaimed Miss Skinner.
I blushed and chewed my lower lip.

Mummy was seated in the library, her ear glued to the radio. "Shush! Sarah, you must be very quiet if you want to remain in the room."

"Why, what's happened?"

A loud voice, attempting to be heard above the roar of a crowd, crackled over the airwaves, shattering the stillness of the library. Speaking in highfalutin' Hindi, which I barely understood, the speaker informed those present of Britain's resolve to "quit India." He mentioned the name of Mahatma Gandhi over and over again and the people cried out "Jai Hind!" repeatedly. It was all very stirring and gave me goosebumps.

"The political situation is like a tinderbox," said Mummy, looking worried, "and our country is in turmoil. The British Viceroy has just announced a new 'emergency' government, headed by Nehru. That was Jawaharlal Nehru himself, addressing the nation from the ramparts of the Red Fort in New Delhi."

"Is he the most important person in India?"

She smiled. "Yes, he is very important."

"Is he more important than Winston Churchill?"

"It's all very complicated, Sarah," she replied, irritably.

In spite of her impatient tone, she continued educating me on what was happening.

"Churchill is important in England, yes, and in India as well, at the present time. But our country is in transition and great changes are taking place at this very moment—changes, dear girl, which will decide the fate of India. Some of them good and others—well, I just don't know…" Her voice trailed away and she sighed heavily. "They want to throw off the British yoke and I can see that happening. However—" she sounded uncertain, torn between British and Indian sensibilities.

"Why are the lodge guests not listening in as well?" I asked. "Wouldn't they like to know what's happening?"

"Oh! They know very well what's happening," she declared. "They read the papers. But, like a lot of old-timers, they choose to bury their heads in the sand, hoping it will all go away. Unfortunately, this time I don't think it will. I don't blame them, of course, poor dears, they are all retired now. Their world is falling apart, fast disappearing, and they can do nothing about it, except try and adjust to the new order, whatever it brings. Besides, all this shouting and hysteria can be very unsettling for them at their age. India will soon be free of Britain, but this much I know, the English will always be welcome here."

"Why?" I asked.

"It's just the way things are," she sighed. "It's the Indian way; I can't explain it."

"Who do you want to win?" I asked. "India or England?"

"Nobody wins in this sort of thing, Sarah. The British will lose India. India will win her independence, but will lose part of her identity if those wretched politicians have their way and succeed in splitting the country in two. The English—wily dogs that they are—after the Indian Mutiny of 1857, in a last ditch attempt at holding on to the subcontinent, devised a way to keep the power. They began sowing the seeds of discontent between Hindus and Muslims, using the stratagem of divide and rule. This political ploy is now going to result in deadly repercussions, I fear. For years the English have been stoking the fires of hatred between the two groups, as a result, they are filled with loathing for one another. If only they would realize they are the same people—but with different religions—the country would be spared a lot of bloodshed. But, as things stand, I fear thousands will die when we are divided and the great exodus begins. And thousands more will be displaced and lose their property—fields, farmhouses, shops. There will be no winners, as I see it, except the politicians." She had tears in her eyes. "Ah! Never mind!" She sniffed loudly into her hankie. "Mine are but the musings of a person on the sidelines. What do I really know about the machinations of government? Let's leave that to the politicians, shall we?" She smiled tiredly.

I placed an arm around her, drawing closer. I sensed her love of India. Although, from what she'd said, I didn't quite understand all that what was going on.

"Mummy, is the Mahatma a politician?" I asked, feeling proud that she had taken the time to explain things to me in such great detail

"I suppose you could call him that, but he is more, much more. He is an idealist, to my way of thinking, and the only true soul among them, with a real love for this country and its people burning in his heart. His is a message of peace, but whether he will succeed in stopping the mindless violence that is sure to erupt, well, that is left to be seen."

Reaching forward, she rapidly turned the dial on the radio. A bouncy tune came rippling through, filling the room with cheery music. "Let's banish the clouds of doom and gloom for the moment. What d'you say?"

"I miss our gramophone at home," I complained. "Grandpa absolutely refuses to allow us to play his."

"You have Miss Skinner and the singing lessons," she appeased, stroking my hair. "By the way, how are they coming along?"

"We are planning a recital and the guests are all invited. But truly, both Moira and I prefer the gramophone. This is all so stiff and starchy.

Of course, we don't want to hurt Miss Skinner, who has turned out all right, so we're both practising like mad."

"H'm … Have you all picked a song to sing?"

"We haven't quite decided yet. Moira likes 'Greensleeves' and I would like to recite a poem, one I wrote about the monsoons."

"Have you completed it?"

I nodded.

"Then recite it for me, Sarah. Let me be the first to hear you."

I cleared my throat and bowed low, as Miss Skinner had taught us to do. "'Monsoon,' by Sarah Watkinson." Then cupping my hands together, I recited:

Black clouds hover over,
Gusts of dusty breezes blow.
Man and beast must run for cover,
As dark and grey the sky hangs low.
Waiting in anticipation—
Dreaming of the aftermath,
When the rain soaks all creation,
In a great torrential bath.
Thunder rumbles, lightning flashes,
Crazy branches sway too low.
Pelting rain the parched earth washes,
As in the sky the rumbles grow.
Pools of water fill the hollows,
Shining bright and crystal clear.
All is fresh and cloaked in beauty,
At this special time of year.

I curtsied and Mummy clapped very hard.

"Why, Sarah, that was beautiful. The guests will love it. Very apt, since we are in the midst of the rains."

I giggled.

"Daddy would have liked to hear it as well."

Sinking back into the old leather chair, she lapsed into silence.

"Speaking of Daddy," she said after a while, "I wonder how he's faring. I haven't had a letter in over a week and am beginning to get anxious. He's in the thick of things, you know, up there in Delhi."

"He's probably okay," I replied and dashed out of the room.

An overseas letter arrived one morning. Grandpa waved it in Mummy's face at the breakfast table.

"Aunt Elsie is arriving on the P&O[59] in a week's time."

"Do I know her?" asked Moira.

"No, you don't, but she's your grand-aunt, Grandpa's youngest sister, who lives in England. I myself have only seen her once, when she came over to spend her honeymoon in India. I was teenager at the time. She's a doctor and, even though she was retired when the war broke out, she served as a volunteer in an army hospital. Oh, yes! I remember Aunt Elsie Lavender, a game old girl, if ever there was one. I think you'll both like her."

"I shan't," Moira declared, decisively.

"Why ever not? You don't even know her. Don't be ridiculous." Mummy was embarrassed at Moira's behaviour.

"What a strange thing for a young girl to say," tut-tutted Grandpa, shaking his head.

"I'll never understand your girls, Emma," was his parting shot, as he strode out of the room and headed for the kitchen.

"I don't like Grandpa and I won't like Grand-Aunt Elsie Lavender." Moira's chin stuck out and I knew she was being obstinate.

"Put that piece of toast down and go upstairs immediately!" Mummy ordered. She was furious. "And stay there until I come up and deal with you."

Moira dropped what she was eating and scooted out of the room.

My eyes filled with tears, for I knew from past experience that it was often impossible to budge her once she made up her mind about something. Besides, she was feeling wretched and wanted to go home—wherever that was. I caught her sobbing in bed one night and pried the truth out of her.

"I want to go home," she bawled. "I hate it here."

By home, I gathered she meant Saltair-By-The-Sea, but that wasn't our home any longer, since Daddy was posted to New Delhi. Our next home would be boarding school, which didn't bear thinking about. The lodge, of course, was no better, with Grandpa ordering everyone around. Not to mention the horrible Dowlings. Maybe Grandpa

Watkinson wouldn't mind us calling his farm home. I resolved to ask him in my next letter. In the meantime: "Cuddle up with Lilibet," I soothed, "it will help you feel better." She did.

Mummy ordered me to follow her upstairs. Closing the bedroom door, she proceeded to give Moira a good dressing down.

"What's the matter with you?" she asked sternly, shaking her. "Don't you know never to judge others before you've had a chance to get to know them? I've a good mind to give you a spanking."

"But, Mummy—"

"Button your lip, Sarah! Your grand-aunt Elsie is a very brave woman. Even though she was retired, all through the war she worked tirelessly in a military hospital, caring for the wounded soldiers brought home from the front. What's worse, she also lost her husband when the bombs fell on London."

We listened silently. I knew it was useless my trying to explain why Moira had said what she did. It had nothing whatsoever to do with Grand-Aunt Elsie Lavender, but everything to do with grumpy old Grandpa Reagan and the fact we had no home. With only boarding school to look forward to, life could be quite frightening.

That afternoon, when I slipped out to play skip rope with Gita, I dragged Moira along with me. As the rope flew over our heads, I made up a song about Grand-Aunt Elsie Lavender. Her name just rolled off my tongue and beat out a rhythm in the dust.

Where have you been, Elsie Lavender, where have you been?
I've been to the war, girls, many battles I've seen.
Where have you been, Elsie Lavender, where have you been?
I've been to France, where they taught me to dance.
Where have you been, Elsie Lavender, where have you been?
I've been to China, where I purchased a myna.
Now will you stay, Elsie Lavender, now will you stay?
If I have a good reason, girls, oh! yes, I may.
If I have a good reason, girls, oh! yes, I may.

Skipping out, I grabbed the rope from Moira and we started the rhyme again. By the end of it we were all shrieking with laughter. Gita, the loudest—even though she didn't understand a word we were saying—, her great, dark eyes brimming with mirth.

Grand-Aunt Elsie arrived a few days later. Leaning heavily on a cane, she walked stiffly up the garden path with Grandpa. The porter followed behind with a tin trunk and a valise. A tall, large-boned woman with strong features, she had snow-white, bobbed hair and clear grey eyes. I noticed a pair of spectacles dangling from a chain around her neck.

We were all there to greet her on the front veranda. I stood beside Mummy and Moira peered out from behind her skirt. Aunty Maggie carried baby Trevor, who squirmed uncomfortably in her arms.

"He kept me up all night with the colic," she sighed tiredly.

Mummy greeted Grand-Aunt Elsie with a kiss and then pushed us forward. We each received a peck on the cheek. Reaching into her purse, she pulled out two bags of sweeties and handed one to each of us.

"Mind you don't eat them all at once, or you'll get a tummy ache. Now, you can run along and play," she smiled; "you'll see more than enough of me in the days ahead."

Grandpa fretted and Aunty Maggie hesitated with Trevor in her arms.

"Jesus, Mary and Joseph! Is this what all the fuss was about?" she inquired of Grandpa. She stuck out her forefinger and Trevor grabbed a hold of it and tried to stuff it in his mouth.

"Got the taste for nicotine already," she laughed. "What d'you call him?"

"Trevor."

"He'll grow into a great strapping lad, no doubt about it. Has a good grip. Trevor Reagan, eh?"

Aunty Maggie nodded.

"Not bad, Margaret Mary, not bad."

Aunty Maggie beamed.

"Now that that's all taken care of, lead me to a chair, Joe, and fix me a stiff drink. Have you any good army rum stashed around here? I'm parched."

Grandpa steered her into the sitting room. Moira and I lurked behind the curtains, anxious to be part of the scene. The guests had fled to their rooms and were nowhere in sight. I imagined them all turned into mice, scurrying about behind the panelling, discussing the new arrival. I chuckled at the thought.

"Sarah, don't act giddy!" Mummy, scolded.

I darted out of the room.

Later that evening we joined Aunty Maggie in her bedroom and sat around while she nursed Trevor. Mummy entered, and soon they were busy discussing Grand-Aunt Elsie.

"She's a right card," said Mummy, "and tough as nails, to boot. It's going to be interesting watching Pa around her."

"He's used to swinging the lead," laughed Aunty Maggie. "He's had everything his own way all his life. Ma could never stand up to him. Emma, d'you recall Aunt Elsie from her last visit?"

"Yes, vaguely. She's had two husbands. When she married hubby number two, they came over and spent a short honeymoon with us; you must have been away at school."

"She didn't seem to mind a bit about Trevor."

"I didn't think she would. After all, the old girl's been around the block a couple of times herself. Besides, she's lived through the war. It must have been hell working in that army hospital and losing a husband as well. They had it bad in England, you know, worse than we can ever imagine. Stuff like that changes a person."

"I guess." Rising, Aunty Maggie placed Trevor in his crib and gently pulled a blanket over him.

Grandpa's guests didn't quite know what to make of Grand-Aunt Elsie. She was an early riser and one could hear her voice resounding through the lodge from before breakfast until way past dinnertime. Rahim Khan was kept on his toes, scurrying between the kitchen and the dining room, with pots of tea, plates of sandwiches and bottles of soda water. Grand-Aunt Elsie had a hearty appetite and enjoyed all her meals, with countless snacks in between.

"Splendid!" she'd exclaim, slathering another slice of bread with a thick layer of butter. "By gad! You're spoiled out here in the colonies. Why, I haven't eaten like this in ages. They don't serve up this sort of grub where I come from; beats army rations any day!"

Rum and water was her favourite drink. She liked beer in the afternoon and could be persuaded to have a peg or two of Scotch before dinner.

"She's not very careful with her cigarettes either; butts them out all over the place," Grandpa complained under his breath to Mummy, as he anxiously watched the column of ash grow.

"Put a sock in it, Joe!" Grand-Aunt Elsie glared at him. "Gin!" she cried triumphantly, beating Doc Stewart at another game of cards.

"The old girl can drink Doc Stewart under the table," Mummy observed to Aunty Maggie.

They were at it again, discussing "the old girl" as they affectionately called her. Aunty Maggie had cheered up immensely since Trevor was born. He was the darling of the lodge and all the guests (except the Dowlings) made an awful fuss of him.

"How long does she plan to visit?"

"Oh! I guess until the rum runs out," Mummy replied.

"In that case, she's here to stay. Old Doc Stewart, being an ex-army wallah, has access to a never-ending supply available to him through the mess and canteen stores."

"I know, he's taken quite a shine to the old girl as well and Pa doesn't approve. I've watched them going at it, playing cards all day. She's got him eating out of her hand—literally!"

"Not planning to marry him, I hope? That would make him husband number three," snorted Aunty Maggie, collapsing with laughter.

"Stranger things have happened. Haven't you noticed he hardly ever goes home these days and when he does, it's only to replenish the liquor supply. It's an awful strain on Pa, the pair of them eating him out of house and home. He was on about it to me the other night and I felt sorry for the old man," said Mummy seriously. "I've written to Reg and he's agreed to chip in, to ease the strain."

"H'm," said Aunty Maggie, "I wish there was something I could do."

"You have enough on your plate, dear sister, looking after Trevor. Pa understands. We can handle the load. Besides, I rather like the idea of Aunt Elsie being here. She livens up the place. Not one bit stodgy. I'm getting rather fond of the old girl and just know she's going to be good for Pa."

Mummy picked up Trevor and cradled him in her arms. "You just watch over this precious bundle. He's all your troubles right now."

Trevor was christened one fine Sunday morning, near the close of the rainy season. Father Gregory arrived to perform the ceremony when mass was over at the local church. Grandpa proudly proclaimed him the first Reagan to be christened at the lodge.

Polished silver and crystal gleamed in the dining room. A snow-white, damask cloth covered the table and each place was set with fine china. A dazzling display! Round tables had also been set up in the garden, each with a floral centrepiece. Moira and I, resplendent in taffeta frocks, refused to wear Granny Watkinson's silk, crocheted socks, because they itched dreadfully. Mummy insisted and, since she was being brutal about it, we gave in, rather than be punished.

Everyone assembled in the garden. The guests, dolled up to the nines, gathered around. Mummy carried Trevor, since she was the godmother. Major Turcotte, who was the godfather, walked beside her. Aunty Maggie, Grandpa and Grand-Aunt Elsie followed behind. Trevor looked magnificent in his christening robe and slept peacefully through the entire ceremony. It was only when Father Gregory sprinkled water over him that he started bawling. The poor little mite must have felt a chill run right through him when he was made a child of God, for he wet himself, and Mummy's dress as well, but she didn't seem to mind.

After it was all over, Moira and I followed her upstairs, to change him. Undoing the tiny pearl buttons, she slipped the christening robe over his head and I picked it up and held it to my nose. It smelled of baby powder and mothballs.

"Both of you were christened in that robe and this was my christening bonnet," said Mummy, gently untying the silken ribbons beneath Trevor's chin. "It was his turn today."

Moira took the robe from me. Smoothing the ivory lace and silk petticoat, "It's beautiful!" she exclaimed. "I can't believe we fit into it, especially you, Sarah."

I glared at her.

"You both did," Mummy laughed.

Coffee, tea, shandy, lemonade and several types of liquor were served out in the front garden, along with curry puffs and an assortment of sandwiches. There were fairy cakes from town and a large, orange-cream christening cake, which was cut into generous wedges and passed around. I piled my plate high.

Grand-Aunt Elsie, noticing my portion, exclaimed, "Goodness

gracious child, your eyes are bigger than your stomach! You're surely not going to consume all that?"

I nodded self-consciously and, finding a quiet corner, plunged into the feast. Everyone was in excellent spirits, even the two Miss Dowlings were smirking. Mr Stanley Dowling sat apart from the others with a plate of sandwiches. He winked at me, but I hurriedly looked away.

Wandering between the guests, I noticed Major Turcotte and Doc Stewart in an animated conversation. They seemed to be enjoying a huge joke, laughing and slapping each other on the back. I decided to join them.

Major Turcotte was a bit wobbly on his feet and had to steady himself against the trunk of a tree.

"Then this other bloke said to her—" he slurred his words, "'Show me your titties.'"

Doc Stewart guffawed and leaned forward eagerly. They both spotted me.

"Dash it all, Sarah, what are you doing here? Gone and spoiled the punchline, you have. Run along and play." Major Turcotte was annoyed.

Darting away, I joined Moira in the sitting room.

Trevor was asleep upstairs in his crib with Radha watching over him. It had become quite hot out in the garden and guests began streaming into the sitting room, plopping down on the overstuffed sofas and chairs. Aunty Maggie wound up the old gramophone and played "The White Cliffs of Dover" and everyone joined in. Father Gregory, looking flushed and happy, sang the loudest when she played "Red Sails in the Sunset." Glasses were emptied and refilled umpteen times. Moira and I, weaving between the guests, who were now mostly all seated, stole a sip here and a gulp there, until she finally passed out on an easy chair. I began to feel green about the gills myself.

Grandpa called everyone to be seated in the dining room for lunch, but the very idea of sitting down to a plate of curry and rice turned my stomach, so I asked to be excused.

"Can I go upstairs, Mummy? I don't feel very well."

"Have a lie-down if you like and take your sister with you." She hiccupped.

"She's asleep in the easy chair."

"Then leave her be." She hiccupped again.

Upstairs, undressing, I lay down in my petticoat and tried to sleep. But my stomach felt queasy. Scooting into the bathroom, I brought up everything I had eaten and drunk all day. Radha came in and started fussing, scolding me for eating too much on such a warm day. She made me wash up and change into a nightdress. Falling exhausted into bed, I slept until well past five o'clock in the evening.

Coming down to tea, I found the entire party scattered all over the house, chatting on the veranda, playing cards or sleeping off the afternoon's inebriation. Father Gregory, who had dropped off on the sofa in the sitting room, awoke and requested a cup of tea.

He waved away the offer of a slice of cake.

"Hair of the dog?" Doc Stewart proffered a bottle. "Perk up that tea."

"No, no, thank you; too early in the evening for that."

"Well, as long as it's not too late. I'll see you home, Father. Not to worry."

"See yourself home first, old chap," snorted Father Gregory.

Outside in the garden, Chinese lanterns had been strung along the low branches of the trees. The rainbow of colours spread a soft, magical glow over the evening. It looked like fairyland. As a brilliant sun dipped below the horizon, fireflies darted here and there in the swiftly descending nightfall. Moira and I chased after them—all around the compound we ran and into the vegetable patch, where I managed to capture a few in the hollow of my hand. Thinking of baby Trevor asleep in his crib upstairs, I asked Mummy if I could show them to him, but she shook her head. "They are fragile and should never be confined," she said. "Marvel at them, Sarah, and let them go free."

Grandpa had arranged a grand spread for dinner, "a real burra khanna." There was pork vindaloo, chicken roast with all the trimmings, fried prawns, masala pomfrets, green peas, mashed potatoes with great gobs of butter, salads, fruit and cake. The list was endless. Delicious odours wafting out from the kitchen all day held a promise of the feast now set before us. Since my unfortunate incident of the afternoon, I was ravenous and my belly rumbled in anticipation.

Major Turcotte raised a toast to King George and baby Trevor.

As Grandpa carved the roasted chickens, Grand-Aunt Elsie remarked, "I can always tell an Indian bird."

"How so?" inquired Doc Stewart. "Every *murghee*[60] looks the same to me." His face was beet red.

"They come to the table with one leg," she observed.

Everyone laughed uproariously.

I was puzzled, never having noticed the chickens out in the back compound hopping around like Long John Silver. I resolved to check it out the next day.

After dinner, guests smoked out in the garden or enjoyed a brandy. The damp night air, however, drove them indoors and soon everyone was gathered around the piano in the sitting room. Miss Skinner fumbled with her sheets of music, while Moira and I stood ready to perform our party pieces. Moira sang "Greensleeves," after which I recited my poem, but sadly most of the guests were not paying attention, for I heard loud snoring and a few snorts during the recital. Mummy said it had everything to do with good food and drink and nothing whatsoever to do with our performance. Nevertheless, I was miffed.

Children are seldom credited with any intelligence. If one sat very still, grown-ups often shared their most intimate secrets with each other in front of you. You could be a fly on the wall, a bump on a log or Toby, sprawled out on the floor; it was all the same to them.

One dull afternoon, soon after Trevor's christening party, Grand-Aunt Elsie was sitting out on the veranda darning a pair of Grandpa's socks, while he chewed his pipe beside her.

"Nice girls Emma has. What's the father like?" she asked.

"An army bloke—has a touch of the tar brush."

"I gathered as much. He's not an other rank, I hope."

"Oh, no; he's a commissioned officer, a Captain."

"What family did Emma marry into?" she continued inquisitively.

"They call themselves *Anglo-Indians*; you know, the new sort. But actually, I suspect the old man is a wog,[61] a native through and through. One of those tombstone A.I.'s. I'm sure you've heard of the type. The parish priest throws a bucket of water over the entire congregation

---

60   *murghee* chicken
61   *wog* western oriental gentleman

and baptizes the lot with a name taken off one of the gravestones. Occasionally, I've heard of overzealous clergymen bestowing their own surname on the faithful. In the South, I believe, there are entire parishes that carry the surname of Smith, Jones, or Brown."

Grand-Aunt Elsie threw her head back and roared with laughter. "Bless me, I can't say I've heard that one before!"

"It goes on all the time, in railway colonies, particularly."

"H'm … And his wife, the old lady?"

"A *cheechee*.[62] She's an upcountry woman. Nice enough, in an earthy sort of way. Ah! The Englishman's mistakes—" He sighed heavily.

"You would know about that, wouldn't you? Fancied that type yourself, as I recall."

"No one could touch my sainted Sheila," Grandpa declared defensively. "Things just haven't been the same since I lost her. Did you know she converted?"

"And I suppose that makes everything all right. Oh, Joe!"

I resented the manner in which they spoke of Grandpa and Granny Watkinson. Quietly sneaking past them, I ran upstairs to find Mummy.

"Daddy's got a touch of the tar brush," I declared out loud. "What's that?"

"Now who in heaven's name have you been listening to, you silly little thing?" She sounded very annoyed.

"Grandpa said so. What does it mean, anyway—'a touch of the tar brush'?"

"Sometimes I really don't know what to do with you," she sounded exasperated. "I have no time for explanations right now, Sarah. If you don't mind, can we keep this for another day? I've got all this packing to attend to and a few letters to write."

"Was your mummy Irish like Grandpa?"

"No, Sarah, she was not."

"Have you got a picture of her?"

"Why, yes; just a moment." She hurried out of the room and came back with a faded sepia print of a young woman in a sari.

"There, that's my mother, your grandmother. Her name was Sheila."

---

62   *cheechee* contemptuous expression referring to half-castes or Eurasians

"So this is Sheila." I examined the photograph minutely. "You look like her, Mummy, and so does Moira."

"So I've been told."

Gazing at the solemn, dusky woman seated uncomfortably on a straight-backed chair, I instinctively knew she preferred the floor. Was this the first time she had had her picture taken? I wondered. Examining each other intensely, it seemed, through large, dark eyes, we bridged generations and the void that separated life from death. Gently, I caressed the glass over the picture and smiled down at her, whispering, "Hello, Granny. This is Sarah."

"Stop mooning over that photograph and hand it back to me so that I can return it to Grandpa's bureau," Mummy snapped. "What's come over you, Sarah? Sometimes you act so strange, I can't figure you out." Snatching the picture from me, she stalked out of the room.

I came to the conclusion that even though Mummy and Aunty Maggie were fair and Trevor had blue eyes with golden hair, they too were "cheechees" and had a "touch of the tar brush," just like Granny Watkinson. And it was plain to see the "sainted Sheila" was Indian and yet Grandpa had loved her very much. Then why did he call Grandpa Watkinson and Daddy names when his own children were cheechees? It was all very confusing. I decided his feelings had nothing at all to do with the tar brush. Grandpa Reagan could be quite weird sometimes and adult reasoning was beyond me. I guessed I would just have to wait until I was grown up myself to understand everything about grown-ups. Besides, Mummy was busy getting our kits ready for school and not in the least inclined to answer any "awkward questions."

Not long after, as I crept out of the bedroom one afternoon and tiptoed down the hall, making my getaway to the back compound for a game of jump rope with Gita, I heard a low, throaty voice, singing:

Lullaby, and good night,
With pink roses bedight,
With lilies o'erspread,
Is my baby's sweet head.
Lay you down now and rest,
May your slumber be blessed!
Lay you down now and rest,

May your slumber be blessed!

The song floated out from Aunty Maggie's room and, since the door was slightly ajar, I peeked in. She was fast asleep in her bed and I was surprised to find Grand-Aunt Elsie Lavender seated on the rocking chair beside the window with baby Trevor in her arms. Looking up, she invited me in.

"Hello Sarah, I thought I'd have a little visit with Maggie, but found her asleep. This little tyke, however, was restless and had thrown off all his covers. So I thought I'd try my singing voice out on him and, as always, it has had the desired effect, for he's now fast asleep."

Rising, she placed Trevor back in his crib and, after covering him with a light blanket, sat back in the rocker. "Of course I've had no experience with babies whatsoever, never having had one myself, and now I'm wondering, perhaps I've missed something."

Plopping down at her feet, I gazed up at her curiously. It felt strange and different seeing Grand-Aunt Elsie, who smelled of rum and tobacco, with her nicotine fingers clasped around little Trevor, as she rocked him to sleep. Fancy that, I thought, one could never tell. I wondered what Mummy would make of it.

"And what, pray, are you doing out of bed at this hour of the afternoon?" she inquired, squinting down at me. "Aren't you supposed to be asleep?"

"I'm on my way for a game of jump rope with Gita, the dhobi's daughter. We're friends, you see, and she waits for me every afternoon under the jackfruit tree, by the kitchen."

"She does, does she? I gather your mother knows nothing about these afternoon trysts."

"No," I replied boldly, instinctively feeling I could trust her. "She doesn't."

Her hearty laughter startled baby Trevor.

"Go along then and don't let me keep you."

I scampered away, thinking, Grand-Aunt Elsie was definitely growing on me. What a sport!

One fresh and glorious evening, at the tail end of the monsoons, Grand-Aunt Elsie invited Moira and me to go for a walk with her. "My daily constitutional," she called it. We trotted beside her, as she moved along at a good clip with the aid of a cane.

"Ah! Nothing beats India after the rains," she exulted, taking in a great gulp of air. "The earth smells divine and the entire place is transformed. It's the rains you see; this country needs them. Gives the place a bloody good bath and washes away all that muck and dirt. Ah, yes! It's lovely."

"Have you been here before?" I asked.

"No, not here precisely, but I have visited India before."

"Can you walk without that cane?" asked Moira.

"I can, but the cane helps me get where I'm going so much faster. I have arthritis, you see."

"When did you get it?"

"It was a long time ago, when I was young woman. Before that I was an all-rounder, very good in sports, top drawer actually. Ah, yes! I had enough time to do all that and more, before I was laid low by this wretched ailment." She chuckled. "I used to ride a motorbike, you know, a Royal Enfield. Can you believe that? Then I became afflicted and it was very difficult for me, at first, to accept what happened. But you get wiser as you grow older and things that once seemed important lose their significance and sort of fade from memory. One learns to make do. Now, of course, you see me as I am: an old woman, filled with wisdom, waiting to die. What a waste, eh?"

"Mummy said you were in the war. Did you see any Japs or Germans?" I asked.

"As a matter of fact, I saw quite a few German prisoners of war."

"Were they dangerous?" inquired Moira.

"Good heavens, no. Poor devils, they were all wounded and, like any other person in a great deal of pain, they were looking for relief and comfort."

"We are off to boarding school in a week's time," I informed her, changing the subject. "Will we see you again?"

"You may, if you don't wait too long to return for a visit. I think I'll be around for a while. And now, if you don't mind, I think I'd like to turn back, I'm ready for a sundowner."

That night, both Moira and I agreed that Grand-Aunt Elsie was a hoot.

We joined "the batch" at Victoria Terminus Station in Bombay. Mummy and Radha were there to see us off and to hand us over to the teacher in charge of the batch of girls all travelling together to boarding school. I tried to put on a brave face, but Moira embarrassed us all with tears and a tantrum. She clung to Mummy's skirt and had to be practically pried away from her, which reduced Mummy to tears. I climbed into the train, took a window seat and gazed miserably out at the pathetic spectacle on the platform. It was a tragic little scene, truth to tell, and one I shall never forget for as long as I live. The teacher, Miss Price, firmly released Moira's hold on Lilibet. After handing the doll to Radha, she steered Moira into the compartment. A weeping Moira came and sat down beside me and, turning her back to the window, refused to wave goodbye to Mummy and Radha. The other students in the batch all seemed happy To be reunited with each other after the holidays. Dry-eyed, they said their farewells and were ready for the off.

When the luggage was all loaded into the brake van, a guard appeared on the platform and waved his flag. He blew a shrill whistle and the train lurched forward, but stopped again. Mummy and Radha hurriedly entered the compartment. Kissing us, Mummy made the sign of the cross on our foreheads. Radha gathered us once more into the ample folds of her sari and whimpered softly. She pressed a silver rupee into our palms before making a rapid exit. The heavy compartment door was bolted shut by the teacher. I clutched the food hamper, while Moira snivelled beside me.

Gazing out as the platform slipped away, I waved frantically, until they were mere specks in the distance. Moira sat with eyes averted. Of course, I was all cried out—since saying goodbye to Aunty Maggie and baby Trevor at the lodge had been a terrible wrench. Most of all I hated the prospect of parting with Mummy. Daddy didn't as yet have a postal address in Delhi and was still billeted at the Officers' Mess. Recalling the agitated voices of the mob on the radio broadcast and Mummy's words, "Our country is in turmoil," I'd been having horrid nightmares all week leading up to our departure. My imagination ran riot and I was sick with the trots before leaving. Lying awake at night, filled with unreasonable fears, I wondered who would care for Moira and me if we were orphaned. How would the nuns find our relatives? Where would they send us? To a workhouse, perhaps, and we would end up being apprenticed to unsavoury characters. Or, worse still, we could be placed in the charge of Grandpa Reagan, who would whip us and never allow us to visit Grandpa Watkinson on the farm. That could spell the start of a terrible feud, for I would most certainly run away and take Moira with me. Shivering involuntarily, I felt someone walk over my grave and hurriedly crossed myself. Somehow, I was confident that I would pull through, since I had overheard Mummy confide to Aunty Maggie: "I'm never afraid for Sarah; she has great resilience and the ability to throw things off."

But, as for Moira, I just knew she'd whine constantly, have tantrums and end up being flogged. How could I ever protect her? Try not to think of it, Sarah, I whispered.

As the train picked up speed, leaving the outlying reaches of the city behind, I opened the hamper and passed it to Moira. She looked away in disgust, but fear and anxiety had made me ravenous, so I found solace in a crumb chop and two hard-boiled eggs.

PART THREE

Saint Anne's

Kasasati pota sati, kasasati pota sati[63]—past fields, forests, nullahs and bridges we raced, moving into the sunset. Gazing out from our compartment window, I watched as a herd of buffalo skirted the shoreline of a parched riverbed, gasping beneath the scorching sun. Grey wisps of smoke rose up in the distance, suggesting age-old rituals before the hearth. As dusk drew the day in the landscape changed to silhouettes of thicket and hedge. Night descended abruptly, leaving me blurry-eyed and sobbing in the dark.

I did not turn my head inward to join the games my fellow travellers were so gleefully playing. Instead, allowing the tears to pour profusely down my cheeks, I desperately tried to wash away the aching loneliness. Moira, curled up in a ball at my feet, had fallen asleep sucking her thumb. This was the first night in our entire lives that we were spending away from Mummy and it felt like hell.

The train slowed as we approached a wayside station. Figures shrouded in yards of khadi littered the platform. Springing to life, they sprinted alongside the carriages: porters, eager to assist alighting passengers. Vendors chanted: "Chai, garam chai. Paan, *beedi,* cigarette. *Kela, santra, naringi. Vada, vada, vada.*"[64] Lured by their cries, hungry travellers poked their heads out from carriage windows and hurriedly made their purchases.

It was a short halt, one of many. Before long, the station master was waving his lantern to and fro and, with a shrill blast of the whistle, we were off again, slipping away from the platform, past transient travellers slumbering beside their luggage. Leaving the winking lights of a railway colony behind, our train gathered momentum, racing furiously into the night.

Moira refused to eat dinner. However, she did share an orange with me. Whilst sucking on a segment, she inquired if I knew how many days would have to pass before seeing Mummy and Daddy again. With a lump in my throat, I told her I didn't have a clue, but it was probably months and months. I suggested making a calendar once we settled in at school, then crossing the days off, one by one (like prisoners counting their time to freedom). She thought it was a good idea.

Fellow students, who seemed quite standoffish at first, proved not to be so bad after all. Sensing our misery, they cheerfully assisted the

---

63   *kasasati pota sati* the sound of a train on the tracks
64   *beedi, kela, santra, naringi, vada* bidi, banana, oranges and savouries

teacher, Miss Rowena Price, in bringing down our bedding roll and laying it out upon the lower berth for us. Moira huddled in a corner and fell asleep with her face to the wall. I lay down beside her, steeped in misery, while our batch mates chattered endlessly. Full of pranks, they shrieked with laughter and tumbled all over their field beds spread out upon the carriage floor. I envied their lighthearted banter, wondering how many years of boarding school was required to ease the wrench of parting with one's family. Squinting up at a bright red chain, high above the window of the compartment, I read the inscription below it: *To stop train pull chain.* It was followed by a warning, aimed at triflers and mischief-makers who dared tamper with property belonging to the Indian Railways.

"Settle down, girls," Miss Price raised her voice above the merriment. "Good night and God bless you."

"Good night, Miss Price," they cried out in unison.

She switched off the light and I immediately fell into a deep, dreamless slumber, exhausted from an excess of emotion.

The next day dawned wet and chill. During the night we had climbed high into the Ghats and the scenery changed dramatically. Slopes of dense jungle rose up on either side of the tracks, their verdant depths blurred by morning mist. Here and there streaks of sunlight filtered through the towering canopy of trees, revealing the lush undergrowth. Wild orchids trailed down from lumbering branches, giving colour to the verdure. Soft, velvety-green moss covered the surface of the rocks facing the tracks. Tiny waterfalls sprayed down and misted my face as I peered out. The engine strained, making its ascent. We passed through several tunnels carved out from the ancient rock.

Miss Price ordered breakfast from the dining car and it arrived as our train came to a halt at the next wayside station. Steaming hot and delicious, the meal was carried in on several trays by waiters who set them down on pull-down tables—savoury omelettes, parathas, spicy vegetable cutlets and thick slices of juicy fried tomatoes, followed by coffee, tea and milk. Fresh fruit rounded out the meal. The combined aromas made my mouth water. I was ravenous!

"If you haven't lost your appetite, Sarah, you're okay." Mummy's habitual reply came to mind and she was right. My eyes hungrily followed the breakfast plates as Miss Price passed them out. I didn't know it at the time, but this was to be the last satisfying meal we were to enjoy for several months. Wolfing down a delicious omelette rolled up in a fresh paratha, nibbling on a savoury cutlet, I washed the meal down with a tumbler of sweet railway tea and burped with satisfaction. Moira refused to eat, turning away in disgust when the food was set before her. After some coaxing, however, Miss Price got her to eat a slice of buttered toast and drink a cup of milk. We later shared an orange.

> Kookaburra sits in the old gum tree,
> Merry, merry king of the bush is he.
> Laugh, kookaburra, laugh,
> Kookaburra gay your life must be.
>
> Kookaburra sits in the old gum tree,
> Eating all the gumdrops he can see.
> Stop, kookaburra, stop,
> Kookaburra leave some there for me.

The lusty singing voices of the batch resounded through the compartment and floated out into the morning air. Smoke billowing from the engine trailed behind in thick, dark plumes, speckling our faces with particles of coal. The chorus of songs continued: "Whispering Hope," followed by "Clementine." Ascending higher and higher into the hills—below the clouds, then into the clouds, where it almost seemed possible to reach out and touch them as they floated by. At around tea time the train chugged into the hill station of Phulamar, which was our designated stop.

Miss Price gave the orders; her manner changing abruptly. Becoming brusque and stern, she directed us to exit the compartment in single file. After stepping down from the train, though, all semblance of order disappeared as we were caught up in the swirl of passengers pushing and shoving in their haste to leave the station. I grabbed Moira's hand and dragged her behind me. A string of tongas tethered to half-starved, knobbly-kneed horses stood outside, awaiting our arrival. They accepted the tin trunks, bedding rolls and us, perched precariously atop the leather seats. Horse bells jangled as we started up the winding road that led to Saint Anne's Abbey.

Walls of thick, grey stone that were at first obscured by the mist now came into view. A mile long and insurmountable they seemed, following the curve of the hill, stretching out into the distance. Bougainvillea creepers clung to their sides and covered the large iron gates that opened to admit us. Once we were inside—tongas, baggage and boarders—they clanged shut. I shuddered, took a sharp breath and examined the surroundings. Our time within the abbey had commenced. Observing Moira seated shivering beside me, tears welled up once more, but swallowing hard I managed to hold back the torrent. Mummy claimed I had a sense of the dramatic and it certainly came to the fore on that chill, damp day in Phulamar!

"Line up, line up, no straggling allowed." A fat old nun with a dragging foot appeared on the scene and began to give orders as we jumped out of the tongas. "Assemble into straight lines, girls, new ones to the left, old ones to the right. That's right, that's right. Wait for me to lead you. No racing ahead!" Turning to "the old ones" line: "You lot know where to go."

"Yes, Sister," they chorused and marched away in another direction.

Turning to us: "You lot follow me!"

Plodding ahead, she led us into a large assembly hall, where we shuffled into rows and gazed up at the stage expectantly. A tall, skinny nun in a snow-white habit stepped out from behind heavy curtains, her rosary beads clicking as she moved.

"Good afternoon, girls," she greeted us. You must be the Bombay batch."

"Good afternoon, Mother," we replied with convent girls' instinct.

"Very good. I am Mother Valerian, your principal. Welcome to Saint Anne's Abbey. I want you all to listen well and pay attention, as I am about to explain the rules and regulations that govern the smooth running of this institution and what is expected of you as good students of the abbey. After our talk, each one of you will receive the school timetable, which sets out in detail your daily routine. You will receive a prayer book as well. If you obey the rules—appreciating the fact that your parents have wisely chosen our establishment to give you a good grounding, without which you will not be able to make your way in the world as decent Catholic women—all will be well. You are here primarily to study, to learn and understand the teachings of the gospels and the meaning of discipline and piety."

Taking a deep breath, she continued: "The routine is the same from Monday to Friday. Since Saturdays and Sundays are holidays, there is a slight variation; check your timetable for the changes. The morning bell will wake you all up at six o'clock sharp. You are to wash your faces, get dressed into your uniforms and line up for mass by six-thirty. Father Murray, our parish priest, says mass in the chapel every morning. He also conducts evening services and hears confession every Saturday from noon to one o'clock. After mass, at seven o'clock, you will all assemble outside the refectory and go directly in to breakfast, which lasts until seven forty-five. After your meal, you have fifteen minutes to collect your books and make your way to the study hall. The next half-hour is to be spent completing your homework assignments. It's playtime from eight-thirty to nine o'clock. You may want to step into the chapel for a few moments of meditation before classes commence for the day. The chapel is always open. The school bell rings at nine o'clock each day, at which time students are required to form a line outside their respective classrooms and enter in an orderly fashion.

"You will meet day scholars attending the abbey, many of whom are not Catholic. Not to put too fine a point on it, but we don't encourage familiarity between day scholars and boarders. And on no account should you ask them to purchase food for you from the market. All your needs will be met here at school and there is nothing extra you could possibly want from outside. Understood?"

"Yes, Mother."

"Very good. Now to continue. At eleven o'clock there is a half-hour break. A snack is available in the refectory for first- and second-class boarders; third-class boarders will spend the break attending to their chores in the nuns' bedrooms and chapel. Classes resume at eleven-thirty and continue to twelve-thirty in the afternoon. It is lunchtime then and the procedure is the same as it is for every meal: You have half an hour for lunch. At one o'clock you are to return to your classrooms and complete your school day, which ends at four o'clock in the afternoon.

"Boarders must go directly in for tea. From four-thirty until five-thirty you are required to attend to your toilette. Every girl will bathe, dress in civvies and rest until five-thirty. You may read or write letters home during that time. Loitering in corners, giggling in groups and indulging in rambunctious behaviour is absolutely forbidden, and will be dealt with severely.

"The good sisters whose vocation it is to serve God and care for you, in that order, need time for prayer and meditation. Therefore, when passing the chapel keep your voices down and tread lightly. Remember, it is the house of God and the sisters may be at prayer.

"At five-thirty each evening you will make your way to the playground, where Miss Price will oversee an hour of games. Everyone is expected to participate and no one will be excused, unless of course you have a chit from Sister Patricia in the infirmary. At six-thirty you are required to file into the study hall, where you will spend a full hour completing the next day's homework assignment. The dinner bell rings at seven-thirty. Sister Griselda presides over all the meals. Remember, if you are late for any meal without a proper explanation you will go without that meal. After dinner every student is expected to attend chapel for a short period of prayer and contemplation. Although not compulsory, it is necessary to give thanks each day—not more than ten minutes, if you please! Then, off you go to your dormitories to undress and get ready for bed. Lights out for juniors and intermediates is eight-thirty and nine o'clock for seniors.

"Sister Angelina is in charge of the first-class dormitory. Sister Patricia is in charge of the second-class dormitory and the infirmary. Sister Griselda has various duties, including the refectory and housekeeping. Sister Germaine is my assistant; she also monitors the study hour. Sister Celine takes care of the rest. Refer to them if you need anything or have a problem. I will now call out your names. Please fall into three lines as I indicate." Moira and I fell in behind Sister Angelina.

Sitting forlornly on my trunk, I surveyed the changed world around me. The dormitory was Babel, with a hive of fellow boarders, talking, giggling and posturing, all at the same time. Busy with unpacking their kits, they tried in vain to fit everything into the miniature lockers beside each bed. I longed for their comfort and ease—not a teary eye among them! Moira who had been designated a bed in the far corner, about three rows down from me, stood gaping at the circus around her.

O Lordy! How different this was from the world we had just left. I thought of Mummy and Daddy in Delhi with no address, of Grandpa and Granny Watkinson struggling with crop failure and of Radha,

Aunty Maggie and baby Trevor. I even spared a thought for Grandpa Reagan, wondering how he was coping with Grand-Aunt Elsie's various appetites and whether she had finally burned a hole in his baize-covered card table. Tears welled up and threatened to spill over, but I managed to contain them with a mighty sniff.

An inquisitive face peered down at me: "I can find a fag for you if you agree to share some of your tuck with her and maybe a few annas from your pocket money every week."

I looked up, bewildered.

"What's that you said?"

"I'm Vera Wainwright. Need a fag? She'll shine your basin till you can see your face in it. Blanco your Keds and what not. Keep old Angel off your back."

"Who's that?"

"Sister Angelina, silly, she's in charge of us and you never saw a more crotchety old biddy. You don't want to get her hackles up: she'd have it in for you then."

"What about Moira? My sister over there." I pointed. "Will she fag for her as well?"

"Can't see why not—double the tuck, though, and money too. I'll check around, see who's willing, and get back to you in a day or two."

"Okay."

Opening my kit box, I started cramming clothes into the tiny locker, not bothering with the stuff that didn't fit. A few uniforms, a nightdress and a couple of changes of underwear would do me for quite a stretch. One towel sufficed for the moment—a couple of pairs of socks and a few frocks. It was a tight fit. Slamming the lid down without bothering to read the list Mummy had pasted on the inside of the box, I shoved it under the bed. I was mighty angry with her at this point, for delivering Moira and me to a fate worse than death!

Walking over to where Moira was sitting, looking dazed and miserable, I offered to give her a hand.

There was a lot to learn. I was glad Vera, in the next bed, had decided to befriend me, although at times I wasn't quite sure of whether to believe all the tales she told or not.

"You'll have to take your licks first, Sarah Watkinson, before you learn the ropes. The seniors will have spite on you and you've got to learn to avoid them. Once a senior picks on you, you're done for!"

I shivered. "Why? How will they know me?"

"Oh, they'll know you all right! You have the look of a greenhorn."

"I do?"

"Pukka—it's pasted all over your face. Your sister's as well."

Every night after lights out, while the nuns were still in chapel, Vera leaned over and we had a whispered conversation through the mosquito netting.

"The most important thing is to imitate others who have been here longer than you—try not to stand out. After the first little while everyone will forget you're here and you can even have a chum fill in for you at roll call. Since the nuns never look up from their lists, saying 'Present' is all it takes. Blend into the background, Sarah, and your name won't come up for anything. Who wants to do anything for the silly old nuns, anyway? Do you?"

I shook my head in the darkness.

"You can get away with a lot if you're not noticed. Secondly, I think I've got a good fag picked out for you and Moira. She'll help you out no end. Some of them have been here at the abbey since God made Adam and they know the ropes."

"How long have you been here?" I asked.

"Simply ages. My parents travel a lot. My father is an ICS[65] wallah, you see."

"Mine is in the army."

"The fags are not first class like you or I; they're mostly all third-class boarders or orphans—'down-and-outers' we call them. Many of them have nowhere to go during the holidays, so, of course, they spend all their time with the nuns. They know this place inside out—and the nuns as well I should think." She chuckled.

"I understand." I didn't entirely, but what the heck!

The very first morning, as we sat down to breakfast, I noticed all the third-class boarders filing into the pantry. A few minutes later they emerged carrying enamelled plates and mugs. Filled with curiosity, I craned my neck in an effort to see what they were eating.

---

65   *ICS* Indian Civil Service

The monitor, seated at the head of the table, gave me a curious stare and asked, "Why are you looking over there?"

"I want to see what they're having for breakfast," I replied.

She snorted: "You do? Then why don't you join 'em? It would have to be the first time in the history of the abbey that a first-class boarder was interested in what the down-and-outers were eating. It's generally the other way around."

Her remarks brought forth a hoot of derisive laughter from the rest of the table. I slunk further into my seat and concentrated on the meal.

As we filled up on buttered toast, fried eggs, a cup of cocoa, and a banana, the third-class boarders hungrily spooned down a plate of dal with two dried chapatis, washing the meal down with a cup of watery tea.

"Ditch water! That's what I call it." Jane Woodman passed judgement on the tea. She had agreed to fag for us and I liked her from the very first.

Moira and I were seated on the top step of the dormitory, busily polishing our shoes. We had a lot of Cherry Blossom boot polish on our arms when Vera brought Jane over to introduce us.

"Here, let me show you how it's done," she offered, taking my shoe and deftly buffing it to a high shine.

Tall and angular with a spotty face, she seemed easygoing and friendly.

"I'm starving," she giggled, not a bit self-conscious.

We shared a couple of annas with her, the remains of Radha's silver rupees.

Falling asleep that night, I felt optimistic; things had already started looking up for us. Soon all would be well.

However, it wasn't that easy. I had difficulty adjusting to the different classes of boarders, as well as to the favouritism and politics that existed within the abbey. Why, I wondered, were second and third-class boarders fed different food? After all, they very seldom had any tuck. Shouldn't they be given extras to compensate? Why were fair girls with *coloured* eyes always chosen to be prefects? Why were they given plum roles in concerts? Why did *certain* third-class boarders receive a special diet, while others scavenged and were forced to perform the most menial tasks in return for a few annas every week? Why? Why? Why?

Try as I might, I couldn't understand a system that favoured students based entirely on their appearance and/or how much their parents could afford to pay. At meals, we sat at separate tables and were served different food. It just didn't make sense and I was miserable. No third-class boarder had a key to the tuck room. During meals, when Sister Griselda rang the bell that allowed us to go and fetch treats from our tuck boxes, you could feel their hungry eyes boring into your back as you entered to retrieve jams, jellies and biscuits. It was beastly.

"Why don't the down-and-outers have a key to the tuck room?" I asked Vera in a loud whisper through the mosquito netting one night.

"What would they do with it, silly?" She rolled all over her bed in a fit of laughter.

The dorm monitor suddenly appeared and, shining her torch through the netting, ordered Vera to sleep at once.

We had a letter from Mummy at the end of the week. She wrote to say Daddy had finally been allotted a tiny bungalow and that they were in the process of moving in. She included the address at the bottom of the page. Delhi was hot, Mummy complained, and very unsettling. Also, Daddy could be posted out again any time soon, she didn't know where to, but promised to keep us informed. For the rest, we should be good and study hard. Everyone missed us horribly. She ended her letter with: "Lots of love and kisses, your loving Mummy and Daddy."

I sobbed under the covers that night and Moira wet her bed.

Sister Angelina discovered Moira's "lapse" and loudly called out for her to stand aside, as we assembled for breakfast. Trembling, she left the line. I watched them disappear in the direction of the dormitory and sat down to eat, feeling heartsick. All through the meal, Moira's place remained noticeably empty. In vain, I tried to get Vera's attention, but she was busy chattering away to another girl at the far end of the table. The meal over, I made a beeline for the dorm, but didn't get further than the front door—for there she stood for all the world to see, my little sister, with a bundle of soiled linen upon her head. She gazed tearfully out at the girls parading past on their way to study hall. I heard a few of them snickering and, in a rage, dashed inside, nearly colliding with Sister Angelina, just as she was leaving.

"What have you done to Moira?" I demanded furiously. "Why does she have bed linen on her head?"

"Mind your manners, missy! Don't you dare use that tone of voice with me. You know very well why. She soiled her sheets last night. Besides, it is none of your concern. Off you go to study class or you'll be late. Moira has to learn to control herself and I aim to make an example of her so others will know this type of behaviour won't be tolerated in my dormitory."

"But, Sister—"

She glared angrily at me and strode away.

Not wanting to face Moira again, I left the dorm through another door. Old, familiar tears welled up and pricked my eyes. During study, they rolled down my cheeks unchecked and stained the reader, but I didn't care. Filled with anger and despair, I found it impossible to concentrate on my history homework or the sums that needed completion. The dread of impending failure was upon me.

Jane Woodman slipped into the seat beside me. "It's not so bad, Sarah," she consoled. "Sister will take the bundle off her head after study hour and she'll be able to join the others in class."

I gazed at her miserably through swollen, red eyes. "Why did Sister have to shame her in the first place? They have dhobis on the premises, don't they? And our parents pay fees. Moira simply had an accident."

"I know."

A few days later, during games hour, Sister Angelina called out our names and both Moira and I rushed over. She handed me a letter—joy of joys, it was from Grandpa Cliffy. I placed it in my uniform pocket and, finding a quiet corner beside the music rooms, we sat down to read it.

Handing it to Moira, I said, "You read it first."

"No, you. Read it out loud, so I can hear as well."

That I did. All was well at the farm, Grandpa wrote, and they seemed to be having quite a jolly time in spite of crop failure, which was expected, since he had hired a wastrel and a drunk to supervise the field hands. Granny was being vindictive, he said, and hadn't stopped harping on it. Moira and I chuckled; it was just as if he was sitting there between us, complaining about Granny. "'How are my two princesses? We hope the good sisters are taking proper care of you. We love and miss you. Pay attention in class and study hard and you'll find the time will fly. Your loving Grandpa and Granny.'"

Moira's lower lip started to quiver and I was sharp with her.

"Stop being a booby. You can reply to Grandpa and give him all your news. I'll write as well and we'll post the letter in one envelope."

This satisfied her. Folding the letter, I stuffed it into my pocket and we joined the others for study hour.

But, try as I might, I could not concentrate on homework. Reminiscing on the familiar scents and sights of home filled me with longing: Granny's Pears soap, the cruet stand with its cracked spout stained with Worcestershire sauce, which occupied a corner of the sideboard at the lodge. Mummy and Daddy, Radha, Aunty Maggie and baby Trevor, Toby, the lodge dog. Treasured memories cluttered my brain and conspired to prevent concentration on the studies at hand.

Finding the centre page of an exercise book, I composed a reply to Grandpa. After giving him a complete rundown on how things were at the abbey, I ended with a poem that reflected my opinion of "The Good Sisters."

Sister Germaine is ever so plain.
Sister Angelina is a real pain.
Sister Griselda is too fat by far.
Sister Celine sports a terrible scar.
Mother Valerian, or Mother Superior,
Thinks every student low and inferior.
We awake to the bell with the rising sun,
With here to the bell, and there to the bell—
Till the day is donè.
I'm always hungry and Moira is sad.
Wish you could save us, dear Grandad.

Hot breath and a wimple grazed my neck, as Sister Germaine peered down at my work.

"What's this? What's this, then? Give it here!"

Grabbing the book away from me, she ripped the pages out. Squinting, she read the poem I had just composed. The large mole beside her nose quivered, its protruding hairs bristling upon her furious countenance. Looking down at me in disgust, she cried, "What have you been up to? This is not your lesson for tomorrow. This is—this is—good heavens, girl, is this what you do with your study time? ... Follow me!" she barked.

I did, to the front of the hall and onto the podium.

"Stretch out your hands!"

Trembling, I stretched them out, palms facing upward. She crossed them with all her might,and I flinched as the edge of the cane came down repeatedly, cutting deep into my flesh. When it was all over, looking out across the hall, I noticed Moira, sitting with her head bowed, seemingly engrossed in homework.

"Stand there." Sister pointed with her cane. I moved under the large wood-framed clock upon the wall.

"I'm going to show this to Mother Superior." She waved the sheet of paper before my eyes. "And you haven't heard the last of it, my girl—count on it!" She glared at me.

When study was over, the girls filed out in silence with all eyes studiously averted. A solitary light burned out in the corridor, but the study hall itself was in darkness. Soon an army of mosquitoes swarmed in and began attacking me unmercifully. Scratching, I inched my way closer to the podium and, plopping down, decided to wait until someone showed up who would give me permission to go for dinner. My hands burned as I rubbed them together and against the fabric of my uniform. Red welts appeared; they were sore and painful to touch. I heard the faraway clatter of plates coming from the refectory, followed by the sound of the dinner bell, which signalled an end to the meal. Snatches of conversation, carried on the night air, implied the girls were now headed for chapel.

The wait seemed interminable. Gazing out at the immense shadowy trees in the compound, I spied will-o'-the-wisp dancing circles around their giant trunks before dissolving into the night. There were mischievous spirits lurking in the dark out there, no doubt about it. Feeling alone and miserable, I escaped in a flight of fancy to where palm trees swayed by the seashore and whispering summer breezes stirred the bedroom curtains at the lodge. I recalled a night strewn with stars when I had fearlessly climbed the rickety stairs leading up to the roof and, looking out at the great spread of the sea, had watched the waves as they rolled in to break upon the shore. Another time, gazing down from that same vantage point, I had thought how pretty the fairy lights strung out in the garden below appeared, framed against the night sky. That was my world and I loved it, but Moira and I had been brutally wrenched away and placed in the care of mean, vengeful nuns. Bitter tears of self pity streamed down and, since I could not find my hanky, I dried my eyes on the skirt of my uniform.

Needing to pee desperately, I crouched into a ball, trying hard not to think of it, but that proved impossible. "When you have to go, you have to go," Grand-Aunt Elsie had once remarked and I needed to go—immediately! A wastepaper basket, standing empty in the corner, beckoned. I was sure nobody would ever find out and, besides, an accident was imminent. Rushing over, I soon experienced a blessed sense of relief!

The sound of a habit swishing down the corridor meant a nun was in the vicinity. Hurriedly moving back to my place under the clock, I was momentarily blinded by a light being switched on—it revealed Sister Germaine.

"You still here?" She sounded surprised.

Where did she think I would be?

"You've learned your lesson now, I hope, and understand that study period is meant for just that. Keep your letter writing for Saturdays and free time. Maybe you're not aware of this, being a new girl at the abbey and all, but every scrap of correspondence that leaves or enters this place is read by Mother Superior. Nothing escapes her. Remember that always and govern yourself accordingly. Run along now and get yourself ready for bed. You hear me?"

"Yes, Sister, but what about my dinner?" I inquired, hesitantly.

"Well, of all the nerve, you cheeky girl! Imagine wanting dinner! Get to bed; there'll be no dinner for you tonight."

I bolted out of there and down the corridor towards the dormitory. Crossing a patch of dewy grass, I caught the scent of night air. Stopping for a second, I gazed into the heavens and spied Moonface smiling down at me.

Climbing into my pyjamas, I tumbled into bed and there she was again—her silver rays, streaming through the barred window, flooded my pillow with glorious light.

Moira's pretty curls proved to be a haven for lice. Sister Angelina yanked her hair roughly one Saturday morning, while going through it with a fine-tooth comb.

"Nits, nits and more nits," she muttered. "You have a veritable colony here! Where's your sister?"

Moira looked over at me, teary-eyed.

"Get here, Sarah. There are nits galore in her hair, although I don't see any lice. In case you're not aware, you are responsible for keeping each other's heads clean. She can hardly be expected to clean it herself. Here is a tin with some kerosene in it. Comb through her hair, remove the vermin and drop them into the kerosene. I want the tin back after you've finished and there had better be some lice in there. There's no smoke without fire!"

Steering Moira towards the dormitory steps, I began the arduous, boring task of delousing. Furious, I gave her hair a good tug.

"Ouch, ouch!" she yelled.

"I wish I had a monkey at this moment," I muttered crossly. "I'd introduce him to your head and he'd make short work of cleaning it."

Parting her locks, I removed innumerable nits, killing a few lice in the process.

Jane Woodman appeared. "What's up, Sarah?" We had run out of tuck, but continued to share our pocket money with her.

"Why are you third class?" I asked rudely.

"Who wants to know?"

"I do."

"I'm an orphan," she replied simply. "I dropped out of the sky one day and the sisters found me lying beside the music rooms with not even a note pinned to my dress."

"Did you have any clothes on?" I inquired.

"Can't remember. Sister Patricia said that God had no intention of giving me parents, but had sent me down to earth to test the nuns' patience. I was just another cross they had to bear. Father Matthias accepted the responsibility of choosing a name for me. He christened me Jane Woodman. Actually, I don't know who I am."

"Maybe you're a lost princess who was kidnapped at birth by evil men who wanted to harm your parents. Perhaps they are wandering the world in search of you and, when they find you, they'll dress you in silk and you'll have loads of tuck. As for the sisters, they'll lock them all in a dungeon deep in their castle and throw away the key. That'll show them!"

"Maybe," she giggled. "But when the sisters get huffy with me they call me a stray. So I guess that's what I really am, a stray."

"That's the sisters; I wouldn't pay any attention to them. Besides, Moira and I will adopt you."

Moira nodded.

"Gee, Sarah, thanks. Move over now and let me show you how it's done. I'm used to cleaning heads for pocket money."

"We're willing to share," I replied eagerly, passing the comb to her. My arms had begun to ache.

"Moira your head is full," Jane muttered, intent upon the hunt. Skilfully removing nits and lice, she dropped them into the tin. Checking it after a while, she leaned back satisfied. "Sister'll be pleased; she always likes to see you've done a fair job of it."

Vera and a couple of her pals swept by and looked our way with pitying glances. I fidgeted uncomfortably, trying not to notice, but Jane didn't seem to care.

"I don't have any lice," I boasted to her, "and I think I know why."

"Why?"

"Well, when you have straight hair like mine, the lice can't find anything to hang onto. As for nits, nits slide right out."

"Not these lice," Jane disagreed. "They're smart little devils and can fly around from head to head. Soon they'll be landing in your hair and, without caring whether it's straight or curly, they'll start to build their nests. Anyway, we'd better get Moira cleaned up or Sister will order a kerosene head bath and they're beastly; she'll stink for days and days."

Vera was cross with me because of "the study incident."

"Now you've gone and done it, Sarah Watkinson!" she declared.

"Done what?" I asked.

"Gone and made a spectacle of yourself, that's what. You're an insect!"

"You're no better," I yelled back. "Besides, I can't see how it's any of your business."

"I'm disappointed, that's all. And, what's worse, I see you and your louse-headed sister have become quite thick with the down-and-outers. We're *katti*[66] for life." She crooked her little finger at me.

"That's okay by me; I'm pukka with a lot of others."

"You'll soon see, they'll all turn out to be tuck friends. That's all they're good for, the down-and-outers. By the end of term, you'll have no tuck and no friends."

Sticking my tongue out at her, I turned and walked away, resolving to ask Sister Angelina for a bed change.

It hurt, but in the end I was relieved to be rid of Vera as a friend. Now I wouldn't have to listen to her whisperings and warnings at night. Besides, she gave me the jitters. After one of her talks, I walked around for days, scared of the nuns and too timid to speak to seniors, for fear of upsetting them—terrified that they would take spite on me. Moira, who was afraid of her own shadow, couldn't handle Vera at all. At any rate, through Jane Woodman we had come to know quite a lot of other girls, down-and-outers, to be sure, but, as time passed, I began to prefer their company.

Moira found the morning wake-up bell impossible to handle. Some days she forgot to brush her teeth and on others she left the dormitory wearing odd shoes or socks. On one occasion, in her hurry to get dressed, she even wore her uniform inside out. This was soon noticed by a bunch of bullies, who teased her unmercifully. Hurrying back to the dorm, she hastily rectified the blunder.

Morning mass was another obstacle. Invariably she'd start dozing halfway through the service and, sliding off the pew, would wake up with a jolt when she hit the floor. Of course, many juniors were guilty of this "lapse," as Sister Angelina liked to call it and mass was often interrupted by their startled cries.

On one particular saint's day, Moira was seated beside Glynis Sullivan during high mass. She tried her level best to stay awake, but as Father Murray intoned the response in his loud baritone and the altar boys swayed their censers back and forth, filling the chapel with incense, Moira's head began to loll sideways against Glynis' shoulder. The communion bells chimed and Glynis rose to receive the host, dislodging poor Moira, who slid down and collapsed in a heap on the

---

66   *katti* broken; not friends

floor. Glynis gasped! I looked up just as Sister Angelina rustled over and roughly righted Moira in the pew again.

Of course, she was called out after service and disappeared once more with Sister in the direction of the dormitory. We had hard-boiled eggs for breakfast that morning and I ate mine with two slices of toast. Moira's seat remained empty, so I leaned over and swiped her eggs from the plate as well. My actions were observed by the table monitor, but she turned away, uncaring, and continued chatting with her friends. After breakfast, Jane and I went in search of Moira. We found her sobbing, curled up in a ball in a bed of marigolds beside the dormitory steps. Although she tried very hard to hide the harsh, red welts on her legs, I spotted them and hated Sister Angelina with a vengeance.

The days passed, becoming weeks, becoming months—all rolled up in miserable time. Hungry and sad, I sought refuge in books and they came to my rescue. Flights of fancy carried me away on dangerous missions with the Scarlet Pimpernel. I rattled through the mean streets of Paris with him, saving aristocrats from Madam La Guillotine. A close friend of the Lady de Winter, I plotted with her and the scheming Cardinal Richelieu. In London, I caught the plague, but recovered and was able to escape to France before the great fire. This other world, peopled with characters from Dumas, Dickens, and Sabbatini, magnificent and fascinating, left me with little or no time for studies.

There was some truth in Vera's words: "Try not to stand out; they'll forget you're even here." However, for me this proved impossible, since I was incapable of maintaining a low profile. Seething with anger at real and imagined injustices, I wanted to smash something, so I broke the rules. Routinely called up along with the other troublemakers to mount the stage, I stoically endured the punishment handed down by Mother Valerian. Staring up at her, omnipotent, as she looked down on us, the rebellious ones stretched out their hands, palms facing upward, never flinching as she delivered her strokes. She meted out punishment in order of severity—each transgression warranted a different number of strokes. We were caned for giggling at mass, for nodding off during study hour, for speaking out of turn, for insubordination, for impudence and slyness. In my case I was also caned for corrupting my little sister, by encouraging her to misbehave.

"I don't feel so lonely up here on the stage with you for company,"

I whispered to Lynette Anderson, who almost always stood alongside of me, waiting for her ritual caning.

"You're incorrigible, Sarah Watkinson!"

"So I've been told."

We elbowed each other, nearly causing an incident, which would have justified a few extra strokes had Mother Valerian spotted us. Fortunately, she was caught up in the fury of the moment, severely caning another offender.

Jane Woodman was continually hungry and would undertake even the most menial tasks for a slice of cake or a cracker with a sliver of cheese on it. She'd jump through hoops for a toffee or a piece of chocolate.

"You must have a tapeworm," I teased.

"Golly, I've got something."

Poor Jane, she was needy and never took offence.

"Sister Patricia says I'm growing too fast and that is why I'm always hungry."

"Why doesn't she tell that to Mother Valerian then; she can arrange for you to have a tonic or some extra grub?"

"Dunno."

Knowing Jane was game for anything that would send a bit of tuck her way, I devised a scheme whereby she could enjoy all the treats her heart desired without having to fag for them.

"Imagine," I said, setting the scene one afternoon as we sat out on the dormitory steps. I passed her a vegetable cutlet that Moira hadn't eaten. "Imagine if you could enter the tuck room and help yourself to anything you liked from anybody's tuck box and never be found out. Wouldn't that be a dream come true?"

"It would!" she exclaimed. "But it's impossible, since I don't even have a key to the tuck room."

"I have a key."

"Why, yes, Sarah, you do. What's on your mind?" She was quick.

"I intend to exact some sweet revenge. Of course, you wouldn't have noticed, but Vera Wainwright has entirely too much tuck, which she shares with absolutely no one. Lately, I've noticed that she hardly ever locks her hamper, just scoops up her treats and rushes to her seat, where she stuffs herself silly. I noticed last week that she received another parcel from home. Now that's a bit much, don't you think? Two parcels in one term. Something must be done to stop her; she's beginning to resemble Porky Pig."

"By golly, she is getting fat!"

"Too fat by far, I feel, and I have a plan. You interested?"

"Count me in."

And so it happened that one evening a few days later Jane and I slipped away from the others, running out onto the games field and crept back into the pantry, which was deserted. Tiptoeing through the refectory where places had been set for dinner, we found it empty and as silent as a tomb. The lights were dimmed and Sister Griselda was nowhere about. She had joined the other nuns for benediction. Stealthily we crept towards the tuck room and I inserted the key, smiling as the lock tumbled easily. Jane, armed with a knife, a spoon and a tin cutter, followed me in, gently closing the door behind her. It was dusk with the only light being the faint rays of the setting sun streaming in through the windowpanes, which were haphazardly painted over a dark green. I was positive this was no war measure, since the nuns were not afraid of Japs raiding the tuck room, but rather they were more fearful of ravenous down-and-outers breaking in and gorging on all the tuck. Armed with an assortment of cutlery, it was possible to ransack the place in no time at all—a case in point, Jane Goodman.

"Ohmygawsh! Ohmygawsh! Oh—my—gawsh!" she exclaimed, over and over again. "Just look at all these hampers full of stuff!"

"Shush!" I silenced her. "If you keep this up, we'll be found out and then I don't have to tell you what will happen next."

We had half an hour to do the needful, to make a sizeable dent in Vera's tuck box and, by the way, to plunder other boxes that had been carelessly left unlocked, which was almost all of them. A delicious array lay before us: cheeses, crackers, condensed milk, jellies, jams and chocolates. Each box held a different variety of goodies.

Rifling through them like bandicoots set free in a dockside granary, Jane and I crammed our mouths full with chocolates and jujubes. I gaped as she hungrily rummaged through the hampers, since I had never seen a look of such unbridled greed on a face before. Plucking a can of condensed milk from out of Vera Wainwright's tuck box, she deftly punctured it and sucked out the sweet, milky contents, without so much as stopping to take a breath.

"Vera's got the best selection," I proclaimed, flopping down on the cement floor beside her hamper. Reaching for a bottle of raspberry jam, I helped myself to some cream crackers. Generously coating each cracker, I polished off the entire package. Jane had sliced off a large wedge of pound cake and was busy cramming it into her mouth.

"Golly, this is delicious!" she proclaimed. "I've filched it from Audrey Jackson's tuck box. I guess she won't mind, she always seems to have loads of pocket money and, besides, she's a snob." Hacking off another large piece of cake, she passed it to me. "Here, Sarah, you've gotta taste this cake; her mother must have made it."

After filling our pockets with chocolates and sweeties, we decided it was time to leave. Jane insisted on tidying up and closing each box. The nuns would get suspicious if the place was messy, she said, carefully placing the empty can of condensed milk back in Vera's tuck box:

"Polished it off in one go, the greedy thing!" she exclaimed.

We giggled.

I buried the half-eaten bottle of jam deep in my hamper and hurried out.

Our little foray was never discovered. At dinner, however, Vera Wainwright emerged from the tuck room bawling her eyes out.

She went up to Sister Griselda: "My tuck's vanished, Sister. Somebody sucked the condensed milk right out of this can and then put it back in my hamper." She shoved the empty can in Sister's face. "What shall I do? It was meant to last the whole term," she wailed. "I think we have a thief in our midst."

A few of the seniors snickered. "Ooh, poor Vera," they teased.

Sister Griselda was unperturbed. "Was your tuck box securely locked?" she asked.

Vera nodded.

Liar!

"In that case, it would be difficult to pilfer, wouldn't it? I notice you've been visiting the tuck room very regularly, Vera, my dear; it's my guess you've eaten it all. Don't come looking to me for any sympathy. You need to portion out your treats and make sure they last you for the entire term. Get back to your seat now and stop snivelling," she ordered. "By the way, has anyone else lost any tuck?" Sister's voice echoed through the refectory.

I shot a glance over at Jane seated below me at the third-class boarders' dining table. She was busy concentrating on the meal, chewing on a piece of dried chapati.

No hands went up and I heaved a sigh of relief.

A rebellious attitude coupled with insatiable hunger caused us to hatch all kinds of imaginative schemes. Enlisting the help of Moira and Lynette, I climbed the mango tree one afternoon and, shaking the heavy branches loaded with raw fruit, watched as they thudded to the ground. Filling pillowcase after pillowcase, I scrambled down and we disappeared into the dormitory in a flash. The following morning I bribed a day scholar to buy us a few annas worth of chili powder and salt, which I blended together. When the weekend rolled around we did a brisk business, selling green mango slices rubbed with the fiery mixture. The dormitory went crazy for the stuff, but unfortunately some of the girls overindulged and got quite ill as a result. My little operation was soon discovered when a bilious boarder spilled the beans to Sister Patricia, who was kept busy administering spoonfuls of castor oil all around. Both Lynette and I were severely caned by Mother Superior, but Moira was spared. Mother said she had been coerced. Looking up the meaning of the word in the dictionary, I didn't entirely agree. Anyhow, for me, the caning was like water off a duck's back, since I was fast becoming thick-skinned and uncaring. In time my notoriety spread, attracting the attention of certain daring individuals; as a result, I was seldom without willing accomplices, especially from within the ranks of the down-and-outers.

Letters home were brief, as I evaded Mummy's prying questions about studies and sports activities. Obsessed with finding ways and means to make life easier, I showed Moira how she could doze through the mass. Each morning she knelt piously beside me at chapel and, with her eyes closed in silent meditation, she snoozed through the entire service, whilst Father dragged on. I poked her in the ribs when she had to change positions. We giggled about it every day at breakfast.

It was difficult on the games field as well. Only the slim, athletic ones were chosen. Not being blessed with either attribute, I was always left out. Miss Price, the games teacher, proved to be quite horrible and completely ignored me. I found her equal to the nuns when it came to playing the game of "favourites." Fed up, one evening I left the field and, needless to say, my absence went unnoticed. Coming upon a tiny trail that led up to the statue of Our Lady, who looked down upon the abbey, I followed it to the grotto and behind. There in the shadows, I came upon a patch of damp, sweet grass surrounded by terraced beds of nasturtiums, carnations, sweet peas and phlox. Now here was a spot I could call my own, where it was possible to sit and read for hours without being discovered. What a find! Immediately I christened it "The Bower."

An ancient mali tended the flower beds, going about his tasks humming softly to himself. He tottered around on spindly legs, moving between the beds like a drunken elf. I chuckled, watching his antics. Best of all, he didn't seem to mind my being there as he pruned and watered the plants. At times a sly smile flitted across his wizened face and he winked when I looked up. I thought he looked like a goblin, a sprite, so I named him Rumplestiltskin and asked his permission to pick a carnation. Nodding, he bent down and plucked one for me himself. It smelled of sweet, spicy cloves and I pressed it in a book.

There were times, of course, when I became quite broody and spent the entire games period staring down at the field below, dwelling on real and imagined slights. Watching my mates at play, filled with hurt at being excluded, I wondered why I never made the cut for basketball, rounders, netball or badminton—but instead always ended up a holdall for cardigans and watches. Sadly, I observed them racing around the badminton courts, smashing shuttlecocks into nets. I wished I'd been born in another place, in another time—slim, athletic and tall. In the end though, I always pulled myself together and counted my blessings. After all, I had my family who loved me and whom I loved in return. We were first class, Moira and I, which seemed all important at the abbey. Our parents had sent us here with the very best intentions, of this there was no doubt. There was no way for them to know the abbey was a vile place with nuns who were mean to us and cruel to the third-class boarders. Mother Superior said nuns had a vocation, a divine calling. Phooey! I thought.

My devotion to Our Lady increased during those evening interludes behind the grotto. Every time The Bower gave me sanctuary, I placed a flower at her feet, feeling safe in her aura, as she gazed calmly down at me. Dressed in a blue and white gown, with a rosary wrapped around her folded hands, she smiled down serenely, without a care in the world.

One Saturday afternoon we were taken to the pictures to see *Joan of Arc*, with Ingrid Bergman playing the part of Saint Joan. She immediately became my favourite actress, displacing Rita Hayworth, whom, I felt, was not a patch on her. Voicing my opinion at the dinner table one evening, I was cuffed on the ear by a senior, who called me "a lump." Henceforth, I resolved to keep my opinions to myself.

A few weeks later, just before the study hour, Sister Angelina called out a list of names, mine included, and we stepped out of line, as was the rule. Marching, we followed her into Mother Valerian's office and silently assembled before the great one.

"Very good, Sister; now you may go," Mother dismissed her. "I shall speak to the girls myself."

Mother Valerian had a regal air about her, which sent everyone hurrying to obey her orders. She was never contradicted and had only to speak for the nuns to stop in their tracks and listen with rapt attention. Meekly they stepped aside as she swept majestically by them in the corridors—like a Spanish galleon on the high seas, I thought. She was the Armada, a force to be reckoned with! My poor friend, Jane Woodman, trembled at the sight of her.

Turning to face us, Mother removed her spectacles and placed them on the desk.

"The time has come for you girls to make your confirmation, to become soldiers of Christ. Accordingly, starting this Saturday at eleven o'clock in the morning, you are all to assemble in the chapel, where Sister Germaine and Father Murray will commence with your instructions. In three months time you should all be ready to receive the Holy Spirit. Each girl is required to choose a saint's name, which will be forever included with her other given names. Please do not consider frivolous names such as Daisy and Doris, Ginger and Ida. Most of the reigning movie stars' names are out of the question. Rather, I would prefer you all to turn to the book of saints' names and choose one from there. This is a holy and important occasion in your lives and I hope you will treat it as such. Searching for a name from the book of saints' names is a wonderful opportunity, for it will give you a chance to meditate upon their lives and compare them with your own. This exercise, I hope, will give you the spiritual direction needed to follow in their blessed footsteps."

Mother continued: "Daniel, the school tailor, will be in to take your measurements and he will sew you new white frocks for the occasion. There will be a confirmation party in the refectory after the service. Does anyone have any questions?"

"No, Mother."

"Very good. You are dismissed."

Fortunately, I didn't have to consult the book of saints' names; I already had my confirmation name all picked out.

Excitedly, I confided it to Moira: "Joan, after Saint Joan of Arc, what d'you think? Sarah Joan Watkinson, it has a certain ring to it, doesn't it?" I asked, pleased with my choice.

"Will you invite me to your midnight feast in the dorm?"

"Yes, silly. What do you think of my new name?"

"It's okay. I like it. Promise you'll invite me."

Moira could be quite exasperating at times.

My grades deteriorated further and I was soon failing in every subject. Continually being called up for detention, I stepped out of line, armed with a storybook, and spent the entire time quietly reading while the nun on duty flitted between the rows of desks. As a result, my mid-term report was dismal and landed me near the bottom of the class. I was second last and would have placed last, except for the fact that Lynette Anderson, my desk mate, scored 19% in arithmetic, while I scored 20%. She got the last place.

"Shame!" Mother Valerian hissed, ordering me up on the stage to stand behind her.

I didn't even get a pass mark in English literature, a subject that for me had always been a breeze. Spelling, poetry, dictation—I had failed in every subject. O Lordy! What had happened? My grades had plunged to new depths, sacrificed to daring exploits, romantic encounters and chivalrous knights. To endless dreaming in The Bower and reading with a torch under the covers at night. All of the above had brought me to this sad end.

Of course, I was not alone; there were others and the line grew, snaking across the entire length of the stage. Gaping out at the teachers and other students assembled in the hall—like a group of village idiots on display—we shifted from foot to foot self-consciously, chewed our lips, lowered our eyes and rolled our soiled kerchiefs into ugly little balls.

Moira received an excellent report card and was commended for her neat handwriting and completion of assignments on time. I grinned at her as she mounted the stage to receive the prize for geography. She completely ignored me.

Lynette Anderson was called up. She climbed on to the stage and stood before Mother, a defiant gleam in her eyes.

"Ungrateful, unworthy little tramp; we don't need students like you here at the abbey. The proper place for you is in an orphanage; your presence lowers the tone of the entire school. Keep your eyes down, miss, when I speak to you!" Mother's voice was harsh and crackled across the hall. Lynette faced her without flinching and received four strokes for insolence and for making "a spectacle of herself before the entire abbey."

From that day forth, I resolved to make her my best friend.

As she squeezed in beside me, I jostled her. Caught off guard, she collided with the girl next to her, creating a domino effect, which sent Arlene Morrison at the very end toppling off the stage. She landed on the floor with a startled shriek. Mother turned and, with a face like thunder, ordered Arlene to pick herself up and come forward. Poor girl, she was caned for the second time and we watched her take her licks, tears streaming down her sad crumpled face. Lynette stared at me accusingly, but I dismissed the entire affair with a shrug, just happy to have created a diversion. That night, though, I felt really miserable about Arlene, especially after I learned her father had died during the war—missing in action, in Burma. I realized I had carried things a bit too far and Arlene had suffered as a result. Silently I said a prayer for her father and repeated Kipling's poem as a tribute:

> Come you back to Mandalay,
> Where the old Flotilla lay;
> Can't you 'ear their paddles chuckin' from
> Rangoon to Mandalay?
> On the road to Mandalay
> Where the flyin'-fishes play,
> An' the dawn comes up like thunder outer
> China 'crost the Bay!

With a shiver, I settled deep under the covers. The night was filled with disturbing dreams.

"Dunce, dunce, double D, forty years in ABC," the bullies chanted. They surrounded me one afternoon a few days later, as I stepped out of study hall.

Brazenly, I stuck my tongue out at them.

"Fatty, fatty, bombalatee, ate up all my ghee chapati," they heckled.

"Sticks and stones—" I replied brazenly, looking them in the eye.

Lynette and I had become the best of chums. We giggled throughout classes, distracted teachers and sent paper aeroplanes soaring through the air during study hour. Composing naughty couplets about the nuns, we circulated them. Through it all, I continued to fail miserably in every subject.

Lynette did not share my love of books. She was athletic with long slender legs and knobbly knees—Captain of the netball team. Determined to include me in a game, she called my name one evening when choosing sides for netball. Rushing over to where her team stood at one end of the field, I hopped around in excitement, waiting for the match to begin. But alas! I proved to be more of a hindrance than a help and by the end of the first half team mates were clamouring for my removal.

"Sorry, Sarah, you stink. You'll have to sit the next half out if we are to win," Lynette informed me apologetically.

So I left the field when the game resumed. Slinking away to The Bower, I found solace in a book.

One evening after study, Lynette ran up to me and placed her arm around my shoulder as we entered the refectory for dinner. Tripping along, chattering away to one another, we were both oblivious of Sister Griselda's proximity. Suddenly and without warning the edge of a ruler came down hard upon my friend's thin arm and she yelped in pain.

"Keep your hands to yourself and look sharp," Sister admonished. "No familiarity allowed. You know the rules." Grabbing Lynette roughly by the shoulder, she steered her to the back of the line. "You're going to walk beside me, where I can keep an eye on you."

Entering the dining room, feeling dejected, I looked down to where the third-class boarders sat and saw my poor friend gazing across the refectory at me with streaming eyes. A bowl of watery dal, two dried chapatis and an overripe banana sat untouched before her on the plate.

Confirmation Sunday dawned. My new white frock on a hanger beside the bed looked pretty much the same as every other white frock in the dormitory. I complained to Sister Angelina that the tailor had paid no attention at all to the pattern I had selected. Furthermore, he had skimped on the material and sewn the bodice too tight.

"You are going to chapel to become a soldier of Christ and not to a fashion parade," she replied, turning away from me.

A tittering Moira pranced around chanting, "I can see your boobies."

I clouted her across the ear. "You're not invited to my midnight feast. Leave me alone!"

Near to tears, I tried in vain to adjust the frock and make it look presentable. I covered the offending "boobies" with a bolero, but the effect was ghastly. Finally, joining the other confirmundi, I trooped into chapel feeling like a clown.

Mummy had sent me five rupees as a confirmation gift and I pooled the entire amount with some others who had ordered food from outside through a day scholar. She was going to pass the grub to us through the back gate of the abbey.

Moira sidled up beside me and whispered: "I'll tell you're getting food from outside."

"You wouldn't dare!"

"I would so."

"That's right, you would!" I replied, turning away in disgust.

That night, after Sister Angelina had made her rounds without detecting that pillows had been placed under covers as substitutes for bodies, those of us who had contributed to the feast huddled together in a dark corner of the dorm. Watching Moira nose around the fringes of our party with her new best friend Jenny Wheeler, I relented and invited them to join in as we unwrapped the packets of chow, *bhujias,* biryani and *jalebis.*[67] Falling on the food like a pack of hungry wolves,

---

67 *bhujias* a savoury *jalebis* big, round, orange-coloured sweet

we demolished the entire lot in one sitting. Hastily scrunching up the evidence, we stored the empty food packets under a bed to be disposed of the next day. Then, taking turns rinsing our fingers under the bathroom tap, we scurried to our beds and pulled the covers over. It was a sight for sore eyes, us girls downing all that grub, sharing our irreverent opinions of the nuns and giggling all over the place. I revelled in the camaraderie and wished the night would never end—convinced the scent of danger, coupled with good friends and good food, had worked a special magic. I vowed to repeat the event.

Horror of horrors! Waking one morning, I discovered blood in my pyjama bottoms. Embarrassed, I hurriedly washed them out in the basin and hung them to dry at the foot of my bed.

"Wet your night pants?" Vera asked rudely.

"None of your business." I shoved her.

Nervous for the rest of the day, I was afraid to visit the lavatory, even when it became imperative. After lunch, however, it was impossible to restrain myself any longer. I simply had to go. There, to my dismay, was more blood, darkly staining my knickers. Tears of fear and frustration flowed freely down my face. How had this happened? What had I done to deserve this terrible affliction? Recalling the woman with the issue of blood from the Bible, I wondered if I was intended to become her modern-day counterpart. Who would save me? Where was Mummy when I needed her most? Oh, darn! Sobbing uncontrollably, I heard the bell for afternoon classes clanging in my ears.

Hurriedly drying my face, I decided to tackle this new challenge as Saint Joan of Arc would have. She had overcome great obstacles without bawling and now it was time for me to emulate my patron saint. Pulling up my knickers, I walked over to the dormitory in search of Sister Angelina,and discovered her embroiled in a heated discussion with Ganga Ram, the dhobi. They were arguing about a discrepancy in the washing account.

Spotting me, she angrily demanded, "Why aren't you in class? Didn't you hear the bell?"

Head bowed, I searched for words.

"Have you got diarrhea?"

"No, Sister, I've got blood."

"H'm, in your knickers, I suppose."

"I nodded."

She didn't seem in the least affected by my revelation.

"Well, I guess that explains your presence here at this time of the afternoon and your pyjama bottoms hanging out to dry over the bed. I suspected something of the sort. Not to worry, my girl. Sit down there—" She pointed to a stool, "And after I've finished with this fellow, I'll attend to you."

Turning her attention to the dhobi once more, she continued with her furious tirade, threatening to sack him if he persisted in losing articles of clothing and shredding the bed linen.

"Sister wanting starch," he offered humbly. "Cockroach also wanting starch—eating *kapada*,[68] making big hole bole." Standing on one leg, he pleaded piteously for Sister to give him another chance.

She shook her head and continued with counting the bedsheets, pillowcases and towels. Unfolding a sheet, she examined it carefully.

"Look at this, just look at this!" She shoved it under his nose. "This sheet is not very old and already it shows signs of fraying. There are burn marks too—from your iron! I'll have to have a word with Mother Superior. You've got to go!"

"You are asking white, clean sheet. My brother Arvind bashing on large stone, using much soap and bleach. Have pity, Sister sahib; bleach shredding bedding every time."

"What about the missing items?" Sister inquired.

"We are still washing petticoat, patloon and pyjama. Bringing soon—tomorrow maybe. Hanh?" he begged, cringing before Sister.

Her look was pure venom. She shook her head disgustedly and, turning away from him, strode quickly over to the far end of the dormitory. A sly smile flitted across the dhobi's face as he wordlessly picked up his bundle of dirty clothes. Slinging it over his back, he ambled out of the dormitory into the afternoon sunshine.

Swinging my legs that didn't quite reach the floor, I smirked. Sister Angelina looked flushed and uncomfortable under her wimple. Somehow, I felt the dhobi had won the day.

"Stop that!" she snapped at me. "You're a young lady now and ladies don't swing their legs. Sit up straight and don't distract me."

I bit my lip in an effort not to giggle.

---

68   *kapada* clothing

The dormitory was quiet at this time of the afternoon—orderly, with the rows of beds all neatly turned down. Fresh linen sat on each bed, ready to be stuffed into the lockers when the girls returned from classes.

"Sarah?"

"Yes, Sister."

Unlocking the large cupboard that stood at one end of the room, she placed her account book in a drawer. Then, taking a package from the bottom shelf, she turned to me.

"Let's get this matter sorted out once and for all. First things first, the blood in your knickers is your period and there is no reason for you to be alarmed. Every young woman from the dawn of time has shared your experience. You will continue to get your periods for a great many years, so settle down and listen closely as I show you how to take care of this problem that will recur every month. Also, you're a lady now and, as such, you must take care to behave with proper decorum—no more tomboy behaviour, you hear?"

"I understand, Sister."

Producing a narrow cotton pad wrapped in gauze, a length of elastic and two safety pins, she continued.

"Here, let me show how it's done. Pay attention."

Tying a knot in the elastic, she attached the pad to either side with the aid of the safety pins.

"Slip this on like you would your knickers and then pull your panties up over it. There will be more pads for you when you return from classes. I'll place them in your locker. See that you change at least three times on the first day, twice on the second and twice on the third. The blood flow should ease after that and completely disappear. Nevertheless, better to be safe than sorry; wear a clean pad to bed every night for the next few days; accidents can and do happen. If you run out, come to me and I'll replenish your supply. Rinse out your soiled knickers everyday when you bathe and, when they dry, place them in the hamper. Used pads are deposited here."

She led me to a covered bin near the bathroom and lifted the lid. I recoiled as the overpowering odour of disinfectant and menstrual blood stung my nostrils. Sister quickly replaced the lid.

I remembered seeing the matherani carrying out the container when she came in to clean the bathroom and clear the rubbish.

Hurriedly changing in the bathroom, I emerged to find Sister waiting for me.

"Here's a chit for you, give it to the teacher and she'll understand. Off to class now and no dawdling along the way."

"Yes, Sister," I replied meekly.

The pad felt uncomfortable and I suffered all afternoon, feeling self-conscious because it protruded too far out in the front, tenting my uniform. All my efforts—running to the bathroom several times to make adjustments—proved futile.

Lynette laughed out loud and teased: "Sarah, why are you waddling like a duck?"

"I'm not well," I replied, hurt.

"What's the matter?"

"I have my period."

"Oh, that! You have the curse. We all get it every month."

"Why is it called a curse?"

"Are you comfortable with it?"

"No."

"That's why it's called the curse." Clutching her sides, she rolled about on the grass laughing like a hyena.

I was not amused.

"When will it go away?" I asked impatiently.

"Never; you'll get it every month for ages and ages. It's also called 'monthlies,' but I prefer curse, because I get awful cramps and headaches on the first day. Do you have cramps?"

I shook my head.

"Lucky. By the way," she whispered in my ear, "d'you want to come to a meeting of the Moonlight Marys? It's a holiday weekend in two weeks and a full moon to boot. All the parlour boarders will be gone for four days and those of us left behind who belong meet under the Mother tree at midnight."

"Where is the Mother tree?"

"It's the tamarind tree behind the music rooms."

"Oh. What do you do under the tree at midnight? Cast spells?"

"No, silly. Cybil Winters, our Head Girl, presides over the meeting and you have to be invited to join. I'm inviting you. Wanna come?"

"Yes," I replied eagerly.

"If we're lucky, we may see the ghost of Celia Stevens taking a walk on the abbey wall."

"Who is she?"

"I told you, a ghost. Ask Cybil."

"I couldn't possibly, she's the Head Girl."

"She's approachable and one of us—a down-and-outer. She's also one of Mother Valerian's favourites. I bet you didn't know that."

I shook my head.

Lynette scampered away, leaving me with a hundred unanswered questions.

The tamarind tree stood at the very end of the playground, its ancient limbs spread across the abbey wall. I had spent some time reading in the shade of its sprawling branches and found it to be a very lively tree during the day. Doves nested within its boughs and, when the tamarind ripened, bright green, rose-ringed parrots swooped down, devoured the fruit and filled the air with their raucous squabbling. At night, though, the tree cast a sombre shadow and a brooding stillness settled in the dark spaces between the wall and its gnarled trunk. Buried in its foliage, an old grey owl kept vigil. One could hear him hooting from time to time.

It was now early November and the nights were chill and clear. Moonface, sailing across the heavens, paused over the tamarind tree. Her rays streamed down, bathing us in light as we sat in a tight circle, huddled under our blankets.

"I've invited Sarah Watkinson to join," Lynette chirped up. "She's a good egg."

"Does she know she has to prove herself?" Cybil inquired.

"How do I do that?" I had obviously spoken out of turn, for the others glared at me.

The Moonlight Marys were all third-class boarders. Jane Woodman was there, Jenny Wheeler, Arlene Morrison and a handful of others I knew. Some seniors were present as well. I didn't dare look at them during the day, but they were smiling at me now, their teeth glinting in the silvery moonlight. I felt privileged to belong.

"Sarah, what's the most important thing to a third-class boarder?" Cybil asked.

"Food," I replied instinctively.

"Yes," she acknowledged. "To prove yourself worthy, on the next full moon when we assemble here, you must steal the fruit from off the nuns' dinner table without being caught. Hide it and bring it to the meeting for all of us to share. You may choose an accomplice."

I looked over at Lynette, who nodded and said, "Will do."

It was all set.

Malvina Cross, a senior, had a poem she wished to recite.

"Hush." We came to order, sitting still, like a circle of stones.

"This is an ode to the Mother tree, who gives us shade and shelter and who generously shares her fruit with us."

Tamarind tree your branches spread out and envelop us.
You hold us close, and we find refuge here.
Your fruit when green is sour, but can be eaten.
When ripe, is soft and brown within the shell.
Oh, Mother tree, we thank you, and applaud you.
For nature's wonder, you have served us well.

"There she is!" Jane gasped, pointing to an apparition some distance away.

The wraithlike figure floating across the top of the wall stopped briefly, turned and continued on. Slight with dark hair that fell to her waist in tendrils, she wore a flimsy gown that billowed in the night air. I gaped, incredulous, watching as she slowly melted into the darkness. O Lordy, my first ghost!

Impulsively, I cried out her name. Once again the others stared at me in disbelief.

"I told her," Lynette owned up.

"She is our very own ghost," Jane Woodman spoke in hushed tones. "D'you know why she walks upon the wall?"

I shook my head.

Lynette left the circle, grabbed a ladder leaning against the tree and climbed into its branches. I could see her thin arms wrapped around its lower limbs, shaking them vigorously. Soon the fingerlike fruit started falling to the ground and each girl helped herself to a few tamarind pods. Peeling off the outer skin, we chewed the green fruit, squinting as the acid juices filled our mouths.

Cybil Winters, being the oldest student of the abbey, was the only one who remembered Celia Stevens. They had shared the same ayah, Rukhmani. Cybil knew the entire story from start to finish, but had to be persuaded to tell it. I was filled with curiosity, but, being the new girl in their midst, didn't dare ask her. Nevertheless, as our eyes met across the circle for a brief second, I detected an anxious expression on her face, which spoke volumes. Instinctively I knew she was aching to speak, if only someone would ask. I nudged Lynette seated beside me and she obliged.

"It's been simply ages since we've seen Celia; maybe she's trying to tell us something."

"Like what?" Cybil asked, leaning forward.

"Well—" Lynette spoke hesitantly, "maybe Sarah Watkinson should know about her."

"Why?"

"I don't know why, but there could be a reason. Who knows? It's all supernatural, isn't it?"

The stage was set. Cybil began speaking softly and we moved closer together, anxious not to miss a word.

"Celia was found one morning by the abbey gates, wrapped in a shawl with her name scribbled on a piece of paper pinned on. The nuns took her in and placed a notice in the local paper asking for her real mother to come forward, but, of course, no one did and so they adopted her. She was a delicate baby right from the start and they gave her as much care and attention as nuns are capable of. All of us gathered here tonight are familiar with their ways, so I need not elaborate. Fortunately, Mother Valerian, who was new to the abbey at the time, grew particularly fond of the frail baby. Realizing she was in need of a wet nurse, Mother hired Rukhmani, the *khansama's*[69] wife, as ayah. It was she who told me of Celia's early years.

"According to Sister Patricia, I was four years old when my mother first brought me to the abbey. Giving the nuns a little money, she asked them to take care of me for a couple of months. Saying she was about to marry a Tommy and, since he was going to make an honest woman of her, she didn't want to complicate matters by showing up with a child. Promising to return and claim me before they sailed for England, she left and, of course, the rest is history, for here I am to this day. Being very young, I, too, was placed in the care of Rukhmani.

---

69   *khansama* cook (masculine)

"Celia was nine years old when I arrived. A delicate child given to coughs and colds, she spent a lot of time in the infirmary. Actually, she was fortunate to have Mother Valerian, who doted on her, because she saw to it that Celia received extras like eggs and cocoa at meal times. I, on the other hand, thrived on abbey food and was soon able to join the other third-class boarders in the refectory for meals."

"Was she pretty?" I asked.

"Yes, she was pale with dark hair and eyes. 'China doll,' the nuns called her and treated her like one. Every morning Sister Griselda spooned a tonic down her throat, and during the winter months she had to have a double dose of *chiretta*[70] to keep the bloom on her cheeks. I remember the tonics very well because we others never got any and I often wished I could try some. Mani—Rukhmani, loved Celia as if she was her mother and her affection was wholeheartedly returned. After all, she was the only mother Celia had ever known.

"Old Father Matthias was the parish priest in those days, but he grew ill and died. I recall it was soon after my ninth birthday that a new priest was assigned to the abbey, Father John Rider. He was young, tall with velvet brown eyes. Celia made her confirmation that year and Father John assisted Sister Germaine with the instructions. We thought it peculiar, the many hours she began spending in the chapel after that. Every evening she would disappear during games hour and one could find her kneeling before the statue of Mother Mary, saying the rosary. Also, she went to confession daily and on one occasion I overheard her sobbing in the confessional. Curious, I asked Mother Valerian why Celia spent so much time in the chapel and she said, 'She has a calling, my dear, and will be joining the abbey as a novice after her Senior Cambridge Examination.' I was in awe of her after that."

"What did she find to confess every day?" I asked Cybil, inquisitively. "She never ventured outside these walls."

"Shush," the others hissed.

Shrugging, Cybil continued: "After her confirmation, Celia's health improved. In fact, she blossomed and Sister Patricia joyously attributed her transformation to the Holy Ghost, whom she said had touched Celia with the heavenly spirit and made her well again. During the summer holidays that year, the nuns went away to the Mother House in the hills and left us girls in the charge of Sister Griselda and Father John

---

70   *chiretta* a horrible drink to bring the bloom back

Rider. By the time they returned, Celia was ill once more. She looked deathly pale and we got used to seeing her thin frame wrapped in a flannel dressing gown, languishing in an easy chair on the infirmary veranda. She also developed a wracking cough and since there was a TB scare about the nervous nuns considered sending her to a sanatorium to recover her health. They forced all sorts of delicacies down her throat—eggs for breakfast, beef tea, chicken for lunch and a double dose of tonic each day. Celia hated the medication. Gagging on it, she threw up violently in the pantry, one morning. I followed her around like a puppy, totally obsessed.

"'I'm possessed,' she confided, as we sat together on the infirmary steps one evening.

"'By whom?' I asked, gaping at her, aghast.

"'I am cursed with the twin demons of lust and temptation.'

"'Who told you this?'

"'I know it in my heart, for it races and pounds when I see that person.' She looked at me, her dark eyes filled with emotion. Beads of perspiration appeared on her upper lip and she seemed flushed and feverish.

"'Have you talked to Mother Valerian about this?'

"'I don't have to, I know what I feel.'

"'Who is this person leading you into lust and temptation?' I asked curiously. 'Give me a name.'

"'I can't tell you, but he and I are both weak and cannot help ourselves. We are damned.'

"'He?' I looked at her, horrified. 'What d'you mean, he?' I couldn't imagine who she was referring to; there were no men around besides the servants and the parish priest. Celia's emotions were quite beyond me. 'Oh! You'll get over it,' I calmed her. 'Just eat all the good stuff the nuns keep feeding you and try not to vomit all the time.'

"'I'll try,' she replied wanly.

"I went to find Rukhmani the following day. Squatting down beside her, I tried to discover what ailed poor Celia, but she would give me no reply. Shaking her head, she looked sadly away into the distance.

"One morning, not long after, the dormitory awoke to a terrible commotion. Mass in the chapel was cancelled—something unheard of at the abbey. Mother Valerian was in a state of shock and the nuns were agitated.

"Nathu, the milkman, whilst walking his buffalo up to the abbey gates that morning, had discovered Celia's lifeless body sprawled across the path and raised the alarm. She was in her nightdress and had just one slipper on. The other slipper they discovered lying beside the wall, right there." Cybil pointed, and we huddled closer together.

"Of course, Doctor Hudson was called in and he arrived with his black leather bag. Unfortunately, there was nothing he could do, but pronounce Celia dead.

"The place was in turmoil and all sorts of stories were doing the rounds. Everyone had a theory, but none of it was the truth. Distraught, I ran to the servants' quarters to find Rukhmani. She, who had known and cared for Celia all her life, was sure to know why this tragedy had occurred. Besides, at that moment I needed to feel her strong arms about me. I found her crouched before the altar of her Gods with the heavy scent of *agarbati*[71] swirling through the room. Her hair was oiled and streamed down her back in a state of disarray.

"'Celia!' I cried.

"She nodded. Opening her arms, she cradled me and as I lay snuggled against her, sucking my thumb, she rocked back and forth. Stroking my hair, she pressed her lips to my forehead time and again.

"'Her tender heart was broken.' Rukhmani's voice was hoarse, but she was dry-eyed. 'That child wanted more. More than what we could give her. After all, she never knew a mother's love and, because she was deprived, spent her time endlessly searching. She did find love, but alas!, it was the wrong kind. Forbidden fruit! How was she to know, poor baby. The gods are jealous of their chosen ones, I cautioned her; no good will come of this liaison. But he was there right before her eyes night and day, a constant temptation. A beautiful man and a girl desperately seeking—it did not bode well for either of them. Besides, she was not worldly wise and all the piety the nuns had filled her head with was not strong enough to restrain her natural instincts. Mind you, there was a time when I thought that perhaps she had heard me and would turn away from him. But it was nothing, just a smokescreen thrown up by the man. Hai Ram! Who is to blame? It was a recipe for tragedy just waiting to happen.'

---

71   *agarbati* incense

"Shifting her weight uneasily, without letting go of me, she stretched out with her back to the wall and continued: 'Night after night they would meet under the tamarind tree and I am convinced that he was as drawn to her as she to him. They were incapable of leaving each other alone. When I first learned that she was with child, I advised her to tell the priest.'

"'Father John Rider, was he the man?' I asked, incredulous.

"'One and the same,' Rukhmani nodded. 'I also advised her to speak with Mother Valerian, who loved her as much as that woman is capable of love. Not much I grant you, but she would have cared for mother and child and put the priest in his place. However, my words fell on deaf ears and they continued to meet. One afternoon, Celia came running to me, tears streaming down her cheeks. She was distraught, wringing her hands in despair. "What is it, child? I inquired. Confide in Mani, I am here for you."

"'"He is leaving, going on a retreat for three weeks. He says we need to spend some time apart. What will I do? How will I manage? I'll die without him."

"'"You will not die," I spoke sternly. "Just listen to me and go speak with Mother Valerian. Tell her of your predicament."

"'But I underestimated the depths of her despair. Thinking she was handling the problem, I didn't seek her out for a couple of days. When Nathu discovered her lifeless body, I knew she had killed herself because she felt abandoned and alone and could not face the consequences of her actions. My heart is broken, for today I have lost my daughter.'

"'Does Mother Valerian know?' I asked.

"'I am sure she is now aware of the facts,' she replied, pensively gazing into the dying embers of the morning's fire.

"'And Father John Rider?'

"'He, too, will hear of it. He is a grown man and a priest. Daily he hears the sins of others and dispenses penance, I am told. I am sure he realizes the enormity of his transgression and will carry the burden of it to his death. That will be his cross to bear. Of course, he is not entirely to blame, for he is but a man and full of frailty. Because he is a priest, it does not mean he is a god and free from temptation. Today I will fast and entreat the gods to welcome Celia baba, forgive her her passion and grant that she be reincarnated into something so beautiful and so loved. It is what she deserves—to walk this earth once more to the fullness of years. I am told the nuns are making arrangements to bury the poor child in unblessed ground, like an outcast. Humph! That is their affair, but I will not stand in judgement over her. For a brief period in her short life she knew and enjoyed love and she has paid the price. The gods see and understand all things. Now, let there be an end to this conversation.'

"Tears streamed down my face and she wiped them away with the *puloo*[72] of her sari. Reaching into a brass *katori*,[73] she produced a sugary *ladoo*.[74] Breaking it into pieces, she fed me like a child, mouthful by mouthful.

"We never did see Father John Rider again; I never learned what became of him. Maybe he was transferred to another parish. Soon after the incident, though, Mother Valerian dismissed the old *khansamah*[75] and Rukhmani as well. She accused them of spreading vicious lies and ordered them off the premises. So, I lost my old ayah. Last year I heard that both she and her husband had died in the village, when their hut caught fire after being struck by lightning."

Cybil's voice was reduced to a whisper as she concluded her story. Her face shone in the moonlight, bright with tears. In the silence that followed her retelling of the sad tale of Celia Stevens, I could hear the soft rush of breeze stirring the lumbering branches of the tamarind tree. It ruffled the feathery leaves that rained down upon us and settled in our hair. It's the cold weather, I thought, and the Mother tree is shedding her pale green foliage, while all around her we humans are bundled up in an effort to stay warm.

The wind increased in ferocity as it swept across the open maidan; it crept under my blanket and caused me to shift uncomfortably. The great, gnarled limbs of the tree swayed heavily, brushing against the abbey wall, casting dark and sinister shadows all around. Seeing a tiny, bent slipper lying forlorn in the gravel where Celia had leaped to her death, I quickly averted my eyes and inched closer to Lynette.

"The wind has picked up and it's getting uncomfortable," said Malvina Cross.

She was the first one to speak. "Besides, it's nearly two o'clock—we

---

72 *puloo* the draped back part of a sari
73 *katori* little brass vessel
74 *ladoo* Indian sweetmeat
75 *khansamah* cook

had better be getting back to our beds." Yawning, she rose. "The last thing we need is for the nuns to find them empty and raise an alarm. By the way, Sarah, I see you've found the little hideaway behind the grotto. That was clever."

Caught off guard, I nodded sheepishly.

Cybil laughed. "We all know about that spot; I buried my pet sparrow in the nasturtium bed. And how d'you like the old mali?"

"I spent the entire night there once," Jemma Brown burst out. "The place smells of flowers and feels comfy."

"We meet again when the moon is full," Cybil reminded.

Rubbing my eyes, pulling the covers close around me, I shuffled back to the dorm.

Lynette grabbed me by the arm. "Well, Sarah, did you like the meeting of the Moonlight Marys? And do you still want to join us?"

"Pukka."

Dozing off in fitful slumber, I dreamed in Technicolor that night. Barefoot, Celia and I floated over the abbey walls and drifted out among the stars. Touching down in a garden filled with bushes of golden *champa*,[76] I kept watch under a *gul mohar* tree as Celia enjoyed a tryst with her forbidden lover.

The throbbing beat of the tabla carried down on the wind from the *dhobi ghat*[77] beyond the abbey walls, awoke me. Startled, I sat up in bed. Walking over to the barred window, I sat perched upon its narrow sill and watched the flames of a distant bonfire leaping out of the darkness, filled with the din of drums. Faraway voices chanted:

Raghupati Raghava Raja Ram Patita Pavana Sita Ram
Ishwara Allah Tere Nam
Sab ko Sanmati De Bhagavan[78]

The bhajan felt strangely comforting. I recognized it as one I had

---

76   *champa* sweet, white jasmine-like flower
77   *dhobi ghat* River bank or well, beside which he washes clothes
78   *Raghupati* ... O king Ram, the most glorious one of Raghu's race. Glory to Lord Ram and his beloved wife Sita, the remover of suffering and sustainer of all by His grace. May your names Allah and Ishwar (Jesus) be cherished by all.

heard Radha singing a long time ago, when Ranga and his scorpions filled the night with terror and Japanese warplanes droned overhead. Mummy had said it was a particular favourite of the Mahatma's. I imagined Rukhmani singing it to comfort the heartsick Celia. Its din and timbre had served as a backdrop all my life and here I was, only just discovering it. The words filled me with a sense of belonging, melding me with the earth and sky.

Crawling back into bed, I allowed the hymn to lull me to sleep.

The wake-up bell set the dormitory bustling the next morning. As my mates hurriedly washed up, got dressed and fell into line for mass, I rolled over and continued to sleep, uncaring. Sister Angelina later discovered me slumbering like a heap upon my bed; rudely she prodded me awake.

"Get up, you lazybones. What do you mean by sleeping in?"

I lay there, staring up at her.

"Answer me at once. What is the meaning of this?"

"I don't feel well, Sister," I feigned illness. "My head hurts and so does my tummy."

"H'm, you haven't been eating rubbish from outside, have you?"

I shook my head.

"Get washed and dressed and go down to the infirmary. Tell Sister Patricia your troubles and she'll fix you up. You can rest there for the day and I'll look in later. Hurry up now, no dawdling!"

I shuffled over and Sister Patricia administered her "cure-all." Insisting I needed a good clean out, she fed me a tablespoon of castor oil. The resulting number of bowel movements thoroughly weakened me. I was ravenous by midday, but my lunch tray arrived with only a bowl of watery dal soup and a slice of toast. Ugh!

Moira came in search of me, but was not convinced of my illness. We got into a row when she accused me of shamming. Indignantly I denied it and advised her to keep away.

"They suspect I may have a contagious disease, in which case if I touch you, you may get it!"

"Will I then be allowed to stay in the infirmary?" she asked cheekily.

I nodded.

"Touch me, please, touch me," she pleaded.

Moira could be an absolute pest. Feeling genuinely weak, I turned away from her and closed my eyes.

Dismissed by evening with strict instructions to abstain from solid food, I dragged myself to The Bower and sought the comfort of its quietude. Contemplating the affair of Celia Stevens and the priest, I pondered at length on the twin emotions of love and lust, the very mention of which sent shivers down my spine. My childish mind, however, was not able to comprehend the depth of desire such passions elicited. Besides, at the moment, hunger was my most pressing problem. Light-headed, I closed my eyes and nodded in the gloaming, dropping off into a dreamless sleep until the bell clanged for study hour. Rumplestiltskin was nowhere around, so, boldly picking a carnation, I laid it at the Virgin's feet and said a prayer for Celia. Mother Mary smiled down on me and I took it as a sign of her approval.

The end of term was near. By golly, we had spent six months in the abbey! With final exams over, the horrible prospect of Report Card Day loomed heavy upon the horizon. Letters arrived from Mummy. She sounded excited and wrote to say she couldn't wait to meet the train at Bombay. Grandpa Watkinson also wrote, but his letter was serious. Granny was not at all well, he said, and he was taking her down by train to see the specialist in Bombay. Her condition sounded grave. Moira's lower lip quivered and a tear spilled down her cheek, but she was silent. Placing an arm around her, I walked with her towards the dormitory. Both of us replied immediately, writing separate letters to Granny, informing her that she was in our prayers and that we intended offering up a mass for her quick recovery. Moira promised to stay awake through the entire service.

No more English,
No more French,
No more sitting on the hard, old bench.
If a sister interferes,
Knock her down and box her ears.
If she says she's going to tell.
Tell her she can go to hell.

The chant echoed up and down the school corridors, on the

playground and around the dormitory, when the nuns were out of earshot. Winter mornings in Phulamar were pale with mist, as the sun played hide-and-seek with the low clouds drifting overhead. Lining up for mass each morning, we communicated in smoke signals. Rubbing chapped hands together, we darted around on the frosty playground seeking sun spots, in an attempt to soak up some warmth. Itchy woollen pinafores, knitted cardigans and thick grey socks replaced the cool cotton uniforms of summer. They were hateful and chaffed dreadfully against our dry skin. But we were luckier than the down-and-outers, for they, poor wretches, shivered in hand-me-downs and ill-fitting, threadbare garments. Mummy had packed a thick woollen pullover and a Fair Isle cardigan in my trunk. Reaching in, I pulled them both out, smelling strongly of mothballs. I wore the cardigan and tossed the pullover at Lynette, urging her to try it on. "Wear it till the end of term," I said, never intending to take it back. She wriggled into it, but being much taller than I, it stopped short at her midriff and the long sleeves were three-quarter length on her. Nevertheless, she declared it comfy as we strode out into the winter sunshine.

"Gee, Sarah, thanks a lot."

I'd explain to Mummy and I knew she'd understand.

Report Card Day found me failing once more in every subject. Of course, I was called up on stage with the other failures to be gawked at by the rest of the assembly. Mother Valerian was in fine fettle and her cutting remarks echoed through the assembly hall. She barked at us and caned a few of the arrogant, stubborn ones for good measure. Upon being called up, I was determined to maintain a low profile and escape a caning. I stood before her with head bowed.

"You again? Why am I not surprised? You can join the line of failures." She jerked her thumb backwards and I fell in beside Lynette.

"Let them stare and let them jeer, I will soon be out of here," I rhymed.

She looked at me, morosely. "Yes, you, Sarah, but not me."

I sighed, wishing there was something I could do to change that. If only I could take her along—with Jenny and Cybil and Jane. We could all spend Christmas with Grandpa Watkinson, on the farm.

Before the last meeting of the Moonlight Marys, the raid on the nuns' dining room was planned and brilliantly executed by Lynette and myself. Everything went off without a hitch. We crept in as Sister Griselda unlocked the door and went off in search of a novice to lay the table. Lynette snatched the mangoes, bananas and a bunch of grapes from a large bowl on the table. I stuffed the fruit into an empty pillowcase—and not a minute too soon. The nuns filed in for dinner before we had a chance to make our escape. Hurriedly, we slid under the table.

Shielded by the damask tablecloth—sitting cross-legged on the floor under the table with black leather shoes arranged neatly all around us—we waited. Dinner was served by the refectory cook and the nuns ate heartily—numerous courses, judging from the prolonged clink and scrape of cutlery against china. The conversation was minimal, only just above a murmur. After the meal, Mother Valerian commented on the meagre fruit bowl and received an inaudible reply from a terrified Sister Griselda. Impatiently, she asked that the box of chocolates on the sideboard be passed round. The rustling of wrappers seemed endless. I guessed they were intent upon downing the lot. Not quite, however, for after Mother said grace and they all filed out of the room once more, we found two hard centres amidst the empty wrappers. Popping them into our mouths, Lynette and I made our escape. Darting up the stairs, we heard the swish of Sister Griselda's habit, just as she returned to lock the dining room door.

It was here at last, the end of term and the last day of school! A chattering Moira, arms linked with Jenny Wheeler, approached the tonga that was piled high with our trunks and bedding rolls. A surly Miss Price was busily organizing the whole affair. I said goodbye to Jane Woodman, agreeing to keep her on as our fag for next term. Saying farewell to Lynette was a wrench. I promised to bring her back a bag of bull's eyes, since they were her absolute favourites. The batch, all ready for the off, waved frantically as the tongas turned down the path and out of the abbey gates, which clanged shut behind us. I looked back tearfully and then pulled myself together. I had no reason to miss the abbey; after all, I was going home to my parents, to Radha, to Grandpa and Granny Watkinson; in short, to all I held dear. Besides, I would be back next term. At any rate, with so many goodbyes in my life, it was about time I learned to control my tears. It all sounded very logical, but, in the end, temperament prevailed!

PART FOUR

Stanton Station

The train pulled out of Phulamar; Moira and I were part of the Bombay batch making the journey home with Miss Price, in charge once again. Herding us into the compartment, she closed the carriage door and bolted it shut. Appearing pale and exhausted, she cautioned us irritably against any unruly behaviour during the journey. Then, climbing into an upper berth and removing a book from her bag, she began to read. Batch mates milled around aimlessly, trying one berth and then another. A squabble broke out and Miss Price sharply ordered everyone to find a seat. We hurriedly found our places and peace was restored. Moira curled up on a lower berth, stuck her thumb in her mouth and fell asleep instantly, while I sat quietly beside her in a reflective mood, mulling over the events of the past term.

The day had started off sunny and bright, but by afternoon it began to rain intermittently and, as we climbed the Ghats, the drizzle persisted, showing no signs of letting up. Gazing out through the open window, catching the damp breezes wafting in, I watched as we rumbled past fields carved out from the hillsides, lush forests and cattle grazing alongside the tracks. By late evening the countryside, shrouded in fog, appeared eerie and mysterious, like a scene from a Gothic novel. I shivered and turned towards my companions, clowning around on their bedding rolls spread out on the floor. Watching them, my sombre mood fell away and I joined in, forgetting my troubles. After all, we were on our way home and every turn and twist of the track carried us further away from the hateful abbey.

Dinner arrived at a wayside stop and we attacked the meal with gusto, polishing off our portions with an enthusiasm never seen in the convent refectory. Directly after the meal, Miss Price turned out the lights and ordered us to settle down for the night. Racing into the darkness, lulled by the rhythm of the train, we were all soon asleep.

A little after daybreak, just as the first rays of sunlight peeped over the horizon, our train screeched to a halt and we were rudely jolted awake. A cow attempting to cross the rails had been struck and killed. We crowded the compartment windows and watched a heated exchange between some villagers, the train driver and a few of the passengers. A passing guard informed Miss Price that it was most fortunate none of the bogies had derailed as a consequence of striking the animal. Disaster was averted, he said, by the experience and quick thinking of the veteran driver. We ate our breakfasts while matters were being resolved and, since I was ravenously hungry, I attacked mine with fervour; even managing to eat half of Moira's meal since she said she had no appetite.

We arrived at Bombay's Victoria Station hours late. As our train slipped into the platform, the crowd surged forward and hundreds of eyes anxiously peered through the windows of the carriage. When Miss Price unbolted the compartment door—at the top of her voice, she ordered everyone to stand back—, pandemonium reigned as the coolies paid her no heed and swarmed inside. Soon they were hauling out the luggage; hampers and bedding rolls were unceremoniously dumped onto the platform. When the brake van's door opened, they rushed over and began hastily unloading trunks, both large and small. In an effort to introduce order, Miss Price asked parents, who were crowding the entrance of the compartment, to stand back; she then allowed us to descend in single file. I spotted Mummy in the sea of faces and, grabbing Moira by the hand, ran towards her. Soon we were gathered into her arms in a great hug.

"I thought the train would never arrive. Everything is in such a mess these days, nothing is ever on time," she complained. "I was in half a mind to go back to the club and have a cup of tea, but Mr Hancock, the station master, persuaded me to hang around for a while longer and I'm glad he did. Just look at you both!"

With two coolies following behind, we made our way through the throng to the army vehicle waiting for us outside. The dozing driver leaped out with a start and began helping to load our luggage into the boot.

"Let's drop this luggage off," suggested Mummy. "Radha can't wait to set eyes on the pair of you. We can all freshen up after that and go out for a nice meal."

It was grand seeing Radha again. Tears of joy streamed down her soft brown face as she hugged us repeatedly. I breathed in her familiar scent of Kanta, betel nut and tobacco.

"Baba log, take bath now, smelling like dirty train. Hai! Hai!"

Bombay biryani, chicken chops, fruit salad and *falooda*[79]; Moira and I bolted down the meal as if we feared it would disappear.

---

79   *falooda* an Indian milkshake

"Had enough?" Mummy asked as the waiters cleared away plates and water glasses. We nodded, satiated.

"Where's Daddy?" I inquired. "Is he not going to join us for the Christmas holidays?"

"Oh! He'll be along. We're going to be staying with Aunty Hilda and Uncle Cyril this year. Daddy's leave doesn't start for a week yet and he'll catch up with us then. In the meantime, I thought we might spend a few days here before going on to Stanton Station."

"Why aren't we spending our holidays with Grandpa Cliffy?" Moira whined.

"Granny is not at all well, as you know, and even as we speak is on her way for a checkup with the specialist."

"What's the matter with Granny?" I asked anxiously. "Grandpa did write and say she was sick."

"We don't know for certain, that's why she has to see a specialist. Besides, there is a surprise coming your way this evening," Mummy continued eagerly, in an attempt to distract us.

"What? What's the surprise?"

"You'll see."

We hailed a taxi and made our way back to the club for an afternoon nap.

"I won a prize at school!" cried Moira excitedly. "Also, I made a tray cloth for you to use when you serve tea." She snuggled up close to Mummy as we drove through the streets of the city.

"Nice. What about you, Sarah? You're being very quiet."

I sat apart, painfully aware of my less-than-perfect conduct at school.

"Aunty Maggie, baby Trevor and Danny Groat will be joining us this evening," Mummy informed us over tea. "And they'll stay with us for two days."

"Danny Groat!" I exclaimed, rolling my eyes.

"Yes, he and Aunty Maggie are married now. Both of them, together with Trevor, will be sailing away to England soon and Aunty Maggie wanted to see you two before she left."

"Why do they want to go to England?" I wailed. "Grandpa Cliffy said it's a mess after the war. Why can't they just stay at the lodge with Grandpa Reagan?"

"Don't take on so, Sarah, everything's fine over there now. Besides, Danny has a job waiting for him as assistant butcher in his father's shop."

"Ooh, butcher! Can't he get a better job?"

"It's an honourable profession," Mummy scowled at me; "and since his father owns the shop, one day it will belong to Danny."

"Maggie Groat and Trevor Groat," Moira sang and we collapsed with laughter.

I found the whole butcher thing difficult to stomach, recalling the one occasion I had visited a butcher shop with Mummy in Saltair-By-The-Sea. She had ordered some special cuts of beef for one of her dinner parties and, wanting to ensure she received the very best, had the driver take her over to the market. I begged to accompany her.

"I don't know why you want to tag along, Sarah," she sounded exasperated. "And what do you hope to find there, may I ask? The meat market is a foul-smelling place and I wouldn't be going unless I had to."

"I've never been to the market and I want to see what it's like, especially the butcher shop."

"I haven't the slighted idea why a butcher shop should interest you. Well, all right then," she relented. "You can come along just this once."

We piled into the car with Hamid and his filthy shopping bags.

"Stay with the driver!" Mummy ordered when we arrived at the market, but I hopped out after her. She glared at me. Following them through the murghee market filled with baskets of squawking chickens, we made our way past the *bania* shop and the *sabzi* bazaar.[80] Crossing a covered sewer we came to a separate building with open drains running along both sides of a tiled walkway. Foul vapours rose up in the baking heat and the air was heavy with the odour of blood and raw meat. Suspended from giant hooks, immense carcasses hung from the rafters with enormous bluebottles buzzing all around. Perched high up in the beams great, black king-crows cawed endlessly. Swooping down from time to time, they snatched up pieces of meat the butchers discarded as they trimmed the various cuts. The butchers themselves in filthy

---

80   *bania* sells dry provisions *sabzi* sells vegetables

singlets, bidis dangling from paan-stained lips, slapped their hunks of beef and cried out:

"Memsahib! Come see this. I make very best cut for you. Come take, choice undercut, round, *kheema—taja, taja!*"[81]

Hamid stopped before a venerable old fellow with a crocheted skullcap upon his flaming head. Mummy examined the cuts of beef he offered and made her choice. We paid him and hastily retreated.

"Why is his hair red?" I asked Hamid.

"Gone to hajj," he replied.

"What about you? When are you going to hajj?"

"Inshallah!" He rolled his eyes heavenward.

I had difficulty picturing Danny Groat in this setting.

Baby Trevor was a butcher's son. He'd be a butcher boy when he grew up. "Trevor Groat, the butcher boy," I sang merrily.

We giggled uncontrollably.

The club, with its manicured lawns and neat rows of cannas and bachelor buttons was a far cry from the wretched abbey. Both Moira and I felt liberated and as free as the breeze; like the hawk circling high in the evening sky, like crows cawing in the gathering dusk, my spirits soared. However, the sadness which had settled deep in my consciousness during those long months at school surfaced from time to time, leaving me with a sense of melancholy at the thought of my dear friends left behind, the down-and-outers. They, poor unfortunates, would never experience this kind of freedom. I hugged Mummy and Radha alternately and they welcomed my embraces. It had been a long, sad parting.

"What's Danny Groat like?" Moira was curious.

"Settle down, you two." Mummy tried to hide her smile. "You'll see."

And we did.

They arrived that evening, Aunty Maggie, Uncle Danny (Mummy said we should call him that) and baby Trevor in the arms of an ayah. I must confess I was not impressed by the tall, gangly young chap who timidly followed Aunty Maggie into the club. I had somehow pictured

---

81 *kheema* ground beef *taja* fresh *king-crows* fat, glossy crows; very bold

him as looking quite different, like Clark Gable. Moira and I were all over baby Trevor, who had grown huge. He gurgled and rolled about on the carpet as we played with him. Aunty Maggie beamed at us; she looked very happy and kept gazing up at Danny Groat with adoring eyes. He had sharp features, a freckled face and masses of curly brown hair. Even though I didn't find him the least bit handsome, he had a cheery smile. Aunty Maggie informed us excitedly that they were off to England and then on to Felixstowe, where Danny would work in his father's butcher shop.

"Why didn't you write to me about it at school?" I asked, pouting.

"Well, Sarah, it wasn't a subject I wanted to discuss at the time. You are happy for me, aren't you?"

"I guess. How's Grandpa Reagan?" I asked.

"He's in good spirits and very relieved that things worked out okay." Nudging me, she winked.

"And Grand-Aunt Elsie Lavender?"

"She's a corker! I wouldn't be at all surprised if she and Doc Stewart tied the knot soon—they're inseparable."

"Go on—" laughed Mummy, "at their age?"

"Yes, at their age. I guess you're only as old as you feel and that old girl is still very frisky believe me; I've seen her in action. She's got him twisted around her little finger, let me tell you."

"But marriage, isn't that a bid extreme?" Mummy shook her head in disbelief.

"Stranger things have happened. She did cheer things up considerably at the lodge last summer, remember?"

"That she did. Come to think of it, her tying the knot with Doc Stewart may be the best thing for the both of them and for Pa as well."

"I have to agree."

"What does Grandpa Reagan think about the love affair?" I asked seriously.

"Sarah, little children should be seen and not heard," scolded Mummy in her sharpest voice. "I'll send you to bed if you speak out of turn."

Slumping further into the chair, feeling hurt and unwanted, I couldn't help thinking Mummy's rebuke had nothing at all to do with my question, but everything to do with my bad grades and behaviour at school this past term.

After dinner, the sisters chatted on in the bedroom. Danny Groat lay on the adjoining bed with Trevor snuggled close by. He was a silent sort of chap and a chain-smoker. I could see the lit end of his cigarette glowing in the dark. Moira was dead to the world and the servants were asleep on their mats. I lay awake thinking about the events of the day, breathing the salt sea air that wafted in through the open window. You could tell the tide was out—the reek of dead fish riding on the wind swept in and filled the room with a horrible stench. A great sadness filled my heart at the thought of Aunty Maggie sailing away to Blighty, but I bet Grandpa Reagan was pleased about it. After all, Danny Groat had returned and made an honest woman of her.

For the next two days, we shopped along the Causeway, enjoyed ice cream sundaes at a swanky new parlour near the Strand and visited the museum. It ended all too soon, for on the third day we said goodbye to Aunty Maggie, Uncle Danny and baby Trevor. I clung to her skirts and wept uncontrollably.

"We'll meet again, you two, sure thing," she consoled. With brimming eyes, she hugged us again and again. Mummy, red-eyed, blew her nose. Baby Trevor started bawling and Danny Groat, looking embarrassed, wandered off to find a cigarette stand — I guess he wanted to have very little to do with this emotional leave-taking. As the train chugged out of VT Station, I craned my neck out of the window and waved until they were mere specks in a sea of people. Mummy kept wiping her eyes and went into the bathroom where I heard her blow her nose again. Radha opened the hamper and passed me a hard-boiled egg sandwich. Chomping on it, I suddenly realized how hungry I was, so I helped myself to a cutlet. Food always made things better!

THE JOURNEY HOME

Rattling over rusting iron bridge,
Ka-tak, ka-tak, ka-tak
Peering at the riverbed below.
Tapti drained of swelling monsoon rains,
Threads sluggishly across the blistered plain—
Parched, panting, pleading with the heavens.
Dust devils, whirling dervishes spin by.

A tangle of babul trees comes into view.
While up above a kite with eagle eye
Circles.
Vast nullahs, gashes in the earth—
Show tufts of bleached grass clinging to their sides.
Open vistas with no place to hide
From unrelenting heat, famine, plague or tide.

Low-rising hills appear on the horizon,
Their swelling mounds, hazy in the distance.
A field of flowering mustard flashes by—
Looking up, golden, laughing at the sky.
Thatched huts trailing melon vines
Cling to fields of jowar, nuts and cotton.
A whiff of dung fire now assails the nostrils.

The land speaks volumes to her native children,
Fettering them with strong unyielding chains.
Old memories, old lives, old deeds restrung.
She holds them fast through life and death and pain.
They live and die, to be reborn again,
And dwell once more upon the seared plain.

With sooty faces and gritty teeth, we gazed out of the compartment window as the Bombay Mail slipped into Stanton Station. Both Moira and I spotted Uncle Cyril chatting on the platform. Two coolies in bright red uniforms ran alongside the train and hopped in as it slowed to a halt. Snatching up our luggage, they hotfooted down the platform before us.

Radha cried out, *"Aree, bhai, kedar jatha?"*[82]

"Watkinson sahib?" they asked, puzzled. Grandpa was well known.

Uncle Cyril brought them to a halt. Dropping the luggage, they hovered in the background as he made the introductions.

"This is Mr Prakash, the new station master."

We nodded in greeting.

"Mr Prakash, this is Emma, my nephew Reg's wife; he is an army officer. And these are my grand nieces. They have come to spend the Christmas holidays with us."

Mr Prakash greeted us with a friendly grin, his head wobbling from side to side.

Mummy smiled tiredly.

"I'll see you around then," said Uncle Cyril, taking his leave. "By the way, where are you staying?"

"Same place as outposted station master sahib—Fibe jeero jeero sevun Badshah Street. Drop over sometime, take tea bee."

"Acha."[83]

Turning to us, he exclaimed, "My gawd, how you both have grown, and skinny too! Didn't they feed you up in that convent school? Or were the nuns *guffing* all the grub?"

Mummy bristled and strode on ahead.

Followed by the coolies, we left the station. Down the avenue of trees we trooped, finally arriving at the old Stanton House.

Aunty Hilda and Uncle Cyril Fenwick lived in the battered old bungalow that had once been our great-great-grandfather Edward Horace Stanton's pride and joy. Begrimed with dust and soot from its proximity to the railway station, the place had, over a period of time, acquired an ancient, weathered look. There was still no electricity or running water. The focal point of the house was an enormous dining

---

82   *Aree bhai, kedar jatha?* Here you, fellow, where are you going?

83   *acha* okay

room filled with heavy furniture that allowed Aunty to seat as many as twenty people for a meal. There were five bedrooms and three bathrooms. Guests were customarily entertained on the front veranda, while a large portion of the rear veranda had been converted into a kitchen. I loved the kitchen best and its close proximity to the main house afforded me the added luxury of being able to visit any time I pleased. Blackened with smoke from the many wood and dung fires that had over the decades burned fiercely, the kitchen's dark interior held in its dim cobwebby corners memories of countless meals, which imparted their odours to the clothing of anyone who lingered too long. Behind the bungalow stood several godowns and a box room, which Moira and I loved snooping around in. But after a large cobra was discovered curled up in a dark corner, Aunty Hilda locked it and refused to relinquish the key. A well at the very end of the property provided water for drinking and bathing. It also served to irrigate the surrounding fields.

On that first morning after our arrival, Maxi, the rooster, crowed outside the bedroom window, waking me from my sleep. Shifting under a pile of coarse, olive-green, army-issue blankets, I turned, settled myself once more into a comforting dip in the mattress and went back to sleep.

Later, perched high on an old kitchen stool, I basked in the early morning sunshine that spilled like liquid butter over the low veranda wall and puddled on the dung-lacquered floor. Pulling my worn flannel dressing gown closer, I shivered in spite of it. Aunty's roses were in full bloom, watered by the constant effluence trickling out from a rusted iron drainpipe behind the bathroom; they put on a splendid show all winter long.

"Beautifying the backside of the house," was her usual reply when complimented on their glorious display.

I looked out towards the cattle shed with its roof piled high with feed and spied her buffaloes, Maisie and Maud, chewing their cud as they waited patiently to be milked. In the yard, amidst fowl droppings, battered sardine and condensed milk cans lay scattered on the rutted earth, a catch-all for feed and water. Dust motes danced in shafts of morning sunlight. The scent of dung, of hay, the glint of dew upon rose petals, suggested fecundity—the ooze of earth, plenteous and productive, which, to me, smelled like heaven.

"Sarah, what are you doing up so early?" It was Aunty Hilda fumbling with the sash of her dressing gown.

"Just looking around," I replied, burying my hands deep in my armpits for warmth.

"At what?"

"At everything."

She removed the cover from Whiskey's cage. He hopped about, cocked his head to one side, and screeched: "Yusouf!"

"Agia, missy baba," a voice cried out from the servants' quarters.

"Duffers, both of them," Aunty declared impatiently.

"Whiskey's frisky, Whiskey's frisky," screeched the parrot and I giggled.

She glared at me. "What's so funny? I have to deal with this damned parrot and that buffalo boy every morning."

"Who baptized Whiskey?" I asked.

"He wasn't baptized, he's a heathen. Some drunken old sot named him, no doubt. Your uncle brought him home one day after a visit to the city, said a friend of his had given him the bird, cage and all. I had a feeling it had something to do with an unpaid loan. Humph."

I didn't mind Aunty Hilda's brusque manner—she was my favourite. She tolerated my inquisitiveness with a gruff indulgence. Grandpa Cliffy's farm and this dilapidated old bungalow were the closest things we had to call home, since Daddy's nomadic army life kept us moving from pillar to post every two years. Besides, our family was deeply rooted in the soil of Stanton Station. Grandpa never tired of telling the tale of Edward Horace Stanton, our great-great-grandfather, who had given the place his name.

I recalled the first time I heard it one breathless night several years ago. Mummy and Daddy had gone off for a stay in Bombay, leaving us behind with Grandpa and Granny, who allowed us to do pretty much what we pleased during the holidays. Even Radha became lazy with her duties, smiling indulgently as we giggled and chatted with Grandpa into the wee hours of the morning.

It was midsummer and the rains were late. By sunset, the blistering dry winds that had breathed fiery gusts across the open plains subsided and Grandpa ordered camp cots to be set up in the compound for the night. Only Granny Connie stayed indoors, sleeping in her great iron bed with the curtains tied back and the windows thrown open. We pleaded with her to join us outside, but she shook her head.

"I'm a creature of habit and a child of the Deccan, quite used to the heat. The stone floor feels cool when I set my feet down on it each morning and my bath water standing in the tub all night is chilled just right, ready and waiting for me when I wake up. Your grandfather loves the outdoors; you girls go along and join him."

I lay on my cot beside Grandpa and Moira, gazing up at a sickle Moonface embedded in deep cobalt-blue sky dotted with a myriad stars that glinted like fireflies in the heavens. Somewhere in the shadows, a cicada whirred its restless wings and I heard the jackals howling down from the hills beyond. Intermittent puffs of hot air billowed the mosquito netting. Moira and I fidgeted endlessly, tossing and turning, scratching the prickly heat rash that covered most of our bodies. From time to time we crept out of bed to quench our thirst with mugs of water from the surahi,[84] which was placed near the front stoop for easy accessibility and to catch the cool night breezes. Taking small sips from the stainless steel cup, I savored the taste of fresh earth and cool water.

"If the pair of you keep parading up and down you will let the mosquitoes into the nets and they'll chew you to bits," Grandpa warned. "Settle down and try to get some sleep."

"I'm hot," whined Moira, "and itchy all over."

"Who was your father, Grandpa?" I asked, changing the subject. "Where did your family live?"

"My old man was a simple clerk of humble origin; he worked in the telegraph office in Pondi, Pondicherry, that is. I was born and went to school there. Our family was poor, but we were happy. Life was a lot simpler in those days."

"And your mother?"

"Mummy was a beauty and the brains in the family. She was the daughter of a headmaster. Mummy made sure that all her children received a good education and she had great hopes for me. They used to say I took after her. I had ambition, you see, and travelled to Bombay as a young man to seek my fortune."

"And did you find it?" asked Moira.

---

84   *surahi* - earthen pot for water, kept outside, to breathe and chill

"I met your grandmother and the rest is history."

"When did you come to live here?" I inquired.

"I was employed by the Bombay Port Trust at the time I met your grandmother and married her; it was good job and the pay was decent. You both know we lived in Bombay, don't you? That was where your father was born. But Granny missed the country life and couldn't get used to the city. When she inherited this piece of land, I decided to chuck it all and took early retirement. We settled here and I became a gentleman farmer."

"Who left her the land?"

"Her father, Reginald Stanton, did. Your daddy is named after him. He divided his land between three daughters—Hilda, Francis and Constance—and each one received her share after your great-grand-uncle Leonard passed on. He was the caretaker of their inheritance."

"Who was Reginald Stanton's wife?" I asked, filled with curiosity.

"His wife, my girl, was a beautiful Muslim lady of noble birth. Her name was Zinat Mahal and theirs was a tragic story if ever there was one. Reginald was a mercenary in the Nizam's army, you see, when he first laid eyes on her. They fell desperately in love with one another and he asked for her hand in marriage. But her father, who held a high position at court, refused his because Reginald Stanton was a commoner and an Englishman to boot. Zinat had been promised to another, he said. Reginald was dismissed and had to leave the state immediately, but he did not go alone. He eloped with Zinat and they were secretly married. He eventually brought her here, where they settled on the land, and he built this house. But their happiness was short-lived, for he was stricken with smallpox and died while still a young man. Zinat Mahal, beside herself with grief, followed him to the grave, leaving behind three little orphan girls who were adopted by his brother, your great-grand-uncle Leonard Stanton and his wife, Marjorie, who were childless. How the Stanton brothers came by this land—now therein lies a tale, which has its beginnings with an Englishman named Edward Horace Stanton."

"Who was he?" Moira inquired.

"Only your great-great-grandfather."

"That's a lot of greats," she lisped, pretending to be childish. "Do I know him?"

"How can you, silly? After one 'great,' you're dead," I chimed in.

"Does that mean I have one foot in the grave and the other on a banana skin?" Grandpa laughed.

"Naw, you're not a 'great' as yet; you're just a grand! … Isn't he the one buried behind Aunty Hilda's well?"

"Yes, Sarah, he is, so are Reginald and his beloved Zinat Mahal. Listen up, you two, the story goes like this…" Grandpa was on a roll. "Edward Horace Stanton came to India in the mid-1800s. He was an adventurous man and it was this spirit of adventure that carried him across the seas from his native England. When he landed in Bombay, he discovered that all kinds of money could be made if a chap was enterprising and had dash and pluck. Army life did not appeal to him, so he declined a commission. Nor did he fancy taking up a clerical position.

"At that time the British were laying railway tracks across the length and breadth of our country. This would make it easier for them to transport their officials and goods from one place to another. Before commencing, however, the land had to be mapped and surveyed and this created many opportunities for bright young fellows. Needless to say, he fell into that category, so when he was offered a surveyor's post he snapped it up, since the job gave him the freedom to travel all over the country and be his own man. That is how one sunny morning he came to be perched upon his shooting stick on a hill not far from here. Gazing out across the rolling plains, Edward was impressed and thought how he would like to get a hold of a parcel of land very much like it. He imagined the forest cleared and acres of ploughed fields as far as the eye could see. He would build a large bungalow with a garden in front and an orchard at the rear. Satisfied with his dream, he set about fulfilling it and, being a savvy sort of chap, didn't waste much time, but got to work immediately. Soon he was in possession of several hundred acres.

"However, it was to be a full five years before he set foot on his investment. In the meantime, he married Olga Purdy, your great-great-grandmother, and brought her to live in a tent under a sprawling banyan tree just outside the village of Shahpur. Engaging the local villagers to build a bungalow, he named it 'Stanton House' on completion and settled down with his wife to raise a family. Your great-great-grandmother had a lot of children, but only two sons survived: Reginald and Leonard. She herself did not live to be very old."

"How did she die?" inquired Moira.

"I think it was heatstroke—or was it typhoid fever? I've forgotten. There was a lot of typhoid fever about in those days. After a brief period of mourning, Edward married again. His second wife, Miss Thelma McDougall, was a parson's daughter. They had no children.

"By the time the tracks were laid and the trains came whistling through, enterprising Edward had branched out and was actively involved in several very lucrative businesses in the area. Oh, he had his finger in many pies! And, given his status within the community, he felt it only natural that the new whistle stop should be named Stanton Station after him, which of course it was. That in a nutshell is how we came to be here, the lot of us. Now, skipping a few generations, I must insist that you two get some shut-eye or you'll be like a couple of wet rags in the morning. Good night, God bless!"

Recalling Grandpa's tale this sunny morning, I felt the thrill of belonging. Not for me the Serendipity Lodge with Grandpa Reagan marching about all day giving orders like a sergeant major. I preferred the easygoing, gossip-filled, rambunctious way of life enjoyed by Daddy's side of the family. Just the memory of events from the previous summer sent a shiver down my spine. Queer Mr Stanley Dowling with his wet, pouting lips and bulging eyes and his eccentric sisters. Even Miss Skinner could be a bit peculiar at times. Of course, both Moira and I absolutely adored Aunty Maggie and baby Trevor, but then they were family. And Grand-Aunt Elsie Lavender was a hoot. Her arrival had changed the atmosphere of the place entirely and I wished I had known her in her "salad days," as she called them.

The delicious aroma of parathas being fried in ghee drifted past my nostrils and my tummy growled as I waited with growing impatience for breakfast. We sat down to omelettes, porridge and great dollops of guava jelly served with generous lashings of cream; both Moira and I were fit to burst after the meal. Clearing away the plates, Sonabhen, Aunty Hilda's beloved old retainer, placed a platter of fruit on the table, but we couldn't eat another bite. It was in every way a perfect start to the holidays.

Aunty fed a pack of pariah dogs that lolled outside in the dust under the trees. Their numbers hardly ever increased, as marauding panthers that prowled the outskirts of the farm at night had a habit of snatching them from the compound. She was unruffled, though, by these nocturnal raids and, when a dog went missing, her only comment at the breakfast table the next day would be: "Sadie's gone. I guess she was carried off last night. But Trixie's still around with her brood."

"Better the pye-dogs than the cattle," Uncle Cyril would remark absently, rifling through the morning paper. "Wish we could keep a pet mongoose to get rid of the bloody snakes hanging around the chicken coop."

Scores of visitors trooped in and out of the house all day. Some dropped in just to read the newspaper that Uncle Cyril had delivered from the station. Tommy Thornton, the enormous station master's clerk, was a frequent visitor at tea time. Whenever Uncle Cyril heard the crunch of his bicycle turning into the gravelled yard, he'd look up over the rim of his cup and exclaim: "Uh-oh! Here comes two-ton Tommy looking for his tea and bhujias."

Moira and I squirmed uneasily in our seats. We detested Tommy. With a wicked gleam in his eyes, he would pinch our cheeks and smirk as we winced. "Now give me a smile from luck to luck, won't you? That's a girl!"

I stepped on his toes once, very hard, then ran out of the house and hid in the servants' quarters.

When Uncle Cyril's friends arrived, they leaned their bicycles against the neem tree out in the compound. Snapping cycle clips from off their pant legs, they placed them, together with their sola topees, on the low veranda ledge. Parking their behinds on rickety chairs, they then proceeded to chew the fat with him for hours.

"Layabouts," Aunty grumbled, "with not an honest day's work done between the lot and that includes your uncle. They spend all their time sitting around drinking that filthy rotgut and gabbing away, counting the hours to lunch."

On weekends the "first families" of Stanton Station congregated in each other's houses. When it was Aunty Hilda's turn to entertain, one could hear her bustling about giving orders from early morning. They came for lunch. PWI[85] Durham and his wife. Dr Pudumjee from the clinic and Mrs Pudumjee. Jimmy Mitchell, a friend of Uncle Cyril's from the old days, who Aunty called "Lickspittle"—I could never understand why. The Reynolds, who officiated as judges at dog shows in Bombay, arrived on horseback. They had a property in Shahpur, a half-hour's ride away. Great-Aunt Fanny (Francis) Foxglove, accompanied

---

85   *PWI* Permanent Way Inspector

by her husband Uncle Melvin, came by horse and buggy. Dressed to the nines, Aunt Fanny entered in a cloud of perfume, her many bracelets jingling as she walked with mincing steps into the house. Aunty Hilda detested Uncle Melvin, whom she referred to as a cad and a bounder, saying she only tolerated his presence for her sister's sake.

A large pitcher of freshly squeezed lime juice with chunks of ice floating in it was placed on a table, together with a bottle of gin, bottles of beer chilling in a zinc tub and a tray of glasses. The men drank beer while the ladies downed countless tumblers of "*nimboo pani*[86] with a splash of gin," as Aunty explained it to me. Mummy snickered at the mention of the word *splash*, but would not elaborate.

An unending stream of gossip flowed from the front veranda through the dining room and out into the kitchen where Sonabhen with Burhan to help her laboured, preparing lunch. Trailing behind Aunty, as she trotted back and forth between the rooms, checking on lunch, instructing the field hands and ordering more limes to be squeezed, I heard the town's gossip as it flowed freely from the mouths of ladies whose lips were loosened by gin. Aunty tut-tutted Lily Van Houghton's free and easy ways: "She's a slut. Mark my words, she'll come to a bad end!"

When informed of the old station master Garnett Gonsalves' retirement, "Good riddance to bad rubbish!" she exclaimed. "He's a skirt chaser and a useless bounder to boot. Cyril tells me his replacement, Mr Prakash, is a decent sort—a little rough around the edges, mind you, but an improvement on the last one."

And so it continued with the stories growing more lurid and intimate as the day progressed. If Mummy discovered me, she'd grab my arm and steer me towards a chair, ordering me to sit tight until lunch was served.

"Don't you dare budge," she'd threaten. "Bah! Children these days, they can be a handful."

Moira, seated cross-legged on the old iron bed at the very end of the veranda, occupied herself with her dolls.

Lunch was served with the grown-ups all seated round the table. A kiddies' table was always set up on the side for Moira and me. Burhan, the cook's helper, entered carrying a huge tureen brimming with a fiery meatball curry, which he placed on the sideboard, alongside an

86 *nimboo pani* lime juice

enormous platter of coconut-scented rice. Grilled green pigeon, dal, pumpkin sabzi, papads and raita completed the menu. They fell on the food with gusto, appetites whetted by a morning of hard drinking. The clatter of plates, followed by the scrape of cutlery against china, drowned out all conversation as the guests tucked in. Serving at the table with a dishcloth draped over his shoulder, Burhan carried away empty plates and refilled glasses of water. For dessert, a platter of jalebis from Ram Lal's sweetmeat shop was passed around—great, orange, crisply fried circles that oozed gooey sugar syrup when you bit into them. I snatched a couple from off the fast-disappearing mound.

After lunch Uncle Cyril would push back his chair, rub his belly and proclaim: "Great grub, girlie, and now it's time to sleep it off!" He yawned. "Anyone interested in a charpoy bash? The spare bedroom's ready. Sleep it off and make your way home after tea. Come on, come on —" he urged his guests, before ambling out for a smoke.

The days flew by and we were already a week into our holidays. Early one morning as I crouched on the kitchen stool, watching a *dekchi*[87] of milk on the boil, I thought it strange that for the past week I had given no thought to the abbey, the nuns or the friends I'd left behind. Like a bad dream, I'd consigned the lot to oblivion. Moving closer to warm my hands before the fire, I heard the call of doves outside that stirred a feeling of sweet contentment in me. A goods train in the station siding began shunting, hissing and spitting like an aggravated dragon. Running to the window, I watched as clouds of steam billowing from the engine filled the early morning air. Taking pleasure in the house's proximity to the railway station, I thought it only fitting, since train journeys were a vital part of our lives, travelling as we did with Daddy from posting to posting. Woolgathering, I suddenly noticed the milk coming to a rapid boil and shrieked: "Yusouf!"

"Aree, aree, aree!" he cried in a panic. Gripping the pot with his grimy *jharan*,[88] he quickly removed it from the *sigri*[89] and placed it on a counter. Then, frantically blowing with a *phuknee*,[90] he revived the

---

87   *dekchi* aluminum pot
88   *jharan* kitchen tea towel
89   *sigri* little coal stove
90   *phuknee* bamboo pipe used to fan the flames

dying coals and placed the dekchi once more over the flames for a second boil.

Since Daddy was arriving later in the afternoon, I knew Radha would be out soon to call me for a bath. It wasn't her, however, who ambled into the kitchen, but Mummy. I ran to her and she bent down and kissed me.

"Up with the lark as usual." She gave me a lazy smile. "Come, Sarah, I want to see your report card before Daddy gets here. He has so much on his mind these days with the possibility of another posting coming up and Granny Connie not being well."

In the bedroom we discovered Moira bent over her trunk with clothing strewn all over on the floor around her. She emerged, triumphantly clutching a badly crumpled embroidered tray cloth, which she handed to Mummy. She also produced her report card. Admiring Moira's handiwork, Mummy thanked her, promising to use it the next time she served tea. Turning her attention to the report card, she read it with a pleased smile. Drawing Moira close, she hugged her.

"Your father is going to be so proud and happy when he sees how well you've done."

Moira preened and jumped up onto the bed beside her. "She's got one too." pointing at me.

"Sarah?" Mummy gave me an inquiring look. "Where's your card?"

I shoved the wretched sheet of paper over and then slunk into a corner of the room.

"Not so fast, missy; come and stand right here in front of me."

With compressed lips, Mummy's eyes travelled slowly down the page, reading each subject, the mark and remarks made by the teacher. Shaking her head with disbelief, she placed my report card on the night table beside her and looked at me with sad, bewildered eyes.

"Why, Sarah? Why?" she asked softly. "For God's sake, child, there isn't a single pass mark in this report. I can understand you failing in arithmetic, algebra and geometry, but in literature, geography, poetry and history? Good heavens! Those were your strong subjects and you always did so well in them. What happened?"

Silent and ashamed, I hung my head. I had no answers. I couldn't bring myself to tell Mummy about the nuns, about all the misery and cruelty I had endured during the term, of continually being hungry and homesick. I felt she wouldn't understand. But, on the other hand, I felt I had to give an explanation.

"I hate boarding school!" I blurted out in a torrent of emotion. "The nuns and teachers are horrible, spiteful creatures and the food tastes awful. You should just see what the third-class boarders get to eat—they're called 'down-and-outers,' by the way. I detest the place." My chest heaved as if I had spewed out a stream of bile.

"I don't think that there is a shred of truth in what you say," was Mummy's furious reply. "As far as I'm concerned, you are a disgrace and I'm thoroughly ashamed of you. When your father and I decided to send you two to boarding school, it was Moira I was apprehensive about, not you. I thought you would adapt easily with plenty of girls your age around, you would make friends and adjust to the routine in no time at all. But I find it's the other way around. Moira has adapted and all you seem to be having is problems." She was pale with anger. The two red spots heightened her cheekbones.

"I don't want to make a scene here, especially since we are on holiday and Granny Connie is not at all well. Otherwise, I would take the strap to you. As it is, your father is going to be very angry and hurt. He works hard to give you both the best education he can afford and is this the way you thank him? What were you up to all those months? Your letters that were quite newsy at the beginning of term became scrappy little notes with no real news at the end. What happened? I want an answer and I want it now," she demanded.

"The nuns read our letters."

"There's nothing wrong with that."

"I don't like it."

Turning to Radha, she ordered her to attend to Moira's bath. They disappeared out of the room. Mummy seemed to calm down.

"You don't like it. What did you want to write about that you didn't want anyone else to read, huh?"

I was silent.

"Well?" she inquired.

"I got my monthlies at boarding school," I mumbled with downcast eyes. "That's a private thing I didn't want anyone to know about."

"I knew about it; Mother Valerian wrote to me. That can hardly be the reason for this report card, your unsociable behaviour at school and those short letters."

She slumped back into the bed, resting her head against the pillows. I stood before her in my worn woollen nightdress, with unbraided hair falling like a tousled mane over my eyes and shoulders.

An awful silence hung in the air between us.

"I've decided to let the matter rest for the time being," Mummy continued. "We'll take it up again in a couple of weeks just before you leave for school. In the meantime, I suggest you think hard about how you are going to improve your performance during the next term. I'll ask your father to be present when we talk again."

I sensed that last sentence was delivered as a threat.

"Go have your bath now and get ready for the day."

I disobeyed her and instead slunk out of the room and found a quiet spot in one of the many empty bedrooms, emerging only when I heard them all go in for breakfast.

Daddy's train was on time and, even though he seemed happy to see us, he looked tired and withdrawn. Mummy said it was the stress and worrying about Granny that did it.

Uncle Cyril paid two visits to the post office and each time returned empty-handed. He was looking for a telegram from Grandpa Cliffy and none had arrived. Everyone was consumed with worry about Granny's condition. It was now more than a week since Grandpa had taken her to Bombay to see the specialist.

"I can't understand Cliffy's silence, it's not like him." Aunty Hilda looked worried as she served Daddy a slice of seed cake with his cup of tea. We were all crowded around him at the dining table.

"Eat up," she urged. "You're looking mighty pulled down. It's no good fretting over things; they always end up as God wills them."

"The same goes for you too, Hilda; take a dose of your own medicine and relax. Cliffy's bound to send a wire soon." Uncle Cyril tried to calm her, although he himself paced nervously up and down the room.

"So, Reg, how are things in Delhi?" Pulling up a chair, Uncle Cliffy sat down.

Daddy took a sip of tea, leaned back and sighed heavily.

"Pretty grim. I was fortunate to be able to get the time off. My CO understood that I had to come home and gave me leave on compassionate grounds. It's a mess out there, let me tell you; you are better off here, far away from all that chaos. The country will soon be split in two and refugees from Pakistan are pouring into the Punjab. There is unrest everywhere and shortages of food and other essential items. Conditions are rapidly deteriorating and I hate to think what will happen next. When Nehru takes office, his new government will walk into an acute crisis; there will be a lot of work to do and I hope they'll be up to the task. Of course, at the moment the Congress wallahs are busy giving endless speeches, which, by the way, all sound like so much rhetoric to me. The nationalist movement has snowballed and Gandhiji has made frequent visits in an effort to quiet what seems to be developing into a highly inflammable situation."

"Did you see him?" inquired Mummy, her voice filled with excitement. I knew she revered the Mahatma.

"Caught a glimpse of him, nothing more … I hear he is dispirited and has lost the will to live. They say he now realizes the INC[91] have absolutely no intention of following his doctrine of peaceful coexistence, but are only using him to further their own ends. I have also heard that he often speaks of death, but outwardly shows none of the despondency he feels. What is to be done? By example he has tried to show the people that freedom is meaningless, so long as prejudice and hatred continue to thrive. But within the party there are a lot of firebrands who refuse to listen to reason and their voices can be heard loud and clear on the podiums, preaching a bold and nationalistic message that the masses are responding to. British rule has caused economic devastation, they say, and we must be freed from the evil clutches of the *Feringhee*.[92] They are advocating a new doctrine, 'India for the Hindus', and the common man is eating it up. 'Quit India' all the banners and slogans read."

"What about the British, how are they taking all this? Have there been many acts of violence against them?" Uncle Cyril asked.

"Not really. I feel this is one of Gandhi's great successes. He has befuddled the English and they do not know how to act against an enemy who does not resort to violence. It has also garnered world attention and brought India into the spotlight. It's a sticky situation all around, no doubt about it. But for the most part the British mood is sombre; they are tired as well, licking their wounds after the bashing

91   *INC* Indian National Congress
92   *Feringhee* white man *dukhan wallahs* shopkeepers

they took during the war. At this point, I feel England is ready to wash her hands of the entire country and approaching independence can't come too soon."

Daddy took a deep breath and wiped the sweat from his brow with his handkerchief.

"In the past few months I have seen history in the making, watching the transfer of power as our country shifts from the hands of the conqueror back to the sons of the soil. And, for the most part, I am happy. However, I have certain misgivings. I feel the pain of partition, as this Utopia that Jinnah so grandly calls 'Pakistan' comes into being and we are split into two nations. I feel it will benefit neither of us, for there will be no peace. Our Muslim brothers are leaving and the niceties that Delhi is so famous for are about to vanish into the past. The gracious way of life, the flowery Urdu speech, will all soon disappear as the rough sons of the Punjab overrun the city. It will be good for the economy, I know, for even as we speak, shops selling everything from a pin to an elephant are springing up all over. Delhi will eventually become a city of *dukhan* wallahs."

Daddy drained his cup and set it down in the saucer. I gazed round-eyed at him as the words continued to spill from his mouth like an unstoppable torrent. For the most part he was a reticent man, my father; to hear him unburden himself in this way was truly amazing. He must have held all his thoughts and feelings in check these many months. As an army officer he had to remain tight-lipped on the job, but here, in the bosom of his family, he was finally free to speak his mind.

"And then there are the anglophiles," he continued. "Diehards, most of them, educated in universities like Cambridge and Oxford. The passing of the old order leaves them saddened and confused. All the trappings of empire, the pomp and ceremony, all this is very close to their hearts. Many of them deplore the state of anarchy that exists at the present time and worry that India will become a third-rate country. Of course, in the prevailing atmosphere, it is dangerous to speak out and so they keep their opinions close to the chest. But catch them at the club and it takes but a few pegs of whisky to loosen their tongues. I must confess that I, too, am sometimes drawn to their way of thinking and feel uncertain of how things will turn out."

"Seeing it all first-hand, I would feel the same way too." Uncle

Cyril cleared his throat and butted out his bidi. "I daresay, the present chaos makes no sense to many, especially since there was no room for confusion in British India, of which you are a product. How do you think a handful of Englishman succeeded in holding masses of Indians in check for over two hundred years? Lording it over them, blithely furthering their colonial aspirations and flaunting their acquisitions in the natives' faces? Discipline, my boy! Discipline! There were any number of princely states and rajahs with great armies, but they could not rid the country of the Feringhee—and why, I ask you? Firstly, they were too busy bickering among themselves and secondly, they lacked the single-minded determination and discipline required to drive them from our shores. It took a half-naked fakir to achieve that, a well-ordered man with a mission. But even he is not strong enough to keep the country together. Today, there is chaos, but, as I see it, this is necessary, for chaos brings change. It has been man's way since the beginning of time. And, as for we Anglo-Indians, born and bred in this country, for the most part we chose to identify with the British, the white half of our whole. Never mind that they think us less even than the Indians and refer to us as cheechees, we still ache to belong, holding all things English sacred. And the colonial power, aware of our weakness, has used it to further their own ends, which again points to their cunning. This is the reason why you are feeling pulled in two directions. But you must banish this ambivalence, since you will soon be serving in the Indian Army. I know you to be a true and honest man, who has chosen to serve India, and that is where your loyalty should lie." Uncle Cyril stared moodily ahead of him.

Mummy looked at him with a new respect in her eyes.

"Wise old head," she said softly.

"Ah, nothing! I am just another armchair politician with too much time on his hands."

"Gone and handed the country over to a bunch of ruffians, they have! What can you expect? Rabble-rousers, the lot of 'em!" Aunty spoke with her usual candor. "For decades people were living side by side at peace with one another, each one knowing their place and keeping it. Then along came these Congress wallahs and that Jinnah, head of the Muslim League, speechifying everywhere, muddying up the waters. And the next thing you know, good sense is chucked out of the window! Hindus and Muslims are at each others throats and there is bloodshed in the streets. Even among the Hindus there are factions on every side. Let me tell you, I have very little time for those loafers. They make my blood boil. I wish them all in hell. Now, the Englishman, he is the devil we know, and I can live with that. They, most often than not, know what to leave and what to look after, but this time I fear they have made a big mistake—shouldn't have let this *Jai Hind!* stuff get out of hand. They should have called in the troops to restore order while the muddle was still a puddle. Now look what has happened? It's a bloody sea of confusion!" She stomped out of the room.

"What troops?" Mummy laughed derisively. "All their troops are Indian with barely a few true British battalions left behind. I read somewhere that most of them were repatriated during the war. And, if in fact there are a few still left, they too will soon be gone. Don't get me wrong, I too miss the old orderly way things were run, but India will be a free country soon and she must be allowed to chart her own course. Her birth will be a difficult one, for these are difficult times. First we had the war with the bloody Japanese on our tails and now there is independence and partition. For better or for worse, I feel Nehru's government must be given a chance to prove itself. I think it's too soon to pass judgment."

"You are right," Uncle Cyril agreed, "they must be given a chance, but with undisciplined power grabbers at the helm, corruption will reign. Believe me, I know the sort. Even now they must be busily carving up the country among themselves with no thought for the future nor for the man on the street. He can die of starvation, for all they care. They will have freed India, not for the people, but for themselves. All that they accuse Britain of doing, they will do and more to their own countrymen. It's the same old story told with a new twist. As for this Nehru bloke, let me tell you, he is a Kashmiri Pandit, an elitist, out to form a dynasty no different from the monarchy. His speeches say one thing, but his very demeanour suggests *gora sahib*[93] to the core. I read the newspaper every day and in them there are countless pictures of him, for he never misses a photo opportunity. He is prominent everywhere and in his element hobnobbing with the likes of Mountbatten and others of that ilk. I am sure he had a say when they established the boundaries that divided up the subcontinent. Everything will favour India and for that I don't blame him. Why

93　*gora sahib* white man

should it not? After all, wasn't it all Hindustan in the first place? As for Pakistan, that country's problems will begin from the moment she sees the light of day. Having us as neighbours will be the biggest impediment. Of course, all this won't affect us to any great extent, living as we do in this backwater. Here things will go on pretty much as they always have for the past hundreds of years. But, mark my words, greed and corruption will eventually erode any good intentions the Congress leaders may have at the moment of independence."

"From north to south, east to west, the country is so diverse—she will need a common foe to hold her together in the years ahead, and she'll have a ready-made one in Pakistan," Daddy declared gravely. "Pakistan will be the glue that holds India together in the future. For one thing is sure, the Hindu populace is united in their hatred of Muslims. Gandhiji understands this need for a common enemy very well. He is a crafty politician. Casting a wide net, he drew the people in under the Quit India banner. Preaching non-violence, he knew full well that his ideal would never be put to the test. When 300 million people are of one mind, the moral force of them alone is enough. He has taught the world a valuable lesson. His theory has worked for us and the British will depart quietly taking what's left of their occupying forces with them, without a single shot being fired. But partition, that's a whole different ball game. This, I fear, will be a bloody separation. Hindu/Muslim hatred has been fermenting for a long time now and the flames burn fiercely, stoked by all these rallies and incendiary actions. The situation is currently very close to getting out of control and I fear that fellow Nehru and his Congress party will not be able to contain it. It is one thing to assume the reins of power, but quite another to hold on to them."

"You are right," said Uncle Cyril. "One word of advice, however, from an old-timer: your duty is to your country, to uphold the system without any reservation. I, on the other hand, can think what I like and air my opinions, free as the breeze."

"Have no fear, I love this country far too much and am totally committed. I never ever wanted to go to England, even when all our friends were leaving. To live like a second-class citizen under the English boot? *Cha!* [94] Not for me." Daddy looked across the table morosely. "Right now the ones I feel the most sorry for are the poor devils who

---

94   *cha* an exclamation of disgust*CID* Central Intelligence Department

are about to become unwilling pawns in this partition game. Ours is an agrarian society, for the most part, and the land is precious. I can imagine the heartache farmers are suffering, knowing they have to uproot themselves, leave their homes and properties behind to journey into the unknown—Hindus to India and Muslims to Pakistan. Already there is a mass exodus with hundreds of thousands on the highways and byways, all on a forced march. Dear God, what a mess! The roads are fraught with danger with dacoits at every turn, not to mention Hindu and Muslim zealots with murderous intentions, waiting to ambush the unsuspecting travellers. The pages of Indian history will be stained with their blood. Such peril is incomprehensible to the common man, but we are privy to this information through the CID, spies and local informants. The slaughter has already begun. Horror stories have started trickling in and the situation I feel will only get worse when partition takes place. This promises to become a problem of gigantic proportions for the authorities, who I fear will be unable to cope with it. In the Punjab especially, where most of this drama is being played out, one can feel tension in the air like a coiled spring. No one will be able to put a stop to it; soon there will be blood everywhere, when the rivers and valleys are carved up to facilitate the birth of a new nation. On my way home from work I pass a maidan and catch a glimpse of refugees before their cooking fires at night. Having fled their homes they live in squalor, exposed to the elements in hastily erected shantytowns. The blasted government, of course, has made all sorts of promises, but is still dragging its feet about giving them proper accommodation. I know it is a momentous task, but I wish they'd hurry up. By the way—" he turned to Mummy, "I left Hamid behind to take care of the house. Even the cantonments are not safe these days; thieves and transients are everywhere."

"You left Hamid?" Aunty gaped at him. "Reg, how could you? What were you thinking, boy?"

"That was foolish of me, I know. I only realized it later when I was on the train, but I never think of Hamid in terms of being either Hindu or Muslim; he has always been my childhood companion and cook. It was a complete oversight on my part and don't think I haven't spent sleepless nights worrying about it. At one of the stops along the way, I got off the train and phoned from the RTO's[95] office. I managed to get

95   *RTO's* Radio Transmitting Officer

193

a hold of Captain Dubey and asked him to keep an eye on Hamid, hide him if the situation became volatile. Dubey promised to go over and look in on him. So long as he doesn't stray too far from the cantonment limits, he should be okay. I'm sure he will be fine; after all, I'm only here for a short time."

"A lot can happen in a short time." Aunty sounded anxious.

The vigorous tinkling of a bicycle bell brought everyone out onto the front veranda. Gavin Pritchard dismounted, cheerfully calling out, "Hello all." Wiping his gleaming pate with a handkerchief, he handed Uncle Cyril a folded sheet of paper from his pocket.

"Mr Malik told me you were at the post office twice today looking for a telegram from Cliffy. It arrived just as I was leaving, after collecting my pension money, so I offered to bring it over."

"Thanks a lot, old chap. Come in, come in," Uncle Cyril invited. "Here, have a chair, take the weight off. Someone fetch him a tumbler of water—or would you prefer something stronger?"

"No, no, water will do."

"H'm," said Uncle Cyril, reading the message. "This doesn't say much, only that they will be arriving by the Bombay Mail tomorrow. Nothing about Connie's condition; I hope that's a good sign." He handed the telegram to Daddy.

"I'll get that back bedroom aired out and ready for them." Aunty Hilda hurried away in the direction of the servants' quarters and we could hear her calling out to Burhan and Yusouf. After giving them the necessary instructions, she joined us again out on the front veranda.

"They can stop here for as long as they like, since I doubt Connie will be in any fit state to attend to things at the farm. Let that good-for-nothing Bill Pigott manage as he has been doing for the last little while. By the way, Cyril, have you been over to see how he's making out?"

"I'll go there directly after lunch."

She gave him a withering look. "You'll go there after lunch, will you? The only place you're good for after lunch is the charpoy. Humph! That's men for you, leave everything for the last. The place could have burned down by now or that sod could have gambled it all away, right under our very noses."

"Shut up, Hilda! I said I'd attend to it. Come on, Gavvy boy, join us for a bite." He steered Mr Pritchard into the dining room. "Burhan will lay an extra place for you."

"Oh Gawd, I hope it isn't the big C she has!" Gavin Pritchard exclaimed piteously. "I stopped over at their place for a visit the day before they left for Bombay. Poor Connie, she looked so pulled down. I'll tell the missus to start on a novena right away. She has great success, you know, with that sort of thing."

"If you believe in that sort of thing, which I don't." Aunty glared at him.

"Honest, I wouldn't say it if it wasn't true, Hilda. Myself, I'm not a praying man, but the wife—now that's another matter entirely. She has great faith. I'll tell her to start praying tonight."

"I guess it wouldn't hurt."

Gathered around the table at lunch, hearing them discuss Granny's illness, I wondered what "the big C" was.

"These venison chops are dynamite!" Daddy exclaimed, reaching into the dish for another helping.

"Help yourself, there's plenty to go around." Aunty was always pleased when she received a culinary compliment.

"What's *the big C?*" I blurted out, unable to contain my curiosity. Mummy scowled at me from across the table.

"Never you mind, my girl," Aunty Hilda scolded. "Little children should be seen and not heard, especially at the table when the grown-ups are busy discussing matters of great importance."

I was silenced with another helping of rice, dal and a venison chop.

"Don't they feed you at all in that boarding school? Both of you look really pulled down." She soaked Moira's rice with a ladle of gravy.

Mummy shook her head in disapproval and stared down at her plate.

Fruit was served after lunch.

That afternoon, feeling rather low, I snuck out of the bedroom and made my way to the well that stood at the back of the farm. It was a magnificent December day with the sky an endless blue. Fluffy, white, cotton-ball clouds scudded by and a poem by Wordsworth came to mind. I recited aloud the verses I remembered.

I wandered lonely as a cloud
That floats on high o'er vales and hills,
When all at once I saw a crowd,
A host of golden daffodils;
Beside the lake beneath the trees,
Fluttering and dancing in the breeze.

For oft, when on my couch I lie
In vacant or in pensive mood,
They flash upon that inward eye
Which is the bliss of solitude;
And then my heart with pleasure fills,
And dances with the daffodils.

A faint breeze rippled the surface of the moat filled with water. Perched on the wall, I gazed across the fields stretched out before me. Thinking of Granny, I said a quick prayer for her to get better soon. Looking over at the tiny fenced plot of land that had served as a graveyard for three generations of Stantons, I felt the icy tentacles of death hovering nearby. Dismissing the fantasy proved futile, as the large stone cross standing prominently at the head of Edward Horace Stanton's grave brought the specter sharply back to me. Several smaller crosses lay scattered here and there. On evening walks with Grandpa, Moira and I loved running in between them, playing a game of tag. We were unafraid, even when he warned us to be careful and tread lightly while playing around the graves.

"You may disturb ancestral bones," he teased. I never knew whether to take him seriously or not. Granny often called him a humbug.

"Will you be buried here?" Moira had asked.

"Yes."

"Can I be buried here as well?"

"It can be arranged."

Remembering Grandpa's tales always made me smile. I missed him and couldn't wait to see them both again.

Spotting Meenakshi, Sonabhen's daughter, seated on a tiny hillock in the distance, I walked over. We were childhood friends, but I hadn't seen much of her this time around since she worked every morning at the doctor's house and watched her mother's goats in her free time.

"Salaam, baba," she greeted me.

"Salaam. *Kaisa hai?*"[96]

"*Teek hai.*"[97] Her melancholy face belied the cheerful response.

Feeling out of sorts myself, I sat down beside her.

"Do you like working for the doctor?"

"Ha!" she nodded. "Memsahib is kind." Changing the subject she confided: "My mother has made a match for me."

"Really?" I was taken aback. Meenakshi was only a few years older than I. "Do you like the chap she's chosen for you?"

She shook her head, eyes welling up with tears.

"Then tell your mother you don't care for him," I advised. "She won't force you."

"It is not so easy. He is the Patel[98] of Moorghao and very influential. Missy baba has already given her approval."

"Have I seen him?" I asked.

She shook her head. "But if you watch next Saturday afternoon you may see him, he is coming to meet with my father. Look for an old man, maybe forty years, with a large white turban. I hear he has had two previous wives, but no children."

"What happened to them, to his previous wives?"

"Both died. I will be the third," she sighed resignedly, "I too will die." She began to weep.

"No, you won't," I replied resolutely.

Watching the goats nibble everything in sight, I chased after them, trying to catch a little one, but it nimbly avoided me and ran bleating to its mother.

"Granny Connie kaisa hai?" Meenakshi inquired, gazing at me through reddened eyes.

I informed her that Granny and Grandpa were returning the following day. But she seemed distracted and didn't hear me, as she turned away to gaze forlornly at the low hills shimmering in the afternoon glare. Sensing she wanted to be alone and since it was nearly tea time, I decided to go in. No use having Radha in a snit with me as

---

96 *Kaisa hai?* How are you?

97 *Teek hai* I'm okay

98 Patel *headman*

well. Promising Meenakshi that I would look out for her betrothed, I left her to her solitude.

Maud, the buffalo, was lowing in the cattle shed and it sounded like she was in pain. I heard her through the bedroom window while having an afternoon nap. That evening, I went to pay her a visit, but was shooed away by a field hand.

"What's the matter with Maud?" I asked Aunty. "Is she all right?"

"She's in labour, that's what she is, and due to give birth any minute now."

That night, just as we were finishing dinner, Yusouf entered carrying a lantern and whispered in Aunty's ear.

"It's Maud's time," she said, rising. "I want to be there for the birth."

I looked up at her expectantly.

"Reg, I'm taking Sarah along with me, if that's all right; she's worried about Maud and I think it will be good for her to witness the birth."

Daddy shrugged and, since Mummy did not look up from her plate, I skipped out behind Aunty.

It was a moonless night, crisp and cold. Inside the buffalo shed, Maud lay on a bed of straw looking wide-eyed and terrified. She shook her head and great gobs of spittle flew all around. Aunty stroked her and she gave a low cry as the calf emerged. Yusouf assisted with the birth, easing the calf into the world gently, he helped it to slip out. Gleaming wet and covered with rough black hair, it lay curled up beside its mother. Within minutes it tried to rise on trembling feet, but collapsed again onto the bed of straw. I watched, wide-eyed with wonder.

"A fine female!" Aunty exclaimed. "What shall we call her?"

"Esmerelda," I volunteered.

"That's a mouthful, Sarah; she'll end up being called 'Melda' by the servants."

I shrugged.

Aunty instructed Yusouf and Burhan on how to clean up the animals and we left the shed.

"How did the calf get into Maud?" I asked hesitantly.

"She was impregnated by Abbas Khan's male buffalo. His was the seed."

"How did the seed get in?"

"The seed entered Maud's body via the same passage through which Esmeralda exited and it's like that with humans as well," Aunty explained in a matter of fact tone of voice.

H'm, I had to really think about that one and now didn't seem to be the right time. Besides, it was nature and everything about nature was wonderful, according to Grandpa. Kissing Aunty good night, I ran to my bedroom, feeling happy and privileged to have been invited to witness the birth of Esmerelda. Moira was timid about such things, but I was afraid of nothing and no one.

Grand-Aunt Fanny Foxglove paid us a visit without Uncle Melvin. She came over riding in a *dumney*[99] and Moira and I ran out to greet her. She twittered with pleasure as she embraced us and I caught a whiff of her perfume—Evening in Paris. Dressed in crisp voile, Aunt Fanny teetered into the house on high-heeled shoes. Traces of her once pretty looks were still evident beneath the mask of powder on her sallow, lined face and in her faded blue eyes.

"And how are, my darlings?" she inquired. "Home for the holidays, I see, and sprouting like weeds. I picked up a pot of *gulab jamuns*[100] on my way over and you can have your fill after dinner, if your mother will allow you. Sarah, my dear, will you carry them in like a good girl?"

Recalling past family discussions on the subject of Aunt Fanny and Uncle Melvin, I remembered how the topic always made Aunty Hilda hot under the collar and, since she detested her brother-in-law, it didn't take much to set her off.

"Could have had any man she wanted, that Fanny; they were buzzing around her like bees around a honey pot," Aunty Hilda fumed.

Granny Connie nodded in agreement.

The sisters loved rehashing the life and loves of their sister Fanny.

"I remember the time that ICS wallah came here all the way from Bombay to court her. Uncle Lenny was impressed and Aunty Marjorie told her to be nice to him. But not our Fanny, she was a flighty one,

---

99   *dumney* a little cart, bringing visitors
100   *gulab jamuns* a sweet

sashaying all over the place, giving herself airs. She totally ignored the poor chap, treated him like dirt and, in the end, he went back to Bombay disappointed. Aunty Marjorie was convinced that she must have led him on during her visit to Cousin Gloria's place that summer. Gloria had those kinds of friends you see, all hoity-toity. It wasn't long after that she took off with Melvin Foxglove. No one knew where that loafer came from and there were any number of stories doing the rounds at the time. That good-for-nothing station master Garnett Gonsalves told us Melvin was put off the train without a ticket and I for once believed him. Uncle Lenny, of course, feeling sorry for him, took him in for the night. The gravest mistake of his life he called it after Fanny ran off. But Melvin was a smooth talker and he did a number on the old people, suckered them in, good and proper he did, sweet-talking them into believing some cock-and-bull story that they swallowed hook, line and sinker. They even found work for him on the farm, but he was not the working type you see, didn't like to dirty his lily-white hands. Every evening he would disappear. Where to, we wondered. It wasn't very long though, before we discovered his filthy little secret. He'd sneak away and spend his evenings with that sod Sam Baldwin, the old mill inspector, and his pal Garnett Gonsalves. Boozing buddies they were, the three of them—kept it up all night. Couldn't walk a straight line at eight o'clock in the morning. Stumble-down drunks, the lot! And how did he repay our hospitality? Tell them, Cyril, how you caught him in the godown with our Fanny in a compromising position. Go on, tell them."

Uncle Cyril grunted and shook his head. Drawing heavily on his bidi he muttered, "Leave off, girlie, it's all water under the bridge now. No use digging up all that dirt."

But there was no restraining Aunty Hilda. "A cobra should have bit him on the arse that day. Uncle Lenny thrashed the living daylights out of Fanny and the pair of them ran off on the train to Bombay the very next morning."

"From where did they get the money?" inquired Mummy.

"Fanny must have given it to him. She had part of her inheritance by then," Granny Connie sighed.

"Hilda, you paint poor Melvin much blacker than he really is," Uncle Cyril reproached her. "He's not such a bad sort, really, and besides, he's settled down now."

"Of course, he has, nothing works and you two have become drinking buddies. Thank God, Fanny still has some money left that she's finally learned to hang on to. Otherwise it would have been the Stranger's Home[101] for him and she would've landed up on our doorstep. Not that I wouldn't take her in, mind you; after all, she's blood."

"I tend to agree with Hilda about Mel," Granny Connie chimed in, taking her sister's side. "It was in Bombay, I recall; Cliffy and I had just moved into the Byculla house. Mel and Fanny were not married very long and she was pregnant with Hazel at the time. Cliffy caught him fooling around with some floozies down at the Starlight Club one night and threatened to beat the living daylights out of him. Never missed an opportunity that Mel; he must have fooled around on Fanny no end. He was a real ladies' man."

Moira and I were lying on the iron cot at the very end of the veranda. Moira had fallen asleep, but I was wide awake and as attentive as ever, absorbed in the grown-ups' conversation.

"And that girl of theirs, that Hazel, why she was hardly out of school when she picked up that shippy bloke and jazzed off to England. I don't think they were even married." Granny Connie shook her head disapprovingly.

"Hazel's a right pretty one, though, I have to say; got her mother's looks and her father's height, besides. Gosh! I remember Fanny and Mel at a New Year's dance one year; they were on the tiles, swaying to the music, dipping and circling around the room." Aunty Hilda's voice was low as she reminisced. "All eyes were on them that night; they were just so beautiful, like a pair of movie stars, I tell you. Yes, Hazel did get it all. She's foxy for sure. But I don't like the way she comes around here talking all plum in mouth, like a gora memsahib."

"Passes for one in Blighty," Mummy volunteered. "My sister, Lillian, in Kent bumped into her one day at the chemist's. Hazel looked right through her, like she was a pane of glass, and hurried out of the shop. Of course, Lillian made inquiries after that snub and discovered that Hazel's husband, Harry Stubbs, had come into a fair bit of money when his father died. I guess that's why she gives herself airs."

"Saucy, very saucy!" Aunty Hilda exclaimed, shaking her head.

"Saucy or not," Granny Connie spoke determinedly, "she can look like the queen of Sheba and waltz around with her nose stuck in the air

101 *Stranger's Home* in Bombay, a place for destitute A.I's

for all I care, but I, for one, won't put up with all that la-di-da nonsense. When she comes over to my place she knows better than to bring her airs and graces with her. And another thing, I don't understand why Harry never comes with her; she's always alone."

"I can tell you why," Aunty sniffed. "Thinks no end of himself he does. He thinks he's better than us—uppity limey loafer!"

"Enough about Fanny!" snapped Grandpa, rising from his chair, "you two with your acid tongues; leave your poor sister alone. She's made her mistakes and which one of us hasn't. But she's a sweet old featherbrain now and Mel's not such a bad sort either. Enough of this gossip!

"Are the girls asleep?" he asked, turning to Mummy.

"They must be," she replied. "It's awful quiet at their end."

Later, passing our bed on his way to the bathroom, he discovered me wide awake. "You little minx," he chuckled.

Now here was Aunty Hilda rushing out to greet her sister.

"Hullo, hullo, Fanny! I'm glad you've come. And I see you've brought your valise as well, that means you're going to stop with us for a while. Good, good. Here, take a seat; you must be worn out from riding in that wretched dumney. How about a sundowner, eh? A spot of gin and lime will perk you up."

Aunt Fanny nodded. "Thought I'd come over. What news of Connie?"

"Cliffy sent a telegram. They'll be on the Bombay Mail tomorrow, that's all we know. I've had the spare bedroom aired out, so they can stay for as long as they like. I don't mind telling you, Fan, I didn't like the look of her the night before she left to see the specialist. She looked so grey and tired and I was afraid for her, if the truth be told." Aunty Hilda sighed.

"There, there, it'll be all right," her sister soothed. "I thought I'd better come around this evening and stay over, if you don't mind. I can be with you all when they arrive tomorrow."

"I'm glad you did. You know, of course, that Reg arrived this afternoon. With Emma and the girls here as well, the whole family's around for them."

"Melvin couldn't make it," Aunt Fanny ventured timidly.

"No matter," was the hasty reply.

That evening, as the grown-ups nursed their drinks on the veranda, Moira and I sipped glasses of freshly squeezed orange juice. We sat on morras and nibbled on the peanuts that were being passed around. The sun set in a fiery ball behind the railway station. With the shades of night fallen, the mosquitoes came out in swarms and sang their shrill songs in our ears. Alighting on exposed parts of our bodies, they thirstily gorged themselves.

"Ouch!" I slapped one, but missed. Moira was busy swatting as well. Burhan entered carrying two kerosene lanterns; one he placed on the table and the other on a low ledge of the veranda.

"Let's move indoors," suggested Daddy after a while. "These mozzies are a plague. Besides, it's time for dinner, isn't it?"

"I'm glad you brought your appetite with you, Reg."

Aunty Hilda called out to Burhan and instructed him to serve dinner. Sonabhen assisted, as we seated ourselves around the table, children and adults together.

"Sarah, come sit here," Mummy patted the chair beside her. I plopped down and smiled up at her. Smoothing my hair, she inquired, "Why so quiet this evening?"

"No reason," I replied.

Potato cutlets, green beans, cabbage foogath, dal, beetroot salad and chapatis with fresh, churned butter. I wasn't feeling very hungry, however, and when Sonabhen piled two cutlets onto my plate, I put one back.

Conversation was at a minimum with everyone concentrating on the meal. All of a sudden and without warning, a gust of wind swept through the room and rattled the old beaded curtains like Mother Superior's rosary when she hurried in to mass.

"I felt a chill go right through me," cried Aunt Fanny in a high, quavering voice. "Did anyone else feel it?"

Another gust blew in from the opposite direction. Outside, the kerosene lantern toppled off the ledge and fell with a crash to the earthen floor. Daddy rushed out, a jug of water in his hand. "It's okay, everybody settle down. I've got it."

It continued to blow very hard. A bat swooped in and circled the room; its flapping wings cast giant shadows on the wall. Aunt Fanny shrieked like a teakettle, as both Moira and I covered our ears. We knew that if it fastened itself to our earlobes, twenty donkeys would have to bray before it would let go. The Ditmar on the sideboard flickered and died. Daddy entered just as a further rush of air caught both sets of dining-room doors and slammed them shut. We were locked in. Paralyzed with fear and in total darkness, we clung to Mummy.

"It's old man Stanton," whispered Aunt Fanny; "he has a message."

"For whom? Don't be ridiculous! Stop that drivel, Fanny," Uncle Cyril spoke firmly. "It's just that, that silly oaf, Burhan, forgot to secure the door jambs. Anybody got a match?"

"This happened once before—" Aunt Fanny continued, but her voice was drowned out by a loud banging at the door.

"*Kohn* hai?"[102] Daddy inquired authoritatively.

"Sahib, *darwaza kohlo*."[103] It was Burhan.

"Matches *lao*,"[104] Daddy instructed. Struggling with the door, he finally forced it open. Burhan entered carrying a lantern.

The lamp was lit and the untrimmed wick shot a jagged flame up through the smoky chimney, throwing grotesque figures that quivered and danced upon the walls. Our family, huddled around the dining table, appeared like a coven of witches straight out of Macbeth. Averting my eyes, I stared down at the plate. Daddy and Uncle Cyril secured the door jambs. Aunt Fanny looked ashen, while Aunty Hilda appeared troubled and preoccupied. Mummy sat rigid with us on either side of her, clinging to her arms.

"We don't want to frighten the children with any fanciful tales, Fanny dear," Aunty Hilda remarked in her no nonsense way. Bustling over to the *doolie,* she inquired: "Now, who's for gulab jamuns? I just hope that spirit, whoever he was, didn't swipe the lot."

Moira and I giggled nervously as she spooned the rich, brown balls into our bowls.

"I wish your grandfather was here, these are his absolute favourites," declared Mummy, lifting a syrup-covered morsel to her mouth.

"We'll get some more tomorrow before they arrive," Daddy offered.

The next morning, whilst eating my porridge, I heard a flutter

---

102 *kohn hai?* who's there?
103 *darwaza kohlo* open the door
104 *lao* bring

overhead, looked up and spotted a bat hanging from the rafters, gazing down at me with horrible yellow eyes.

Upon their return, Granny Connie was confined to her bed. Curled up on a chair beside her, I watched as Dr Pudumjee entered carrying his black leather bag, which he placed on the bedside table. He spoke to Aunty Hilda in whispers, requesting a special diet for Granny. After examining her and administering an injection, he left, promising to return the following day. The house was in a state of utter confusion, everything was topsy-turvy, since Aunty Hilda was occupied most of the time with taking care of her sister, while Aunt Fanny spent her days sitting out on the front veranda, knitting cardigans for Moira and I. She allowed us to choose the colour of wool we wanted. Moira chose peppermint green and I chose yellow, blue, red, green and white.

"Why, Sarah, that sounds to me very much like a coat of many colours," she laughed.

I nodded. "I want all the colours of the rainbow."

"Choose one colour, dear, or two at the very most and I'll work them into a pattern for you."

"I choose red and blue."

On winter evenings a deep mist hung low over the land, veiling the hills in the distance. There was a distinct chill in the air. After tea, Mummy and Daddy, with Moira and I in tow, took long walks along the rutted cart tracks through fields of cotton and groundnut, up and down nullahs, until we came to the verge of the forest. On reaching Neel Pani,[105] a tributary of the great river that threaded its way through the surrounding plains, we stopped and wriggled our toes in the shallow pools of crystal clear water, before heading back. Daddy always carried his gun into the jungle and shot green pigeon along the way, bringing them home for the pot.

On the surface, things looked pretty normal, but an undercurrent of sadness marred each day. Grandpa Cliffy had lost his funny bone and wandered around the house looking confused and helpless. Soon after breakfast, he rode his pony, Cinnabar, over to the farm, returning by afternoon. Most of the time we were left to our own devices with Radha paying scant attention since she had found a new love—Gulab,

---

105   *Neel Pani* blue waters

the porter. I doubted very much whether we were going to have any Christmas celebrations at all that year. Hopes and plans for a splendid holiday had somehow turned dismal. I voiced my disappointment to Mummy one night after dinner.

"Man proposes, Sarah, God disposes," she replied philosophically.

I wondered if that qualified as a hackneyed phrase, but dared not ask.

Gazing out of Granny's bedroom window one lazy afternoon, I watched a flock of parrots swoop down and settle in the guava trees. Brilliant feathers shimmered in the afternoon sun as they flapped their wings, squawked and buried their sharp beaks into the ripening fruit. Moira disturbed my reverie, whispering in my ear that she knew what the matter was with Granny.

"What?" I asked impatiently.

"Promise you won't tell."

I promised.

"Cancer."

She darted out of the room.

The big C! I knew she was right. Staring intently down at Granny as she lay pale and wan under the covers, my worst fears were confirmed. She seemed asleep, but little moans escaped her lips from time to time. With a heavy heart, I rose from the chair and left the room. Words could not begin to describe how I felt. I tried to think of other dead people I had known, but only Harry De Boer came to mind and he too seemed so far away—a ghostly friend that had faded with time into the distant past.

Perched high on the uppermost limb of the custard apple tree, I watched as a figure came pedalling down the dusty trail towards the farm. Furiously ringing his bell, he scattered a herd of goats that ran bleating in every direction. Swinging down through the branches, I blocked his passage and boldly inquired: "Who goes there?"

"None of your business and get out of my way, unless you're Hilda Fenwick."

"I'm Sarah Watkinson; Hilda Fenwick is my grand-aunt."

"Ashley Durham; PWI Durham is my father."

"You'll find her in there." I pointed him in the right direction.

Leaping onto his bike once more, he disappeared down the path leading to the kitchen. It wasn't long though, before he was back under the tree again.

"Did you find her?" I asked.

"Yes."

"Where do you live?"

"Not far, on the other side of the station. Are you a boarder?"

"Yes."

"Me too. Ta for showing me the way."

He was gone again and I scrambled back up into the tree, just in time to observe him as he turned down a path before a babul thicket, finally disappearing into the distance. Dark curly hair and flashing grey eyes—I was instantly smitten. Ashley, I thought; even his name had a romantic ring to it. His mother must have read *Gone with the Wind*. Mummy wouldn't allow me near her copy of the book, but I had read a few chapters surreptitiously under the covers at night. Sighing deeply, I prayed I would catch a glimpse of him once again, soon. Climbing down, I went in search of Aunty Hilda.

"Did you get your message?" I asked.

"Yes, Sarah, the Durham boy brought it over. I have a million things to attend to, my child." She sounded distracted, but I trailed her.

"Haven't you got a book to read?" she inquired.

I found it impossible to concentrate all afternoon as thoughts of Ashley Durham raced through my mind. Grabbing a note pad, I sneaked out after lunch and made my way to a shady spot beside the well. Here, in solitude, I penned a poem of love, my first.

Appearing like a knight from a different place in time,
You captured my heart, confused my senses,
So I could hardly find words that rhymed—
With your curly hair and eyes so grey,
Will you come again, dear Ashley, another day?
We can carve our names on the trunk of a tree
And declare our love for all to see.
If you love me, as I love thee.

Pleased with my impromptu effort, I leaned back and dreamed of moonlit strolls through the jungle with Ashley by my side and of great dinner parties held at the farm with me presiding as hostess.

That evening Mummy found me curled up in an easy chair, scribbling away.

"What are you up to, Sarah?" she asked, peering into my pad.

Caught off guard, I quickly turned the page. "Oh nothing, it's just a poem I'm working on."

"You must let me read it when you're done," she remarked absently.

The kitchen was a hive of activity since Mummy had taken charge of Christmas preparations. Large basins of cake batter were poured into baking tins lined with coarse brown paper. Extra choolahs were fired up and the delicious aroma of fudge and coconut toffee wafted through the air. Grandpa cheered up as Granny's condition seemed to improve and she was even able to join us for tea one afternoon. Aunt Fanny was busily putting the finishing touches to Moira's cardigan that looked pretty and delicate with pearl buttons down the front. She left the house by dumney early one morning, returning later in the day with Yusouf in tow, carrying a large brown paper bag.

"I've just come from the post office, Sarah," she squealed with delight. "Your wool has arrived from Bombay and I can't wait to open the package. I also asked them to send some silk thread over, so I can crochet a couple of pairs of socks each for you girls before you go off to school."

Ooh, not that! I shuddered at the thought of crocheted socks, remembering what they did to my feet. Anyway, since I'd be away at boarding school, I need never wear them. Opening the package, she examined the skeins of red and blue wool, individually wrapped in tissue paper. Dropping a skein over the back of a dining-room chair, she skilfully began rolling it into a ball.

It was a chill evening, a week before Christmas, and Radha insisted we wear warm sweaters and woollen socks. As the grown-ups sat silent in the gloaming, each one busy with their thoughts, sipping drinks and smoking cigarettes, Moira and I, bundled up against the cold, played cards on the iron bed, enjoying a glass each of Aunty's special punch.

The recipe was a secret, she informed us, one she herself had concocted for invalids and children with the shivers.

Even though Christmas baking was in full swing, somehow I sensed a lack of cheer all round. I knew Granny's condition weighed heavily on everybody's mind. Dr Pudumjee had visited earlier in the day to give her another injection. She always drifted off into a deep sleep after it and was her old cheerful self for a while when she awoke. Most days, however, her spirits floundered and sometimes she seemed to slip away from us entirely. I took to sitting with her for long periods of time each day. As thin as a wraith, shrouded in a heavy flannel nightdress, she lay on the bed hardly breathing. A cup of soup or a dish of custard stood untouched on the table beside her. Moira visited, but didn't linger; I sensed she was afraid. When Dr Pudumjee arrived she scooted out of the room, while I, on the other hand, just eased myself further into the chair and covered my face with a book.

"Are you afraid of Dr Pudumjee?" I asked one night as we lay in our beds.

"He may grab me and give me an injection."

"Tosh!"

It was pitch dark outside, the only illumination being the gas lights from the railway station shining through the leafy branches of the trees. Burhan entered carrying two lanterns, depositing them as he always did, one on a table and the other on the front veranda ledge. I was brooding about Granny lying in the next room, deathly ill with cancer, and hastily sent up a prayer to Mother Mary and Saint Joseph, pleading with the pair of them to intercede on her behalf. Sister Angelina at the convent had mentioned more than once that I should pray to Saint Jude, since he was the patron saint of hopeless cases—I was sure she considered me one. So I offered up a prayer to him as well for good measure. Suddenly the dogs started howling, all of them together, each in a different pitch as pye-dogs tend to do.

"What's that infernal racket?" Uncle Cyril inquired, rising from his chair and peering into the darkness.

"Careful," Grandpa cautioned, "there may be a panther out there."

"Missy baba, missy baba." A thin voice cried out from the direction of the cattle shed.

"Kohn hai?" Aunty Hilda marched out into the compound, carrying a lantern before her. She was afraid of nothing.

Two scruffy individuals in ragged clothing emerged from out of the darkness. Between them they half-carried, half-dragged a third person who was obviously wounded. A bloodied bandage was wrapped around his arm and, below a tattered pant leg, his left foot hung limply off the ground. Aunty Hilda motioned them into the house. Bending, they lowered their companion to the floor, and sat huddled in a heap beside him.

"Mangat!" Aunty Hilda gave a cry of recognition. "*Kya hogia?*"[106]

With a faint smile of acknowledgment, he looked up at her with limpid brown eyes.

Daddy poured a couple of stiff drinks and handed them to the shivering pair. They gulped the amber liquid down in silence.

Hurrying into her bedroom, Aunty Hilda emerged a short time later carrying a large wicker basket and an old bedsheet, which she passed to Mummy.

"Tear this up for bandages."

Cutting away his ragged sleeve, she exclaimed: "My God, he's been shot! You bloody goonda! *Haram chor!*"[107] she abused, unravelling the blood-soaked bandage.

"Hilda, be careful, the girls—" Uncle Cyril cautioned.

"This is no place for children; send them into the bedroom."

No one stirred. All eyes were on Aunty as she dabbed the wound with antiseptic. Mangat winced and looked up at her with pain-filled eyes.

"Right through the arm," she observed, "and another shot has grazed his leg. I'll clean it up as best I can, then apply a tourniquet to staunch the flow, but Pudumjee will have to look at it in the morning."

He moaned as she tried to turn him.

"Pass me a shot of that rum." Pointing to the bottle. Laying Mangat's head on a cushion, she carefully poured the contents of half a tumbler down his throat. He passed out. Lying sprawled out on the floor, as pale as a ghost, he looked quite dead.

"Gone and killed him," Uncle Cyril stated matter of factly.

She fixed him with a murderous glare.

---

106 *kya hogia?* what has happened?
107 *haram chor!* bloody thief

Meanwhile, the menfolk were busy questioning the pair huddled on the floor about the shooting. They seemed hesitant to talk at first, but Grandpa quickly pointed out that it was in their best interest to make a clean breast of things.

"If you don't speak," he warned, "we will have no alternative but to hand you over to the police in the morning."

The younger of the two started bawling. Tears flowing down his begrimed face, he pleaded with Uncle Cyril, crying out that he was Dilip, Mangat's brother. Falling at Aunty Hilda's feet, he begged her to remember him. How he used to draw water from the well for her bath, how every day he weeded her vegetable patch and her rose bushes. Grovelling, he implored them not to turn him and his brother over to the police.

"We have come here because everyone knows the loving heart of missy baba," he sobbed.

"Dilip?" Aunty Hilda leaned over and peered into his face. "By gad, it's him all right! Why, I haven't set eyes on this rascal since he ran off with my bazaar money. Look at him now, gone and become a goonda like his elder brother."

"Who are the parents?" inquired Mummy.

"Both of them are dead, poor souls. Good honest servants, they were with us for ages."

"He is called Sandu," Dilip cried, pointing to his mate.

The story slowly unfolded. It seemed that Mangat was the head of a gang of six dacoits who operated in the Moorghao village district. They had hatched a plot to hold up a local grain merchant, but somehow he had been tipped off and called the police in. Ambushed, they lost three of their members in the shootout that ensued. Mangat was wounded, but managed to make a getaway with the other two helping him. That was three days ago; since then they had been on the run, hiding out in villages where sympathizers gave them food. Even though Mangat's injuries impeded their progress, he was determined they should make their way to the Stanton bungalow.

"How very considerate of the rogue!" Uncle Cyril scoffed. "This is all your doing, Hilda; your fame has spread far and wide for giving refuge to every good-for-nothing that turns up on our doorstep. You can settle this."

Aunty was silent.

"Now that we know what happened, what d'you plan to do next?" asked Daddy.

"We throw ourselves at your feet and beg your mercy." They prostrated themselves before him.

"Good Lord!" he exclaimed.

"Are they really dacoits?" I asked Mummy in a hushed voice. I was thrilled beyond measure to be part of such an adventure.

"Yes, they are, Sarah. Poor devils, they're just starving young men who have turned to a life of banditry because they can't get proper work. I feel sorry for them."

"Don't be fooled," Daddy corrected her, "some of them actually enjoy the danger and notoriety that goes with the life of a bandit."

"Like a highwayman?' I ventured.

"Exactly."

"Yusouf!" Aunty bellowed.

He emerged from his quarters, looking tousled and droopy-eyed. She instructed him to clear the last godown and, with Burhan's help, to make up a bed for Mangat.

"Use the blankets from the box room," she ordered. "The other two can sleep in there as well, but the wounded one will need the blankets. It's a cold night and he's lost a lot of blood."

"Are you sure that it's wise to harbour these thugs on the premises, Hilda?" Aunt Fanny ventured timidly. "The police will surely trace them to this place in a day or two and then we'll all be locked up as accomplices."

"Twaddle! I won't turn them away, not for anything. These boys were born on the premises. We knew their parents."

The godown was made ready. Uncle Cyril followed Dilip and Sandu as they carried Mangat in and laid him on the bed. I trailed behind, filled with curiosity. Sonabhen emerged with three platters of food, which she placed on the floor, before hurriedly departing.

We sat down to dinner at around nine o'clock that night. An air of excitement still lingered as Grandpa Cliffy recounted tales of other such incidents from the past.

"Police Inspector Mr Chandra Gopal must have some clue as to their whereabouts." He looked up at Aunty. "He's as wily as a fox, that fellow, and I'll warrant he'll be on your doorstep in a day or two, mark my words. Better have your story ready, Hilda, old girl."

"What story? We'll give him a bottle of rum and a thick feed. End of story. But I'll have to get Pudumjee over tomorrow and have a talk with him; he's going to have to fix the wounded one up."

"Are you sure he'll be willing to attend to these fellows after the story breaks in the papers?" inquired Mummy.

"Sohrab's a good egg," replied Uncle Cyril. "We were boys in Byculla in the old days, spent countless hours together flying kites. Nearly got run over a couple of times chasing the damned things out onto the street. Oh! But it was fun. His father was the chemist, I remember, and we were always nicking cough lozenges from his shop. When Sohrab applied for the job as Mill Doctor, of course, I put in a good word for him. With him there'll never be a problem, but I only hope for Mangat's sake that he can fix him up, because a hospital is out of the question."

I shivered with excitement.

The next morning we discovered the dacoit named Sandu had run away and nobody knew where to.

Grandpa was right. The following afternoon a police jeep swerved into the compound and Police Inspector Mr Chandra Gopal stepped out. A tall, paunchy man dressed in neatly pressed khakis with umpteen medals gleaming across his chest. He looked like a person of great importance, but when Aunty came out to meet him, drying her hands on her apron, he clicked his heels and bowed to her.

"Come in, come in, Inspector sahib," she greeted him cheerfully. "What brings you here today? Actually, you're just in time for a beer and Sonabhen has prepared her famous mutton curry for lunch. Will you join us?" Aunty waved him into the house.

"Thank you, Mrs Fenwick, but this is not a social call." He swaggered in after her and sat himself down on Uncle Cyril's camp chair. "Actually, I have come to warn you, madam, of dangerous criminals on the loose."

"Around here?" she asked, surprised.

"Notorious dacoits tried to hold up a poor grain merchant in Moorghao, but luckily we got wind of it and ambushed them, killing three of their number, but three escaped. One of them, the leader named Mangat, I believe is known to you and I am given to understand

213

that he was once in your employ. His younger brother, Dilip, as well is a gang member."

"My, my, Inspector sahib, today you are a veritable font of information. Surely you don't suspect I would give shelter to such unsavoury types? And how did you come to discover all these facts, if you killed three and haven't as yet set eyes on the other three?"

"No, no, madam, I am not accusing you of giving shelter. It's just that you have such a vast property, they could be hiding anywhere. As for how I discovered their whereabouts, we have our ways, and we use them to get to the truth. One of the escapees has already been apprehended and is presently locked up in the police *thana*.[108] The fellow calls himself Sandu, although that is not his real name. We surprised him early this morning, hiding in the fields behind a well, quite near his mother's house. My men gave chase immediately and he was caught. It wasn't long after that he spilled the beans. You won't mind, I am sure, if I have a look around. I'll be able to sleep better at night knowing I have given honest upright citizens like yourself and Mr Fenwick sahib our very best protection."

Uncle Cyril emerged from the dining room, carrying a tray that held two frothing bottles of cold beer and a couple of glasses. He had been tippling since early morning and was in high spirits. Looking surprised to find the inspector in earnest conversation with Aunty, he exclaimed cheerfully, "Good day to you, Inspector sahib. What perfect timing! How about a cold beer? My nephew, Captain Watkinson, his wife and children are here visiting with us. He brought over a full case of beer from Delhi. Capital stuff, if I may say so," he laughed out loud and continued. "We are well stocked this Christmas season with liquor of every description—a drinking man's delight. No prohibition in this house, eh? Come, come, what'll it be? A tot of rum perhaps with a chaser of beer?"

Inspector Chandra Gopal's eyes lingered longingly on the amber liquid spilling into the tankard. The anticipation of chilled brew sliding down his parched throat was just too much for him. Accepting the brimming mug, he drank deeply, wiped away a frothy moustache and sat back satisfied.

"Bottoms up!" Uncle Cyril urged, raising his glass. He beamed at the inspector. "Thirsty work rounding up criminals, eh?"

---

108 *thana* station

The family gathered around, it was time for the routine drink before lunch. Mummy agreed to Moira and I having a shandy each.

"Just a dash of beer for the girls and top it up with plenty of lemonade," she instructed Grandpa.

"The season is once more upon us," rejoiced Uncle Cyril, settling back comfortably in an easy chair. "What *tamasha!*[109] Unfortunately this year my sister-in-law is very ill."

"Has she seen a specialist? Bombay is the place to go," suggested the inspector.

"They have just returned. It is cancer and Sohrab Pudumjee is administering the drugs."

Aunty Hilda solemnly brought him up to date with all the news. "They are stopping with us for the time being. Cliffy goes over to his place everyday and returns by noon, but my sister cannot be moved."

"I'm so sorry to hear about your good wife, Watkinson sahib. We will be offering up prayers for her swift recovery," he commiserated with Grandpa, who had stepped out carrying two glasses of shandy for Moira and me.

Grandpa acknowledged him silently.

Eased by libation, everyone relaxed and turned to lighthearted banter, as Uncle Cyril teased the inspector who took the ribbing in good humour. Everyone laughed uproariously at one of Grandpa's jokes. Aunt Fanny didn't join in, however; she sat rigid and tight-lipped, a little apart from the rest of us, knitting furiously.

"Getting back to the matter of these dacoits..." The inspector looked directly at Aunty Hilda. "As I was saying, that fellow Sandu spilled the beans and we have good reason to believe the other two may be hiding out here on your farm. After all, the surrounding fields, godowns and outhouses are intimately known to them. Inadvertently, Mrs Fenwick, you could be harbouring criminals."

"Surely you don't think they would slip back here?" Grandpa asked. "It doesn't make any sense, since this is the first place you would come looking for them."

"True, true, but who can know how these rough fellows think? Sandu was, I am sure, going to visit his mother—a logical place for a police lookout, wouldn't you think? But not that oaf; he walked straight into the trap. I am afraid for Mrs Fenwick; she doesn't want to come

---

109 *tamasha* big confusion, noise

upon them unawares, hiding in an outhouse or in the cattle shed. They can be dangerous and do grave harm. This was my first instinct, Watkinson sahib, so I came here, post-haste, to do a little scouting around." He examined his watch. "I asked a couple of my men to join me here in about an hour; we'll just check around and soon be off."

"In an hour!" Uncle Cyril slapped him heartily on the back. "Why man that gives you plenty of time for lunch. So let's have no more talk of harbouring bandits for the time being and have Burhan set an extra place at the table for you."

Aunty Hilda trotted out to the kitchen and I tailed her. "The sooner we get this over and done with the better," she muttered. "Harbouring bandits, indeed. Such cheek!" she declared indignantly. "Sarah, child, slip out to the back and see if Meenakshi is anywhere about; if you find her, bring her back in with you."

I ran to Sonabhen's quarters, but Meenakshi was not there. Then, remembering the goats, I made for the fields and found her, as usual, perched on the hillock, preoccupied with her thoughts. We hastened back. Aunty Hilda shooed me out of the kitchen and they huddled in a corner. After being of service, I was disappointed at not being included.

Back in the dining room, lunch had progressed with a sizable dent made in the platter of rice and only a few mutton bones swimming in the curry dish. Sliding into a vacant chair, I served myself, adding a vegetable cutlet to my plate.

Topping up the policeman's drink, Uncle Cyril jovially inquired, "I say, Inspector, what are you and the missus doing on Christmas Day?"

"Nothing. Why?"

"In that case, you are invited to come over here for lunch. If you haven't caught your dacoit wallahs by that time, who knows, you may even find them serving at our table." He snorted.

The inspector, his face flushed red as a beet, fixed him with a baleful eye.

"Surely, you are joking, Fenwick sahib," came his slurred reply.

"Honestly, anything is possible."

Aunty Hilda, fussing with the fruit salad and custard sauce, froze. She glared at Uncle Cyril—this time he had gone too far. Mummy shifted uncomfortably in her chair. Aunt Fanny dropped her fork that fell with a clatter to the floor, excused herself and left the room. Uncle Cyril tittered, hiccupped and was silent.

Two jeeps rolled into the compound just as we were finishing the meal. Aunty Hilda raced out onto the front veranda.

"I think I hear my men out in the compound." Pushing back his chair, the inspector followed Aunty, nearly colliding with her as she rushed back into the room.

"Your men are here," she breathlessly informed him.

Stepping out into the brilliant sunshine, Police Inspector Mr Chandra Gopal adjusted his glare glasses, turned to Aunty and requested she hand over the keys to the godowns, box rooms and outhouses.

"I would rather you did not accompany us, Mrs Fenwick; after all, we are apprehending criminals and this sometimes is a dangerous job."

Moira and I tagged along beside Grandpa, but we were stopped by Mummy who firmly steered us in the opposite direction towards the bedroom. Radha drew the curtains as we lay down in the darkened room. Moira giggled nervously, while I settled myself comfortably under the blankets. We heard the loud slamming of doors as the inspector's men searched the premises. That they had entered the henhouse was evident, for the birds squawked and fluttered all over in confusion. Murmuring voices passed our bedroom window, followed by silence. After a while we heard the police vehicles as they started up and rolled down the gravelled path out of the compound. They were gone! I was sure they hadn't found Mangat and Dilip. Moira dropped off to sleep, but I lay awake, wondering and worrying. Mummy and Daddy entered the adjoining room and I hurriedly pulled the covers over my head, not wanting them to find me awake.

"Whew! That was a close call," exclaimed Daddy. "It was touch and go for a while there."

"Where d'you think she hid them?"

"I don't know and I don't want to know. The old girls full of tricks, and she's got balls; I knew they'd never find the pair of 'em."

"Hush, Reg—the children!"

"They're sleeping. Care to slip under the covers with me?"

With eyes shut tight, I wondered where Aunty Hilda kept her balls.

Even though Mummy had charge over the Christmas baking, she grumbled to Daddy about Aunty Hilda's constant interference. She was furious to find her recipe for Christmas pudding revised with the changes neatly penned in red ink. Also, her fudge turned into a gooey mass.

"Needs more stirring," Aunty instructed. "It hasn't reached soft ball as yet; you were in too much of a hurry to take it off the stove. Put it back in the pan and keep stirring over a low flame. Mind it doesn't catch though and remember to keep a saucer of cold water beside you. Nothing beats cold water for making sure the toffee's done. Drop a lump into the water and see how it hardens."

I was preoccupied with thoughts of love. Still mooning over Ashley Durham, I added his name to my Christmas card list. Moira and I always made cards for family and friends that we handed out on Christmas Day. Sitting out at the back veranda table, busily drawing and pasting cut-outs from old magazines, I noticed a bullock cart approaching. It rattled down the path leading into the compound and came to a sudden halt beside the kitchen. A hefty individual with handlebar mustachios and a large white turban eased himself out, followed by a chokra carrying several garlands. The bullock cart driver grabbed the youth by the collar and weighed him down further with boxes of sweetmeats, while the portly one strolled into the kitchen with an air of great importance.

"This must be him," I said aloud.

"Who?" asked Moira.

"Meenakshi's intended."

"Intended for what?"

"Hush!" I waved her away.

Sonabhen, on seeing him, called out to Aunty Hilda: "Missy baba, Hari has come to greet you and also to meet with Cyril sahib and Meenakshi's father."

"What does he want with me?" Aunty emerged from a bedroom, looking annoyed. "I thought the matter of Meenakshi's wedding was all settled."

"True, true," the burly Hari smiled ingratiatingly at Aunty. "Missy baba's festival is coming up soon and so I have come with garlands and sweets for her and sahib." Folding his palms together, he greeted her and then placed a garland around her neck. Moira and I abandoned our project and ran into the kitchen.

"Ha, baba log!" he exclaimed on seeing us. "I hear the Captain sahib and his family have also arrived from Delhi." Since Uncle Cyril was nowhere in sight, we were garlanded instead and presented with a box of sweetmeats each. Aunty thanked him and hurried away. Out of the corner of my eye I spotted Meenakshi slipping out of her quarters and disappearing behind the godown. Hari sauntered over to where Pandurang, Sonabhen's husband, sat sunning himself. They exchanged greetings and sat together for a while out on the stoop, sipping cups of tea and basking in the afternoon sunlight. Aunty Hilda had branded Pandurang "a drone" since he hadn't worked a single day after his brush with TB.

Christmas cards forgotten, Moira and I examined the boxes covered in brightly-coloured foil, gleaming like shot silk in the morning sun.

"Shall we open them?" I ventured.

Moira giggled excitedly. "Shall we?"

"We'll open one, but which one?"

"Yours."

I slipped the gold tie with red tassels gently off the box and removed the cover. A delicious assortment of sweetmeats lay nestled within: *gulab jamuns, doodh pedhas, gajjar halwa, balushahi, ladoos,* and *cham chams.*[110] The cloying scent of *kewra* essence and cardamom assailed my nostrils. I salivated. Moira peered over my shoulder. Her eyes lit up.

"Take one."

Quickly snatching up a doodh pedha, I bit into it. A milky, sweet sensation permeated every corner of my mouth. Moira chose a ladoo. Radha appeared out of nowhere and watched in silence as we prepared to help ourselves to another sweet morsel each. Snatching my box away from me, she relieved Moira of hers as well, disappearing with them into the dining room. We next set eyes on the sweets when Aunty Hilda passed them around after dinner.

"Who brought these?" Grandpa inquired.

"That fellow Hari, the Patel from Moorghao. Sonabhen has fixed him up with Meenakshi, and they are going to be married next year."

---

110   *doodh pedhas, gajjar halwa, balushahi, ladoos, cham chams* sweets *kewra* essence of pandan

"He's been married before, hasn't he?" Uncle Cyril reached over and fished a *cham cham* out of the box.

"Yes, twice. Both wives died childless. This time he hopes for success with Meenakshi."

"Must be firing blanks," Grandpa chuckled. "What does Meenakshi think of the whole affair, has anybody cared to ask her?"

"She wasn't too happy about the prospect at first," Aunty Hilda informed, "but lately she seems to have perked up. I suppose she's accepted the inevitable."

"H'm, he's the patel, you say. In that case there's no point in asking Police Inspector Mr Chandra Gopal to investigate the deaths of his previous wives. The fellow's probably got the entire police force in his back pocket. Strange though, both wives dying like that. I, for one, wouldn't be marrying my daughter to him. But that good-for-nothing Pandurang, why he must be relieved just to get the poor girl off his hands and to a big shot no less, certainly a feather in his cap. But if you say Meenakshi seems happy, well then—" Uncle Cyril shrugged his shoulders.

"She's probably resigned to her fate," Mummy volunteered.

Dr Pudumjee felt Mangat was on the mend. One afternoon he cornered Aunty Hilda and whispered loudly, "That fellow Mangat will soon be well. What are your plans for him after that? He can't remain hidden here forever."

"Is he strong enough?" Aunty inquired.

"Not as yet, but very soon."

"I'll cross that bridge when I come to it." She dismissed him.

"Reason with her," he pleaded with Uncle Cyril. "The crossing of the bridge is imminent."

Uncle Cyril smiled, shook his head and invited his old friend into the dining room. "Have a drink, Sohrab, let's celebrate, it's nearly Christmas."

I thought Meenakshi's behaviour certainly very strange, as she furtively slipped in and out of the godown countless times a day. Peering in one afternoon, I caught her hurriedly adjusting her sari. Then someone pulled her down onto the floor and I heard moans followed by scuffling sounds. I craned my neck in an effort to see what was going on, but it was useless, since my view was obstructed by a piece of gunny sacking covering the window. Meenakshi herself seemed changed in the past little while. At first she was timid and afraid to take food in to the fugitives, but, as the days passed, she didn't seem to mind the chore at all. These days she sauntered into the kitchen, her eyes darkened with kohl, fresh *mogras*[111] threaded through her hair, and casually picked up the enamel plates of food for the two dacoits. Nor did she beat a hasty retreat, but lingered to chat and flirt girlishly in the doorway. Sonabhen, preoccupied with affairs in the kitchen, was oblivious of the goings on, but not so Radha. With time on her hands and years of experience in the game of love, she paid close attention. Leaning against the veranda wall, chewing paan, spitting volleys of crimson into the dust, she watched the drama unfold.

Braiding my hair one morning, she whispered in my ear, "Baba, warn Meenakshi that she is playing with fire. I have been keeping an eye on her these many days and I fear she has fallen desperately in love with that fellow Mangat. He is handsome, no doubt, but it is a dangerous game, for he will only bring her grief. After all, he is a dacoit and it is known everywhere that inspector sahib has put a price on his head."

"I know, I have seen her too." Confirming Radha's fears, I shivered as the full extent of what could happen suddenly dawned on me. I listened attentively as she recounted for me the many times she had spied Meenakshi leaving the godown, her tousled appearance and trailing sari betraying her secret. Romantic love was just too much to bear, I decided, and in Meenakshi's case it was dangerous as well. Radha and Gulab—pish! Nothing would ever come of that. Ashley and I, the same story. But Mangat and Meenakshi, now that was another matter altogether.

"I'll try and talk to her," I whispered, "though I don't know how far I'll get, for she seems different these days." Yanking my braids away, I darted out to find Meenakshi.

"Hurry!" she cried out after me.

I knew all about Radha's many men friends. After all, she had been my ayah since birth, watching over Moira and me as we travelled the length and breadth of India with our parents. Mummy, too, I suspected was aware of her amorous adventures, but had chosen to turn a blind eye. She knew Radha was totally devoted to the family and wouldn't dream of running away with any of her lovers.

---

111   *mogras* a flower

That afternoon, I spotted Mangat's brother, Dilip, herding Sonabhen's goats out in the fields. He was startled, as I came upon him unawares.

"Does missy baba know you're out here?" I asked importantly.

He looked away, shaking his head. Seeing him for the first time in the light of day, I noticed that he looked quite fit. He was sporting a bushy mane and thick beard which made me a little afraid of him.

Meenakshi kept avoiding me; it was difficult to get a moment alone with her. All day she worked for the doctor's wife and in the afternoon she was up to hijinks in the godown, I suspected. One evening, however, I cornered her in Aunty's bedroom, as she tidied the linen cupboard.

"Why have you been avoiding me?" I chided.

She shrugged indifferently. "I am always busy."

I mentioned having met her intended.

"What do I care?" she replied insolently, tossing her head.

Quite the opposite, I thought, of the sad-eyed, forlorn creature of the previous weeks.

"You'll have to care when he's married to you. Besides, I hear you are overly friendly with Mangat, the dacoit. Be careful, people are watching you," I warned.

"What of it? We are childhood friends. Besides, missy baba gave me the job of bringing his meals. I do what I am told, nothing more."

"Well, all right then."

I detected a subtle change in her manner, a new arrogance. Mannerisms picked up from a swaggering dacoit, no doubt.

Right after breakfast one morning, Uncle Melvin suddenly appeared on our doorstep with a field hand in tow, carrying a metal trunk. Since he wasn't a frequent visitor, we were surprised to see him so early in the day. Uncle Cyril looked pleased and, wishing him a cheery good morning, ushered him inside, dusted off a chair and asked him to park himself.

"What brings you here, Melvin, my man? Fancy a bit of Fanny?" He laughed uproariously at his own joke.

Aunt Fanny glared at him and stiffened visibly.

"Joker!" Uncle Melvin smiled weakly. "I've come to wish you all a

Merry Christmas, since I'm off to visit my sister in Nasik and won't be around for the celebrations."

"You have a sister in Nasik?" Uncle Cyril was in good humour. "Why, that's the first I've heard of it. Where have you been keeping her all these years, man? I always thought you were an orphan, without a relative in the world."

"Naw, naw. Come on, Cyril, you old windbag, you know I have a younger sister Dolly. She's married to Bobby Patterson, who was a guard on the GIP. You've met him. They have three kids, all grown now. I never did get to see much of them because, being on the railways, they travelled around all over the place. Now that old Bob has retired and taken a house in Nasik, I thought I'd go and look them up. No need for Fanny to come along though; I see she's happy here with her sisters and the children. Eh, Fan?"

"Suit yourself, Melvin Foxglove." Aunt Fanny didn't look up from her knitting.

"How about a teeny tot to see you on your way? It's nearly Christmas after all," Uncle Cyril coaxed.

"No, no thanks. Too early in the day for me, besides my train is at ten o'clock, so I better be pushing off." He kissed Moira and I, apologizing that he didn't have a couple of "chips" to spare for Christmas presents.

"So, Fanny, I'll see you in a couple of weeks then?"

With needles clicking furiously, she totally ignored him.

"Merry Christmas all!"

"See you later, old chap." Uncle Cyril patted him on the back, a hint of sadness flitting across his face.

We watched Uncle Melvin disappear down the avenue of trees that led to Stanton Station. A tall spare man dressed in shabby clothing. I, too, felt sorry for him.

"Aren't you going to miss him?" I asked Aunt Fanny.

"Not a bit," she replied. "This shawl I'm knitting for your grandmother is coming along very nicely, don't you think?"

Aunt Fanny had completed my cardigan with a lovely blue pattern knitted into a red background. She sewed pearl buttons down the front. Moira and I each had a new pair of white crocheted socks as well, which I secretly planned to lose at the very bottom of my kit box.

Christmas Eve and the place was humming with activity. Uncle Cyril brought the old gramophone out from the storeroom, dusted it off and played a tune by Bing Crosby. The record was old and badly scratched. Bing sounded like he had a sore throat, but Moira and I didn't mind; we took turns playing records all day. Granny Connie seemed a bit better and Grandpa carried her out onto the veranda and settled her into an easy chair. Wrapped warmly in a shawl with a blanket over her feet, she sat with us, smiling weakly when she recognized a tune. I played "Now Is the Hour" and her eyes lit up with that old spark of mischief.

"Maggie's song," she whispered softly.

Meenakshi was recruited to help out in the kitchen every afternoon, while Dilip snuck out from the godown and watched the grazing goats in the fields. Dr Pudumjee called it sheer lunacy. The inspector could have spies planted all over the property, he whispered to Aunty, who accused him of having an overactive imagination.

"And another thing, Mangat's wounds are now completely healed. What do you propose to do with him?" he asked.

"Your job is done, Sohrab, and I thank you. I'll look after things from this point on."

"But—aree! Hilda, he's a wanted man and Police Inspector Mr Chandra Gopal has posted a reward for his capture all over the town. Every nook and cranny is plastered with his ugly mug. Dear lady, let good sense prevail! He has nowhere to go, but to jail or to the gallows. Actually, you have made him better for a worse fate. A paradox, is it not? Even if he runs away into the hills, someone will give him up. Those villagers are dirt poor and a five thousand rupee reward is an unbelievable sum to them. Many will sell their own mothers for far less. The truth will come out and you and Cyril will be automatically implicated. I have been a friend and helped you out, now I plead with you to be equally my friend and give him up to the authorities. Please—" he begged.

"Thank you, Sohrab, thank you, thank you—please leave it with me. Your bill I'll settle with you at the end of the month. Now I have a hundred things to do with Christmas almost upon us. My nephew's wife tries her best in the cooking department, but—" Aunty shrugged and, pushing past him, made for the kitchen.

I felt sorry for Dr Pudumjee, as I watched him look helplessly after her.

He must have appealed to Uncle Cyril and Grandpa as well because the subject of what to do with Mangat and Dilip was brought up again at the lunch table.

"Hilda, I want you to send the pair of 'em packing." Uncle Cyril spoke firmly. "Their continued presence poses a danger to us all. Now that Mangat is sufficiently recovered and his brother has some meat on his bones, it's time they cleared out—the sooner the better. I don't want to know and I don't care where they go, just get rid of them."

"Cyril's right." Grandpa Cliffy spoke up. "Get rid of them—fast!"

"Sohrab's been bending your ear, hasn't he? Silly sausage!" She glared at them.

Christmas Day dawned clear and sunny with a distinct chill in the air. Aunty Hilda, Mummy and the servants had been busy bustling around the old house since daybreak. First came the family breakfast. Later guests would start arriving for lunch. The previous day Moira and I had watched Burhan as he tried to lure a couple of large ducks into his gunny sack.

"Ah! Ah! Ah!" he called out, chasing after them with a handful of grain, but they refused to be tempted. Losing patience, he changed his tactics and began furiously pursuing them. Padding away on webbed feet, they flapped their wings in alarm, but failed to elude him. He cornered them against the chicken coop and, swooping down, grabbed one and then the other, forcing them into the gunny sack. A frantic fluttering ensued behind the kitchen wall, followed by a triumphant "*Bismillah!*"[112] as he beheaded them. Peering over, I watched, fascinated, as he stepped back, triumphant, a broad grin pasted on his face, thoroughly enjoying the spectacle of the wretched birds dancing in the throes of death. Aunty arrived on the scene just as he plunged the pair into a large pot of water boiling on a makeshift wood fire nearby. I joined her and together we watched as Burhan deftly plucked and gutted each bird.

"Duck vindaloo!" she exclaimed. "You've got to be quick about getting the job done and, I must confess, the boy's got a knack. I've

112 *Bismillah!* for Allah; rendering them kosher

been fattening this pair up all summer; they'll be good eating. Ha!"
She looked satisfied.

There was no tree to decorate at Stanton House, no garlands to
string up, nor Chinese lanterns.

"I don't hold with fripperies," Aunty Hilda informed Moira when
she asked about a Christmas tree. "It's the Lord's birthday and he was
born in a stable, not in bloody Buckingham Palace."

The dining room was dressed up, however. On the sideboard pretty
doilies were placed under Aunty's few pieces of crystal. Aunt Fanny
had neatly mended all the holes in the lace tablecloth and the table
was set with Aunty Hilda's best Meakin china. The gifts were brought
in before breakfast, each parcel neatly wrapped in tissue paper and
tied with string. Mummy placed a gift on every seat. Moira and I were
barred from the room, but we peeked in and noticed more than one
gift each on our seats. The servants' "packets" were put in a basket on
the back veranda to be handed out before lunch was served. Family,
friends, servants and field hands all sat down for the afternoon meal at
the same time. Burhan served at the table, while Sonabhen remained in
the kitchen. They were rewarded later with extra baksheesh.

But first came breakfast. The yeasty fragrance of fresh-baked bread
drifted out from the kitchen, permeating the rest of the house. Aunty
was busy carving thick slices of salt hump. A large bottle of gooseberry
jam was placed on the sideboard, beside a dish of fresh cream. Sonabhen
carried in a platter of mixed grill: mutton chops, tinned sausages,
bacon, eggs fried sunny side up and kidneys on toast.

Mummy had a *durzee*[113] sew our Christmas dresses in Delhi, but
she hadn't counted on us sprouting like weeds. The dresses were short,
in spite of the hems being let out. Mine was a plaid pinafore with a
white voile blouse. Moira wore a different plaid and her blouse had
puffed sleeves and a pretty lace collar. Using Mummy's powder-puff
to dust some Coty's all over my face, I glossed my lips with Vaseline,
imitating the seniors at boarding school. Radha braided our hair. Moira
agreed to have a pair of butterfly clips set into her braids, but I refused.
Mummy dabbed cologne on our kerchiefs and we were ready to meet
the day.

Good heavens! I couldn't believe the number of gifts I received.

---

113   *durzee* tailor

Four lace-edged handkerchiefs and a purse with a tiny compact mirror from Mummy and Daddy. The cardigan and socks from Aunt Fanny. *Deerslayer* by James Fennimore Cooper and *The Cremation of Sam McGee* by William Robert Service from Grandpa and Granny. Best of all, both Moira and I received a gold bangle from Aunty Hilda and Uncle Cyril. Slipping the circlet of gold onto my wrist, I watched in wonderment as it caught the light, glittered and gleamed.

"Thank you, thank you." We jumped up and ran around the table kissing everyone. The room was overflowing with love and Christmas cheer. Aunty was right, we didn't need a tree.

"Mind you look after those," she warned as we hugged her. "I had them made up from one of your great-grandmother Zinat Mahal's heavy bracelets. You do know that she was the daughter of a lady-in-waiting to a begum?"

"We do," I whispered in awe.

"I'll make you girls each another one next year, if I see you've looked after those. In the meantime, breakfast's getting cold, so tuck in."

Later, I asked Mummy if I could wear my bangle to boarding school. She looked at me crossly and said, "Not a chance!"

The day was a feast at every meal, with umpteen snacks in between. Moira and I took turns playing the gramophone. "You'll Never Know," "That Old Black Magic," "Lili Marlene," and "I'll Be Home For Christmas." Mummy and Daddy did the foxtrot and Uncle Cyril, well into his cups by midday, danced with a broom handle, swaying and dipping very low as he circled around.

"Big dipper, stingy tipper," Grandpa teased.

"Never fails to make an ass of himself," Aunty Hilda remarked.

"Oh! Let him alone, old girl; he's just clowning around." Grandpa defended Uncle Cyril. "Besides, it's Christmas Day."

"Humph!" She hastened away.

The guests started arriving around midday. The Durhams were the first. They came without Ashley, who had the mumps.

"Such a nuisance, having him laid up in bed on Christmas Day," his mother complained.

I wasn't very disappointed, however, since my ardour had cooled considerably in the last little while.

Inspector Mr Chandra Gopal, his wife and two children roared into the compound in a police jeep. Aunt Fanny's jaw dropped as she watched the inspector strut into the house carrying a large box of sweetmeats that he presented to Aunty. His wife and daughters followed meekly behind.

"Didn't think he'd take old Cyril up on the invite," she declared with a look of distaste. "My, but the natives are becoming very uppity."

"Sohrab and Nasreen Pudumjee are here as well," Mummy reminded her pointedly.

"Ah, but they're different! Parsis don't count; they're much like us."

"Are they?" Mummy shook her head in disbelief.

All the "first families" of Stanton Station were represented. They made themselves comfortable, seated out on the front veranda. Soon the dining room was emptied of chairs as the guests overflowed, spilling out onto the compound. The menfolk leaned against the giant neem tree, laughing, joking, smoking their cigarettes and doing some serious drinking.

Lily Van Houghton, who I had never set eyes on before that day, but whom I recalled was the hot topic of conversation at Aunty's Sunday lunches, arrived by tonga with a pale, skinny man dressed in a shiny suit. He wore a sola topee. On removing it, I noticed a few strands of limp blonde hair clinging to his otherwise bald pate. She introduced him as Freddy Darling, her man friend. Our guests nodded knowingly. He plonked himself down on a folding chair and never stirred until lunch was served. Downing glass after glass of beer, he was a silent drunk.

Lily, a woman of ample proportions, wearing a loud, flowered dress, insisted on greeting everyone with a kiss. When her scarlet lips brushed my cheek, I was overpowered by the combined fumes of alcohol and cheap perfume. She collapsed in a chair opposite and I examined her carefully—brassy curls and dewlaps of fat rolling over her neck. She seemed a jolly sort, though, and, as the afternoon progressed, kept everyone in stitches with her off-colour humour. By lunchtime she was decidedly the worse for wear. Spilling her drink down the front of her dress, she shrieked as a lump of ice got lodged between her breasts. Tommy Thornton dashed to the rescue. Stuffing his handkerchief down her cleavage, he tried in vain to retrieve the melting ice. We children crowded around and watched in amazement as Lily's enormous blush-red bosoms jiggled uncontrollably. If Mummy had spotted us we would surely have been sent outdoors to play, but, as it happened, she was in a merry mood herself, giggling with the others as they egged Tommy on with lewd suggestions.

Moira and I imbibed our share of shandy that afternoon. Ignoring the inspector's prissy daughters, who sat apart watching the shenanigans with sickly smiles pasted on their thin embarrassed faces, we joined in the adult hijinks. The inspector, I noticed, wasn't above a little fun himself; he moved over and sat very close beside Lily. Laughing uproariously at her ribald humour, he gave her a hand up as she staggered to the table to replenish her glass.

"Inspector sahib, I see you have a way with the ladies," Uncle Cyril remarked with a huge wink. "You fancy them large, eh? This one definitely has a jiggle in her wiggle," he tapped Lily on the bum. Uncle Cyril had an audience and he was on a roll. Turning to Tommy Thornton—"Tommy boy, I was glad to see you were *up* to the occasion!" The company roared with laughter. Uncle Cyril crowed and got ready for another round of banter.

I was in my element, jigging around, snatching furtive little sips from abandoned glasses, cranking up the gramophone, playing the old records over and over again.

Aunt Fanny though, was in a sour mood. She sipped her drink and sat a little apart from the rest of the party, her lips pursed in a thin line of disapproval. Remembering tales I had heard of her gay youth, I was disappointed to see her this way. I wondered if she was missing Uncle Melvin. Granny Connie was unable to join the party, for she was having one of her bad days and had to remain in bed. Radha kept a vigil beside her all afternoon, eating her Christmas lunch seated on a mat spread out on the floor.

Lunch was served at around three o'clock that afternoon, an ungodly hour according to Aunty. Everyone was invited into the dining room. Jimmy Mitchell—Lickspittle—disgraced himself. Sozzled, he slumped forward in his chair and snored loudly into his plate. Grandpa put him to bed to sleep it off.

Aunty outdid herself. Mutton korma, *jeera*[114] pulao with raita. Venison chops, pickled pork, green beans, cabbage foogath dressed with a sprinkling of toasted coconut and beetroot salad. Finally, the piece de resistance arrived: duck vindaloo—succulent morsels swimming in a

---

114 *jeera* cumin

rich, dark gravy. All eyes followed Burhan as he gently lowered the dish onto the centre of the table, taking great care not to spill even a little grease. Heavy fumes rose up from the steaming tureen, filling the air with pungent odours—impregnated with garlic and a fistful of spices ground in vinegar. A mound of *phulka*[115] chapatis followed and was passed around to sop up the rich sauce. Salivating, each guest dipped into the dish and helped themselves. Uncle Cyril fished for the pope's nose and giblets, his favourites. Mummy served us with portions of meat and gravy.

Smacking their lips, the guests devoured the tender joints of duck, gnawing on the bones to extract the last bit of taste from them. Lifting their tumblers with greasy fingers, they washed the meal down with quantities of beer. Moira and I, seated at the kiddies' table, giggled and laughed with the other children. Eating with abandon, the company shifted vast amounts of food that afternoon. A harassed Burhan, sweat pouring down his face, was kept on his toes serving at the table, topping up empty beer glasses, clearing plates and passing the different dishes around to diners who, after a time, had difficulty rising from their seats.

Servants and field hands assembled at the back to receive their packets, as Daddy filled their tumblers with hefty pegs of army rum. Enormous dekchis of mutton korma, fiery chicken curry, pea pulao with all the accouterments covered the table. Lining up, they served themselves and then sat on the floor to enjoy their meal.

When lunch was cleared away, a large basket of fruit—the Reynolds' contribution—was placed at the centre of the table beside Inspector Chandra Gopal's box of sweetmeats. Dainty cut glass trays, filled with slices of shortbread, fudge, coconut toffee and dark plum cake, were passed around. But, since most everybody was filled to bursting, there were few takers. Even though it was a cool afternoon, they all perspired profusely. A surfeit of food and liquor undoubtedly had something to do with it. Mrs Durham fanned herself and patted her face all over with a large handkerchief, smearing her lipstick in the process. But she was past caring. Aunt Fanny piled her quarter plate high with several pieces of cake and fudge. She didn't drink much, but had an incredible sweet tooth. I watched in amazement as she downed one dainty morsel after another between sips of tea. Intelligent conversation was at a

---

115   *phulka* unleavened bread made on coal fire

standstill, as a feeling of lethargy descended on the gathering. Outside in the compound a racket started up as the pye-dogs began fighting over mutton bones thrown to them by the servants.

The meal over, guests slumped in their chairs, sluggish and heavy. Languidly, the men rose and followed Uncle Cyril out onto the front veranda for a smoke. The womenfolk, gathering up their children, descended on the bedrooms. Flopping down wherever there was a place, sharing two or three to a bed, they were all soon snoring. Moira and I shared her bed that afternoon, since mine was occupied by Mrs Pudumjee. Flushed with food and drink, Moira was asleep instantly, but I lay awake, listening to a train chug slowly out of Stanton Station, then drifted off when its shrill whistle cried out in the distance.

It had been a glorious Christmas Day and it wasn't over yet. Early evening tea was a subdued affair. Cake, bread, butter and jam were passed around, but most of the ladies settled for a simple cuppa. At dusk guests began their farewells and pushed off home before night descended. A few diehards remained, however, "to squeeze the last drops from the bottle," according to Aunty.

It was late. As Moira lay beside me on the iron cot, cuddled up with her old rag doll, I squinted by lantern light, examining my books over and over again. Uncle Cyril, having his last puff of the day, coughed and I could see the glowing end of his cigarette at the far end of the veranda. A tired Aunty joined him, collapsing into an easy chair.

"Well, old girl, I have to say it was a helluva lunch, a burra khanna, in the true sense of the word. You look beat; come sit by me." He pulled her closer.

"It was nice, wasn't it? I hope everybody had a good time, especially the girls. Christmas is for children."

"They enjoyed it and more. The bangles you made up for them were dazzling. By the way, I haven't given you your gift as yet." He reached over again, but she slipped away from him laughing in a girlish voice that totally surprised me.

"Keep it for later, old man; right now you're all mushy with drink. I'll see you later."

She disappeared into the dining room.

That night, lying in bed, recapturing the day's events, I caught my breath as a silvery Moonface, beaming in through the open window, flashed across my gold bangle, turning it into a brilliant circlet of light. "Zinat Mahal!" I whispered her name: "Granny."

Never having heard our parents quarrel loudly before, Moira and I were naturally terrified to wake one morning to the sound of their raised voices. Shivering with fright, I ran to the bathroom, shut the door and sat on the commode for what seemed like an eternity, waiting for the noise to die down. But they were still going at it, hammer and tongs, when I peered out after a while, so I decided to wash up and get ready for breakfast. Daddy was due to return to Delhi in a few days and it wouldn't be long after that Moira and I would have to join the batch at VT Station. Oh, golly! I wish I knew what the hullabaloo was about.

I found Grandpa seated in the dining room, eating a solitary breakfast. Pulling up a chair, I sat down beside him. Moira soon joined us. Aunt Fanny, Uncle Cyril and Aunty Hilda where nowhere in sight and I thought this rather strange since Aunty Hilda rose early each day to take care of things around the farm.

"What's going on with Mummy and Daddy?" I asked Grandpa.

"Don't worry about it; just a storm in a teacup. It'll all blow over in a little while."

Radha served breakfast, but neither of us were very hungry.

"Eat up, you two," Grandpa urged. "Don't waste your porridge and eggs. Remember, you'll be back with the nuns soon enough and wishing you had some."

"We do have porridge for breakfast," Moira informed him, "but it's lumpy and the eggs are oily and the bread is dry and the bananas are black and squishy."

"Enough, enough—I get the picture! I have some lumps of sugar here in my pocket. Eat up and we'll go out and feed Cinnabar. You can each have a ride around the compound after that."

I never did find out what the quarrel was about, but was happy to find Mummy and Daddy sitting quietly beside one another that evening, holding hands. Things were back to normal.

Daddy caught the train to Delhi, promising to return and visit Granny again very soon. He looked sad and kept staring down at her, seated frail and deathly pale on an easy chair beside her bed.

"Be good, you two, and study hard. Especially you, Sarah," he warned sternly. "I don't want to see any more bad report cards, you hear?" I nodded mutely. He kissed us and, taking Mummy by the arm, followed Yusouf and Gulab, who were carrying the luggage down the avenue of trees that led to Stanton Station. I was relieved. No lectures, no beatings, no fuss.

A few days later we were awakened by a great hue and a cry in the back compound, as Meenakashi ran bawling into the house, calling out for Aunty in a strangled voice.

"What the bloody hell is going on around here?" Aunty came rushing out, nearly bowling the shivering Meenakshi over with the force of her exit. With tears flowing, Meenakshi cried out that the godown was empty.

"They've flown the coop!" Aunty exclaimed.

"Good riddance!" Uncle Cyril declared, joining them. "I don't see what all the fuss is about; we are well rid of that pair of thugs." Turning, he went back into the bedroom.

Mummy nodded in agreement.

Not wanting to be discovered, I huddled on the milking stool beside the kitchen table.

"What were you doing in the godown at this hour?" Aunty questioned Meenakshi. "And why are you crying so hard? Have they harmed you?"

She shook her head.

"I took them mugs of tea, which my mother gave me," she explained, blubbering. "The door was ajar and they were gone."

Shaking her roughly, Aunty ordered her to compose herself, but she continued sobbing uncontrollably.

"So they are gone. But why are you crying?" She looked puzzled for a moment. Realization suddenly dawned on her and she fixed Meenakshi with a knowing look. Something else was obviously the matter.

"Get Sonabhen!" she ordered to no one in particular.

In a fever of excitement, I dashed into the kitchen to obey her.

Grabbing Meenakshi by the arm, Aunty dragged her into the spare bedroom and slammed the door shut.

Returning with Sonabhen in tow, I heard loud voices, followed by a sharp slap. Uncle Cyril knocked on the door and demanded to be let in. Mummy, her face a mask of disgust, collapsed into one of the old cane chairs. I crept back to the milking stool.

We could hear Uncle Cyril's loud accusing tones: "Hilda, you are wholly to blame for this mess. First, you allow those two dacoits to remain here on the premises. Then you send this young girl in with food for that murderous pair. Something was bound to happen. So why beat her now? She is not at fault and neither is her mother. Sonabhen is busy in the kitchen all day attending to the meals and she takes direction from you. For God's sake, when does she ever get a chance to keep an eye on her daughter, working as she does from morning to night? As for her husband, that lazy oaf Pandurang, why, he's of no use whatsoever; he's horizontal most of the time. As I see it, the best way to resolve this problem is to rush the wedding plans. Hari will have his child, if my suspicions are correct, and he'll be a doting husband because she will have given him what no other wife could. So, enough of these dramatics. Let's get on with it, there's no time to waste!" He stomped out of the room and yelled for his morning tea.

"Cyril's got what it takes when the chips are down," I heard Mummy mutter under her breath.

Sonabhen, followed by a petrified Meenakshi, exited the room and made their way to the servants' quarters.

Dabbing her eyes, Aunty confided: "I'm afraid those two will be discovered by nightfall and strung up before you can say Jack Robinson. It won't be long before the inspector will get a whiff of them; his spies are everywhere."

Mummy nodded in agreement.

After that fateful day, I hardly ever set eyes on Meenakshi; she kept out of sight. One evening, after giving Granny her injection, Dr Pudumjee slipped into Sonabhen's quarters and discreetly closed the door. Radha, who was taking her ease in the back veranda, no doubt waiting for Gulab to return home from work, eavesdropped and the next morning, while braiding my hair, confided: "Meenakshi is with child. They are hurriedly making her marriage plans to cover the pregnancy."

"Who is the father?" I asked, wide-eyed.

"Guess."

I was dead curious to find out how this came about, but didn't dare ask.

Burhan took over the kitchen duties and Uncle Cyril was not happy about this new arrangement. Curry spices were ground too coarse, he complained, and Burhan rolled out his parathas with a heavy hand. Aunty informed him that he had better shut up and put up, since Sonabhen and her sister, Parvati, were busy with wedding arrangements. I did catch a glimpse of Meenakshi one afternoon. Bucket in hand, she was making her way to the well. On seeing me, she pulled the cowl of her sari low over her head and averted her eyes. I scampered off in the opposite direction.

Aunt Fanny had nearly finished the shawl she was crocheting for Granny, who grew sicker by the day. "You'll be off to school in a week's time, Sarah," she peered at me over her glasses. "I hope my old man doesn't visit with his sister too long; I'm getting tired and need to sleep in my own bed."

"I thought you didn't care about Uncle Melvin," I ventured boldly.

"Oh, but I do. There are different kinds of caring you know."

The day before the wedding, Moira and I watched as the servants and field hands assembled a *shamiyana*[116] in a clearing behind the house. Inside, they erected a stage on which was placed two rows of folding chairs with lanterns on either side. By afternoon bullock carts loaded with enormous cooking pots creaked into the compound. A makeshift kitchen was set up for the wedding cooks who came trooping in at dusk. They created quite a racket, bawling at their helpers and playing loud "filmi" music. Drawing buckets of water from the well, they made kettles of tea and smoked countless bidis. That night from my bedroom window, I watched the glow of their cooking fires as they prepared the evening meal.

"Who is paying for all this?" I asked Grandpa.

"Neither you nor I, so why worry?"

All was in readiness for the marriage.

At dawn the next day the wood fires were kindled. Enormous cooking pots brimming with quantities of mutton curry, dal and

116 *shamiyana* huge tent set up for weddings

vegetables simmered over them, sending tantalizing aromas floating through the morning air. Soon, scores of curious onlookers were drawn to the sight—with great guffaws they jostled one another and mingled freely with the invited guests, some of whom had arrived early. The scene resembled a village *mela*,[117] only the stalls and acrobats were missing.

That afternoon the groom arrived, riding into the compound on his marriage horse. His turban was braided with tassels of silver and gold that hung down over his eyes and glinted in the morning sun. Garlands were draped round his neck and covered his portly chest as well. The horse was led by a skinny youth in a braided uniform. He was followed by a band of young men playing on several musical instruments. They created one hell of a din, passing through the compound to the shamiyana erected behind the house; Grandpa called it "a veritable cacophony of sound." Enthusiastic clapping arose as the groom dismounted and entered the large tent. Our family was ushered in and offered seats at the front. The place was ablaze with lights from a hundred Petromax[118] lanterns. It was unbearably hot and the odour of attar mingled with sweat hung heavy in the air, as guests and inquisitive onlookers crowded in.

"Huzoor."[119] Hari bowed low and greeted Aunty Hilda and Uncle Cyril with palms folded together.

Meenakshi, her slight figure draped in a magnificent sari (a gift from Uncle Cyril and Aunty Hilda), weighed down with jewellery and garlands, found it difficult to climb the dais and had to be helped. The ceremony was performed and the celebrations began. When it was all over, Aunty heaved a sigh of relief as she and Uncle Cyril made their way back to the house, where they found Sonabhen and Pandurang waiting for them. Wiping away tears of gratitude, Sonabhen bent low and touched them on their feet. Aunty's face crumpled with emotion as she slowly helped her loyal servant up off the ground and embraced her.

"It is not necessary for you to do that. What happened was good—very, very good. You take your ease now for the next few days," she instructed her weary retainer. "Burhan and Yusouf will take care of

---

117   *mela* a fair
118   *Petromax* a pump kerosene lamp
119   *huzoor* a term of deference

things around the house." They salaamed us and disappeared in the direction of their quarters.

While tucking me into bed, Radha, with a knowing smile, declared the marriage a wonderful deliverance.

The next morning, Meenakshi departed with her husband for the village of Moorghao.

Waking early, I ran to Granny Connie's bedroom and found Grandpa fussing with her covers. We were leaving by the afternoon mail train for Bombay and I wanted to sit with her for a while. He bundled her in warm blankets, lifted her out of bed and carried her into the back compound. Setting her down on a recliner within sight of Aunty Hilda's rose bushes, he adjusted a Japanese parasol to shade her ravaged face from the sun. The morning air, filled with birdsong, smelled rich with the essence of life. I sat on the dewy grass beside her, happy to see her smiling down at me. Reaching for a few leaves from the lime tree, I crushed them in the palm of my hand and inhaled the citrus scent. Mixing them with a clump of earth and grass, I placed the lot in Granny's hand, but they sifted through her limp fingers. A sob escaped my lips, for in that moment I realized I would never see my grandmother alive again. Wrapping my arms around her, I clung to her thin shoulders.

Gently patting me on the back, she murmured, "There, there."

Moira joined us. Holding Granny very close, she repeatedly kissed her on the cheek.

"Petty Boo," Granny whispered, using her pet name for Moira. With tears running down her ravaged face, she held her close. I had always known that Moira was her favourite.

After a while Radha came out and hurried us inside to bathe and get dressed.

Wishing them all goodbye was a wretched experience and I renewed my resolve that day to always remain in one place when I grew up. Grandpa, looking tired and worn out, kissed us silently, but had no parting joke.

"Write, will you?" he whispered hoarsely, as he bent down to kiss me. "Think of me," his eyes pleaded.

Aunt Fanny handed us each another pair of socks.

Aunty Hilda and Uncle Cyril looked faded and expressionless, like shadowy figures in a negative. I felt like bawling just seeing them that way.

"Can we come back next year for Christmas?" I asked.

"Can we?" Moira echoed.

"If you like," Aunty whispered hoarsely. "I've packed tiffin for you all for the journey."

Hugging them, we ran out into the afternoon sun, following Mummy, Radha and two coolies carrying our baggage—down the avenue of trees that led to Stanton Station.

Clickety-clack down the track. Will I ever journey back?

"What's the matter?" I asked, gazing at Mummy as she leaned, wilting, against the leather compartment seat.

"I've had a wretched Christmas, Sarah," she sighed wearily, "and I'm feeling all washed up. Glad that's over and done with."

"Why?" I asked, incredulous.

"Well, Sarah, it's just that your father's side of the family tires me out. Too many comings and goings, too much confusion—they're loud, loud, loud."

"And I love them," I declared fervently.

"I know."

"I prefer them—" I bit my tongue.

"To whom?"

"To stuffy old Grandpa Reagan," I blurted out.

"Me too—" Moira nodded vigorously.

PART FIVE

Down-and-Outers

The new term started off in pretty much the same way as the last one did with piles of luggage scattered all over the dormitory and Sister Angelina clutching her endless lists, bellowing at us at the top of her voice, designating beds and lockers. Moira, happily reunited with her friend Jenny Wheeler, had no problem adjusting to the convent routine and I was glad of that—no more tears and snivelling. Our fag, Jane Woodman, however, seemed the worse for wear after the Christmas holidays. She had come down with a cold and fever and was laid up in bed for much of the time. Of course, being so thin and undernourished didn't help either—poor Jane, as skinny as a beanpole, kept blowing her dripping nose into sheets of toilet paper that shredded on contact. She rolled them into little balls and stuffed them into her pocket.

"Haven't you got a hankie?" I asked.

"No, Sarah; lend me yours."

"Here." I felt sorry for her. "Keep it."

"Ta."

Jane complained that Santa had not put in an appearance that year. "He just plain forgot us," she declared mournfully. "But Christmas breakfast was a treat with bacon and eggs and for dinner we had roast chicken and salad with sticky toffee pudding for dessert. Each of us girls got a new dress and a pair of sandals. We must be grateful, you know, for what God gives and not expect too much," she concluded, echoing the nuns.

A bright winter sun shone down, piercing the morning chill, and light breezes carried the scent of dung fire from the dhobi ghat in our direction. Jane sat hunched over on the top step of the dormitory, a cardigan pulled tight around her frail body. I was reminded of a nasty verse the bullies chanted whenever she passed by.

Plain Jane, skinny and white,
Gives us all a terrible fright.
With her spotty face all red and sore,
Plain Jane's a frightful bore.

"You don't believe in Santa Claus, d'you?" I inquired.

"We-l-l ..." she looked away.

"My Aunty Hilda says Santa's a lot of rubbish, but, of course, you can believe whatever you like; it's most probably what the silly sisters have told you, anyway. As for me, I know my parents arrange the whole Christmas thing and, in your case, it's the nuns. Who else is there? And that explains why you never got a gift this year; they just plain forgot you."

"I guess they did," she replied simply.

I had been cruel for no reason at all and immediately regretted it. Seeing her sad, pinched face, I suddenly felt awful, but it was too late to take back my words. She gazed at me with brimming eyes and my heart ached. Impulsively grabbing her by the arm, I insisted she sit still until I returned.

"Where are you going, Sarah?"

"Hold on; I'll be back in a minute."

Rushing into the dormitory, I hurriedly rummaged through the kit box stored under my bed, throwing clothes and linen about higgledy-piggledy. Finally, finding the bag of candies, I took from it a couple of packages of bull's eyes and chocolates, before racing out again.

"Here!" I exclaimed, dumping them in her lap. "See, I never forgot you. Bull's eyes and chocolates, all the things you asked for."

"Gee, Sarah Watkinson!" she exclaimed in disbelief. "Ta so much." Popping a chocolate into her mouth, she shivered with delight at the delicious sensation. "Gosh, they taste grand! You must have bought these at a first-class confectionery store; they're not stale or anything. Ta again!"

"I was saving some of my stash to share with the Moonlight Marys at our next meeting," I informed her, "but most of it was for you and Lynette."

"How was your Christmas by the way?" Jane asked, blinking up at me in the bright sunlight, a bull's eye rolling around in her mouth. She was gobbling them down at an incredible rate.

I didn't have the heart to tell her about my gifts, the sumptuous breakfast, lunch and dinner. However, I did speak of Granny's grave condition.

"Oh, Sarah, poor you. Is your Granny expected to die very soon?"

I nodded silently.

"I wish I had a Granny," she sighed wistfully. "I would spend a lot of time with her and I am sure she would knit me cardigans and socks like yours did."

"You most probably have one, Jane, only you don't know her."

"I guess you're right." She sneezed mightily into the handkerchief I had given her.

We sat for a while in companionable silence with thoughts of Mummy running through my mind. She had looked sad and distant the day we joined the batch at Victoria Station. I figured she was worried about a lot of things and Christmas at Aunty Hilda's had been rough on her, although I couldn't figure out why. Of course, Radha wept buckets. I was determined not to shed any tears and, after we said our goodbyes, I climbed into the compartment and sat silent and aloof throughout the journey. Moira, as usual, curled up beside me and went to sleep.

"What's the matter with you, Sarah Watkinson?" one of the batch had inquired. "Cat got your tongue?"

Refusing to take the bait, I turned away.

A fortunate thing, I was assigned a bed at the other end of the dormitory, quite far away from Vera Wainwright. I heard that she had requested a bed change.

Good riddance! Both Lynette and I agreed it was a stroke of luck. I was pretty sure Vera was Sister Angelina's spy, for she had begun to watch my every move towards the end of last term.

Finding myself back in the same grade after having failed the year, I was joyfully reunited with the other failures. Huddled at the back of the classroom, we chatted animatedly as the newly promoted ones entered, looking shy and suspicious. We ignored them.

"Book-bashers, the lot of 'em," Jemma Brown proclaimed, gazing scornfully in their direction. "I daresay they've been advised to steer clear of us." Jemma, a third-class boarder, got away with murder at every turn. She was often rude to Sister Griselda and Sister Celine declared her quite impossible at times, but they did nothing at all about it, just smiled good-naturedly, shook their heads and looked the other way. Watching her shenanigans, I often wondered how she managed it. A tomboy, Jemma had laughing green eyes, a turned up nose and long blond braids that hung down nearly to her waist. Short, athletic and wiry, she was up for any mischief we planned, but miraculously escaped the punishment meted out when we were discovered.

During the holidays I had made numerous resolutions to change my ways, to be obedient to the nuns and to study hard. But upon my return to school I discovered the nuns hadn't changed one iota and the same old rules were still in force at the convent. Besides, I was branded as a major troublemaker and so decided to live up to my name.

A copy of *Forever Amber* lay gathering dust on Aunty Hilda's bookshelf. I couldn't believe my eyes; the very thing I was looking for. Swiping it, I had placed it in my satchel that lay at the very bottom of the kit box, and it travelled with me to school undetected. At the first opportunity, I made for The Bower and hid my book on a shelf in Rumplestiltskin's cluttered garden shed. The next day, even though classes went ahead at a decent pace, I could hardly contain my excitement. When the bell clanged for games period, I bounded up the path, retrieved the book and settled down for a good read. Examining my prize, recalling how Mummy had taken every precaution to keep her copy away from me, I chuckled because Aunty Maggie, while reading it at the Serendipity Lodge, had shared segments of the story with Moira and me. She even planned to call her baby Amber, if it was a girl.

Golly, I thought, so much has happened since then. Aunty Maggie, baby Trevor and Danny Groat were now in England, well established in Felixstowe, no doubt. She hadn't written for ages, but I guessed that was because baby Trevor must be taking up all her time. Granny was deathly ill and Moira and I, separated from Mummy, Daddy and Radha, were alone and miserable, captives of the horrible nuns at Phulamar. Groaning, I crouched deeper into the bed of sweet, damp grass, wishing the earth would open up and swallow me whole and in so doing deliver me from the dreadful sisters.

Mummy had explained that every year the Church catalogued a list of books good Catholics should stay away from and it was a mortal sin to read a book from the list. Rifling through the pages, I wondered if *Forever Amber* was on the list and, if so, would I have to confess having read it to Father Murray? Not likely!

Set in England against the backdrop of the Restoration, the story chronicled the adventures of Amber St. Clare and her dashing lover,

Bruce Carlton. I had never read anything so bold and explicit in all my born days and was completely absorbed as the story flew off the pages and settled deep into my psyche. Transported to another place in time, reliving Amber's birth, her introduction to the city of London, her daring exploits, I devoured page after page, oblivious that dusk had fallen. Squinting into the book in the fading light, I resolved to bring my torch along the next evening. A bell clanged in the distance, breaking the silence. Was it calling us to study, or for dinner? I was confused.

Low-lying clouds obscured Moonface and night breezes brought with them a touch of damp. Scrambling, I hastily hid the book and made my way down the path to join the others assembled outside the refectory. Lordy! I had missed the entire study period and my absence had gone undetected. Shivering, I squeezed in beside Lynette.

"Sarah, where have you been?" she asked gruffly.

"None of your business; I was busy."

"Doing what?"

"Reading, silly. You know I'm hopeless on the games field."

"Sister Angelina was looking for you."

"And?"

"Well, she found Moira and gave her the letter, but she may still question you."

I was troubled at dinner and later, lying in bed, practiced a hundred different excuses in the event Sister cornered me the next morning. Fortunately, she didn't.

It was Saturday and since we were allowed an extra half-hour in bed, the bell clanged at six-thirty. Dressed in civvies, we lined up for breakfast after chapel. Freed from classes, we jostled each other and giggled uncontrollably. Sister Germaine, the tall angular one with huge mannish hands, strode by looking severe. Reaching the end of the line, she turned and faced us. Retrieving a sheet of paper from her pocket, she proceeded to read out a list of names, mine included.

"Step aside," she barked.

"You lot can go," she dismissed the others. "And you lot, follow me."

Bewildered, we obeyed. Lynette winked at me, but I was watching Moira—her eyes were studiously averted as she dragged her feet and moved with the others towards breakfast. I shrugged, uncaring.

Sister sailed on ahead, propelled by her starched wimple and flowing habit. We hurried behind her. Passing the "banquet hall," so named for the multiple courses habitually consumed therein by the good sisters, I noticed the gleaming mahogany doors were shut tight against prying eyes. This was the inner sanctum, where the nuns lived and prayed, planned and plotted. Peering in through the open door of Mother Valerian's office, I noticed it looked bright and cheery inside, hardly intimidating without her august presence. Shafts of morning sunlight streamed in through the glass-paned windows and rows of potted plants, resting on the sill, nodded gently in the morning breeze. Sister Germaine came to an abrupt stop at the chapel entrance and, turning, faced us.

"Mother Valerian has asked me to speak with you," she said severely. "She is fully aware of the main instigators and troublemakers here at the abbey and, since this is the beginning of a new term, she is determined to put an end to it. Amongst you there is a very disturbing element at work, constantly trying to undermine the authority of the nuns and impede the smooth running of the school. And, as for the rest of you, you follow the ringleaders like a flock of sheep lacking direction." She took a deep breath and fixed us with a steely gaze. I shuddered.

"Mother Superior will not hesitate to enforce discipline and, since most of you are familiar with her ways, I need say no more. She feels that a day of prayer and meditation is in order and will prove beneficial. So, follow me into the chapel where I would like you all to kneel in the very first row, in plain sight of your Creator. I am going to leave you here and it is my hope that you will take this opportunity to implore our Father in Heaven to show you the error of your ways and help you turn over a new leaf." With that she strode out, leaving us strung along the entire length of the pew like a decade of rosary beads.

Left to our own devices in the chapel lit by numerous white tapers and heavy with the scent of incense, we sat in awkward silence, gazing up at the magnificent altar. My thoughts wandered as I examined the statues of saints keeping a silent vigil in the darkened niches all around. Which one would I choose to intercede on my behalf? Who had the power to make me a better person? None of them, I decided. Instead, I resolved to continue praying to the Virgin of the Grotto who always smiled down on me. Besides, at that moment, prayer was the last thing on my mind, as my stomach growled and I began to feel the overpowering pangs of hunger. Maureen Standish, kneeling beside me, heard the rumblings in my belly and started to giggle. She was a fidget and couldn't sit still. Suddenly the missal fell from her hands and landed on the floor with a loud thud, which echoed through the chapel right up to its vaulted ceiling. Petrified, we waited expectantly for a nun to appear, but when no one did, we continued with our whispered conversations.

After what seemed like an eternity, Mother Valerian, entered, and ordered us all upstairs, since the letter-writing hour had begun. That meant breakfast and lunch had come and gone.

Moira grabbed me as I stepped out into the brilliant afternoon sunshine. "Here," she said, shoving a crumpled hankie at me. It held an oily fried egg wedged between two slices of bread.

"Where'd you get this from?" I asked, attacking it voraciously.

"Your breakfast," she replied; "I swiped it. Are you in loads of trouble?"

"Uh-huh."

She giggled. I put an arm around her shoulder and we went in to letter writing together.

The sandwich, however, didn't sit well in my tummy, so I asked to be excused and threw up in the lavatory. Back in study hall, staring down at the blank sheet of letter paper, I was at a loss for words and unable to write a thing. It was soon spattered with tears, crumpled and thrown in the wastepaper basket.

Vera Wainwright cornered me one evening after benediction. "Er, Sarah?"

"Yes."

"What's the matter with you; your face is all spotty?"

"None of your business," I replied, self-consciously touching my pimples. "Leave me alone."

"Okay, if you say so, but the nuns have got it in for you."

"How d'you know? Are you best friends with them?"

"I just know. Remember what I told you at the very beginning? You can get away with a lot if you're not noticed. Well, you have made yourself noticed and now they are out to get you. You're a troublemaker and an instigator. The rest of us have been warned to stay away from you."

These were Sister Germaine's very words.

"Why are you telling me this? What do you care, Vera Wainwright? I happen to know you are Sister Angelina's spy."

"Just watch it, is all I have to say." She darted away.

I confided in Lynette.

"She's out to frighten you, that's all. Someone must have put her up to it. By the way, Easter holidays are coming up and the parlour boarders will all be out of our hair. That weekend there's a meeting of the Moonlight Marys. You coming?"

"Count me in."

"We need a couple of chips for the kitty; there's something special planned. You got anything to spare?"

"Catch me on Saturday."

Resisting a trip to the tuck shop, I would give them my all.

The parlour boarders all departed for the Easter holidays, leaving the classrooms and playgrounds silent and empty. Freed of routine, the days were easy and carefree, since we were not required to attend classes or go for study. The only bells we answered were for meals, dormitory duties and chapel—always chapel.

Easter week commenced and with it the obligatory Lenten duties that required us to attend chapel twice every day and three times on Good Friday. My knees were wobbly and worn out from all the kneeling. In the sweltering heat, we followed Father Murray through the Stations of the Cross. Good Friday was a day of abstinence—breakfast was a cup of weak tea and a slice of toast. As the day progressed I began to fully appreciate how the down-and-outers felt, for this was their everyday fare. Rachel Kerr fainted during service that afternoon, landing with a thud on the marble floor. Mother Valerian looked severely in her direction, for she hated a scene in chapel. Sister Patricia rushed to Rachel. Grabbing a silver pitcher from the side altar, she splashed it over her face.

"A second baptism," I giggled.

"Yes, it's most probably holy water," Jenny Wheeler whispered back.

That night, after a meagre dinner of soup and a banana, I lay awake with the Latin prayers racing through my head. Lynette occupied the bed right next to mine, for we had planned on having a lengthy chat since the dorm was half empty. Sister Angelina was nowhere in sight; she was with the other nuns at chapel, reciting endless litanies, no doubt. All of a sudden I began to feel sick and light-headed and, turning to Lynette, moaned, "Ohmygawsh, I'm dying!"

"You are not, you silly goose," Lynette prodded me. "Spoiled, that's what you are. You're just very hungry and it's making you ill. Here, take a sip of water."

I did, but felt it rush right up again and I barely made it to the bathroom sink. After brushing my teeth, I gargled and returned to bed. Unfortunately our chat never materialized, for we fell into a drugged sleep after that, brought on by excessive heat and hunger.

Hot, hazy April winds gathered up the dry leaves and swept them against the convent walls. Afternoon heat was unbearable, but by evening Phulamar, a hill station, cooled down, making it comfortable for sleeping at night. The Moonlight Marys skipped out of the dormitory as soon as it was safe to do so. They assembled beneath the tamarind tree, clutching pillows or trailing sheets and counterpanes behind them. Strange rustling, chirruping sounds emerged from within the branches above, as fruit bats and other nocturnal creatures feasted on the ripening tamarind. Wisps of clouds drifted below a pale Moonface, who smiled down at us from a starry sky.

We sat in a tight circle. I searched the faces round me and discovered they were all there, the same ones from our last meeting: Cybil Winters, Glynis Sullivan, Malvina Cross, Arlene Morrison, Jenny Wheeler and Jemma Brown, her golden hair free of braids, streaming down past her shoulders. Cybil cleared her throat and spoke.

"Girls, after the Cambridge exams this year both Glynis and I will be leaving the convent and that just leaves you, Malvina, to head up the Moonlight Marys." She smiled at the tall, pale girl sitting across from her. Sedate, with very little to say, Malvina displayed a quiet assurance that inspired trust. I caught her watching me with sad knowing eyes one morning at assembly, as Mother Valerian raked me over the coals. Our paths did not cross often, but whenever she was near I felt her friendly presence. She bobbed her head in acceptance.

"I am pretty sure that by the end of the year there will be more of us," continued Cybil. "Remember, when you nominate someone to join the group, that you are sure she will fit in. After all, we are a very privileged lot. The first-class boarders do not and will never understand us. Except for you, Sarah Watkinson, you seem to fit right in."

I smiled sheepishly.

"Where will you go?" asked Arlene Morrison.

"Both Glynis and I will travel to Bombay, where the nuns have arranged accommodation for us in the Mother House. The shorthand, typewriting course we were told takes a little over a year and after that I suppose we'll find jobs, settle down and maybe even get married." She smiled shyly.

"Ooh, married," teased Jemma.

Missus what's-her-name—
Where do you live?
Down the lane.
What number?
Cucumber.

We broke into peals of laughter at Jemma's silly rhyme.

"Hush, don't be giddy, this is a serious matter. Many of us don't know too much about what goes on beyond these convent walls. I can't remember the last time we were invited to the Mother House for holidays and then too we were never left alone, but always escorted everywhere by the nuns. I think it's going to be a wonderful experience to be left alone to discover the world for ourselves, don't you, Glynis?"

"My aunty in Bombay," Glynis joined in, "says we can go over to her house for lunch every Sunday. She has a radio and a gramophone with tons of records."

"For coconut rice and ball curry?" Jemma rolled her eyes. Her laughter was infectious. We were brought to order again by Cybil.

"The years spent at the convent have been harder for some of us than others. You, Arlene, still have your mother and can go home for holidays at least once a year. Lynette, Jemma and Jane never leave this place. Neither do Malvina and I. The nuns have been our parents, for better or for worse, and we have had to put up with them and they with us. I will be sad to leave and most of all I'll miss you, my sisters, who are my family. These have been my best times, spent here under the Mother tree together with you, my Moonlight Marys."

Caught up in the moment, my eyes misted over. We held hands

and silently vowed to always be there for each other. Lynette started bawling uncontrollably and so did Jenny Wheeler. Breaking the circle, the pair of them went and sat on either side of Cybil who hugged them. I saw the tears roll down her cheeks.

"We have a special treat planned for tonight." Malvina regained her composure. "Thanks to all those who pitched in, we were able to pay the baker for several loaves of bread that I have here. And thanks to those unnamed Marys who raided the tuck room, we have plenty of good things to eat it with." Spreading a towel, she spilled the contents of a pillowcase onto it. Cans of cheese and butter, bottles of jam and condensed milk, boxes of biscuits and chocolates fell out, followed by oohs and aahs. This was a considerable haul and now I didn't mind so much not having shared my chocolates and sweets with them— Jane and Lynette got the lot. Arlene, busy with a tin cutter, efficiently removed the tops from all the cans. Both she and Jane produced knives and spoons they had nicked from the refectory. Hunks of bread were passed around and magically all the sadness disappeared as we tucked in to what was to be a feast to remember.

I pictured the sullen faces in the refectory when the parlour boarders returned from their Easter holidays and discovered their tuck boxes had been ransacked. Sister Griselda, though, would give them scant sympathy. I believed she was secretly on the side of the down-and-outers and may have been one herself, for she never investigated the mysterious disappearances. Recalling some of her comments, I smiled to myself.

"You're sure now that you didn't eat it all? You certainly look as if you have.

"So, your tuck's been stolen, has it? Now why do I find that difficult to believe?"

And, best of all: "Maybe the rats got in. Are you sure you locked up the last time you were there?"

Her remarks always caused a ripple of laughter amongst the down-and-outers, consuming their meagre rations at the other end of the refectory. I wondered how much had been filched from our tuck box, Moira's and mine. Guiltily, I hid a package of biscuits and a large portion of cheese in my pillowcase to share with her.

Cybil looked over at me. "Sarah, has Vera spoken to you?"

"Yes," I replied, taken aback. I had no idea Vera was even aware of the existence of the Moonlight Marys. But, then again, she had been at the abbey for ages and was privy to everything that was going on.

"Good. You and Lynette are seeing entirely too much of each other, getting up to all kinds of mischief I hear, upsetting the nuns. You don't want to be drawing too much attention to yourselves. Otherwise, life will become unbearable for you. In future, I don't want to see you line up beside Lynette on the way to class, nor sit next to her in the study hall. Please, please do remain friends, but control yourselves.

"As for you, Jemma, I don't suppose Mother Valerian has taken you to task about your unruly behaviour?"

"No, she hasn't," Jemma replied boldly.

"What?" I turned in amazement to Lynette.

Lowering her head, Lynette whispered, "Jemma is Mother's favourite, her fag, sort of. She tidies Mother's room and fetches for her. Mother braids Jemma's hair on Saturdays and buys her clips, ribbons and things. Jemma can do no wrong. And that's the truth, Sarah; that's the way it is."

I had long suspected Jemma was a favourite.

"Does Mother know she's a Moonlight Mary?"

She shrugged. "Jemma can get away with anything, but don't get too upset, she's on our side."

The meeting broke up and we made our way back to bed. I had learned a lot and my mood was pensive. Lying awake in the half-empty dormitory, I let my thoughts drift to Stanton Station and last Christmas—to Granny, Aunty Hilda and Aunt Fanny. I prayed that Granny's health would improve, even though in my heart I knew she was dying. Longing for that carefree life away from boarding school with its drudgery and its politics, I drifted off to sleep with the scent of smouldering buffalo pats in my nostrils and dreamed of Maisie, Maud and Esmerelda.

Dressed in our Sunday best, we attended a fete held on the cathedral grounds. Sister Germaine herded us into a line and we left the convent with her in the lead, walking briskly ahead.

"Keep your eyes in front of you; look neither to your left nor to your right," she instructed in a gruff voice.

Happy to be out and about, oblivious of the heat, Moira trotted on ahead with Jenny Wheeler, while I brought up the rear, one of the stragglers, cavorting with my chums, all of us chattering like magpies. Not a leaf stirred in the trees above and the street was deserted with the exception of a few pariah dogs lolling in the dust. A crow cawed, jarring the early evening stillness. We passed a couple of tonga wallahs sitting in a circle on their haunches, chatting, smoking bidis and drinking tea. Their emaciated horses fed from a stack of hay nearby. Huge bluebottles buzzed around the mounds of horse dung, the odour of which, coupled with the acrid stench of bidi smoke, stung the nostrils. Sister Germaine pressed a kerchief to her nose, but the rest of us walked on, uncaring, accepting the smells as natural to the surroundings. Turning the corner onto the main road that led to the cathedral, I watched as lethargic shopkeepers leisurely rolled up their shutters and began setting up for evening business.

All of a sudden a group of men emerged from out of a side gully and quickly spread across the road. Half-naked and writhing with religious fervour, they beat themselves with switches and chains. Sister Germaine froze. Moving rapidly, she tried desperately to shield us from the sight, but we peered out at them, fascinated. Dust billowed as they churned the parched earth with their frenzied feet. Some of them fell delirious to the ground, but were hastily helped up and continued chanting and thrashing themselves. In a flash, a lithe, animal figure sprang out from their midst and landed on his feet with perfect feline grace. His entire body was marked like a leopard and he wore a mask over his face. Strange guttural sounds came from deep within him as he grimaced and pranced about on all fours. We stood rooted to the ground. The wind picked up, blowing in our direction sporadic gusts of blistering heat, which scorched my face and neck. Looking over at Sister Germaine, I was sure she suffered much more than any of us. Her plain Irish face was beet red with beads of perspiration trickling down the side of her wimple. The mole beside her nose quivered uncontrollably. Making a rapid sign of the cross, she ordered us in a hoarse voice to stay clear of the road until the party had moved on. A few chokras with sticks brought up the rear, doing their own imitation of the flagellants. Rolling their eyes, whirling around like dervishes, they laughed excitedly when they caught sight of us.

"Faith and begorra!" a thoroughly unsettled Sister Germaine cried out. "Straight ahead to the church, girls, step to it!" she ordered. "And keep your eyes on the road. Since this is your day of outing, after benediction we will visit the fete for a short while, but by six o'clock I want to see you all assembled at the entrance of the church. In this way, we will be safely back in the abbey by dusk." She was clearly unnerved.

Meeting a day scholar friend at the fete, I excitedly recounted our adventure, but she was unimpressed.

"Ah! It was nothing, just a party of Muslims preparing for *Mohurrum*.[120] Don't be silly, Sarah Watkinson, you know they wouldn't harm you."

"But why were they thrashing themselves?" I asked.

"For penance," she stated simply.

Sister Angelina distributed the mail every evening before games period. Since my birthday was fast approaching, I hung around on the lookout for cards and letters, but nothing arrived. I was just about to give up hope when I heard my name called out and Sister handed over an envelope addressed to me in a strange scrawl that I didn't recognize. It was a letter from Aunty Hilda, into which she had folded a five rupee note.

"To our darling Sarah on her birthday," the letter read. "Enclosed is a small gift towards the purchase of a sweet treat. I pray you are being a good girl and studying hard. How is Moira? I hope she has given up the bad habit of sucking her thumb. We missed you both after the Christmas holidays. Attend to your studies, dear girl, and don't give the good sisters any reason to get angry with you. Our united love to both of you, from all of us here at Stanton Station—Grandpa Cliffy, Granny Connie, Uncle Cyril and Aunty Hilda."

I was surprised. How did she know about my birthday? Had Grandpa told her?

It brought them all vividly back to me. Folding the letter and placing it back in the envelope together with the money, I made for The Bower and there, crouched behind the grotto, bawled like a baby. Aunty Hilda had made no mention of Granny's condition and I hoped that was a good sign. Why had Grandpa not written? He never forgot my birthday. I wouldn't have cared if there was no money in his letter. In an effort to change my mood I tried to read, but it was useless, I

---

120 *Mohurrum* Muslim festival

couldn't concentrate and ended up spending the entire games period feeling sad and dejected.

My birthday arrived and still nothing from Mummy. Moira had her theory.

"I think she's punishing you, Sarah, for being a troublemaker. The nuns must have spilled the beans and now you've got nothing for your birthday."

"I do so have," I replied defiantly.

That evening Jane and I spent Aunty Hilda's entire gift at the tuck shop. I shared my bounty with her, Lynette and Moira.

Forever Amber was proving to be a most absorbing novel. As a matter of fact, it was so engrossing I quite forgot myself in class one afternoon and cried out "Lord Carlton" instead of Lord Cornwallis during the history lesson. Miss Price glared at me.

Mummy found Queen Elizabeth very lovely and, I suppose, she was, but with dull old George on the throne and not a trace of scandal about, I would have preferred to belong to the English court in the time of Charles II. Born in the wrong place at the wrong time, I thought. The Restoration was the place to be, a romantic and exciting period in British history, when a vixen like Amber St Clare with her womanly wiles could get away with murder. I fancied her looking like Elizabeth Taylor with violet eyes and a double row of lashes. Yes, Amber was most definitely she.

"Sarah Watkinson … Hang on …" A breathless Arlene Morrison tackled me on the way to lunch. "Sister Angelina is looking all over for you; she wants you right away in the dormitory."

"Why?" I asked nervously. "What did I do?"

"Dunno, but she asked me to tell you to come right over."

I found Sister overseeing a pair of convent ayahs as they swept away the cobwebs from the crevices and corners of the dormitory.

"Ah, Sarah, there you are. A parcel has arrived for you from home." She handed me a fairly large package covered in cotton cloth with my name and the school address neatly printed on. I recognized Mummy's handwriting.

"I want you to take it over to Sister Griselda immediately and she will place it in the tuck room for you. You may open it at the dinner hour. Now, hurry along or you'll be late for lunch."

Turning, she walked rapidly over to the ayahs and, after giving them further instructions, departed. I watched her disappear in the direction of the music rooms.

Placing the package on my bed and examining it at length, I was in two minds whether to take it over to Sister Griselda or not. I decided not. After all, I had spent the last few weeks in feverish anticipation, waiting for something to arrive from home and, now that it finally had, it hardly seemed fair that I should have to turn it over to a silly old nun. Mummy had sent no card, nor made any mention of the parcel in her letters. This was a complete and absolute surprise. Tears of happiness spilled down my cheeks and I decided this couldn't wait.

Taking a pair of scissors from my locker, I cut away the cloth covering, revealing a roughly-hewn wooden box hammered together with nails. I pried it open and in the process littered the area around my bed with pieces of wood and packing straw. A letter addressed to me lay right on top. Stuffing it into the locker drawer, I decided to read it later, as the contents of the parcel spilling out on the bed claimed all my attention. There was a bottle each of guava jelly and gooseberry jam, a can of cheese, two cans of condensed milk and a package of jujubes. Gloating, I imagined the look of surprise on Moira's face when I showed her the treats. Unmindful of all around, I sank down on the bed to savour the moment.

Feeling a pair of eyes boring into my back, I turned and looked straight into the furious face of Sister Angelina.

"You! You disobedient little wretch," she shrilled.

I backed away. The ayahs nervously exited the dormitory.

"Didn't I tell you to take that parcel over to Sister Griselda?"

I nodded.

"And you chose to deliberately disobey me. Why? Answer me!"

I made no reply.

"You army brats are all alike, horrible, undisciplined creatures," she yelled. "Forever upping stakes and moving with your parents from pillar to post like gypsies, you know nothing of stability. Finally, not knowing what to do with you, they pack you off to boarding school and we nuns are given the responsibility of educating you and teaching you manners." She spat the words out at me.

"Sister, my parents pay fees and Moira and I are first-class boarders." I stood up to her. But my insolence only served to enrage her even further and, picking up a plank of packing wood with sharp nails protruding at one end, she laid it with a will on my back and legs. "No, Sister! No! Please!" I pleaded, but, having worked herself into a fury, she didn't hear me. The plank came down repeatedly and the sharp nails caught my uniform, ripping it to shreds in several places. I fell, cowering to the floor, as the blows rained down on my back. Finally, flinging the weapon aside, she strode out of the dormitory without a word.

Crouched between the beds with my face in my hands, I sobbed uncontrollably for what seemed like an eternity. Then, rising with shaky legs, I made my way to the rear of the dormitory and exited through the back door.

A grove of ancient trees covered the slopes leading up to the classrooms. On holidays we spent many pleasant afternoons playing hide-and-go-seek beneath the canopy of their entwined branches. Now they beckoned, cool and inviting, an oasis of solitude. Sinking down, I leaned against the trunk of a giant jackfuit and examined the welts that covered my body. The skin was bruised and cut in several places with blood trickling down. Hastily I dabbed the abrasions with a tear-stained handkerchief.

Afternoon classes came and went. Uncaring, I spent the entire time with my eyes closed, dozing, dreaming, waiting—waiting for what, I didn't really know. Evening shadows shrouded the blighted day, the dinner bell clanged and a light, switched on outside the refectory radiated through the darkness. Rising slowly, painfully, I dusted myself off and joined the others shuffling in for the evening meal. But the plate of stew did not tempt me, it remained cold and untouched until Moira leaned over and asked if I was hungry. Shaking my head, I shoved it towards her. Quickly exchanging plates, she polished off my portion.

Back at the dormitory that night, I noticed all evidence of the afternoon had been cleared away—contents of the parcel, pieces of wood and straw were all gone. My counterpane was folded and placed at the foot of the bed and the mosquito net was neatly tucked under. Past caring and with a face on fire, my back and legs covered in welts, I trembled feverishly. Undressing was a painful task. Crawling beneath the covers, I found oblivion, falling into a deep, dreamless sleep.

Awakening in the infirmary with Sister Patricia peering down at me, I gazed in perplexity at my changed surroundings.

"Ah! There you are, Sarah. We were worried about you. The doctor is here to see you."

I looked up at her in confusion.

Tubby old Doctor Hudson, his stethoscope dangling around his neck, peered down at me through horn-rimmed glasses. Slipping a thermometer into my mouth, he removed it after a minute or two and declared I had a high fever.

"Some of those cuts and abrasions on her back and legs have become infected. I've dressed them and given her an injection, but it will take time to act. Sister, please arrange for a sponge bath, but be careful she doesn't catch a chill. She's burning up and we must bring the fever down. You can't be too careful in these cases. By the way, have the parents been notified? She's quite a sick girl."

Sister mumbled and I didn't catch her inaudible reply.

How long had I been laid up in bed? I felt it was useless to ask. I drifted in and out of delirious slumber as the days merged one into the other and a dreadful lassitude descended. Clinkers from the bowels of the earth bore through the covers and set my body afire as I lay pinned to the bed. Drenched with perspiration, I felt helpless as Sister Patricia and the infirmary ayah cooled my burning body with cologne-scented towels. Night winds rushed through the infirmary, wildly tossing the curtains and billowing the mosquito netting. Everything appeared strange and distorted. Feeling hot and cold by turns, I burrowed deep under the blankets and lay shivering there for hours when the ague seized me. Was it winter already? I wondered. Had I slept all summer long? Questions without answers raced through my fevered brain as I tossed and turned in uneasy, restless slumber. Feeling the sharp prick of a needle in my arm, I slept.

"Good morning, Sarah." It was Sister Patricia's gentle voice I recognized, smiling weakly up at her.

"There's someone here to see you."

Moira, her lips quivering, peered down at me.

"Hello, Sarah; are you feeling better?"

"I'll leave you two to visit," Sister said, moving away to the other end of the infirmary.

"What happened to you?" Moira asked. "How did you get so sick?"

"How long have I been here, Moira?" I croaked.

"Oh! I don't know, for days and days, two weeks perhaps. I took Mummy's letter from your locker and read it. She mentioned a parcel. Where is it, Sarah? Did you eat it all up? And is that why you're sick?"

I shook my head.

"Who has it?"

"Don't know."

"What d'you mean, you don't know?" She stared at me in disbelief.

"I don't."

"They wouldn't let me come see you at first, but today Sister Patricia said I was allowed. Jane and Lynette are not permitted near this place and neither is Jenny. Pity you can't remember where the tuck is," she continued, perching on a high stool, swinging her legs that didn't quite reach the floor. I was poor company, however, so after an interval of uneasy silence, she hopped off and, promising to come again the next day, dashed out into the afternoon sunlight.

A few days later I spotted Daisy, the convent hairdresser, coming towards me with a wheelchair. She had her apron on with scissors and combs in the pocket.

"I going to cut your hair," she proclaimed. "You get better very soon. Mother Valerian says long hair taking all strength from the body. You need strength."

I was too weak to object.

Wheeling me out onto the back veranda, she draped a sheet around me and deftly proceeded to give me a short bob. I watched as my long dark braids fell to the stone floor to be swept away by the matherani, who gathered them up in a pan and deposited them in the dustbin.

However, cropped hair did not have the desired effect, for I hovered on the precipice for what seemed like an eternity. Eventually, cuts and abrasions healed, closing over, but a low fever persisted as emotional scars lingered. A different sort of poison had taken hold and was slow to relinquish my body. I longed for my parents, Radha and the farm. Feeling Granny Connie's presence, I reached out to her. Elusive, she drifted off into the long, whispering night. Amber St Clare, an apparition in silk, cavorted with Bruce Carlton, who flung a velvet purse of Spanish doubloons in her direction.

During my waking hours I was aware of Doctor Hudson and Sister Patricia's continual ministrations. Ayah fed me soup and refreshed my burning limbs with her sponges.

Tossing and turning beneath the covers, casting them off and then drawing them back up to my chin again as the fever gripped me, I hovered in a state of limbo.

Awakening late one evening, I sat up in bed. Searching the clear night sky, I spotted Moonface sailing past, pale, gold and radiant. She was magical and I recognized the healing properties in her rays pouring down, which drew me to her like a magnet. Loosening the tie of my night dress and slipping it away from my shoulders, I pressed my body against the barred window, inviting her silvery beams to penetrate as I breathed in the night air. An owl hooted and winged past on its way to some unknown destination. Pye-dogs howled in the distance and beneath me I felt the earth shift. Falling in a swoon back into bed, I reached for the tumbler of water on the nightstand and heard her call my name, "Sa-a-rah," with the *a* drawn out, and then "Sa-a-rah," again. It was Celia Stevens, floating in a gown of pristine white outside my window, her pale face pressed against the bars, her dark, haunted eyes pleading. "Let me in," she implored; "please let me in." I froze and instantly fainted, dead away.

The next morning Sister Patricia beamed as she read the thermometer. My fever had broken. Soon I would be able to enjoy a breakfast of bacon and eggs with fried bread on the side, she teased. My stomach lurched at the thought, but I smiled weakly up at her.

"It's been weeks and weeks, Sarah, but you've rallied and I'm so proud of you." She plumped the pillows, asking if I felt like sitting up in bed. I nodded. I felt listless, but my brow felt cool to the touch and my spirits were lifted.

Cybil Winters paid me a visit a few days later. I was feeling better and rose on unsteady legs to greet her. I wondered how she had come to know that I was in the infirmary. It certainly wasn't Moira—maybe it was Lynette, or Jane.

"Oh, Sarah, you look so pale and pulled down. How are you feeling?"

"Much better, thank you." I smiled weakly at her.

"We were all worried about you. Sister Patricia said it was touch and go for a while there. It's all over the abbey what happened; one can't keep a secret in this place. I'm here primarily to see you and to find out if there's anything at all I can do. If there's something you'd like to confide, go ahead, I can assure you it won't go any further. And if you'd like to send a letter to your mummy, that can be arranged as well. You don't have to worry; the nuns won't get their hands on it. I'll have it posted on the outside through a day scholar."

"How did I get here?" I asked.

"Sister Germaine carried you over. Old Angel came and got her. She's banished, of course, to God only knows where. Mother Valerian was stewing for days after that, but things have calmed down since."

I looked away in silence.

Impatiently rising, Cybil grabbed a hand mirror from the dressing table and shoved it in my face.

"Look." she said, "you're as pale as a ghost. Sister Patricia tells me ayah has to force feed you. Do you want to die here?"

"Celia came to me, you know," I whispered.

She gaped at me, wide-eyed.

"She asked me to let her in, but I fainted."

"Dear Jesus! Of course she would. This is her bed you've been lying in. She spent a lot of time in the infirmary and particularly liked this spot beside the window. From here she could look out at the banyan tree and watch the langurs up to all kinds of tricks. They made her laugh. Would you like a bed change?"

"No. Celia was dressed in a gown of white, pure and simple. Cybil, the nuns should not have buried her in unhallowed ground. Who were they to judge her? She looked like an angel, although a troubled one."

"Poor, poor Celia." Cybil gazed out of the window with a faraway look in her eyes. "They tried so hard to save her, Sister Patricia especially. She, poor dear, spent so many sleepless nights beside this very cot, but nothing helped. I guess it was just meant to be. Don't let her spirit bother you, Sarah; I know she haunts the abbey. There have been sightings of Celia all over the place, and why not? This was the only home she knew. I hope she is resting in peace, poor girl, although I sometimes wonder.

Her short life was marred by so much unhappiness—the obsession with Father John Rider, the child she conceived but never bore. By burying her in unconsecrated ground, the nuns consigned her soul to limbo like a common criminal. It was all too much really and I wouldn't blame her if she haunts them at night. But rest easy, she would in no way harm you. Celia was a gentle creature who never wished anybody ill. If she comes to you again, ask what she wants; maybe she'll confide in you. I just know you are strong, much stronger than she ever was, and you are on the mend. Now, what about that letter? Would you like me to send it?"

"You can if you wish. By the way, how are Lynette and Jane? And why are they not allowed to come and see me?"

"Lynette and Jane cannot visit you, Sarah, I'm sorry. The nuns won't allow them. Sister Patricia is a special friend of mine and that is why I was able to sneak over. Does Moira have your home address?"

I nodded.

"I'm going to drop your mummy a line and tell her that you've been deathly ill. I'll swear her to secrecy, of course. The nuns will never inform your parents; they're hoping you'll get better soon and the whole thing will blow over. Rukhmani's niece, Asha, told me what happened in the dormitory; she saw it all."

"Is Rukhmani's niece one of the ayahs?" I asked.

"Yes, but the nuns don't know that."

"What about the parcel? I received a parcel from home and that was what all the fuss was about. Can you get the tuck back and give it to Moira?"

"You've found your voice, Sarah," she grinned at me. "There's nothing like a bit of tuck talk to get a hungry boarder going, eh?"

We chuckled together at the truth of it.

"At this time I would rather not ask too many questions; we don't want the nuns getting suspicious. As it is they are jumpy and things haven't been easy for some of us third-class boarders. They tend to take it out on those they don't like when the going gets rough. In the meantime, I would like you to eat all your meals and get strong, or you'll wither away in this place. You hear me?"

I nodded.

Rising, she hugged me, her eyes moist. "You look even skinnier with your hair all shorn off."

Back at the dormitory, a new nun, Sister Bertha, was placed in charge of the first-class boarders. Upon my discharge from the infirmary, she walked over and tucked me under the covers.

"You're to stay in bed for the next little while and you can read if you like. Ayah will bring your meals to you and mind you eat everything. I want no fussing; you need to get your strength back," she admonished in a no-nonsense manner. "We'll discuss getting back into a regular routine next week." With that, she hurried out of the dormitory.

And so it was that I did whatever I pleased for the next week and, when the week was over, attended classes sporadically, returning to the dorm for a lie-down every afternoon. There seemed to be no set routine for me at this point. The nuns were accommodating and I think in a quandary, wondering how best to deal with my situation. Filled with loneliness and boredom since my friends Lynette and Jane avoided me and even Moira on occasion turned and looked the other way when she saw me coming, I soon left reality behind and retreated into the murky recesses of my mind. Deciding the nuns were watching all the time, giving me plenty of rope to hang myself, I resolved to outwit them. Plodding through school days, staying away from The Bower, never speaking out, I gave them no cause to challenge my behaviour. We were both on guard.

As time passed, I grew stronger. Soon I was attending classes and chapel regularly. Of course I failed miserably in all subjects, but was never taken to task about bad marks. Leading a charmed life, I dozed in study hall, ate what I pleased and in general did pretty much what I wanted. Handing over the keys of the tuck box to Moira, since food repelled me, I gave her free reign. Mummy continued to write her weekly letters and I wondered if she had received anything from Cybil, but dared not ask. Dear Jane, saying very little, continued to fag for us, doing countless extras for which I never could pay her enough. Lynette now had a new best friend, though sometimes I caught her watching me from the other side of the classroom with sad, troubled eyes. Jemma, on the other hand, being Jemma, cared nothing about what others thought and, placing her arm through mine one evening, walked with me to chapel.

Awaking from a nap a few days later, I was surprised to see her face beaming down at me. Tugging at the covers with an impish grin, she asked, "Sarah, old chum, can you talk?"

"Uh-m-m." I stretched. "Fancy seeing you here, you should be in study hall. What d'you want, Jemma?"

"Not a thing. Just thought I'd pay you a little visit, that's all. The others are scared and it's like you hexed the nuns as well; they're afraid, too, in case you fall ill again and die like Celia Stevens, but in your case it will be worse. Celia was an orphan, so it was easy to hush the whole thing up, but you're different, you have parents. Lordy! I can imagine what a fuss they would make if anything happened to you in this place. They might bring the police in and then the nuns would all be locked up. Can you imagine them in jail, having to eat bread and water for the rest of their lives?"

Peals of laughter echoed through the empty dorm.

"I can't," I shook my head. "Imagine Mother Valerian being caned for insubordination and Sister Griselda slim as a reed?"

"By the way, Cybil sent the letter."

"Oh! You know?"

She shrugged. "That's the message."

"Hurry up and get better, Sarah, and then we can have loads of fun. I know it must be a pain and you're missing your mummy and daddy, aren't you? See, I don't know what that feels like, since I've only had to deal with the nuns all of my life. This is my home. I have an aunty and uncle in Poona who I sometimes visit during the summer holidays, but they don't feel like family to me. They're just people I see occasionally, for a change. They don't write to me or anything. It must be wonderful to have a real family. I plan to have a husband and lots of children one day," she said longingly. "Tell me, why do you sleep so much? Are you still feeling weak?"

Picking the lint from my flannel nightdress, I nodded. "This old thing keeps me warm and comfortable when I get cold."

"Cheer up. You know we are all rooting for you. The Moonlight Marys are, at any rate. And now I must run along and bash the books. So ta-ta for the time being." With pigtails flying, she darted out of the dorm.

I started sneaking up to The Bower again during games period, but it was not to read, since *Forever Amber* had lost its charm. (It would be several years before I picked up the book again, to read it from cover to cover.) I found comfort amongst the flower beds, where butterflies fluttered and heavy-headed dahlias nodded in the evening breeze. Burrowing into the soft, dark earth, I whiled away the time reflecting on the events of the past week.

My cuts and abrasions healed, leaving scars that ran along buttocks and thighs like fine tendrils. But a heaviness of heart persisted, which, for some uncanny reason, I began to associate with Celia Stevens. Occupying her bed those many weeks, I wondered, had I absorbed some of the pain she suffered during the last tormented days of her life? Baggage that even in death continued to weigh her down and which she sought so desperately to cast off. On that pale moonlit night when I had bared my chest to Moonface, she had appeared and pleaded to be let in. Had my spirit unwittingly reached out and drawn her in, thereby setting her free to find another brighter existence? If so, I was glad of it, for being stronger I could wrestle her demons to the ground. But for now they sapped my strength, leaving me feeling dull and disoriented sometimes. I couldn't speak to anyone about it, for I didn't know a soul who would understand. I would have to continue living this strange detached existence between the real and spiritual world.

By the middle of May the heat was unbearable. Classes were cancelled and we were herded into the dormitory for a nap every afternoon. Sprinkling water on our baking sheets, we lay down on them in an effort to cool off, but nothing worked. The sun, a blazing sphere, shone down each day from a pale, washed-out sky. Tempers flared as the nuns, covered from head to toe in their flowing white habits, felt the heat more intensely than we did. The down-and-outers bore the brunt of their discomfort, as canings and other punishment increased, and the food they were served was inedible—coarse-grained rice that was poorly husked, overripe bananas, tasteless dal mixed with pumpkin, leathery chapatis and mouldy bread. Flies settled on everything and I pushed my plate away in disgust. Even Moira lost her appetite. I was pretty sure, though, that the heat wave would not last since Phulamar, a hill station, was known for its temperate climate.

And I was right. One morning we awoke to gusting winds that blew the branches of the trees around wildly, bending them down almost to the ground. Dark clouds, pillows of rain, banked the horizon, hanging low over the distant hills. Lightning streaked across the sky and the trembling world waited, anticipating the deluge.

When the rain came pelting down in huge droplets, burrowing into the parched earth, howling winds moaned through the trees and twisted them in a mad dance of joy. I watched in wonder as a forked whip of lightning crackled and leapt across the sky. Coming down in sheets, it poured nonstop, drumming on the dormitory's corrugated roof for a whole day and into the night.

The next morning a watery sun filtered through the clouds, bringing with it a delightful scent of renewal, as the damp, moist earth released a dark and delicious odour, somewhat like chocolate cake. Ignoring the bell, I slept through chapel and abstained from classes. Since nobody cared, no one came looking for me. Creeping out at midday, I wandered through the grove behind the dormitory and found it strangely quiet there. For trees and foliage, saturated with moisture, the greening had begun. Uncaring, I squatted down upon the rain-soaked earth and wallowed in its steamy scent, like a buffalo in a swamp on a midsummer afternoon. Mosquitoes sang in my ears and I swatted a few. I had brought along a book of Wordsworth's poetry and was soon engrossed in one of his baffling "Lucy" poems.

> She dwelt among the untrodden ways
> Beside springs of Dove,
> A Maid whom there were none to praise
> And very few to love:
>
> A violet by a mossy stone
> Half hidden from the eye!
> Fair as a star, when only one
> Is shining in the sky.
>
> She lived unknown, and few could know
> When Lucy ceased to be;
> But she is in her grave, and, oh,
> The difference to me!

Wordsworth could have been writing about Celia Stevens. Memories of her came rushing back to me. Making a mental note to read up on Wordsworth's life, I whiled away the hours reading poetry, leaving the abbey world behind. As evening approached, birds bickered in the foliage above and the undergrowth hummed with the night sounds of the insect world. Deciding to wash up before the dinner bell, I rose and was making my way towards the bathroom when I heard Moira call out my name as she raced along the corridors leading to the classrooms. Dismissing it as my imagination, I continued on, but then I heard a frantic Sister Bertha.

"Sarah, where are you?" she cried out in a high alarmed voice.

Hurriedly washing up, I rushed out, quite forgetting to change my uniform that was muddy. Joining a group of girls milling around as Sister Griselda attempted to bring order, I slipped into the line forming outside the refectory.

Mother Valerian, an imposing presence standing at the head, spotted me.

"Sarah!" she cried out.

"Yes, Mother," I replied in a panic. Her voice always had that effect on me.

"Come here, child." Something about her tone was not right. With head bowed, I shuffled forward. A squirming Moira stood beside her and, in the shadows, Mummy.

My heart raced as I hesitated, unsure of what to do next, but Mummy pushed forward.

"It's me, Sarah, I've come for you." She hugged me to her and a strangled sob escaped her lips. Dazed, arms dangling by my sides, I watched the others troop into the refectory.

Pulling Moira closer, we clung to each other for a long moment. Smoothing my hair, she gasped, "What in the name of God happened here? You look as pale as a ghost and your hair—who cut your hair off?" I hung my head.

Turning to Mother, she asked severely: "I can't believe my eyes. Sarah appears changed. Why were we not informed?"

"Not here," Mother said firmly; "let us go into my office."

We followed her into the inner sanctum, and there, after examining me closely, Mummy demanded an explanation.

"Sarah's had a bad go of viral fever and we were concerned for her health, so we decided to cut her hair. Long hair has a tendency to sap the strength and is difficult to comb out every day when someone is as sick as she was." Mother spoke in firm, even tones. "As to why you were not informed—it is not our policy to unduly alarm the parents. Young girls tend to get very high fevers, but with proper medication their temperatures drop just as rapidly. I was confident that Sarah would get better with Doctor Hudson, our able physician, in attendance and Sister Patricia, our excellent infirmary nurse. That, coupled with good food and plenty of rest, assured me of her quick recovery. Since she was transferred back to the dormitory, Sarah has been on a relaxed schedule and is allowed to rest whenever she gets tired."

"I still feel we should have been notified of her condition," Mummy stated coldly. "I find what you say very difficult to believe and refuse to accept your explanation. As for her hair, you had no right to touch it unless she was infested, which she clearly was not."

Mother Valerian coughed. "Well—"

Mummy rose. "I've heard enough. I'll hear Sarah's version and then I'll take this up with your Mother House. Believe me, this matter is not closed. I am taking the girls away with me right now and will arrange for their kits to be sent over tomorrow morning."

"As you wish," Mother replied stiffly. "By the way, how did you discover that Sarah was ill? Did she write to you?"

"She did not."

Turning to us, Mummy ordered: "Get your nightclothes and a clean change for the morning. Sarah, your uniform is filthy; it looks as if you've been rolling in the mud. Change into something else. Run along now, you two, I want to have a few words with Mother in private."

Moira hurried, but I dawdled, taking a long, last look at a place I knew I would never see again. Even though I was filled with joy at the proximity of Mummy, I nevertheless felt a few pangs of regret. Her arrival presented another set of problems that were even now beginning to take form—endless questions and explanations.

Carelessly I threw together a set of clothes. Discarding my soiled uniform in a heap on the meticulously turned down bed, I stuffed my socks into muddied shoes and, slipping on a pair of sandals, exited the dormitory without waiting for Moira. Outside my eyes swept past the classrooms and the infirmary with its bright lights shining through curtained windows. Passing the grotto, I wished Our Lady goodbye, knowing in my heart she would follow wherever life led me. And

Rumplestiltskin, I wished him well, and a long life tending his beloved flowers. Out on the playground, I cast a last lingering gaze towards the Mother tree, brooding and silent in the gloaming with its branches sprawled across the convent wall. A deep sorrow welled up within me for the friendships I had enjoyed under its canopy, which now would be lost to me forever. I had once heard Grandpa Reagan candidly inform Mummy that I was often away with the fairies. I now fully realized the truth of his words.

"Jane, Lynette, Cybil, Jemma, Malvina, Arlene, Jenny and Celia—goodbye," I whispered, as Moira joined me and we slowly followed Mummy to the car waiting at the abbey gates. They clanged shut behind us and it was a silent ride to the tiny hotel at the foot of the hill, where Mummy had rented a suite of rooms for the night.

I spent a comfortable night in an old iron cot that creaked between sheets that smelled of sunshine. Waking the next morning to monsoon weather, I watched the low clouds drift past my bedroom window, surprised at the different scene that greeted me. This was still Phulamar, I realized, and the abbey lay just up the hill. If I followed the path it would lead me to the gates and, if I rang the bell, Rumplestiltskin would admit me, for we were friends. It felt unreal, like a dream—this room and being here with Mummy and Moira. And, if it was a dream, indeed, would I want to wake up? I wondered. What for? For some strange reason perhaps—to once more see the faces and visit the secret places that I knew existed within the abbey gates. I knew I would never know anything quite like it again in my life. "Thank heavens," I said aloud, but the phrase sounded hollow, echoing through the empty room. I felt my voice betrayed a strange and troubled heart.

Mummy entered and sat at the edge of my bed very quietly. "Let me look at you," she said, holding me away from her. "Are you feeling all right, Sarah? Would you like to rest here for a few days before we move on?"

I shook my head. Moira joined us.

"I slept with Mummy in her bed," she informed me cheerfully. "We didn't want to disturb you."

"What about some breakfast for all of us?" Mummy asked. "We'll have it sent up to the room and then we can take our time about bathing and getting dressed. I have to go down to the station later on, maybe you girls would like to come along, it will be a pleasant walk. I have to check the timetable."

"To where?" I asked.

Clearing her throat, she said, "I thought we might go and see Grandpa Cliffy." Hesitating, she continued: "I didn't know when would be the best time for me to break it to you girls, but Granny Connie has died."

Moira ran bawling to Mummy, but I rose from the bed, walked over to the window and stood gazing out at mist-shrouded Phulamar.

"She was gravely ill for a long time," said Mummy in a small, sad voice, "but God is merciful. They were having a heat wave when she passed away in her sleep a few weeks ago. Grandpa Cliffy is naturally devastated; he has not gone back to the farm and is still living with Aunty Hilda and Uncle Cyril. I think he'll remain there for some time yet. Daddy is there as well and I sent Radha on ahead."

"Is she buried behind the well?"

"Yes, Sarah."

"Beside Reginald Stanton and his Zinat Mahal?"

Mummy nodded.

I could hear her now as if it were yesterday: "I'm a child of the Deccan, quite used to the heat."

"What's the matter?" Mummy's voice faded away as she looked wide-eyed at me.

"Ohmygawsh! Ohmygawsh!"

"Have no fear, madam, she is coming around now. There, there…"

Mummy was rubbing my arms compulsively.

"What happened?" I asked.

"You fainted," Moira informed me. She was sitting cross-legged on an easy chair beside the bed. "We had to get a doctor in to examine you. Here he is." She pointed to a slim young man busily writing a chit at the dressing table.

"Ha! She is awake now. Tell me, child, are you feeling better?" Shining a torch into my face, he lifted my eyelids one by one and peered in.

"Nothing to worry about, Mrs Watkinson, she will be all right, just a shock to her system. But I am sorry to inform you, dear lady, that looking at the state of her, she appears badly undernourished and weakened. Also, she has cuts and bruises. I would investigate and try to find out how she came by them. These are not very old scars," he observed, lightly running his finger down my thigh and leg. "Sarah needs plenty of bedrest and a good pick-me-up. Various tonics are available and I can recommend a few good ones. But for now, just give her two of these pills every three hours with a cup of milk or soup and I will have my compounder fill this prescription and bring it along to you by afternoon. Maybe no travel for a few days, hanh? If that is possible. I will be in this evening to check on the patient."

"I'm sorry, Doctor; I didn't think the news of her grandmother's death would have this affect on her. The old lady was suffering with cancer for some time and the girls knew it."

"Anything can cause upset, madam; after all she is in a weakened state. One needs to be careful."

"Thank you, Doctor Aziz; it was very kind of you to leave your practice and come here at such short notice. Yes, I'll delay our journey by a day or two and, as for the bruises on her legs and back, I'll try and get to the bottom of it. We can talk about how she came by them later this evening when you drop by for your visit."

Mummy walked him to the door and I heard his footsteps disappearing down the long hallway.

Three days later Doctor Aziz gave us the green light to travel and Mummy booked a coupe on the evening train. Our kit boxes arrived from the abbey and were set down, ready and packed, in one corner of the room. Moira was in a bath; I could hear her splashing in the tub. Getting my toiletries together, I was preparing to follow her when Mummy entered.

"Did you get the parcel I sent you for your birthday, Sarah?"

"That was what all the fuss was about," I replied.

"What fuss?"

"I disobeyed Sister Angelina by opening the parcel, instead of handing it over to Sister Griselda, like she told me to. It was wrong of me, I know, but I was very excited to receive something from home. Sister was furious and called me the worst example of an army brat. She said our parents, not knowing what to do with us, had sent us to boarding school for the nuns to look after and educate."

"Did you reply?"

"Yes." I repeated our exchange of words. "Sister became very angry and, taking the piece of wood with nails from the packing case, she beat me."

"My darling girl, when will you ever learn to hold your tongue? In such instances, you must learn that discretion is always the better part of valour."

I shrugged.

"I will have to take this up with the Mother House, you know that, don't you?"

"Please, Mummy, don't," I begged. "I wish to forget the incident and don't want to discuss it any further." Turning away from her, I busied myself with setting out my clothes.

She sighed and looked on helplessly.

Our train steamed into Stanton Station and a sad-eyed Daddy was there to meet us. He greeted Mummy with a peck on the cheek and helped Moira and I down onto the platform. "What happened here?" he asked, ruffling my hair.

Mummy looked tiredly up at him and shook her head. "Let's get home, Reg; we'll discuss it there."

"Sarah, you okay to walk?" he asked.

I nodded.

They were all assembled on the front veranda, Grandpa Cliffy, Aunty Hilda and Uncle Cyril. Radha eased herself off the floor and enveloped us in a huge hug.

"Sarah, let me look at you." Aunty impatiently pulled me towards her. "What have they gone and done to this child?" she asked in a loud querulous tone. "Dear God, look how pale and run down she looks! And her hair, what happened to her long silky braids? Don't tell me they cut them off at that convent." She next grabbed Moira and examined her closely. "You too are looking peaked. What's all this about, Reg?" she asked sternly.

"I have yet to hear the whole story," Daddy replied wearily. "We had a letter from one of Sarah's friends at the abbey and that's what took Emma there. She wrote to say Sarah had been very ill."

"You found out about her condition from another student?" Aunty asked, incredulous. "You mean the Mother Superior never wrote to you informing you of her illness? What were they waiting for?"

"For her to recover, I suppose, and the whole thing to blow over."
Uncle Cyril shook his head. "What's the name of that place again?"

"Saint Anne's Abbey," said Daddy quietly.

"Abbey, shabby!" Aunty exploded. "I don't care what sort of
highfalutin' name they gave the place. As far as I'm concerned, it's just
another money-making scheme dreamed up by the Catholic Church.
What do nuns know about raising children, I ask you? They've never
had any of their own, frustrated old biddies. Oh! I could think of a
few choice names to call them right about now, but I'll hold back on
account of the girls."

At that moment I would have liked to have fled to the safety of the
bedroom, but Aunty held onto me with an iron grip.

Grandpa Cliffy shuffled over. He had aged since I last saw him.
Taking us both by the hand, he led us into the dining room. "Let's see
what Sonabhen has rustled up for lunch, shall we? The grown-ups can
argue all they want; I'm just glad to see you both. Are you famished?"
he asked, winking at me.

We were back at Stanton Station, but with Granny gone a blanket of
sorrow lay over the place and our arrival had only served to create more
confusion. From the outset, the grown-ups seemed to be continually
at odds with one another, for the heat was unbearable and tempers
flared. After his initial joy at seeing us, Grandpa Cliffy lapsed into a
brooding sadness that he didn't seem to be able to shake. I desperately
wished he'd cheer up and would have given a lot just to hear his old
familiar chuckle or one of his "cock-and-bull stories" as Granny called
them. But he was distracted all the time, gazing into space, unable to
concentrate on anything. Each morning after reading the paper, Uncle
Cyril pointedly left it folded on Grandpa's chair. But all Grandpa ever
did was pick it up and, after a cursory glance at the headlines, set it
down again.

I knew Daddy was worried about him, for I heard him voice his
concerns to Aunty Hilda in the kitchen one morning.

"Your father needs time," she informed him. "Theirs was a long
and very loving relationship. He worshipped her, you know, and even
though Connie never showed it, Cliffy was her everything. I can
remember how desperately they tried for a child during the early years
of their marriage and she had three miscarriages before you finally came
along. Your birth—it was a joyous occasion—seems like yesterday," she

sighed. "You were the unexpected gift that made their family whole. So give it time, my boy, give it time. Forty-three years of living and loving together can't be forgotten in a matter of weeks."

"I know, I know," Daddy agreed impatiently, "but I hate to see him like this. Even the girls, who generally cheer him up, haven't done it for him this time."

"Well, Reg, what do you expect? He has just lost your mother and then seeing Sarah like that. By gad, even I can't get over it. I truly believe there's more to that place than meets the eye. The abbey should be thoroughly investigated. I am sure the authorities will unearth all kinds of skulduggery if they give the place a good going-over. You may actually be able to have it shut down and none too soon either is my way of thinking."

"It's not that simple," he continued in hushed tones. "Sarah doesn't want Emma to take it up with the Mother House, she especially asked her not to pursue the matter and we respect her wishes."

"Ah! What does she know, she is just a child? I'm all for going after them."

"I disagree with you. I don't think that's the way to go. Besides, as uncaring as they seem to be, I know for a fact they look after countless little orphaned and abandoned children, feeding, clothing, and educating them. Young Anglo-Indian girls just like ours would be out on the streets, but for the nuns. What really worries me, though, is that Sarah seems different, she's somehow changed. Something happened there, Aunty. I don't know what exactly. But she's become strangely self-possessed, while at the same times she appears more fragile. Do you know what I'm getting at?"

"What d'you mean? D'you think they brainwashed her or something? I'd demand Mother Superior's head on a plate for that!"

"Nothing of the sort. Rest easy," Daddy calmed her. "All I know is, she won't enter into any discussion about the abbey with her mother and there's no use questioning Moira either, she gets all funny and evasive. So we've decided to let sleeping dogs lie. After all, Sarah's been through enough, so why regurgitate the whole business, eh?"

"H'm, if you say so."

"By the way, how are things down at the farm? I didn't want to bring it up with the old man since he's not in the right frame of mind."

"Your father hasn't been back to the place since your mother passed on, but Uncle Cyril has been making the farm 'run' and doing a fair job of it, if I may say so. He actually managed to get rid of that good-for-nothing Bill Pigott and has hired a new overseer who seems to be working out very well, an ex-railway chappy called Thomas Alvarez. Cliffy goes over to check up on him all the time. It's always good to show up because its when they think you're not coming they get lazy and the place goes to pot. Don't I know it."

I was pretty sure that Daddy and Mummy had been to visit Granny's grave and I understood how Daddy would want to spend some time with his mother alone, but was, nevertheless, disappointed that they hadn't asked Moira and I to come along for a special visit. After all, she was our grandmother and we missed her terribly. Of course, I could always go by myself since the family graveyard was just behind the property, but that wasn't the point. I for one would have liked to go there for the first time accompanied by my parents or Grandpa Cliffy. I didn't feel it right that Moira and I should have to make that first visit on our own. Speaking to Moira about it, I found her indifferent.

She shrugged her shoulders, saying, "I don't care; we can go together if you like."

"But don't you agree," I repeated, "it would be nice if someone else was there?"

"Why?" she asked.

"Well then, why don't you go alone?"

"I was waiting for you."

"So you do agree—to go there alone would bother you."

"Sarah, don't be tiresome." She turned away from me with her nose in the air—a good imitation of Mummy, I thought. Moira's behaviour sometimes was past all understanding.

And another thing, I couldn't understand why the grown-ups avoided making any mention of Granny in the house. It was as if she had never lived, nor been part of this family. I questioned Mummy about it and she felt that it was out of consideration for Grandpa—no one wanted to upset him. I disagreed, feeling he wouldn't mind in the least, and neither would Granny. I imagined her flitting around unseen, guarding us from danger, touching our lives and performing countless little miracles on the farm. It was actually a very exciting notion. But since no one bothered to ask Grandpa how he felt and being timid to broach the subject myself, we just avoided it altogether.

A few days later, in the cool of evening, I asked if we could be taken to visit the grave. Grandpa hurried inside as if he hadn't heard me, but Uncle Cyril rose from his chair and agreed to walk over with us.

The last glorious rays of evening sunlight streamed through the grove of mango trees, tingeing the leaves with gold. Matherani was sweeping the compound and dust motes, swirling high from her broom danced in the orange sunset. Cowbells tinkled as the cattle came in from grazing and I watched Pandurang lazily herd his goats into the lock-up for the night. Servants salaamed us and we returned their greeting. Old familiar sights and sounds continued unchanged, in spite of one of us not being here.

Uncle Cyril hurried us. "Come along, girls, it will soon be dark; you can dawdle all you like on the way back."

Standing beside Granny's grave, I thought, how sad and pathetic it looked—a mound of fresh-turned earth with bunches of withered flowers strewn all over it. It was difficult to imagine Granny lying silent and cold beneath.

"How deep is it?" Moira wanted to know.

"More than six feet," Uncle Cyril informed. "We dig the graves deep so the jackals and other scavengers can't get to the body."

"Will there be a stone slab over it?" I asked.

"Yes, in time. When the earth settles, your Grandpa will have a headstone erected with your Granny's name on it, her date of birth and death and perhaps some beautiful sentiments inscribed below."

We lapsed into silence, preoccupied with our thoughts. Looking out across the fields into the distance, I felt this to be the most perfect spot for Granny to rest in peace. Bleached grass, torched by the setting sun, rippled down the slopes of the low hills. Countless *Anjun* trees[121] with bottle birds' nests hanging from their branches dotted the landscape; while the earth, having just given up a crop of groundnut, appeared dry and unyielding. Reunited with her parents and other members of the Stanton clan, Granny was now resting as she would have wanted, buried deep in the soil of the Deccan she loved so dearly. A small company of birds settled in the fields and proceeded to feed, keeping up a constant

---

121 *Anjun trees* found at the base of the Saptura Hills

chatter that distracted. I smiled, recognizing them as the seven sisters, or *sat-bhain*,[122] as Radha called them. It all seemed so perfectly natural, the cycle of life and death being played out before our eyes.

"I should like to rest in a place such as this when my time comes," I said, looking up at Uncle Cyril.

"Hopefully, that's a long way away, Sarah, girl," he patted my head. "I pray this place will always be here for both of you when you need it, so you can return any time you please."

"I too hope it never changes." Moira looked droopy, her eyes wet with tears.

I placed a protective arm around her.

"Pray God, it doesn't. These fields have been ploughed over and harvested for generations. The land has never been allowed to rest and, as such, is not worth much, except, of course, to we who live here."

As the sun disappeared behind the low hills, we turned for home in the short twilight. Uncle Cyril walking alongside us was lost in thought, but, before we reached the house, he spoke: "Do not be afraid to visit your grandmother's grave alone in the future. I know for a fact that she would love it. Besides, it's a comfort just knowing she is always near."

Radha rolled a mat out on the baked dung floor and, placing an enamel plate piled high with curry and rice on it, pulled me closer. She proceeded to feed me with her hands, one mouthful at a time, in the same way she had all those years ago when I was a baby first learning to take solid food. I watched her face grow hard as she gazed at the now faint scars criss-crossing my skinny legs. "*Hai, hai, hai!*" she exclaimed. "*Yay dekho. Kya halath hogia. Mera baby ka bal be sub cart thia, sister pishter log!*"[123]

I smiled at her. Dear Radha, she took everything that had to do with both Moira and me very personally. I knew for a fact that she nursed a grudge against Mummy and Daddy for having sent us to the abbey.

Carrying my empty plate into the kitchen, she rinsed her fingers

---

122 *sat-bhain* seven sisters; birds
123 *Yay dekho. Kya halath hogia. Mera baby ka bal be sub cart, thia sister pishter log* Look at this. What trouble has befallen you, and they have even cut off all your hair.

and returned with a bottle of coconut oil, which sported a picture of a young woman with luxuriant, jet-black hair rippling down to her waist. "Come, my baby," she coaxed, pouring a palm full of the heavy oil on my head and rubbing it in vigorously. Slowly she began massaging my scalp with her strong bony fingers. I squirmed and tried to get free of her, but she grabbed me by the shoulders and, uttering a base threat, continued with her ministrations.

Later, I complained to Mummy about the cloying scent that clung to my hair despite two rinses with hot water. She smiled indulgently.

"Be patient with her, Sarah; she is determined that you grow a head of hair as abundant as the lady on the bottle. I doubt very much that you can escape her."

"Once a week then; please talk to her, Mummy," I pleaded. "She never listens to me."

"I'll have a word."

Rummaging in her suitcase, Mummy produced a package from which she removed two brassieres.

"These are for you, Sarah. Try them on, will you? I want to see if they fit properly."

Hurriedly taking them from her, I disappeared into the bathroom.

"How do they fit?" she asked.

"Uncomfortable and restricting," I replied.

She assured me I would get used to them in time.

Moira, curled up on the easy chair, couldn't stop giggling. "Ooh, Sarah, booby bras," she teased.

Mummy looked at her severely. "You're next, my girl," she threatened.

Preferring the soft outline of a petticoat, I felt awkward and self-conscious in a bra, since it tented my frocks and blouses, making my breasts stick out all stiff and coming to points. No one seemed to notice, however, except Aunty Hilda, who, placing an arm around me, playfully asked, "So Sarah, how does it feel to be a young woman?"

Refusing to let the matter of the nuns and the abbey rest, Aunty Hilda kept harping about it every chance she got. This infuriated Mummy and bothered me as well, for I wished it all away and things back to normal as they were before. Piling my plate with great portions of food that I found difficult to consume, she rattled on, calling the nuns wicked, unnatural creatures.

"Just look at my poor darling," she'd say in passing. "Now who gave those God forsaken creatures permission to chop off all her hair and break her spirit to boot? Who, I ask you? The good Lord certainly did not. Convents—I detest them!"

"We thought it was the best thing to do at the time," Mummy spoke up, defending her decision. "Our lives were thrown into a state of confusion when Reg was transferred to Delhi and then put on a waiting list for family accommodation. Living in the Officers' Mess out of boxes is no life for children; they need stability and a routine. Boarding school was the next best thing. Saint Anne's Abbey at Phulamar came very highly recommended."

"By whom?" asked Aunty. "Lucifer himself? I can imagine what goes on in places like that. Those nuns with no outlet for their frustrations take it out on their students. It's unnatural, I say, and something should be done about it."

"It's over and done with," Uncle Cyril butted in impatiently, "so let's move on. Are you planning to take them back to Delhi with you?" He looked across the table at Mummy.

"Yes," she replied stiffly.

I knew she was furious, for her cheeks were flushed and her eyes bright and glassy. Mummy could never hide her anger.

Turning to Daddy, Aunty continued: "And why didn't you think of leaving them with us until the accommodation problem was resolved? After all, we are your flesh and blood, Reg. Are we not good enough?"

"That's not the point." Daddy cleared his throat, shifting uncomfortably in his chair. "The girls need an education and, as Emma has told you, we did research the place very thoroughly before we sent them there. They were first-class boarders, all the extras were covered."

"How many classes did they have, hanh? More than one, from what you're saying. Humph! I can imagine what the other poor wretches must have to go through."

Uncle Cyril fixed her with a menacing glare. Banging the table, he sent all the plates clattering. "That's enough out of you, Hilda!" he exclaimed loudly. "This is none of your business."

Moira and I were taken aback and I spilled my cup of tea all over the tablecloth.

Sonabhen stopped dead in her tracks with a platter of banana fritters and quickly used her jharan to mop up the spill.

"What's done is done," he continued. "It doesn't help us as a family to be divided in this way and bicker in front of the children. Reg and Emma acted in the best interest of the girls, of that I am sure. Things don't always work out the way we want them to. But they are safe now and I can vouch for Sarah, she has sufficient spirit in her to get through this. Children are more resilient than we give them credit for. So let's put this matter to rest, once and for all, and try for happiness instead. Enough has happened already."

A morose and silent Grandpa never once looked up from his plate of food.

Mummy was livid and later in the bedroom I heard her complain to Daddy. "They have no right, Reg, to meddle in the way we are raising the girls. It's nobody's business."

Daddy heard her out in silence before replying. "I agree, she shouldn't interfere, but she loves the girls, especially Sarah. I too got a jolt seeing her looking that way and pray each night that she bounces back to her old self. Believe me, I would rather have a rambunctious inquisitive daughter than a sad-eyed downtrodden one. Anyway, I've had it with boarding schools, Emma, and Catholic ones are out of the question for the future. I would prefer keeping them as day scholars, even if we are uprooted a thousand times. They do much better in school under your supervision and help each evening with their homework. At first I was afraid Moira would be the one most troubled going to boarding school and am actually surprised that Sarah proved to be the casualty. At any rate, we must shower her with love and bring back her smile. Incidentally, I've invited my father to come spend time with us in Delhi when we are settled; it will be good for him and for the girls."

"That's fine with me," Mummy consented.

That evening, in spite of midsummer heat searing the plains, I broke into a cold sweat, feeling all jumpy and anxious. Imaginary fears swirled in my brain and took hold. I was in a panic for no reason at all, wondering how much the family really knew of what had actually transpired in Phulamar. Did they, for instance, know about the beating? I hoped not. If the fact that I was ill and had my hair chopped off had created such a flood of emotion, I hated to think what effect knowledge of the beating would have on them. I had begged Mummy not to speak about it to anyone; surely she'd respect my wishes. Dressed in my old flannel nightgown, I crouched, brooding and pensive, in a sunny corner of the veranda, soaking up what was left of the day's lingering heat. Nobody was around, since Mummy and Daddy with Moira in tow had gone for their usual evening walk.

Uncle Cyril and Aunty Hilda emerged from their bedroom deep in conversation, going over the afternoon's events.

"Don't you think Emma's acting very uppity these days?" Aunty asked. "I for one think she needs to be put in her place. I don't like what she's doing with the girls, avoiding her responsibilities, sending them off to a convent to be neglected and ill-treated. I am sure their heads as well were being filled with all that Catholic mumbo jumbo. Ah! But what am I saying? She is, after all, the daughter of that two-bit Irishman. How could we have expected any different?"

"Listen to yourself, Hilda; just stop for a moment and listen!" Uncle Cyril raised his voice. "It's all about what you think, as usual; never taking anyone else's opinion into consideration, just yours. You are deliberately driving a wedge into the family by interfering in matters that are none of your business. Stop it, woman, before you cause a rift! Sarah and Moira are not your children; they belong to Emma and Reg, who very kindly bring them here for holidays so that we old-timers can enjoy some family life. I do agree with you, partially, but I feel we should keep our opinions to ourselves until they are gone. Besides, it is a time of mourning in the house. Out of respect for your dead sister, their grandmother, hold your tongue. Cliffy as well must have peace in order to heal. He is suffering, poor man, and you are adding to it all with your *buck buck*.[124] Show Sarah all the love I know you feel for her, but keep your own council, for God's sake!"

I heard her loud sigh and, after a while, "Sorry, my dear; you are right," spoken in low, contrite tones.

I was flabbergasted!

The oppressive heat continued, as the sun, a gaseous orb of fire,

---

124 *buck buck* constant nagging

blazed down on the plains, baking the earth's crust, driving both man and beast to shelter. Rising early, Moira and I escaped the stuffy bedroom to sit outside on the old iron cot within the veranda. Enjoying the early morning birdsong and the odd cool wisps of breeze that drifted by, we became engrossed in a game of draughts. But not for long, as our attention was soon diverted by a bullock cart creaking into the compound. Hari, the Patel of Moorghao, jumped out. Moving to the rear of the cart, he helped a very pregnant Meenakshi down. We gaped at her, but she, catching sight of us, looked away and pulled the cowl of her sari close over her face. Following her husband, she moved towards the servants' quarters.

Aunty bustled out. "What now?" she muttered to herself. And, stopping Hari in his tracks as Meenakshi slipped inside, "Kya hogia?" she inquired. Hari salaamed her.

"Huzoor, I have brought my wife home a little early because the midwife in the village is saying she is in the last stages of her pregnancy and, besides, she is not feeling very well. Please, if missy baba wants to speak with her mother she can come to know exactly what the problem is."

Aunty turned and made for the kitchen. Moira and I followed. Exciting moments such as these were not to be missed. There we found Aunty and Sonabhen deep in conversation with Hari seated on a chair, slurping down a cup of tea. He smiled benignly at us, asking, "Baba log *chootee par* agia?"[125] Disappointed, we went back to our game.

That night at the dinner table, Aunty pulled a chair in beneath herself and declared, "Meenakshi's back."

All eyes looked up from their plates and Daddy asked teasingly, "Is there a problem? Or did your little plan backfire?"

"No, nothing of the sort. She is spotting and, according to the village midwife, the baby's head seems already to be in place. Curious, it's still a little too early by my calculations. Naturally, Hari has been beside himself with worry and, of course, that old harridan, the midwife, she can't afford to have Meenakshi lose the baby, since I am sure there is a big baksheesh in it for her."

"Ah, but she is not privy to the secrets that dwell deep in the

---

125 *Baba log chootee par agia* Have the little girls come for holiday?

heart of the Fenwick homestead, is she?" Uncle Cyril asked with a mischievous gleam in his eye.

"Of course not, but I have a hunch that we as well may have been hoodwinked. These latest developments throw a different light on the whole affair and I've been giving the matter a lot of thought. To begin with, it's strange how that fellow Mangat and his brother felt confident enough to arrive here on our doorstep, after having disappeared into the jungle to live like dacoits for more than a year. Meenakshi herding those goats out in the fields near the verge of the forest could have run into them very easily; after all, they were childhood friends. So it is only natural to assume that when they were being hunted down by the police, she would direct them here—"

"Knowing the kind heart of missy baba," Uncle Cyril completed her sentence.

Aunty ignored him and continued piecing the facts together, as if completing a jigsaw puzzle: "If, as the midwife thinks, the baby's arrival is imminent, well, our little girl may be even more of a minx than we first took her for. Hijinks in the jungle is what I am getting at; they had all the time in the world for it and ample opportunity. Heaven knows when it all started, in which case the midwife may be right: Meenakshi is ready to deliver."

"We have a veritable Miss Marple in our midst." Grandpa had been listening intently and now he smiled across the table at Aunty. "You're most probably right, my dear, but you'd better watch what you're saying; there are servants about. You wouldn't want any of your excellent deductions leaking out now, would you?"

"Yes, Radha's foxy and has a nose for gossip." Daddy cautioned.

I smiled.

"Anyway, whatever the story is, I'm just glad that Hari brought her here. In that way we can keep an eye on the girl," Aunty Hilda declared in a matter-of-fact tone.

"By the way, was Mangat ever caught?" inquired Daddy.

"No, the brothers disappeared into the jungle and have not been seen since. I am sure, if they were captured, Police Inspector Mr Chandra Gopal would have been by to inform us."

"And strut around the place like a bleedin' peacock. I can't abide that fellow!" Uncle Cyril exclaimed.

"Yes, we know how you feel about him from the way you acted at

Christmas—nearly gave the whole game away. Your infernal banter could have landed us in hot water." Aunty glared at him as she made her way to the sideboard to retrieve a marrow spoon. "Our poor Fan almost had a nervous breakdown."

"It doesn't take much to get Fan going," observed Uncle Cyril.

Grandpa nodded in agreement.

Mummy sat silent through the entire discussion, a look of disapproval pasted on her face. Later she complained to Daddy about "Aunty's tasteless conversation at the dinner table, exposing the girls to common farm gossip."

"What d'you want, Emma? They're country folk with common country ways. Life has been hard for them—eking a living out of the soil. They haven't had a lot of spare time to develop la-di-da manners. Salt of the earth, true blue they are, and I for one wouldn't have them any other way. The world is not all tea and crumpets, m'dear, so please step down from your high horse and stop being so sensitive about every little thing. I told you about my family before we were married, even before I brought you here to meet them. I love them dearly and so do the girls. As far as I'm concerned, that's all there is to it."

I heard Mummy blow her nose and wondered whether she was crying.

A few days later Radha gave me, between snippets of servant gossip, her take on the whole Meenakshi affair. While massaging my scalp, she whispered, "She is spotting. I have calculated she must be in her seventh month—still too early. I wonder if that Hari was leaving her alone. A pregnant woman must be left to herself."

I rolled my eyes; Radha was talking in riddles again.

"What are you speaking about?" I asked.

"Woman's problems, woman's talk. I thought after attending girls' school you would have learned something, enough at least to understand and follow what I am saying to you. What did they teach you, the sister log?" She aimed at the veranda post a volley of blood-red spittle, which found its mark. "Make promise now not to talk this with Moira baba." She wagged her finger at me. "She is still too young and Mummy too will be angry; she must not suspect that you are aware."

"Of what?" I asked impatiently.

"It takes nine months for a baby to come, you know that, hanh?

Considering all matters, Meenakshi is only at the end of her seventh month. Sonabhen says she is here because she is passing blood and that in itself is not strange, for it has been known to happen to pregnant women. Generally it goes away, but sometimes not. Hai Ram! I hope her husband has not interfered with her too much, causing her to lose the baby. If she does, I fear she will not get another from Hari."

"Why ever not?" I asked.

"Bah! He is useless. One needs fertile eggs to hatch strong chicks. Hari has had two previous wives, young women who did not bear him any children. But the third wife, she becomes pregnant immediately after wedding. How is that, have you thought? For him, that is a miracle, no? So when there is the least little fear that she may lose the child, he hurriedly brings her home to her mother. Mark my words," she continued darkly, "if Meenakshi does not have a safe delivery, he will leave her here and try his luck with another."

"Why?" I asked. "If she got pregnant once, she can get pregnant again."

"How? Where is the means? The means is roaming the Satpura Hills, stealing and spilling his seed every night in a different bed."

"You're too much," I laughed out loud. "I don't believe a word you say. That bhang you chew is going to your head."

"You think it is Hari's child that Meenakshi is carrying? Don't you recall the tamasha in the godown on the day Mangat ran back to the hills with that useless brother of his? Remember Meenakshi's state?"

I nodded.

"Why was that? Hurry burry her wedding date was set in a minute. Why I ask you? Why? *Bas!*[126] I am saying no more."

She leaned back and looked away in disgust.

I squirmed uncomfortably and was about to rise and go inside. However, she was not done with me as yet.

Glaring at me with hurt-filled eyes, she dragged me down and admonished: "Very smart you think you are, making fun of me in that way." She yanked my hair. "Menstruating, wearing bra, everything like a woman, but the most important thing you don't know. For a young healthy female, she needs a strong man like a young bull with gentle eyes. He must impregnate her and fill her womb with fertile seeds, so that she can bear him healthy children. Now you understand?"

---

126 *Bas!* Enough said

I nodded.

With a look of disgust, she removed a wad of tobacco from the cloth purse at her waist and, shoving it to the back of her mouth, settled down for a good chew.

Struggling free, I ran from her. I was very tempted to share with her Aunty's excellent deductions, but held my tongue.

That night with Radha's words ringing in my ears, I couldn't get to sleep. How dare she accuse me of ignorance. She was not privy to my secrets. From reading and real-life experiences I had learned something of love, sex and lust. Of course, I hadn't given it much thought until now, since the very concept of love seemed scary with tragic consequences for some. My mind raced back to Celia Stevens.

When love came to me, I hoped it would be a romantic experience that would transport me to another dimension; floating on air on the wings of love, was my illusion.

What Radha didn't know was I did have an understanding of lust and sex. The image of Stanley Dowling goosing Jamal out in the curounda field flashed through my mind. I knew that act was horribly wrong and had nothing at all to do with love, but everything to do with lust. Mummy and Radha could not always protect Moira and me. On our journey through life, we would be exposed to different situations and have our own private experiences. Besides, I had read things, seen things and formed my own opinions. In the case of Mangat and Meenakshi, I decided it was equally love and lust on Meenakshi's part, but just plain lust on Mangat's part. After all, he had run away and left her behind, hadn't he? Lust dominated, I decided, and was a very important part of life. There was lust for gold, lust for life and lust for sex as well. Both men and women experienced it. Love and lust were often intertwined, I concluded.

Then, of course, there was the matter of Hari's missing fertile eggs; both Grandpa and Radha had alluded to them. Very perplexing indeed! I understood nothing at all about that. Nevertheless, I felt sorry for him and was sure that having Meenakshi's baby to call his very own would make up for the loss. That would be his reward for marrying her. I smiled in the dark, satisfied with my conclusions. Henceforth, I resolved to pay greater attention when grown-ups spoke of sexual matters. Satisfied, I turned over and fell asleep.

Cuscus tats were lowered and doused continually. The old house turned dark and cool as Yusouf and the lazy Pandurang fetched water from the well in relays. Visitors were few and far between these days, as no one ventured out in the searing heat. Sunday lunches were on hold since the household was in mourning and Moira and I took it in turns being bored. She teased Whiskey in his cage, stealing his piece of cuttlefish away from him, and received a nip for her trouble. Aunty berated her, but Mummy came to Moira's defence, saying it was because she was bored. "We are all bored," she sighed tiredly. I looked up from my book of short stories and, for what must surely have been the first time in my entire life, was held up as an example to Moira.

"Sarah's busy reading, staying out of trouble and minding her own business. Why can't you pick up a book? Go read, child!" Aunty scolded.

But Moira was stubborn and continued sulking. Actually, I knew she was missing Granny, who always petted her, for they had a special relationship. I gently reminded her that Granny was with us, even though we couldn't see her.

Moira's eyes misted over. "I know," she agreed, "but I still miss her."

"Well, cheer up, old thing; you have me," I offered, "and the whole family besides."

"It's not the same," came her teary reply.

"Of course it's not the same, silly. What about a game of Snakes and Ladders after tea?"

She stuck her thumb in her mouth and turned away from me. I wished Mummy had thought to bring Lilibet along. At this point even Ronny the rag doll would have comforted her.

Waking one afternoon after tea from a drugged sleep to the drip, drip, drip of the cuscus tats, I walked out onto the veranda and sat on the front stoop. Noticing storm clouds gathering on the horizon, I realized the wait was over. The perennially late monsoons had decided to make an appearance and refresh the parched plains and I joyfully informed Aunty of the fact.

"I know, I know," she acknowledged. "I can feel it in my bones. Thank heavens; we need some respite from this wretched weather."

It came down in buckets for the next few days and the earth grew wet and steamy from the incessant downpour. Confined to the house, everyone was on edge and tempers were short. Mummy and Daddy had to give up their evening walks and Uncle Cyril didn't make the farm run for a week or two. Grandpa Cliffy was moody and irritable. The situation became quite intolerable.

A few days later, when a break in the clouds allowed the sun to filter through, I decided to visit Granny's grave and go by way of the buffalo shed, since I hadn't set eyes on Esmerelda for a long time. Yusouf was milking Maud, who gave me a baleful look before turning away. As I patted little Esme, I noticed she had grown considerably. Planting a kiss on her shiny wet snout, I hurried over to the back of the house.

Standing before the damp mound of earth that was Granny's grave, I whispered a prayer for her and offered up another for peace to return to the family. I had heard Mummy mutter that her nerves were stretched to the limit and was afraid of an awful row.

Beside the well, a patch of fresh new grass looked inviting. Sinking down, I gazed out at the hills on the horizon and wondered what Mangat and his brother were up to. I was sure they were oblivious of the upheaval their stay had caused here at Stanton House. If Mangat did know of Meenakshi's pregnancy, would he care? I doubted very much—ignorant dacoit that he was.

Slipping a stalk of grass between my teeth, I turned my mind to other things, like "budding womanhood." Mummy claimed I was entering a new phase in my life and this was proving to be somewhat of a dilemma. Even though the prospect was filled with exciting possibilities, I was unsure of how to conduct myself in this new arena. I would have loved to adopt the dreamy, languorous look of the romantic heroines, like the Lady of Shalott, for instance. But the problem was, I didn't fit the mould, since I looked nothing at all like Elaine of Astolat from the paintings of her I had seen in a book.

However, the idea persisted and I couldn't put it out of my mind.

Questioning Aunty on the subject proved to be quite useless. Scoffing at the idea of budding womanhood, she dismissed it as a lot of silly nonsense.

"Don't let anyone fill your head with rubbish, Sarah," she informed me in a matter-of-fact tone of voice. "Keep both feet planted firmly on the ground, my girl, at all times. Dreaming is for fools. For the most part, life is difficult and hardly a fairly tale. A lot will depend on your attitude and whom you marry. Take your uncle and me, for instance;

we may not have a lot, but we are happy and content. I keep a good, strong hold on the accounts and Uncle Cyril has his duties. It works out perfectly."

"I thought Uncle Cyril was a lazybones," I interrupted. "Even Whiskey the parrot calls him that."

"Don't mind that silly bird; he's got nothing to do all day but spout rubbish."

"That he learns from you." I laughed out loud.

"Don't be cheeky, Sarah; be serious and you'll learn something," Aunty Hilda admonished. "Take your Grandpa Cliffy for instance—now he's a good sort, but was always a bit of a dreamer. Fancied himself a country squire, he did, and left the upkeep of his property in the hands of an overseer who robbed him blind. As a result, your grandparents had very little money and had to fall back on your grandmother's meagre inheritance to pull them out of many a tight spot. But the prime examples of ineptitude are, of course, your uncle Melvin Foxglove and our airy-fairy Fanny. Now, there's a good-for-nothing loafer, if you ever saw one. Why, he hasn't done a hand's turn all his life. Lived off his wits he did and Fanny likewise—squandered her inheritance. Oh yes, she puts on all kinds of airs nowadays, like butter wouldn't melt in her mouth, but the pair of 'em went through everything she could lay her hands on. Gambling, carousing, living like there was no tomorrow. They owed all over the place and were nearly run out of town. Of course, when all the money was gone and without a pot to piss in, they came back here to try and make a go of it on the land. Thank heavens, your great-grand-uncle Leonard, knowing what kind of a wastrel Fanny had run off with, wisely invested a portion of her inheritance; something Melvin couldn't get his sticky fingers on. She should be eternally grateful to him, for it is that little nest egg that today pulls them through from month to month. And, of course, their daughter Hazel got lucky; she made a good marriage and is able to send them something from Blighty every month. So, there you have it, my girl; every kind of fool represented in this very family."

Aunty made a lot of sense. But looking over at Granny's grave, I knew that, even though her life had been hard, she had been happy with Grandpa. "We get by," I remembered her confiding in Aunty Maggie one far off afternoon in Saltair-By-The-Sea. How different the sisters were, I thought. There was Granny, who was practical, but had a soft side to her. Then there was Aunty Hilda, as tough as nails and, even though I loved her dearly, I knew she could be too much sometimes. Maybe she had to be because she wore the pants, according to Mummy. I didn't entirely agree with that either, since Uncle Cyril always had his way when things went too far, like the other day at tea, for instance. And finally, there was Aunt Fanny—dear, sweet, silly Aunt Fanny, forever timorous and dithering, unable to make up her mind about anything. Smiling to myself, I realized I loved them all equally, in spite of or because of their differences. This time spent here at Stanton Station had healed me and I felt lucky indeed to have my family around, smothering me, cosseting me and drowning me with love. I hardly thought of the abbey anymore and the nightmares had disappeared. I had dreamt of Jane Woodman a few nights ago and cried into my pillow, remembering her pale, pinched face. Would I see any of them again, ever? I guessed not.

The person standing over me cast a long shadow and, looking up, I saw a lanky Ashley Durham squinting down. "Hello, Sarah. Imagine finding you here?"

Scrambling to my feet, I hastily dusted off my frock and noticed how tall he had grown. Handsome, with skin burned a biscuit brown. Taking it all in with cool grey eyes, he seemed pleased to see me.

"Hello, Ashley." I used my best Scarlett O'Hara voice, wishing I had Amber St Clair's double row of lashes to cast a half-moon shadow on my cheeks.

"Is your aunty home? My parents would like you all to come for Sunday lunch next week. Are you going to be around?"

"I suppose so. You'll find them all in the house."

"Walk over with me, will you? I could use a glass of water."

We ambled over and all the while I couldn't still my rapidly beating heart.

"There's Aunty," I pointed to her giving Yusouf orders on the back veranda and turned to leave.

"Not so fast," he cried out after me. "What about that water?"

"Get it yourself from the chatty," I replied, before disappearing into the house.

I was definitely smitten and knew it.

Later I casually asked Aunty whether she had accepted the invitation.

"Oh, yes," she replied. "Have you a party frock for Sunday? It will be nice for you girls to get out from under this cloud of mourning and have a little fun. We've all been cooped up here for too long. With the heat and everything else, life's become a drag and it shouldn't be like that for young things like you and Moira. We shall have a nice time at the Durhams'; she serves an excellent lunch. And, of course, there's Ashley." She winked at me.

Radha set out fresh voile dresses for Moira and me and, thank goodness, they were not the identical print or pattern. My dress was loose and the sash, after going around my waist twice, trailed on the floor. Eyeing me, Mummy declared I could do with a little meat on my bones and Daddy suggested a tonic, Kepler's Malt or Waterbury's Compound, perhaps. Since I was settling into my new skin and hoping to remain thin and vulnerable looking, I turned away from them to admire my angular figure in the mirror. The prospect of the return of "plump Sarah" filled me with fear and firmed up my resolve to keep away from sweets and cake in the future. From now on I would cultivate a lilting voice and work on looking wistfully distant all the time. Setting a ring of daisies in my hair, I could then become very like the Lady of Shalott.

I shared my thoughts with Mummy one afternoon. She gave me an odd look and asked if I didn't feel that was too extreme.

"You know what happened to her, Sarah, don't you? She died from unrequited love for Sir Lancelot and ended up floating down the river in a barge. You wouldn't want that for yourself, would you?"

"No."

"I didn't think so; you're far too sensible," she declared, with a searching look.

Who is this? And what is here?
And in the lighted palace near
Died the sound of royal cheer;
And they crossed themselves for fear,
All the Knights of Camelot;
But Lancelot mused a little space
He said, "She has a lovely face;

God in his mercy lend her grace"
The Lady of Shalott.

Moodily, I recited the last verse of Tennyson's poem to myself.

Thankfully, my hair had grown out a little and the oil massages seemed to have worked wonders. Brushing it out in long strokes, I was pleased to see it looking sleek and shiny. Mummy passed me her perfume and we climbed into the dumney at midday.

Ashley lounged in a long-armed railway chair. We had one at the house and I remembered Grandpa calling it a "Bombay fornicator." An odd name, I thought, for a chair. Looking up the word *fornicator* in the Oxford dictionary, I was even more confused by its meaning. The chair obviously had multiple uses. Surreptitiously admiring the height and grace of Ashley Durham, I kept my eyes glued to the floor. His mother rushed out to greet us, thanking Aunty profusely for the venison roast she had brought along as a gift.

"Nothing beats cold venison," she simpered. "A few slices in a sandwich with a smear of mustard, heavenly! So thoughtful of you, Hilda."

Mummy took a seat on the cane settee and Moira and I plunked down beside her. Soon the room filled with guests, many of whom we didn't know. But after the drinks were served and the gramophone wound up, it didn't matter anyhow, since the mood changed and everyone relaxed. The Durhams' had a large railway bungalow and a sitting room with ample space for dancing. "Drinkin' Rum and Coca-Cola" on the gramophone broke the ice, as sweaty couples rose to take a turn on the floor. Sitting a little apart self-consciously, I watched Moira giggling with new-found friends. They pranced around the floor, bumping into the adults.

"Sarah! What happened girl?" It was Aunt Fanny. "You're as thin as a reed and grown tall too. Where is Moira?"

I pointed, as she planted a kiss on my cheek. I was happy to see both her and Uncle Melvin—he in an old shirt and wilted tie, while Aunt Fanny was resplendent in silk with an armful of bangles and a matching broach.

I hugged her and she asked in a loud whisper: "Feeling better now, are you? Aunty Hilda told me you were quite ill at that abbey. I, for one, never trusted nuns. Give me a good old Protestant school anytime. I sent my Hazel to one and never regretted it. Anyway, that's all behind you now and I see you've turned into quite a young lady." She winked, as I smiled self-consciously. She settled into a chair beside me and her wrinkled, rouged face suddenly turned mournful.

"Sad about our dear sweet Connie, your granny," she sighed heavily. "Poor angel, she just slipped into a coma one afternoon and never regained consciousness. We were all there, you know, even your Uncle Melvin. Doctor Sohrab Pudumjee was attending. Of course, we knew the end was coming as she grew weaker by the day, but still one is never prepared when it finally does arrive. Cliffy, your poor grandpa, took it very hard. Your grandmother was the love of his life, you know. Oh, he was inconsolable for days and days after that; hasn't recovered yet, I don't think."

"Grandpa is still very sad and broody," I agreed mournfully.

"And Dr Pudumjee—why that dear, dear man wouldn't take a pie from your grandfather for all the time he spent coming and going from his clinic. He's a brick. The man's a veritable saint, I tell you!" Aunt Fanny rolled her tear-filled eyes heavenward. Taking a scented hankie from her bag, she blew her nose loudly. "I couldn't stay long after she passed on, my dear, all that emotion, it just got me down. I felt drained and had to run home. Haven't been back since. I'm one of those that takes long to recover from grief and the loss of dear Connie laid me low for weeks. She was my favourite, you know," she whispered, leaning close. "Your Aunty Hilda is the strong one, so I didn't feel too bad about leaving. Bless her, she made all the funeral arrangements, since Cliffy wasn't up to it. Our family, of course, has a firm footing in this place and is very well known. Naturally, absolutely everyone came to the funeral, everyone who is anyone, at any rate, here at Stanton Station. Your poor, poor grandpa—" she sighed, dabbing her eyes periodically.

I nodded, trying to picture that sad day when Granny died and happy that Moira was not around to hear Aunt Fanny's recounting of it.

"I have the shawl, dear, the one I was knitting for your Granny. Remember?"

"Yes."

"I'd like for you to have it, Sarah."

"Give it to Moira," I said. "She's missing Granny something awful and may like to cuddle up with it, knowing it was hers."

"Then that's settled, she shall have it. Of course, you're not going to be left empty-handed. I've been working like a beaver all these months and have several pairs of socks for the two of you. Now that your grandmother is no more, I shall take over the knitting duties."

Shuddering inwardly, I recalled my patterned feet. "Thanks, Aunt Fanny," I smiled. "Oh, look! Here's Daddy."

He invited her and Uncle Melvin to stay at Stanton House for the next week, since he was going to be travelling back to Delhi soon after. I was happy about that, hoping their visit would help cheer things up at the farm.

Eyeing Ashley seated at the far corner of the room, I caught him a couple of times throwing furtive glances in my direction. Sharing a joke with his cousin Ian, who was operating the gramophone, he seemed to be enjoying himself. A chilled jug of shandy on a teapoy nearby proved hard to resist. Moira and I downed two glasses each, after which I began feeling light-headed and giddy.

"Come dance, Sarah," one of her new-found friends pleaded. Bold and uncaring, I rose and joined the crowd on the dance floor. Giggling, we moved in a circle, following the adults in a Paul Jones—collapsing on the settee in a fit of laughter at the end.

Lunch was served and it was as magnificent as Aunty had predicted. A glistening platter of pea pulao with chicken korma and mutton chops. A red-hot curry of trotters was passed around with an ample supply of parathas to sop up the gravy. Fish rissoles, cauliflower foogath and countless side dishes enhanced the meal. It was a truly wonderful repast. The company attacked the platters of food that were replenished time and again. Feeling ravenous, I indulged to excess, hoping Ashley was too busy to notice. Looking across the table at him, I was comforted to see his plate piled high with trotter bones. Leaning back, he gave me a bold wink. I looked away, blushing. For dessert, ice-cold wobbly jellies and a blancmange that had been chilling in a zinc tub of crushed ice were placed on the table, together with a rich custard sauce and a cut-glass bowl of canned fruit in heavy syrup. Even though I was full to bursting, I couldn't resist. In the future I promised myself, I would just toy with the food and leave the table feeling half full. Fortified by an excellent meal, I found it easy to make such vows.

The grown-ups, sated after the lunch, flopped down wherever they could find a place to sleep off their excesses. I decided on some shut-eye as well and curled up in a rickety old armchair in the corner of the veranda. Dozing off, I felt a hand on my arm.

"Hey, Sarah, how about a game of cards?" It was Ashley.

I shook my head.

"Can we just sit and talk then?"

"Okay."

And we did. This was his last term in school, I learned.

"Will you be going back to boarding school after the hols?" he asked.

"No," I replied. "My father is transferred to Delhi, so Moira and I will be day scholars there."

"Oh nice, I'm sure you'll like that better."

"Do you like boarding school?" I asked.

He shrugged. "It's not that bad. I'm school captain."

I gave him an admiring look.

"You believe that?" he asked, laughing, with a mischievous glint in his eye.

I nodded.

"Geez, Sarah, then you'll believe anything. I would have liked to have been, but I'm not."

We exchanged secret smiles.

"Your parents are great. Your dad's an army officer and your mummy's pretty."

"Yes, they're all right."

"I'd like to be an officer. Actually, I'm thinking of entering the Military Academy."

"You should, you'd make a great officer."

"What about you? What would you like to be?"

"A journalist, maybe. I would like to travel the globe, reporting on world events."

"You'd make a wonderful journalist."

I burst out laughing. "How would you know?"

Aunty was standing over us. "So what does one have to do around here to get a cup of tea?" she asked.

"Hold on!" Ashley rose. "I'll have the cook put the kettle on for you." He dashed off in the direction of the kitchen.

"Sorry, Sarah, but I was dying for a cuppa."

Daddy was leaving for Delhi the next day. The evening prior, our entire family was gathered, as always, on the front veranda and I felt happy to see everyone in such a mellow mood. Daddy and Mummy were cozied up on the old settee, romantically holding hands, while the others, busy with their own thoughts, nursed their drinks and had very little to say. The sun set on Stanton Station and, as night fell, I closed my book of short stories. It was pitch dark outside, except for the flicker of lantern light. A couple of flying foxes, who had spent the day in the crevices under the eaves, flew out on a nocturnal errand, squeaking and quarrelling among themselves. Moira and I had at one time tried to dislodge them with sticks, but Uncle Cyril had come to their rescue, admonishing us.

"Don't disturb the bat population," he said; "they have their purpose in life."

"What's their purpose?" Moira inquired.

And he quickly informed us of how they helped keep the mosquitoes under control and enjoyed eating beetles and flies. Satisfied, we decided to leave them alone.

There was a hook in the ceiling designed to hold a lantern, but lazy Burhan almost never used it, preferring to place the lamp on a ledge. My eyes were now drawn to it as I spotted one of them suspended upside down from the hook, gazing down at me with demon eyes. I shuddered and, recalling a rhyme from Macbeth, leant towards Moira and recited it in menacing tones:

Eye of newt and toe of frog,
Wool of bat and tongue of dog,
Adder's fork and blind worm's sting,
Lizard's leg and owlets wing.

Screaming, she ran to Mummy.

"What are you on about, Sarah?" Aunty asked.

"Look, a flying fox!" I shivered, pointing to the hook.

"Perfectly natural; it's time for them to go about their business. After all, they are creatures of the night."

Just then, a thin wail came from Sonabhen's quarters, bringing all conversation to a halt.

"Sounds like it's Meenakshi's time," Uncle Cyril observed, looking over at Aunty.

She rose, as another sharp cry rent the air. Sonabhen, hurriedly drying her hands on her sari, emerged from the kitchen, and meeting Aunty halfway, they hurried over together.

Daddy called for dinner and, as we assembled around the table, there was much speculation on whether it was really Meenakshi's time or simply another false alarm. She had experienced a few of them.

"You seem to be having never-ending problems with that girl," said Aunt Fanny, squinting at Uncle Cyril from across the table. "What's the latest?"

"The latest, Fanny dear, is, I think she's in labour," Uncle Cyril stated plainly. "That fellow Hari, her husband, brought her back to be with her mother a few days ago and that's as much as I know. Now, if you would like all the sordid details, I suggest you had better have a talk with your sister; she'll fill you in."

"H'm. Very interesting. I can't imagine why Hilda is paying so much attention to a mere servant girl. But then again, on second thoughts, it does make sense. After all, she's never had a child of her own," Aunt Fanny sniffed.

A secret smile crossed Mummy's face and I felt she rather relished the catty remark.

During the last week I had had occasion to observe Aunt Fanny and Uncle Melvin and notice how she bullied him. Actually, if it wasn't for Uncle Cyril going out of his way to make him feel comfortable, life would have been intolerable for the poor man, especially since Aunty Hilda ignored him completely. When he was not at Aunt Fanny's beck and call, Uncle Melvin retreated to a corner of the veranda and spent the entire time playing solitaire, sipping rum and water from a thick tumbler. I now understood why he seldom came to stay.

"It's going to be a long night for Meenakshi," said Mummy, as further cries rent the air.

"I suppose, if Hilda is going to get mixed up with servants, it may as well be with her own," Aunt Fanny declared. "I for one don't want to know anything about their private lives; we have enough on our plate as it is."

"There's something you've forgotten, Fanny dear." Uncle Cyril leaned over and looked directly at her. "Many of them were born right here on the property and have served us loyally for most of their lives. Don't you think that warrants a little bit of caring on our part?"

"I agree with Cyril," Grandpa Cliffy spoke up. "Meenakshi was born in that very same servant quarters and so was her mother before her. They are Stanton retainers and the daily comforts we take so much for granted wouldn't be here but for them."

"You have a point," Uncle Melvin agreed.

"We pay them a fair wage." Aunt Fanny fussed with her napkin, smoothing it out on her lap. "And, of course, if it's a little extra they need from time to time, no one grudges them that. But to actually roll up one's sleeves and get right into their problems—why, I draw the line at that."

"Well, Fan, that says a lot. Maybe it explains why the likes of Sonabhen and Yusouf have hung around here for so long and you can't seem to find anyone to stay for more than a few months. I know that for a fact from the many little chits you send over to your sister, asking her to recommend someone." Uncle Cyril was being brutally honest. "We treat our servants with the respect due to loyal retainers and try not to confuse the word *servant* with *slave*. Come to think of it, we are *interdependent*." Uncle Melvin cleared his throat and continued eating.

I knew that Aunty had supplied all that was necessary for Meenakshi's delivery and that the midwife was already on the premises. She had arrived by bullock cart that afternoon. Moira and I, seated on the kitchen steps earlier in the evening, had watched intently as she downed a large meal of curry with chapatis, in anticipation of the long night ahead.

Before retiring for bed, Moira and I peered in the direction of the servants' quarters, but could see nothing, except a few shadowy figures on the veranda in the pool of lantern light.

Radha shook me awake early next morning. "Come," she cried excitedly, "see Meenakshi's baby boy."

I hurried over with her, my slippers flip-flopping on the smooth dung floor. There, in a spare room beside Sonabhen's quarter, on a string charpoy covered with a thick quilt and a plain white sheet, lay an exhausted Meenakshi. Smiling up at me tiredly, she moved aside to let me see her son and, to my amazement, I found myself gazing into the limpid brown eyes of Mangat, the dacoit.

Later that day, Mummy gave me a packet with some money in it to take over as a gift and Moira followed, since she had not seen the baby.

Yusouf served lunch. It was the day of Daddy's departure. We would follow up later on in the week with Grandpa, who had decided to accompany us right away.

Mummy was restless and in a foul mood; I don't think she relished the idea of remaining behind without Daddy for even a few days. But he had insisted on going on ahead to get things straightened out before our arrival.

Aunty had outdone herself once again and my resolve to eat sparingly fell by the wayside.

"I'm glad you've got your appetite back," Aunt Fanny observed as I piled my plate high. "You'll be back to your old healthy self in no time at all."

I bristled, knowing she meant "fat." O Lordy! This was not exactly how I wanted things to go, but, once again, I was just being me.

"I would like to remain slim," I confided in Grandpa, "but I get so hungry."

He nodded sympathetically. "Old habits die hard, Sarah child," he replied, smoothing my hair. "To stay away from food takes a lot of discipline and hard work. Anyway, you don't want to be joining the ranks of Pharaoh's lean kine, now, do you? I love you just the way you are."

"Moira remains scrawny in spite of eating like a pig." Filled with envy, I spat the words out.

"We are all different," was his wise reply.

Even though I looked out for Ashley every day, he never came again, not even for a visit. I felt rejected. "Men," I had once heard Aunty Maggie say, "can be exasperating!"

"What are you mooning about, Sarah?" Mummy asked.

"Nothing," I replied.

"Then stop daydreaming and come help me sort out your clothes. I don't want to carry what doesn't fit you all the way to Delhi. We may as well make a bundle for the servants' children as we are about it."

Mummy was busy packing up in earnest. She spent all her time going through our kit boxes and discarding stuff we didn't need. Aunt Fanny gave us four pair of socks each and I asked Radha to hide mine at the very bottom of the trunk.

She smiled knowingly as she took them from me. "You wear party time in Dilli, okay?" she teased.

I glared at her.

As the days moved rapidly ahead, I was filled with sad confusion at the thought of leaving Stanton Station. I knew that I would not be seeing the place for sometime, since Mummy had had her fill of the Fenwicks and the Foxgloves and was already turning Daddy's mind towards holidays in other places.

"Since we are going to be up north, Reg," she coaxed, "it would be nice to visit Kashmir, Simla or Darjeeling; you know, explore the hill stations." Touching her face lovingly, he smiled, understanding exactly what she meant.

On our last evening, Moira and I paid a visit to Granny's grave and there we discovered Grandpa bent over that sorry mound of earth, sobbing quietly. Backing away, we were ready to leave the scene, when turning, he spotted us.

"Come," he whispered softly and we did. Huddled together, our arms wrapped around each other, we tearfully wished our grandmother goodbye.

The next afternoon they were all assembled before our compartment, sunlight glinting on old grey heads. My heart stopped as I gazed at them and I prayed, "Dear God, please keep them safe until we meet again."

The luggage was stored and tiffin carriers handed into the carriage, together with a basket of oranges. We received innumerable soft wet kisses and expressions of love, then our train steamed out of Stanton Station, gathering momentum as it hurtled across the plains of Central India.

EPILOGUE

End of an Era

A fog rolls in, blurring the outline of the old fishing boat gently knocking against the dock. The plaintive cry of a loon echoes across the lake and a heavy splash suggests a bass has broken the water's surface, reaching for the stars. My vision is clouded at the best of times and with dusk approaching I see even less—not the mist hazing the shoreline, nor the loon, nor even the fish. But their images are sharp in my mind's eye. Dear familiar sights and sounds that stay with me and speak of other times, of glorious youth, of strong limbs and warm, rough hands beneath the woollen blankets.

Those early years were a struggle, but they were good. A young woman with a family of my own, I was driven to follow a dream, to explore a new land with a lean, hard man who entered my life like a rush of invigorating air. And even though the spark of youth has long since dimmed, I can still feel the strong clasp of his firm hand. Evoking his chiseled features, etched into my memory, I have no regrets.

Arriving in Canada without a penny, we came filled only with our dreams and made this country our own. I wrote a tribute to Toronto once, labouring long and hard to bring the rhyme to perfection. Submitted it everywhere, wanting to share my sentiments, but without success. Wasn't good enough, I guess, but I loved and memorized it, reciting the poem to myself whenever our car sped along the Gardiner Expressway towards the CN Tower, into the city. Now, the old familiar words roll off my tongue and I am once again Sarah, with a pocket full of dreams.

Seated out on the deck, shrouded in a heavy shawl whose fringes fall softly around my knees, I shiver as night winds breathe a distinct chill into the air. Leaves of orange, gold and red trail earthwards, their rustling an omen of winter's tightening grip on the land.

Our Randy's ashes rest in the icy depths of the lake, together with the fish and logs of long-submerged timber. I recall that summer evening we sprinkled the ashes over the gently lapping waters and a tear spills down my cheek. I impatiently brush it away.

We skimmed the surface of the lake in a high-powered boat, the whine of its engine drowning out Led Zeppelin's "Stairway to Heaven," which was blaring from a ghetto blaster set out on the picnic table by his friends, who had all gathered to wish him farewell. Howie, his face streaming, his hand outstretched, scattered his brother's remains over the churning water.

Randy died two weeks earlier on a mid-summer day which was bright and brassy. He was on a motobike. Behind him Howie drove his car with Andrea, their two children and myself in it. All of us were on our way to the cottage for a long weekend.

Traffic clogged the highway, but speedsters continued to zoom in and out between the cars, daring man and God to swipe them off the road. Randy on his bike was one of the speedsters.

It started to rain; swollen drops disgorged from pendulous clouds hanging low overhead. A thunder shower turned the road into a slick, wet ribbon of gleaming asphalt. Almost impossible to negotiate, it dared you to live past the experience—one man didn't.

From inside Howie's car we heard a crash of metal ahead of us. Traffic came to a grinding halt. Randy had been hit by a car and thrown off his bike. A mother's cry rent the air, startling curious onlookers gaping through car windows as they headed north. Standing by the side of the highway over my dead son's body, I pressed Howie's arm and wept. Andrea followed mutely behind us with a pair of trembling children clinging to her sides. We stayed with Randy's body till an ambulance arrived. Then we stumbled back to our car and followed Randy's remains to the edge of the earth. My wild and wonderful son had made a fiery exit, cramming the experiences of a lifetime into thirty short years.

High-pitched laughter, loud chatter and the tinkle of glassware spills out from the open windows, dispelling memories of that dreadful day, bringing me back to the present time. Howie and Andrea are entertaining friends who live in a cottage nearby. Children dart between the guests; escaping through the screen door, they scamper into the darkness, making mad playful sounds. Brandy chases after them, suddenly tires and settles panting at my feet. I lean down to pat his silken head. Amidst the rough and tumble of their lives, I am alone with my thoughts and I feed off them.

Searching the skies, I see no stars, but know them to be there. On clear nights such as these, they grace the heavens in thick, bright clusters. A simple little rhyme I wrote for my sons once long ago comes to mind and I recite it to myself in a high tremulous voice. A child stops at my elbow, caught in a shaft of light shining through the open dining-room window. I see his wide, questioning eyes gaping at me. He darts into the shadows—crazy old woman!

Perhaps.

"Granny, would you like to come in now? Dad wants to know."

It's Stuart, my grandson.

"No, dear, I'd like to sit out for a while longer. It's a lovely night and the breeze has chased all the mozzies away. You can run along; I'm just fine."

He scoots indoors and seriously informs his father: "She would like to stay out for a bit longer."

"Well, all right then."

Pine trees release the scent of their gummy resin. I regurgitate the past, going back to a time before this grand, high-beamed structure towering over the lake changed the landscape. It was a simple, tumbledown cottage then, sitting on a plot of reclaimed land, purchased for a song. All we could afford at the time. He and I had spent endless days reinforcing, priming, painting and laying new flooring—fixing it up, as it moaned and rattled when high winds off the lake swept through its draughty interior. In those days I saw the world in Technicolor. We enhanced the rooms, painting them in different hues, and cluttered them with pieces of solid wood furniture purchased from second-hand stores.

A terrible storm once tore parts of the roof away in the dead of night and the cottage moaned as we lay huddled in our beds, praying it would subside. But the level of the lake kept rising and soon we heard water lapping against the concrete supports. Dressing hastily, we made ready to leave; but my men were ravenous, so I hurriedly fried up bacon and eggs as they milled around me in a fever of excitement. We lost hydro soon after and it was a meal that had to suffice until sundown. Now there are generators and other sophisticated pieces of equipment installed in a separate room at the rear of the cottage, ready to meet any emergency, but emergencies are few and far between in this technologically-advanced age. And, as for me, I've lost all my muscle and am now a mere whisper, a trembling leaf about to blow away.

"Burra khanna," he said; "let's have one and invite our new friends from around the lake."

"Why not? I'll make a great big biryani with all the trimmings."

"Sounds good to me."

Finding Hamid's recipe which had been carefully preserved these many years in an old cigar box filled with ancient sepia photographs, I examined the list of ingredients. Hamid made a grand biryani, it was his specialty. However, the poor fellow was seldom given the opportunity of impressing guests with his magnificent creation, for Mummy rarely included it in the bill of fare when entertaining her la-di-da friends. Perhaps she never quite forgave him for his ineptitude where other dishes were concerned. Didn't she realize, though, that without a teacher and unable to read English, he would find it impossible to recreate the gourmet recipes so lavishly illustrated in the British women's magazines?

I can still picture them as if it were yesterday: Mummy seated at the dining table, with Hamid standing before her, fidgeting nervously, scratching his grizzled head. "Ha, memsahib," he would acknowledge, his head wobbling from side to side as she gave him orders on how he was to go about creating the epicurean delights pictured in the pages before them. Daddy's faithful retainer, who had accompanied him on every posting—until that winter morning in Delhi, when Radha found him curled up on his mat in the kitchen, cold and dead as the ashes lying in the grate beside him. We took him so much for granted; it was inconceivable to think that a day would come when we would not be awakened by Hamid performing his morning ablutions under the garden tap. He had not complained of feeling ill, so Mummy was mystified as to what had caused his sudden demise. Grandpa was pragmatic about it, saying he had most probably died of heart failure. Philosophically he explained that since Hamid had lived a good life, he was now, no doubt, where all worthy Muslims yearned to be, in the arms of Allah! But Daddy was overcome with grief and wept unabashedly when Hamid's body was carried out of the house for burial in the Muslim cemetery. I walked around in a daze all day, feeling lost and alone and that night wept bitter tears, sensing that with his passing my world was changed and would never be the same again.

Reading through his recipe, I noted the ingredients and ordered several pounds of fresh lamb from the butcher. Trimming away the excess fat, I proceeded to marinate the meat in a mixture of yoghurt and spices. The next day, whilst plucking fresh herbs from earthen pots nurtured all summer long, I crumbled a sprig of mint and held it to my nose, inhaling its sweet fragrance. Memories came flooding back of a clear winter morning long ago, when crushing a lime leaf, I had mixed it with earth and placed it in Granny Connie's near lifeless hand, so she could get a whiff of it. She smiled and I watched helplessly as the soil sifted through her limp fingers. Moira and I were off to boarding school that day; little did we know it would be the last time we'd see her alive.

The cottage smelled divine with the heavy scent of spices wafting through the air. Guests gathered around; cordial, subdued greetings were exchanged. The experience was new to us all. I served dinner and the salver of gleaming rice embedded with succulent morsels of lamb took pride of place. A bowl of creamy raita, a platter of masala fried potatoes, fresh sautéed green beans, papadums, chutneys and pickles—the table was groaning with food. Hovering anxiously over our guests as they hesitantly sampled the fare, I heaved a sigh of relief, watching as they returned time and again to refill their plates. Taste buds titillated, they ate with gusto, eagerly partaking of the various dishes. It was a night to remember and the start of a trend; friendships forged that evening lasted a lifetime.

Summer holidays at Grandpa Reagan's Serendipity Lodge—hair flies in my face, and salt spray bites my lips. Moira is being stingy with her pail and shovel. I lost my set the day previous to the receding tide.

"It's a fish's home now," she yells at the top of her voice, as the thundering waves come crashing in to beat upon the shore. "Mummy said you were careless, so you'll have to wait if you want to borrow mine, as you can see I'm busy."

"I've changed my mind and don't need it anymore, I'm going to read my book," I reply huffily, walking away from her. Climbing onto the flat rock, I spend the entire day absorbed in a tale of high adventure. As the sun dips into the Arabian Sea, I contemplate the things that make me happy:

Story books, fireflies, brilliant starlit nights—
Mango trees, morning breeze and Mummy by my side.

Mummy kept promising every time she received a letter from her father that we would make a trip back to the Serendipity Lodge. But her promises didn't amount to a hill of beans according to Daddy because her intense involvement with the bridge club left very little time for anything else.

One morning after breakfast we received a telegram from Grand-Aunt Elsie Lavender, who informed us that Grandpa Reagan had keeled over and died of a heart attack while shooting grouse on the open maidan behind the lodge. Arrangements had been made for his burial. Would Mummy be attending?

"Poor Pa," she sniffed into her handkerchief; "at least he didn't suffer."

The estate was settled by a Bombay lawyer and Mummy came into quite a bit of money. The lodge was purchased by Grand-Aunt Elsie, who was now married to Doc Stewart. One evening I returned home from school to find a gleaming mahogany sideboard in our dining room with an intricately patterned silver tea service prominently displayed on it. There was also a pair of silver candlesticks and other bric-a-brac that Mummy said was part of her inheritance. These pieces, which now graced our house in Delhi, brought back vivid memories of that summer we spent at the lodge. The eccentric Dowlings, Miss Skinner and Major Edmund Turcotte. In retrospect, I felt sorry for the old dears, not being able to return home upon retirement. Faded by the blazing Indian sun, their energy sapped from years spent working in the *mofussil*, they were just too tired to pull up stakes and make the long trek back to England. Besides, in most cases, there was nothing to draw them back. I recalled a conversation between Mummy and Miss Skinner that took place on the front porch of the lodge one lazy afternoon, during that summer long ago. Mummy inquired whether, now that she was retired, Miss Skinner was considering a holiday in England. Dolefully she shook her head.

"I don't think so, since everything I knew and loved has been destroyed by the war. I am an orphan, my mother died in the London Blitz. She was ninety-four years old, poor dear. I don't doubt that she would have lived to see a hundred. My friends are scattered and I have no living relatives remaining. This country suits me just fine; it is my home now. I'm not afraid of the flag-waving masses or of being murdered in my bed. For better or for worse, I've opted for India."

Mummy clucked sympathetically and patted her hand.

I guessed it was the same with the others. Being ruled by Grandpa Reagan, who made every decision at the lodge, seemed preferable to living a hand-to-mouth existence in a tiny flat or retirement home in Britain, spending endless days drinking tea and gazing out at the dreary weather. Settling into the routine of set meals at set times, Grandpa's guests were content to lead a laid-back existence.

That was, of course, until the arrival of Grand-Aunt Elsie Lavender. Coming like a bolt from the blue, she changed the tenor of their lives. Grandpa's younger sister, drinking, chain-smoking, laughing raucously and telling bawdy tales, not only unnerved her brother, but also his guests, sending them scurrying to their rooms at first. After a time, however, they got used to her, enjoying her anecdotes and rude songs that she sang whilst accompanying herself on the piano. Staring glassy-eyed into the distance, shifting uncomfortably in cane-bottomed chairs, they watched as she downed three fingers of rum and told Grandpa off in her no-nonsense voice. I wondered how many of them appreciated the fresh air she had breathed into their musty lives. Doc Stewart certainly had! He was smitten and proposed to her soon after we left for boarding school. Grand-Aunt Elsie accepted and, after a decent interval, they were married. Mummy declared it to be "the best thing all around." They were now the new owners of the lodge and I was sure they would do a bang-up job.

So much water has flown under the bridge since that time long ago; I have a lifetime of memories to catch up with.

"Mum, you had better come in; it's getting quite chill out here." Howie's concerned voice reaches through my reverie.

"I have my shawl, dear; it keeps me warm."

"Let me help you to bed." I feel Andrea's firm hold on my arm.

Wrenching free, I stumble forward. "I can manage quite well on my own, thank you."

She sighs. "Okay, but watch your step; Brandy's by the door."

Entering through the rear door, I try to remain inconspicuous, not wanting to break up the party. Laughter reaches me as I undress by the night light and make ready for bed. Only Howie feels close; the others are as nothing—even the grandchildren are lost to me. I am just their ancient relative taking up space, waiting to die. Funnily enough, in my youth, I never saw "the old ones" in that light. Ties were strong and enduring; we belonged to one another. Besides, Moira and I shared a curiosity about the past, about the way things were and how they came to be that way. When my nose was not buried in a book, I continuously buzzed around them like a noisome bee, pestering with countless questions. I realize things are different now; time has become a precious commodity and that rare inquisitiveness has been traded for the instant gratification afforded by other distractions.

"Sarah, sit still and allow Radha to braid your hair."

"It's Saturday, Mummy, can I please not have braids just for today?"

"You must braid your hair every day, child; it looks very untidy streaming down behind your back."

As Mummy leaves the room, Radha yanks me by the shoulders and forces me to sit down in front of her.

"I make pretty plait, Sarah—two ribbon and two clip."

"I don't want two clips," I reply huffily.

Radha, our dear sweet ayah, who bullied, pampered and comforted us by turns—leaving her behind was a terrible wrench. I see her now, clear as daylight, standing a little apart from the rest of the family, gathered at the airport to wish us goodbye. We were leaving, emigrating to Canada, being carried there by the stuff of dreams and an irresistible urge to explore the Great White North.

Dressed in a shimmering sari with a garland of jasmine set at a jaunty angle in her hair, Radha held me close and her thick frame shook with sobs. It was more than I could bear. Whispering goodbye, struggling free, carrying away the cloying scent of Kanta upon my clothes, I rushed to follow *the man*. Moira had decided to employ her to take care of little Stella and this had made me happy. Years later on a visit back, I found her again, squatting against a pillar on the back porch of my sister's home. Grey and stooped, chewing her endless paan, she squinted up at me. Overcome by a great surge of love, I leaned down and pulled her close to my chest and inquired about her health.

"I am content," she assured, "spending my retirement years doing very little, enjoying winter sunshine."

Producing an earthen pot of gulab jamuns from under the folds of her sari, she shoved it in my direction, smiling slyly.

"Here—take, eat, Mummy no looking."

I giggled. "Don't be fooled, she sees us."

Tears spilled down my cheeks and she hastily dried them with her puloo. I was a child again.

Howie and Andrea's friends have all departed and the children are asleep. Lying in my bed, I can hear the wind soughing through the pines. Pale rays of moonlight stream through the sheer curtains and Zinat Mahal's bangle, a slender circlet of gold upon my aging wrist, catches the light and flashes with the same brilliance as before. I never did receive the pair to it, for there were no further Christmases celebrated at Stanton Station. Mummy wouldn't hear of it and came up with umpteen excuses when Daddy suggested a visit back.

"Some other time, Reg, but please, not at Christmas," she pleaded. "Besides, the girls are older now, and there is so much more for them to do here in the city. They would just get bored to death, quarrel with each other and end up driving me crazy. I couldn't handle that."

"I won't get bored," I replied with alacrity, "and I don't think Moira will either. Shall we put it to a vote? Wait, I'll get Moira."

"You'll do nothing of the sort, Sarah; stay out of this." Then, turning to Daddy, "Christmas is always such a busy time here with friends and all. Anyway, your old man is with us; what more do you want? Let's plan something for next summer, shall we?"

He glared at her and stomped out of the room, without bothering to reply.

We arrived in New Delhi a week after Indian Independence was declared. At the stroke of midnight, August 15, 1947, India emerged free after more than two hundred years of British colonial rule. From every mast the new tricolour flag flew, unfurled, buoyant, glaring into the bright Indian sunlight. "The dawn of a new day," newspapers proclaimed and it seemed to me everywhere there was an air of joyous expectancy. I was thirteen years old and filled with the optimism of youth.

Gazing out from the army vehicle that carried us to our new home, I observed, "Everyone looks so happy, Mummy, so it must have been all for the best. Getting rid of the British, I mean."

"That is a naive observation, Sarah, coming from you. After all you have read and heard on the subject, you should know better than to think India's troubles will miraculously disappear just because she is independent. True, people are optimistic for the future, but independence is just the beginning and there is still a lot to be accomplished. In Old Delhi there are still thousands of Muslims who have opted to remain and become part of the new India. In spite of their decision, they must be filled with fear and uncertainty, not knowing what the future holds for them in a country hostile to Mohammedans. There are shortages of food and other essentials and the consequences of independence and partition have created monumental headaches at the top level of government. Even though we would like to think that the departure of the English is the end of our troubles, nothing can be farther from the truth. The entire country and this city in particular seethes with unrest."

Settling into a small bungalow not far from the cantonment, we lived like gypsies for the next little while. Daddy was very busy at work

311

and we only saw him at the dinner table each night. It was a time of flux, not only for us as a family, but everywhere there was change and instability. Grandpa especially suffered, since this was all new to him. Daddy explained that after being a gentleman farmer, it was difficult for Grandpa to adjust.

"His life is radically changed and, for the moment at least, he seems to have lost all interest in his surroundings. I don't know whether it was a good thing asking him to come along with us so early in this posting. Maybe we should have waited a bit and requested him to join us at a later date. What do you think, Emma?"

Mummy shrugged. "You didn't want to leave him behind; this was all your idea. But, given time, I think he'll come around."

Daddy sighed. "I'm so busy and everything is at sixes and sevens here. I know he misses the freedom of not being able to place a gun on his shoulders and walk into the jungle on a whim to shoot a couple of green pigeon before dinner. He mourns my mother and the loss of his independence. In the past it was okay for them to visit because they always knew they could return whenever they chose. This time it's different."

Besides, the city wasn't safe and Grandpa, not knowing his way around, stayed home. At times it seemed to me as if the very life had gone out of him. Always an early riser, he now slept in until way past nine o'clock every morning. Mummy said he was depressed and gave strict orders that he was not to be disturbed. But when he sat staring vacantly before him, she would urge us to distract him. This we did and in time he improved, becoming almost like his old self again, although not quite.

Since Mummy was nervous to let us out of her sight, Moira and I spent the early morning hours completing homework assignments she had set us the previous day and playing silly games out in the compound. The heat was incredible and every afternoon after lunch we sank down to sleep, exhausted, until it was time for tea. Radha did the marketing and Hamid remained in the kitchen, cooking our meals and smoking his endless bidis on the steps of the back veranda.

"It's safer that way," said Daddy, "Hamid staying close to home, until tensions ease."

As time passed Grandpa slowly regained his interest in the newspapers and, daily, he gave us a running commentary of the birth pangs of our newly emerging republic. After informing us of the whereabouts of all the major politicians, he would pick the most chilling articles of murder and mayhem to read out aloud, which troubled Mummy, although she never did say anything. Moira and I, though, took great pleasure in all the gory details and embellishments he added as a postscript to every story.

The days passed with the same monotonous routine until one evening when Daddy came home with the news that he had been allocated officers' quarters near the heart of town. Since Mummy had never fully unpacked during that brief unsettled time, we were ready to push off at a moment's notice. Moira and I were excited; the move meant new surroundings, a new school and new friends. At this point, we were ready for a change.

A Mogul garden, surrounding an ancient tomb dedicated to some long-forgotten saint, was within walking distance of our new home and here we came to take the air each evening, accompanied by Radha. Moira soon made friends, but I was going through a phase and, not anxious to make new acquaintances, kept pretty much to myself.

Wandering among the magnificent peacocks trailing iridescent feathers as they strutted across the lawns, I watched them prance and pirouette, their shimmering tails glinting in the sunshine. From time to time they shattered the evening calm with shrill cries, as fluttering upward they came to rest on the crenellated walls and gate of the garden. From this vantage point, gazing imperiously about them, they surveyed their world of tranquility, set in the midst of a city throbbing with fear and friction.

During the winter months, the silk cotton trees burst into bloom. Scores of them along the avenues and roundabouts leading up to the garden, they coloured the landscape with vibrant splashes of red. When summer breezes breathed fire, the cotton balls released their seeds. As light as air, trailing fibers behind them, they caught the wind and drifted heavenwards and we children chased after them. With the passing of time, these evening interludes took on an almost magical quality and I looked forward to visiting the garden each day after school.

Our outings were cut short, however, and our visits to the garden came to an abrupt end. One evening, as Moira and I lay sprawled out on the grass chattering aimlessly, waiting for Radha, who was as usual gossiping with a group of ayahs seated nearby, a tattered band of chokras suddenly came marching past. Waving ragged banners and shouting unintelligible slogans, they raised their fists and made threatening gestures. Without further ado, a nervous Radha gathered us to her side and we hurried home.

"They were just a group of ragamuffins," I tried reasoning with Mummy, but she wouldn't hear of it.

"I'm sorry, Sarah; the place is out of bounds for the next while. I am forever reading in the papers about such demonstrations—of hoodlums performing all sorts of acts of vandalism, burning effigies and desecrating holy sites. A Muslim saint's tomb lies in the heart of that garden and it may well become their next target. We're living in turbulent times and things haven't settled down as yet."

I wept into my pillow that night and tried to grasp the enormity of what was happening. "Turbulent times"—just contemplating the fact that we were actually living and breathing history gave me goosebumps. Thinking about it night and day, I became obsessed and began spending my evenings poring over history books borrowed from the library.

Moira and I attended the same convent in the city. But we were very different in our choice of diversions. She sat with her group at the very front of the bus, giggling and chattering all the way to school, while I took a seat at the rear and spent my time gazing out at the throngs of people as the bus bumped and rattled along. Dust clouds churned up on the congested streets and blew in through the open windows. Bullock carts often snarled traffic, bringing it to a halt, but patience, the virtue of all Indians, prevailed. Tempers seldom flared, order was slowly restored and everyone continued on their way again.

Delhi was dotted with old ruins and they appeared at every twist and turn of the road. I fell in love with the city during those long bus rides and absorbed its ambience like a sponge. Mummy was right, though, we were living in dangerous times and ample evidence of this unfolded before our eyes every day during the journey to school and back. We often saw orderly groups of men in white dhotis and Gandhi caps marching down the road, chanting slogans. At other times the processions were not so tidy, as ruffians in tattered garments leapt out from the alleyways and ran helter-skelter and screaming into the streets. They threatened the shopkeepers, snatched foodstuffs from vendors, broke bottles and caused a disturbance. We sat huddled in our seats, nervously watching the acts of vandalism, as our driver skillfully maneuvered the bus through the crowds. Graffiti and slogans on walls dripped blood-red paint and jeeps with loudspeakers swerved through the populace delivering rabble-rousing messages. I couldn't quite grasp all they were saying, but it was evidently intoxicating stuff and had the desired effect. Some pedestrians averted their eyes and hurried out of the way, while others jumped into the jeeps or ran alongside, crying out *"Bharat mata ki jai!,"*[127] *"Jai Hind!,"* and *"Vande Mataram!"*[128]

After dinner one evening, I sat on the carpet at Mummy's feet and shared with her some of the incidents we encountered on the way to school. She looked at me anxiously and smoothed back my hair. "The blasted politicians are to blame; they are responsible for getting the crowds worked up!" she exclaimed. "I don't know when this will all end. At this point in time I wish your father had been posted anywhere else but here. Each day I watch you both get into that bus and worry myself sick until I see you safely home again." Tiredly she rose from her chair and, turning to me, said, "Sarah, it's time for bed; go brush your teeth."

Insatiably, I devoured the history of Delhi, from its inception in 1450 bc, to the present day. How the ancient city of Indraprastha, emerging from the mists of time, had grown to become the capital of numerous empires. Its inhabitants, having lived under the boot of

---

127 *Bharat mata ki jai!* Hail to Mother India!

128 *Vande Mataram!* Hail to the Mother(land)! "Bengali Vande Mataram" is the national song of India, composed by Bankim Chandra Chatterjeee in a highly Sanskritized form of the Bengali language. First appearing in his book *Anandamatha,* published in 1882 amid fears of a ban by British Raj, the song was written six years prior, in 1876. "Vande Mataram" was the national cry for freedom from British oppression during the freedom movement. Large rallies, fermenting initially in West Bengal, in the major metropolis of Kolkata (Calcutta), would work themselves up into a patriotic fever by shouting this slogan. The British, fearful of the potential danger of an incited Indian populace, at one point banned the utterance of the motto in public forums and jailed many freedom fighters for disobeying the proscription. To this day, "Vande Mataram" is seen as a national mantra describing the love of patriots for the country of India. *Yamuna* the largest tributary of the Ganges, flows through Delhi and Agra

successive conquerors, had, over a period of 5,000 years, witnessed the rise and fall of successive monarchs. Each one had erected palaces and citadels to proclaim their power and magnificence, only to be brought down to defeat by further hordes of invaders. It seemed Delhi was bad luck for any who sought to conquer and hold her. This was evident from the scattered ruins of at least seven cities that lay strewn upon the land—bounded by the Aravalli to the north and west and the river Yamuna to the east. Marvelling at the people's resilience, I felt a great surge of pride in belonging and shared my enthusiasm with Mummy one evening.

She looked up at me, perplexed and remarked, "Sarah, my girl, you baffle me sometimes. If you could only put as much effort into your studies as you do into those musty history books, I think you would come first in class. As it is, Sister Rosita tells me that you show absolutely no interest whatsoever in any subject except literature and now, of course, history. She despairs of you ever passing this grade. Why don't you try and pay equal attention to your arithmetic, algebra and geometry? It will help you get better marks."

"But Mummy—"

"I know, I know, you find math boring."

Settling back in her chair, she picked up the book she was reading and I was dismissed.

I would have liked to spend my weekends wandering through the many tombs and forts that I passed on my way to school, but Mummy wouldn't hear of it and kept me on a tight rein. We could only see the sights on guided tours, she said, accompanied by herself and Radha. Daddy was often too busy.

"The city is a dangerous place," she repeated time and again, "filled with refugees and transients."

On one occasion, both Mummy and Daddy planned an all-day excursion. Starting early on a Saturday morning, we would visit the Qutb Minar, a magnificent tower soaring to a height of some 238 feet, where, from the top gallery, it was said one could view the entire city spread out like a map. Once that was over, Daddy promised to take us to the Officers' Mess for lunch before returning home. Moira pulled a face and said she was not one bit interested in seeing "crumbling ruins," but I was excited. When the weekend arrived however, I awoke to find myself feeling quite ill and knew immediately the reason why. The night previous I had gorged on too many gulab jamuns and was now paying for my greed with a queasy stomach and headache. I begged Mummy to allow me to stay behind, but she was adamant that I accompany them. Arriving at the site, I once again asked if I could be excused from climbing to the top, but she would have none of it.

"Sarah, you are constantly clamouring to be allowed to go out and see the sights. Well, here we are now, so I won't have any more of your whining. You must come along and view the city from the vantage point at the very top."

And so I lagged behind them, climbing round and around up the circular flights of stairs with my head swirling and my knees trembling like jelly. I was exhausted, arriving at the top. Gazing down from the projecting gallery with the city spinning around me, I felt my stomach heave and instantly threw up the morning's breakfast to the embarrassment of the entire family. Mummy and Daddy quickly stepped aside and Moira looked away in disgust. Radha grabbed a handkerchief and wiped my face, then cleaned the vomit from off the front of my dress. Daddy looked sternly at Mummy.

"Why did you insist Sarah climb those stairs when she complained of not feeling well? Some people just can't handle heights. Now let's climb down before there's another accident."

Radha grabbed hold of my hand, helping me negotiate the endless turns on the way down. Needless to say, our sightseeing was at an end for that day. When we arrived home, I hurried in for a bath; then, changing into my pyjamas, spent the entire afternoon lolling around in bed, reading a book. For supper I was served a watery gruel with a piece of dry toast.

When the lunch bell rang at school each day, Moira followed the boarders into the refectory, where she was served lunch by the convent cooks. This suited her, since many of her friends ate at the same table. I, on the other hand, created quite a scene when Mummy proposed the same for me. Daddy looked up from his newspaper and, shaking his head, glared at her. It was decided that I would take a packed lunch to school each morning and eat it with Padma at her home, since she lived nearby. Padma was the daughter of a brother officer in Daddy's regiment and my classmate. Mummy reluctantly agreed to this arrangement and her decision proved to be the best break I ever had. Padma and I were two of a kind and it didn't take long for us to become fast friends. Bolting down our lunch, we bounded out of her house to explore the surrounding labyrinth of lanes and alleyways that crowded the vicinity. Wandering through the teeming streets, we pressed our noses against windows and inquisitively entered all types of strange and wonderful shops, selling everything from jewellery to heavy incense and perfume. During the sweltering summer months with perspiration trickling down our faces, we often sought the shade offered by sprawling peepul and neem trees lying scattered around an old grave site nearby. Peering into the cavernous interiors of some of the tombs, we found many of them occupied or just lately vacated by displaced refugees driven from their homes during partition. I noticed smoke from their cooking fires had crawled up the walls, leaving sooty stains behind. There was rubble everywhere—the detritus of ages scattered all round. Here and there we came across ancient, gnarled trees, crooked and disfigured with time, standing like silent sentinels overlooking vacant, desolate courtyards. I disturbed an old man once as he sat on his string charpoy pulling on a hookah. He gazed at me with a distant look in his eyes and I scampered away. On these excursions we often lost all sense of time and had to race back to school in order to be there before the last bell. While the teacher's face was turned towards the blackboard we slipped into the classroom just as the period ended. My grades suffered as a result and I was once again "a bloomin' disgrace."

Living in New Delhi was exciting, since we were at the very heart of things. The subcontinent had come through a bloody time; carved up and hemorrhaging, it was now two countries: India and Pakistan. Spurred on by the seeds of hate planted by the conquerors who had sought to divide and rule and thus keep control of the empire, Hindus and Muslims went on a bloody spree, rampaging through the streets, settling old scores, as age-old hatreds came to the fore. The Feringhee had stoked the fires well and left behind a legacy of loathing, which, after simmering for ages, now reared its ugly head. But we endured for this was Mother India, an ancient land who had known multiple deaths and scores of new beginnings at the hands of numerous invaders. Mulling these facts over in my mind stirred up a whole host of conflicting emotions, as I eagerly devoured every propaganda pamphlet and newspaper I could lay my hands on. Suddenly the longing to be like Rita Hayworth with tawny hair or the languid Lady of Shalott evaporated and I felt reborn as Rani Lakshmibai of Jhansi, who fought so valiantly for Indian Independence against the British and was killed in the Mutiny of 1857. Reincarnated as the "best and bravest of the rebel leaders," I walked around for weeks serious and determined to do something, anything that would make a difference. Eventually, sadly, I realized the struggle was over and India had her freedom.

Even though the British were gone, we were still studying English history as a subject at the convent. Why? I wondered. Shouldn't we be studying Indian history instead? I questioned Sister Lourdes, our history teacher, but she didn't take too kindly to my quizzing her and brusquely informed me that it was none of my business. I was here to study and not waste her time by asking ridiculous questions. I turned to Grandpa and he gave me his honest reply.

"You need to know English history, dear girl, because it's a subject required to pass the Senior Cambridge Examination, which, incidentally, is an English exam. We are not done with the British, nor will we ever be. Indians set great store by English degrees. Why do you think every babu[129] with a few extra shekels in his pocket packs his eldest son off to Oxford or Cambridge to obtain a degree? Those degrees carry a lot of weight, not only here in India, but all over the world. So you'd better buck up and put your nose to the grindstone."

If all things English were so much in demand, why did India need to be free of England? Wouldn't she be better off riding on her coattails, basking in the limelight of the Raj? Why had the Mahatma fasted nearly to death? Why had millions marched? Why? Why? Why? I searched for answers with the naïveté of an adolescent trying in awkward fits to solve the riddle. I had overheard relatives and friends of my parents' state that life was good, safe and orderly prior to independence.

Aunty Hilda Fenwick was fond of saying, "With the English there is a place for everything and everything is in its place. Of course, they help themselves to the best, but that is the price we have to pay for law and order. Besides, there is justice for the lower classes and very little bribery and corruption. What more can a person ask for?"

What more indeed, I asked myself. Maybe she was right because,

---

129   *babu* clerk

now that we were independent, there was certainly a lot of confusion and troubles everywhere. In a quandary, I broached Mummy on the subject.

"A country needs to be free to govern itself, no matter what the consequences. Freedom is everything. It's going to be a rough ride, Sarah, but I am sure things will settle down. At least I hope they will."

Her voice trailed away and I somehow felt she too was struggling with the truth, but, not wanting to burden me with her biases, had given me the textbook answer.

Lately, Mummy had been spending a lot of time reading the teachings of Mahatma Gandhi, some of which she shared with me. I listened intently, although I could not grasp all the subtle meanings of his message. I knew he was instrumental in getting India her independence without striking a blow, but was unable to stop the country from being divided. Mummy felt that he had never quite recovered from the shock of it and the continued violence and killing between Hindus and Muslims made him very sad. He had gone on a fast to try and prevent it.

"The Mahatma is a great thinker," she said, "a mystic, a true and honest soul, above politics." Mummy hated politicians. "Politics and corruption," she once remarked, "go hand in hand."

At that point Gandhi was spending a lot of time in the city, travelling between the sweeper colony and Birla House, the home of one of the wealthiest men in India.

"Why can't he stay in one place?" I asked.

"Well, he lives in the *bhangi* colony,"[130] she explained, "to show us that all men are equal. One of his main causes is to liberate the lower castes. At the same time he has a lot of official business to attend to and dignitaries to meet, so Mr Birla has very kindly allowed him to use his residence for these functions and for his prayer meetings."

Pretty decent of Mr Birla, I thought.

It wasn't long after that a shot rang out one cold January day, killing her beloved Mahatma. Grandpa Cliffy was the first to hear of it on the radio and came rushing into the bedroom, his voice choked with emotion. Mummy looked up from her sewing.

"What's it? What has happened?" she asked.

---

130   *bhangi* sweeper, the lower caste

"It's Mahatma Gandhi," he declared hoarsely; "he has been assassinated."

"Mary Mother of God! By whom? Who did it?"

"It only just happened; I don't really know who the assassin is," Grandpa replied, as they rushed together into the sitting room. A solemn voice, filled with grief, came trembling over the airwaves; it was Pandit Jawaharlal Nehru speaking before the hushed Constituent Assembly, solemnly declaring, "The light is out."

The next few days were chaotic. There was confusion on the streets of Delhi and at home. We were kept from school as news from the city was grim. They named the assassin as one Nathuram Godse. In the news they said he had shot Gandhiji as he was about to mount the steps of the podium for his prayer meeting. With folded hands the Mahatma had greeted his audience, just as a young man pressed forward. Bending down in a gesture of respect, he removed a revolver from within his coat and pumped three bullets into the great one's chest.

A bleak day. Moira and I wept alongside of Mummy. Seated on the sofa on either side of her, we watched her fingers move mechanically from bead to bead, reciting the rosary. Over the years so much of memory collapses into other memories, but that day in history I can never forget. Weeping all day and into the night, she refused to be consoled, even by Daddy. The next evening I heard her in a shaky voice suggest to him that perhaps we should all go away, leave for England by the next boat out of the country. "A kinder gentler place," is how she described it, "where the girls can grow up and have a decent life. Marry decent men." Daddy patted her hand and shook his head. Rising, he walked out onto the front porch.

Fear gripped my heart. Why was she thinking of leaving? It was a contradiction of all her sentiments voiced on the subject of independence. Besides, what did she know of England? Of course, we had family there, but Mummy had never expressed any curiosity to go and visit. Was not the Englishman the enemy whose whisperings resulted in the division of our country? Was all that was written in the newspapers about them just a tissue of lies? "A kinder gentler place"—was it really? I wondered what Mummy meant by that. It was her divided loyalties, I decided, pulling her in two directions while she was caught up in the fear and hysteria of the moment. We all were. I knew she wasn't like a lot of other Anglo-Indians who yearned for England, a country many of them had never set eyes on; imagining it to be some sort of Utopia. Nevertheless, Anglo-Indian sentiments were deeply rooted in her—and in me too I realized. Perhaps that was why she struggled when giving me the reasons for independence. A conundrum, since I knew for a fact she loved India and revered the Mahatma. On the other hand, there was no mistaking the curl of her lip and the look of contempt that sometimes crossed her face when she discussed certain topics related to things Indian—dirt, violence and corruption in particular. Contemplating her motives, I found it difficult to decide whether she agreed with the idea of an Independent India because she honestly felt it would benefit the country or simply out of loyalty to Daddy, who served as an officer and was staunch in his allegiance. Perhaps it was to spite Grandpa Reagan. Notwithstanding the sainted Sheila, I knew he had thought all Indians beneath him. I recalled his derogatory remarks concerning some of Daddy's relatives.

In questioning Mummy's prejudices, I began to question mine. After all, I was a part of her and she had raised me. Did I really dislike the English or was I being conditioned by the media and all that was going on around me? After all, I loved English history, English literature and the white cliffs of Dover, although I hadn't set eyes on them. Vera Lynn's song gave them a magical quality that made me long to sail by on an ocean-going vessel, on my way to England. Utterly at odds with myself, I ran to find Grandpa Cliffy and poured my heart out to him.

Placing an arm around me, he tried to calm my fears. "Sarah, why are you so afraid? You mustn't dwell too long on such topics and make yourself miserable. There will be time enough when you are older. Life can get very complicated and there are seldom satisfactory answers to tricky problems. Now, look at your sister Moira; why don't you try to be a bit like her? She hasn't got a care in the world beyond choosing a pattern for her next party dress. Besides, she studies and does well in school. I want you to chuck all those history books out, clear the cobwebs from your head and settle down to studying in earnest; it won't be long before your exams."

I sat beside him, stubborn, silent and resisting. "What do you think, Grandpa?" I asked doggedly.

He sighed and gently gave me his take on the Anglo-Indians' dilemma.

"To begin with, we are mixed, Sarah, which complicates things, because one feels pulled in two directions. We have also lived with two hundred and fifty years of British rule and, as a result, have been brainwashed into thinking white is right. I don't know that we will ever be able to unload that baggage. Come to think of it, neither will the Indians who have driven the Englishman from these shores and sent him packing to his island home. No, Indians will still bow before visiting white faces and place them on a pedestal above their countrymen. And that, in a nutshell, is what I think of it. As far as your mother is concerned, I wouldn't worry too much about her. She is overwrought and unhappy with the unsettled conditions and Gandhiji's death has brought all her unhappiness to the surface. Your father understands this and he will calm her. He'll do the best for her and for us as well. Now run along and start bashing those books, will you? I know you can ace every subject if you only put your mind to it."

Taking his advice to heart, I settled down to my studies in earnest.

Soon after my seventeenth birthday, we received a telegram from Dr Pudumjee, informing Daddy of Uncle Cyril and Aunty Hilda's untimely deaths. The details were sketchy and efforts to contact the doctor by telephone proved futile. Moira and I wept bitter tears and moped around the house for days, as Daddy and Grandpa made preparations to leave for Stanton Station. Mummy, in a fit of remorse, allowed me to accompany them.

A morose-looking Station Master, Mr Prakash, and Dr Pudumjee greeted us on the platform. Grandpa hugged his old friends warmly, while Daddy stepped aside to speak with Chief Inspector Mr Chandra Gopal, who was also there to meet the train. The old house had burned down, he said; Aunty Hilda and Uncle Cyril had perished in the blaze. The fire that had started in the kitchen in the back veranda had raced through the place, consuming everything in its path. It happened at night and Aunty Hilda and Uncle Cyril were asleep in their beds, so they didn't stand a chance, poor things. The next morning two charred bodies were recovered, burned beyond recognition.

Gazing solemnly at the blackened patch of earth, I felt a shiver go through me. Whiskey's mangled cage lay in the rubble. There were shards of glass everywhere as I tiptoed through the debris, trying in vain to find some reminder of my beloved aunt. Nothing remained, however, which even remotely suggested she had but lately tended this property and touched the lives of those around her with generosity and love. An ancient Sonabhen held me in her arms, tears streaming down her worn face as she tried to console me. Impatiently I wrenched free and ran to the cattle shed where I discovered Maisie, Maud and Esmerelda patiently chewing the cud. Maud fixed me with one of her baleful stares.

Sprawled out on the dirt, leaning against the crumbling wall of the old well, I gazed despondently at the pathetic little graveyard looking barren and neglected in the summer heat. Two mounds of freshly turned earth with withered flowers scattered over them broke the symmetry, but I knew that would not be for long. Soon they too would blend in with the graves alongside, topped by teetering gravestones. My heart ached and tears streamed down my face as I began to feel deeply the loss of Aunty Hilda. She was irreplaceable. Growing angry with Mummy, I blamed her for having kept us away from Stanton Station for so long. Her bridge club came first, not to mention the fact that she didn't like Daddy's relatives. Zinat Mahal's bangle on my wrist caught a ray of sunlight and winked up at me. Now the other heavy bracelet would never be melted to complete the pair for Moira and me. It was doubtless lying in the charred rubble, mangled beyond recognition.

Squinting out at the hills through the afternoon haze, I watched as they shimmered like a mirage in the distance. A burning wind picked up and came whistling across the fields, carrying with it skeletal bushes and other rubbish, which it plastered against the crumbling sides of the well. Sweat poured down and ran in little rivulets into the creases of my body, as I sat uncaring, contemplating their deaths. It was fitting that those two had died together, along with their talkative parrot, Whiskey. Like a mascot, he had accompanied them into the great beyond. I thought of how simple their existence had been and how content. Life breathed into dust, they had eked out a living from this land for all their married years. And now they had returned to the soil from whence they had come. Aunty Hilda with her blunt manner and forthright speech would not have taken kindly to my "snivelling." "It's over and done with, child; why are you moping?" she would ask. I could almost hear her voice speaking to me from beyond the grave. Suddenly, miraculously, I felt my spirits lift and the need to grieve for the pair lying side by side below the arid soil disappeared. I realized they were happy and free from care, resting in peace, surrounded by their loved ones.

We also paid a visit to Aunt Fanny who lived in the convent. She had surrendered what was left of her inheritance to the nuns and they, in turn, took care of her. Having quite lost it, poor dear, she kept calling me Hazel, who, according to Mother, hadn't visited her mother in years. Aunt Fanny was impatient with the good sisters, referring to them as troublesome busybodies who continually poked their noses into her affairs. Nevertheless, they were sweet and patient with her and ignored her rude remarks.

Uncle Melvin Foxglove had died of heatstroke the previous summer and was buried in the Stanton graveyard. Grandpa hoped he was resting in peace surrounded by generations of Stantons, some of whom had looked on him as a good-for-nothing bounder.

"Death, the great leveller," he philosophized, "brings us all together in the end, doesn't it?"

We said our goodbyes and Grandpa laid a fond hand on Aunt Fanny, planting a kiss on her forehead. "Take good care of yourself, Fanny, old girl." With tears misting his eyes, he hurried out of the room.

Death had a way of snatching our loved ones away from us in little clusters, with long intervals of "nothing" in between. It happened in quick succession. Our world began to crumble and Moira and I were helpless to do anything about it. Mummy was the first to go …

My first year at university and I was buoyed by the fact that I had actually been accepted and was on my way to a career in journalism. Each day was filled with lectures, friends and diverse distractions. Still a dreamer, but with a purpose, I put my nose to the proverbial grindstone during the last years of high school, scored excellent grades and graduated with flying colours. Moira too was in her teenage years. With bright eyes and a winning smile, she was the darling of grownups and peers alike. Busy with poodle skirts and buckram petticoats, she had discovered boys. Titivating endlessly before the mirror, she pinched her cheeks and glossed her lips, before racing out of the house to be with her giggling, scatterbrained chums. Radha clucked like an old mother hen and complained that she had very little spare time since every moment was occupied with handwashing, ironing and fussing over our clothes. Daddy as well was very busy and maintained a hectic pace. Eating on the run or at the mess, he hardly ever sat down to a weekday lunch with Mummy. It was a time of whirlwind activity and, somewhere in the hustle and bustle, Mummy seemed to fade into the background. Since she was always there, we tended to take her for granted. Complaining of tiredness, she quietly retreated into the shadows, forsaking her teas, bridge parties and friends. Seldom going out, she preferred to draw the curtains and spend her days stretched out on the sofa with a book. Radha knew of her fatigue and the nagging cough that shook her slender frame. One evening she confided her concerns to me and I questioned Mummy, but was dismissed with a smile.

"You know how Radha likes to over-dramatize things. It's nothing; just my change coming on."

But she was eating less and less and over a period of time lost her appetite entirely. Gazing at her across the breakfast table one morning, I was taken aback by her pale, waxen appearance. Her hand trembled, raising the cup of coffee to her lips, and her high-bridged nose and cheekbones seemed even more prominent in a tiny oval face, framed by limp brown hair. She looked worn out and I was worried.

"Mummy, are you feeling okay?" I inquired, concerned.

"Yes, child," she leaned over and touched me. Her palm felt clammy on contact.

A few weeks later, just before we sat down to dinner, she became quite short of breath and we rushed to her. This was followed by a spasm of coughing that would not quit. Removing her handkerchief from her mouth, we noticed the frothy flecks of blood that she was not quick enough to hide. Daddy steered her towards the bedroom, while Radha rushed to get a hot water bottle ready. After feeding her a cup of beef tea, he emerged and joined us as we sat around looking helplessly at one another.

"I should have taken notice of that cough; your mother has had it for some time now. I told her to go and see the doctor, but she kept assuring me that it was just a passing thing and that she would soon be better. God almighty! I've been so busy these last few months; I should have made the time and taken her to the hospital myself. First thing tomorrow, that's where we're headed and let the devil take the army!" He sighed heavily.

"Don't go blaming yourself too much, Reg. Come now; let's have our dinner and after that a good night's rest will help you to see things clearer in the morning. You have a long day ahead of you. Whatever it is, we'll see it through together as a family. I too feel partially to blame; I noticed when her routine changed and she began spending her days resting on the sofa. Come to think of it, I mentioned it to her once or twice; but you know Emma, she brushed it off as if nothing was wrong. 'Just tired,' she said. The heat was exhausting."

The news was not good and the prognosis worse. Mummy was suffering from a particularly virulent type of tuberculosis and would have to spend a year at a sanatorium in a hill station. The doctors assured Daddy that they would do what they could for her, but in their estimation she was too far gone. Since Moira and I were barred from visiting, we never saw our mother alive again. Her death came as a sudden, brutal shock and I never did get over it. Missing her terribly, we sobbed into our pillows every night. Radha comforted us by turns and in the bargain didn't get much sleep herself. An old crone now, I find myself repeatedly going back to that place in time—there was no closure, no goodbye. Decades later, Randy was snatched from our midst in much the same way.

We lost Daddy a year later. He went into a deep depression, which I felt was brought on partly by guilt, since he blamed himself for not taking better care of Mummy. "I should have paid more attention to that cough," he would repeat over and over again. "She let it get out of hand. If I had only taken her to see the doctor sooner, they would have nipped it in the bud and she would be here with us now." Retreating into himself, he had difficultly communicating with us. Continuing to work as hard as ever, he felt no joy, even when he was promoted.

The routine of the household continued undisturbed as it always had and it was just as well, since Daddy didn't seem capable of making even the most trivial decisions. I found a wellspring of strength within me and, stepping forward, took the reins from him. Managing the household accounts and other incidentals, I learned that Moira and I had been well provided for in the event of anything untoward happening. Daddy slipped away one night in his sleep to join the woman he loved.

The doctors claimed it was a heart attack brought on by overwork and hardening of the arteries, but I somehow thought differently.

During those long lonely months after his death, I became aware of the yawning chasm that lies between the living and the dead. There were no stepping stones to bridge the gap, no salve to ease the aching heart. Death was brutal and definite. For a long time afterwards I kept searching for something, as I did with Randy later on in my life. A look perhaps, or a dear familiar smile. At times I felt a presence flit by me, but on reaching out, grasped only thin air. Smoke and mirrors; those little tricks the mind played for the benefit of gullible humans.

Feeling abandoned, orphaned, Moira and I fell into a routine. Only Grandpa Cliffy remained with us, lingering on for years, growing deafer and nearly blind with the passage of time. His eternal optimism and cheerfulness kept us going through those dark days and we, in turn, took particular care of him, pampering and spoiling him, catering to his every need. He seemed happy enough and in good spirits. One Sunday morning though, as we sat around the breakfast table of the rented bungalow we now lived in, he hesitantly asked if he could be taken back to Stanton Station.

"To live where?" I inquired, since the properties had all been sold.

"With the nuns at the convent," he replied. "A couple of months ago, after we lost Aunt Fanny, I wrote to them about the possibility of my returning some day and they assured me there would always be room for me. I have a little money tucked away and it should do. I don't imagine it's going to be a very long stay. You girls have to get on with your lives."

"Are you leaving us in the lurch?" Moira asked, a hurt expression crossing her face.

"Not a bit of it; I'm simply going home to die."

The arrangements were soon made and we caught the train, travelling to Stanton Station in the sweltering summer heat. I stayed with him for a while, not wanting to let go, but the day finally arrived when I could no longer postpone my departure.

"I'll see you soon." Kissing him, I tried to remain cheerful. "Moira and I will come and spend the holidays with you and it will be like old times. We'll even bring Radha along, since I hear her old flame, Gulab, is still knocking about."

"That will be nice, but don't forget to check on me from time to time to make sure that I'm still *knocking about.*" He smiled mischievously with that old twinkle in his eye.

"I see you've not lost your funnybone."

"Be the best you can be, Sarah," he hugged me close and I rushed out, leaving him fragile and bent, but still clinging to the flickering life force within.

Grandpa developed a chest cold at Christmas, which quickly turned into pneumonia. Moira and I hastily packed our bags and journeyed to his bedside, but we were too late, arriving at Stanton Station just in time to bury him beside Granny Connie.

Brittle clumps of soil welded to the earth resisted the sons of Burhan and Yusouf who worked hard at digging the grave. The fields were bare, for a crop had just been harvested. Only this tiny plot was Stanton land now; all else had been sold. Moira and I had wanted to build a fence around it, but Mother Superior dissuaded us, thinking it an exercise in futility.

"They will steal the chain links," she declared simply, "and may even dig up the graves. Leave it as is."

Shivering in the pale winter sunshine, I looked past the graves at the denuded hills in the distance, where deforestation had begun to wreak havoc on the land. Feeling helpless and filled with a great sadness at seeing how the place had changed, I realized it mattered little now. What was all-important was ensuring Grandpa Cliffy's body was put to rest beside his beloved Connie. The defiant earth offered up a challenge, but in the end, they persevered, these men, sons and grandsons of fathers who had all been born on Stanton soil. As with her grave, they dug his grave deep, so the jackals wouldn't get to the coffin, and we laid him to rest with a pastor in attendance to pronounce the blessing. I did not weep that day for Grandpa Cliffy, but looked straight into the wind as it blew grit in my face from off the dead hills. I did not flinch.

The next day, while our train steamed out of Stanton Station, something died in me as I gazed out at the fleeting countryside for the last time. It was the end of an era; there were no Stantons left. The stalwart men and women of a generation had all passed away. I wept bitter tears for a time gone by.

Now there was just Moira and I with Radha to keep house. And this she did admirably, attending to our needs, growing more rotund with age. I can still hear the rattle of her pots and pans and see her smooth, round face, ruddy with the light of the kitchen fire, as she prepared our evening meal—chapatis, dal and chicken curry. She had become a passable cook. One evening I found her weeping copious tears, which mixed in with the dough she was kneading. "My life will soon be over," she sobbed. "Everyone I loved is dead. Soon baba log will get married and go to your own houses. What will become of Radha? What about her old age?"

"We will care for you," I assured her. And we did.

Drifting into soft slumber, lulled by the sound of lapping waters, my mind is at rest. All in all, I have had a good innings with few regrets.

Hello! There's Moira, seated on the curve of a crescent moon. How did she get up there? Moonface is mine, I think, possessively. The room is filled with light as meteor showers illuminate the darkness outside and I can see again. Grey shadows have fled. Light as a feather, I slip through the window and soar up to the heavens on a moonbeam, my hands outstretched, reaching for the light. I lose a slipper in the ascent and watch my wrap float away to freedom. Night winds are bracing and Moonface bright and cold, as I grab hold of her silvery tip and gently ease myself up. Gathering in the folds of my gown, I cross unshod feet and turn to Moira seated nearby.

She asks, "Now, isn't this grand?"

I have to agree.